Slay Ride

Marilyn C. Long

Slay Ride

Marilyn C. Long

PEAR
TREE
PUBLISHING

Slay Ride

By Marilyn C. Long
Copyright © 2019 by Marilyn C. Long

Published by Pear Tree Publishing
www.PearTreePublishing.net

Second Edition
Proudly published in the United States of America

Long, Marilyn C.
Slay Ride / by Marilyn C. Long – 2nd Ed.

ISBN 978-1-62502-016-1
Library of Congress Control Number: 2018949582

1. Novel – Author. 2. Novel – Fiction: Suspense. 3. Novel – Civil War
4. Novel – Equestrian 5. Novel – Murder
I. Title II. Long, Marilyn C. III. Novel: Fiction

Cover design by Marilyn C. Long, Christopher P. Obert and Laurel Larivee
Cover art by Laurel Larivee

1 2 3 4 5 6 7 8 9 10

Dedication

My book is dedicated to three loving souls who have now passed over the Rainbow Bridge: my beautiful horse, Indy, 'Reene's' incredible dog-of-nine lives, Andes, and her beloved Shennan. Our treasured animals brought us such joy and love that our lives will never be the same without them.

Do animals have souls? Yes, they do. If only humans could act as they do, the world would be a better place.

Thank you Indy, Andes and Shen for letting us love you and for loving us in return.

Prologue

Williams Farm
Westbrook, Massachusetts
August 1865

Nineteen-year-old Josephine Taylor Williams had just won the Civil War. The day President Lincoln issued his Emancipation Proclamation, she realized her people were still not free. Because she had dared to take a risk, this former Negro slave's heroism changed her country's way of life.

"No one could force my people into slavery ever again," Josephine had declared when the war ended. "My people are really and truly free." She received no medals, but her reward was the letter clutched in her hand.

Years ago her master, recognizing her intelligence, had taught her to read and write. Now safe in her new home she read again and again the letter her husband had brought back from town. The unexpected letter thrilled her and her fierce sense of pride grew stronger.

July 18, 1865
Regimental Headquarters

My dear Miss Taylor,

Your contribution to our victory has not gone unnoticed. Your gallant actions in the field while carrying messages to the North at great personal risk have saved hundreds of lives.

I have been authorized by the Federal Government to provide you with payment for services rendered. A money order is enclosed· If I may be so bold, I wish this amount could be increased a thousand fold·

From a grateful Nation,
Yours sincerely,
Captain Richard Ellsworth
37ᵗʰ Massachusetts Infantry Regiment

As she refolded the letter and placed it back into the envelope, her thoughts drifted back to the day that had changed her life forever.

Belle Meadows Plantation, North Carolina
May 1863

Before the war Josephine Taylor, like so many other Negroes, belonged to a plantation owner. A slave who had no rights, no say in whatever happened to her. Even though her master treated her well, she couldn't endure plantation life any longer. At the age of seventeen, she decided to run away.

The marshal in the next town caught her and brought her back. Terrified she'd be punished, she huddled, trembling, in her cabin. Would she be whipped? That was the standard punishment given no matter what slaves did wrong in the eyes of their White owners. But when her master called her into his study, the scene that unfolded amazed her.

"Master, I didn't mean to cause you no trouble! Please forgive me!" Josey pleaded.

"There's nothing to forgive."

When she could only stare, he continued, "Josey, I've been well aware of your unhappiness. However, you are an intelligent girl or I wouldn't have taken time to teach you to read and write. I sympathize with your situation more than you think. Even though I was born and raised here, I loathe the idea of keeping slaves to do my work. If my friends and business associates knew how I felt, I could be in real danger of losing this plantation. Do you understand?"

"Yes, Master."

"I'm asking you to trust me. Today I met a man who is looking for Negroes willing to help the Union Army. Would you be interested in what he has to say?"

Before she could reply, a heavily bearded man stepped from the shadows.

"Miss Taylor, my name is Allan Pinkerton. I represent the Union Intelligence Service under General McClellan. Your master has assured me that you are bright and eager to learn. Am I correct?"

"You are, Mr. Pinkerton."

"Your master has also told me you have a way with horses. I would like you to pose as a stable boy to infiltrate Southern ranks," Pinkerton explained. Pinkerton covertly assessed her as he spoke. Tall and slender, her boyish build, coffee colored skin and high cheekbones made her gender uncertain.

"You will be the eyes and ears of your regiment," Pinkerton continued. "Miss Taylor, by the sparkle in your eyes, I'm certain you'd like to accept my challenge. May I continue?"

Intrigued with Mr. Pinkerton's plan, Josey agreed. Within a fortnight, she found herself reporting to Captain Richard Ellsworth of the 37th Massachusetts Infantry Regiment positioned near Chantilly, Virginia.

However, Captain Ellsworth had made it painfully clear that he hadn't given Allan Pinkerton's strategy to use a Negro as a spy much merit. As she left his tent after her first meeting, she overheard him tell another officer that he did not believe Negroes were smart enough to discover important information behind enemy lines, much less carry information back to their regiment. And a woman besides!

Later that afternoon when he summoned her to his tent, Josey decided to prove the stubborn captain wrong. She went to his office dressed as a boy and slouched and shuffled before him.

"You axted to see me, Cap'n, Suh?" she drawled in a low voice.

Captain Ellsworth's face went rigid with disapproval, but he remembered his military rank.

"No, I'm expecting a young woman. Where is she?"

"Don' know, Suh. Wan' me go look?" When she scratched her behind and hitched up her pants, the captain almost had apoplexy.

"This is exactly what I feared. Ignorance. Unreliability. Mr. Pinkerton feels that girl he sent me—wherever she is right now—can spy on the Confederate Army and report information to her contact. Can you give me one good reason why I should trust her with this important job?"

Josey coughed loudly and he fixed her with an icy stare. Then she changed her voice again. "Why, yes, Captain Ellsworth," she replied demurely. "I believe I can."

Before he could respond, she straightened up to full height, dragged off her cap and shook her kinky hair free. She quickly reached out and scooped up paper and pen from the captain's desk.

"I fooled you by pretending I was a lazy, good-for-nothing Negro. You also thought I didn't have a brain in my head. And best of all, you were sure I was a boy! Should I write this down for you, sir?"

For a moment she feared she had gone too far. It appeared this Yankee officer had no sense of humor. He drew himself up in full military attention, but then his eyes twinkled and he laughed at the sudden turn of events.

"Young woman, I believe you have satisfied me with your qualifications as a spy for the Union Army." He bowed ceremoniously, his eyes still merry.

In return she dropped him a curtsy worthy of any plantation belle.

After their high-spirited meeting, Captain Ellsworth told Josey he would assign her to the Virginia First Cavalry near Waynesboro. He requested that she join him after mess.

During that meeting he said, "Miss Taylor, I want to go over the details of your assignment with you and your contact, my aide Lieutenant Peter Williams. It is vital that you and he remain in close accord. Your safety depends on him." Ellsworth opened the tent flap and called to one of his men. "Private Licqurish, tell Lt. Williams I wish to see him in my tent."

"Yes sir."

Josey perched on a camp stool and waited for the lieutenant to arrive. *Will we get along or will he and I fight like cats and dogs? What if he thinks I'm not smart enough…*

When the tent flap parted, a young officer ducked inside. He stopped for a fraction of a second when Josey sprang to her feet and she forced herself to meet his steady gaze. Immediately he came to attention and saluted.

"At ease. Lt. Williams, I'd like you to meet Miss Josephine Taylor. Mr. Allan Pinkerton of the Intelligence Service recruited her to do a little spying for us."

"Sir?"

"Must I repeat myself, lieutenant? Mr. Pinkerton believes she can be of service by posing as a stable boy. I am now convinced his plan can work. Miss Taylor will report to you any and all information she finds. I trust I can count on you to assist her in every way possible?"

"Of course, sir. I will do my best to make sure Miss Taylor fulfills her obligations." He bowed to Josey. Piqued by his discomfort, she extended her hand.

The lieutenant made no comment but with obvious reluctance he took her hand. His face registered shock at the roughness of her palm, but he strengthened his grip.

Determined to win him over, she offered him her biggest smile. "A pleasure to meet you, Lt. Williams. I can't wait to get started."

Chapter 1

Billerica, MA
Present Day

"Lissa, I had the dream-to-end-all dreams last night! We bought an old farmhouse and turned it into our to-die-for horse bed and breakfast. We fixed up the barn so perfectly *we* could eat off the floors. Customers were galloping up to our door."

"On what corner of the planet was this farmhouse hiding?" Lissa asked. "The ones we've looked at so far give new meaning to 'handyman special'."

Lissa sighed. She and Reene had been widowed within months of each other and in their grief, had bonded closer than sisters. Their late husbands' life insurance had left them financially sound, but they decided to make the money work for them doing something they'd always dreamed about.

"Yeah, the paper-thin walls on some of those houses couldn't stop a sneeze," Reene admitted. "It's so frustrating. When we didn't have enough cash, beautiful houses were flooding the market."

"Get back to bed and dream up a house we can live in. Call me back in the morning."

In the morning turned into many mornings. Reene finally called, her voice shaking with excitement. "Girlfriend, remember that dream I had a few months ago? Well, you'd better start packing."

"Another handyman special?" Lissa groaned.

"Does a rambling farmhouse in Westbrook, Mass, complete with barn, pond and 150 acres qualify?" Reene asked. "Last night I spotted the ad in a real estate booklet I picked up. When I read the description, I felt like I'd found a pony under my Christmas tree."

"Hold your horses, woman. Let's check it out first. Running a B&B is a ton of work. And we're including horses! Are you sure we're ready for this? And where on God's green earth is Westbrook?"

"Not far off the Mass Pike. In the central part of the state. Lissa, we can do this. We know all about taking care of horses. We'll be doing something we love. How hard could it be?"

If only they had remembered, 'Be careful what you wish for'.

Two weeks later muffled in fleece jackets and pants, Lissa Martin waited with best friend Reene Anderson for their real estate agent, Allan Chapman, outside Westbrook's Town Hall. They had scheduled this meeting to view the farmhouse. If the property turned out as advertised, they planned to pool their resources for the $450,000 mortgage and set up their dream business.

"Where is that real estate guy?" Reene complained. "My toes are frozen."

Lissa sympathized. At five-foot-almost-nothing, her friend's petite frame didn't hold enough pounds to give her extra warmth.

"Be patient, woman. When your toes fall off, we'll call him."

Lissa settled her black ear muffs closer to her head. Her short brown hair barely reached her ears and was no help in winter weather. But her English toffee colored eyes danced in anticipation.

As Reene stamped her cold feet in frustration, Lissa used her five inch height advantage to watch for their realtor. Happily, a Lincoln Town Car rolled down the street and stopped in front of them. The Lincoln creaked noticeably as Allan Chapman climbed out of his car. A huge barrel-chested man, he towered over the two women. His eyes twinkled behind gold-rimmed glasses as he extended his hand. "Mrs. Anderson? Mrs. Martin?"

"Reene and Lissa will do just fine, Mr. Chapman," Lissa said.

"Why, then, it's Allan to you lovely ladies. Were you waiting long?"

"Not too long," admitted Reene. "We've been admiring your town square."

"It is impressive, isn't it? In September we celebrate Yankee Homecoming Days on the green. There are vendors, crafters, food booths and games. Our major attraction is the parade down Main Street to the Grange Hall. We're trying to retain our small town character in a growing population."

"We hope to start our own bed and breakfast in Westbrook," Lissa explained. "We want to cater to horse lovers."

"Equestrians? What a novel idea! I believe this property is just what you're looking for. The old farmhouse has three floors, if one counts the attic, and attached sheds that stretch from the back of the house to the barn. The outbuildings should be of special interest to you. Sad to say, the ancient barn looks like a stiff breeze would knock it over."

"Allan, if the house is sound, we'll build a decent barn and the rest will fall into place," Reene assured him.

"Shall we head out to the farmhouse?" Allan suggested. "It's located on Breckenridge Road, about twelve miles out of town."

Lissa linked her arm with Reene's. "At your service, Allan."

When they arrived at the house, the friends dashed from room to room like kids in a toy store, exploring and exclaiming in delight. Lissa discovered a lopsided portrait of a Civil War soldier presiding over the fireplace. With a proprietary grin, she reached up to straighten the dust-covered frame.

"Lissa, check this out!" Reene called from another room. "One-step landings go off the main staircase into all the other rooms!"

"This is typical of old farmhouses," Allan commented. "A front and back staircase allowed easy access to both sides of the house."

Reese yelled, "The back staircase leads to the kitchen. That clenches the deal for me."

"I love this place! Allan, could we have a few minutes alone to discuss our next step?"

Leaving Allan beside the Civil War portrait, Lissa met Reene in the kitchen. Moments later she returned with her friend.

"Reene and I agreed; we want to make an offer!"

Allan looked astonished but delighted. "Well, my dears, I couldn't be more pleased. I will submit your offer to the broker. As a matter of course, you must have the property inspected and checked to see if there are any liens against the estate. I doubt it. However, the bank will handle that when a title search is done." He checked his massive Rolex. "I'm due in town for another appointment. Before you go, let me tell you about many unique features you may have missed. I wouldn't feel I'd done my job if I didn't. You won't be bored, I assure you."

And they weren't. When the salesman described the stone spring house, coffin door and twin chimneys, they were more in love with the place than they thought possible.

But on the way back to Reene's house, Lissa felt doubts begin to creep in.

"Reene, do you realize what we've just done? Other than offering to buy an old farmhouse in dire need of repair. What do we really know about running a bed & breakfast? Or any business for that matter? What if it's all a mad scheme?"

"That's just buyer's nerves," Reene assured her. "We'll pick it up as we go. Most important, we'll be in charge."

37ᵗʰ Massachusetts Infantry
Chantilly, Virginia
May, 1863

Briefed by Captain Ellsworth and the distantly courteous Lt. Williams, Josey prepared for her journey to Waynesboro. As she packed her scanty possessions, the captain paid her a surprise visit.

"The Virginia First Cavalry is composed of companies of horsemen from all over the Shenandoah Valley," Captain Ellsworth explained. "Their commanders have led them through intense battles and skirmishes from Bull Run to Gettysburg. Therefore, it is imperative you glean all you can from these homespun but brave soldiers. You should slip easily into their company."

He paused and looked away, sudden emotion working on his face. "In another time or another place, I would be honored to ride with them. That will be all. Good luck, Miss Taylor."

During the next few bone-jarring days as the wagon jolted over the rough road to Waynesboro, Josey thought about the captain's words. The responsibility weighed heavy on her mind. *I won't let him down!*

She also kept half an eye on Lt. Williams who rode ahead of the small column of soldiers and wagons. She noticed how he sat his horse, relaxed in the saddle but alert for trouble. She also noticed how his blue uniform clung to his lean figure.

Abruptly the lieutenant reined back to her wagon. "Miss Taylor, we're coming soon to a crossroads that will take you to the Virginia First Cavalry's camp. I regret we'll have to send you on your way alone. But Confederate soldiers are used to having darkies groom and tack up their horses. In your present disguise, you should be safe."

Josey's heart skipped a beat. Now that she'd be left on her own, she felt a surge of panic. For the first time she fully grasped the dangerous situation she'd eagerly volunteered for.

Lt. Williams must have sensed her fear. He leaned down and awkwardly patted her shoulder. "Good luck. Report to me next week as we discussed. If anything important happens in the meantime, you know how to reach me."

Josey nodded. Her voice stuck in her throat. She watched him wheel his horse and ride back to the head of the column.

"Thank you," she whispered.

Captain Ellsworth's prediction proved correct: Josey fit right in among the First Cavalry. When she straggled into their camp, hot and dusty, she found the men in charge of the horses and begged them to let her stay.

"Josiah, he cain groom and saddle up yo' horses, suhs. Please suhs!"

Soon they took her for granted as she came and went, cleaning stables and running their errands. She hid her kinky black hair under a tweed cap and wore layers of loose shirts and men's trousers. Her clever disguise fooled them so completely she almost felt sorry for them.

After she whined "Yas suh" and "No suh" and "Josiah, he don' no iffin he cain do that" more than a few times, the Confederate soldiers didn't pay her much mind and spoke freely in front of her. Those proud but ignorant farm boys thought she was nothing more than a good-natured simple-minded darkie.

Josey reported to her serious minded young officer later that week. She guessed he was about twenty, and she suspected his sturdy New England upbringing instilled his initial distrust in her and other Negroes who had volunteered to help the Union win the war. To her dismay, the empathy he'd shown when he left her at the crossroads had disappeared.

"Lt. Peter Williams, I've done everything you asked. But you still don't have faith in me. Why?" Josey seethed as she repaired a broken rein in the Confederate camp. She'd won over the captain, but she soon realized the lieutenant couldn't forget that she was a Negro.

"Stubborn! One thing you can't ignore: we both love horses."

During their ongoing meetings, Josey's eyes glowed whenever she spoke to the lieutenant about Confederate horses she cared for, and her heart ached when one of the animals became injured or was killed in battle. Eventually she was pleased to discover that out of this shared love, their cautious friendship grew, although they continued to address each other by their formal names.

With each report, it seemed that Lt. Williams' respect for Josey increased. Her attention to detail helped his unit keep track of Southern movements. She made lists of stores, ammunition and animals that

16

showed a clearer picture of what the North was up against. After her latest foray, he began to talk to her about his life in Massachusetts.

"Our farmland was covered with rocks and trees. That first winter we almost didn't make it. We suffered..."

"Suffered! You don't know nothin' about suffering!" Josey cried. "Long hours laboring in the hot Southern sun. Babies crying from sickness and hunger. Seeing your momma and daddy sold off without a word! A plantation horse or mule was worth more to the master than one of us! That's why I ran away. That's why I'm here now."

The lieutenant remained silent a long time as if he could find nothing to say. But her horrifying revelations opened his eyes and his attitude toward her softened.

Now that they were on more pleasant terms, Josey slipped personal notes to him in her official courier pouch. Touched by her sweet gesture, he reciprocated with notes of his own. Eventually notes became long letters, eagerly anticipated.

One morning the lieutenant led his own horse, Shiloh, a spirited chestnut gelding, over to her.

"Josey, would you like to use Shiloh for your next assignment? I'd trust him with my life and I know he'd take excellent care of you."

"Oh, Peter, I couldn't take him away from you!" she cried in a tone that clearly said 'Don't you dare change your mind!' Their eyes met, alight with laughter, and she realized they'd finally used each other's first names.

"But you must be careful, Josey," Peter counseled. "You know the penalty for stealing a horse. However, I've made arrangements with a local farmer who is sympathetic to the Union. He will keep Shiloh in one of his outbuildings that is close by. Remember, you must act the part of a dim-witted darkie whose only job is to run errands for his Confederate masters."

In a short time, Shiloh, who carried her back and forth safely behind enemy lines, changed his allegiance to Josey and nuzzled her whenever she came near.

One day Peter told her, "I would be jealous of Shiloh's loyalty, but I can see you've formed a special bond. And it reassures me to know you're safe. Shiloh knows his job better than most soldiers know theirs."

Josey needed all of Shiloh's skill and courage the day she was assigned to carry vital information to headquarters from the regiment locked in battle outside Vicksburg, over thirty miles away. Her detailed map proved useless. Familiar landmarks, there just days ago, had been destroyed. Staying on the main roads proved too risky, and she often hid among dense trees as scouting parties hurried by.

"I can't carry a gun dressed as a stable boy!" Josey worried. "If I'm caught, they'll drag me off to prison camp! And if soldiers saw a Negro riding a fine horse, they'd shoot me!"

As they rode along a back road, young men, no older than she, lay dead and wounded in ditches and fields. Some had legs and arms blown off. Out of nowhere, images of Peter lying bloody and still made her heart stop.

"Oh dear Lord!" Josey cried. To escape this frightening picture she spurred Shiloh. But when they rounded a bend, Shiloh spooked and almost bolted.

"Shiloh! No!" When she dragged his reluctant head around, she saw what had scared him.

Two dead horses lay outstretched between the traces of a wagon. The cannon the horses were pulling had been blown apart. Heartsick, her eyes filled.

"Those poor animals!" she sobbed. "Thank the good Lord they never knew what hit them."

Josey anxiously scanned the road in both directions. No soldiers were coming, but she didn't dare stay longer.

She gave Shiloh his head and they thundered away from the carnage. Wending their way past small farms and burned-out plantations, Josey kept a constant guard. At last they galloped into camp. Shiloh, winded and lathered, headed toward the corral. She flung herself out of the saddle before he came to a stop.

Pvt. Licqurish spotted her and ran to help.

"Please take care of him!" Josey begged. "I'll be back quick as I can." Mindful of her mission, she hurried into Peter's tent.

"Josey, what's wrong? Are you all right?"

"Peter, I was so afraid! The things I saw! Dead boys, dead horses! It was awful!"

Without another thought, she threw herself into his arms. For a split second, Peter hesitated and then crushed her to him. His lips found hers and she returned his kiss, her fingers clutched tightly in his hair.

When he released her, he looked deep into her brown eyes. "Josey, we can't get caught in each other's arms. Not now."

But his actions belied his words. He stroked her cheek and covered her mouth with his a second time. She cuddled closer, kissing his neck, murmuring his name.

18

"Come back after mess," he said as they pulled apart. "I'll make sure we're not disturbed. That's a promise."

Josey remained in the Union camp for as long as she dared. Under the pretense of discussing potential enemy locations, she and Peter enjoyed quiet meals in the privacy of Peter's tent. She stole out in the dead of night to return to her Confederate regiment, but she took with her the memories of passionate lovemaking. Those stolen moments intensified the love that had sprung so spontaneously between them. Still, Josey was worried. She realized a White officer in the Northern army might fraternize with a colored girl in the line of duty, but they were treading on dangerous ground.

When she managed to slip away from under the not-too-watchful eye of the Confederate soldiers, she and Peter escaped the confines of the camp and rode out on reconnaissance missions.

"We must keep our love a secret, sweetheart," Peter cautioned Josey as they walked their horses down a secluded trail. "My men need to trust me and look to me to lead them. I could lose their respect if I went around acting like a moon-struck calf."

Seeing her crestfallen look, he grinned and pulled her head down to his. "Like to kiss a moon-struck calf?"

Two years later the disastrous war between the North and South dragged to a close. Josey prepared to return to headquarters and laid out her clothes for the trail. She tugged a cotton shirt over her head and touched the small doeskin pouch that hung from a leather cord around her neck. Her fingers traced the outline of the ring inside. She remembered their last night together when Peter had removed the onyx ring from his hand.

"Sweetheart, my father gave me this ring. Now I'm giving it to you. I love you with all my heart and soul and I want you for my wife."

Her eyes had filled as he slipped his ring on the ring finger of her left hand.

"Oh, yes, Peter! I will be your wife. I will love you for the rest of my life!"

Peter had framed her face with his hands and lightly kissed her lips. Then they had clung to each other. She knew nothing was certain until the war ended. Unspoken between them stood their difficult life together once they left the South.

Three heart-wrenching days later, it was almost time to leave. Josey picked up the daguerreotype Peter had given her. His sweet face looked so somber. She missed the special smile he reserved just for her. She loved him so much. If only he were here with her! After the South surrendered, he had gone north ahead of her as soon as his regiment disbanded. She longed to be with him again but dreaded meeting his parents. She knew her life would not be easy once she joined Peter and his family at their Massachusetts farm. No matter how hard he tried to reassure her, she could not stop worrying.

"What's wrong with me?" Josey sniffled. "Peter knows about my condition and said he couldn't wait to see me. Tears fell from her eyes. Tomorrow I'll board the northbound train in Richmond to make a connection to Boston."

Peter had sent her money so she could hire a private wagon to take her the rest of the way. To her delight, Peter had sent Shiloh home by train a few weeks earlier.

It'll be a long while before I'll be able to ride him again, but I'm so glad he's safe.

The trip she now faced would be long and tedious, unlike the adventures she'd experienced during the last three years of the war. Hope flowed through her as she began her new life. Her life with Peter.

Early next morning she packed her few belongings, including her stable boy clothes, into a carpetbag and set off for the railroad station. She also packed the letters Peter had written. Peter had surprised her when he confessed he too had saved every scrap of paper she had given him.

"Thank you, Lord, for giving me someone like Peter!" Soon the train would be taking her to him.

She didn't have long to wait. The train pulled in right on time and she climbed up the steps from the platform.

"Please, Lord," Josey prayed as she watched the miles roll along from the train's window, "let his momma like me."

She gently placed her hand on her tummy and smiled.

"Like me or not, I'm carrying her first grandbaby."

Chapter 2

Barn Swallow Inn
Westbrook, Massachusetts
Present Day

"It's nine o'clock! We're late feeding the kids," Lissa exclaimed. "They're probably banging their feed buckets against the bars like criminals in an old Warner Brothers' gangster movie."

"You crack me up. Will you throw Shen some carrots with her grain? I'll take care of our other four-legged critters."

"No problem," Lissa replied. Trekking out to their brand new barn, she remembered the day the dilapidated original collapsed under the weight of its rotted timbers. Fortunately, the only inhabitants had been nesting barn swallows which had inspired their new inn's name.

"Allan Chapman warned us," she muttered. "But we found the right guy to replace the relic. I'm so glad he was able to shore up the outbuildings. Now the new barn looks like it's always been there."

The right guy turned out to be local contractor Lou Consoli. During their initial visit to his shop, he had laid pictures of possible designs on his worktable. "How do you want your barn to look? Traditional? Modern?" Consoli asked.

"We're into rustic," Reene had answered. "Lots of wrought iron hooks for hanging lead ropes and bridles. And make it look like the farmhouse gave birth to a miniature version of itself."

"Speaking of tradition, we'd like a hay boom over the main door," Lissa had added. "We'll need a warm room, a place for our tack and hay and a porch might be nice ..."

"In other words, the Taj Mahal, New England style," Consoli interjected.

"How soon can you start?"

Lissa rolled back the heavy wooden door and fumbled for the light switch. Even at this hour, her over-fifty eyes needed all the help they could get as she squinted at feeding instructions posted over the barrels of grain.

"Morning, Brav. How's the pretty girl, Shen? Sissy, be patient! I'm coming as fast as I can."

A chorus of deep nickers and whinnies issued from the stalls at her greeting. Lissa's gelding Bravo demanded his breakfast. He was a Registered Quarter Horse with a white star and blaze on his handsome face, and an attitude. It wasn't a question of his stepping over the line: he wanted to draw the line himself.

Giving Bravo a lesson in manners, Reene's mare Shenan acted like a perfect lady and asked for her grain politely. She dressed like a lady as well, her liver chestnut coat complemented by a flaxen mane and tail. Shenan's kind eyes watched Lissa through the bars of her stall door.

"Sissy, you're such a sweetie," she crooned as she moved on to the next horse. Reene had found Sycamore's Folly, unhappy and underfed, at the racetrack. "If Reene could only rescue one, I'm glad it was you."

Under Reene's loving care—and rechristened Sissy—the mare had gained weight and her red roan coat shone, but she hadn't lost her fear of neglect. Reene had patiently worked with her until she gained her trust and respect.

As Reene always wanted a driving horse, finding a wonderful girl like Sissy made her eyelashes curl. Ever the bargain hunter, she bought driving tack for less than half price from a retired driver. She had even sweet-talked the guy into throwing in a dozen decorative brasses for parade or show. Then the hunt was on for an appropriate wagon.

Two weeks later her search had ended. Reene's one-horse wagon, brass fixtures shining like gold, hugged the opposite wall. Now rechristened Lord of the Barn, the oak wagon's short bed was ideal for storing grain, groceries or whatever.

"You're a beauty, Your Lordship," Lissa told the unheeding hunk of wood while setting buckets on the grain bin, "and you must have cost her a fortune. Reene keeps changing the subject whenever I ask how much she paid. She claims you give her a comfortable ride, but that leather-covered seat ain't thick enough to suit my bottom."

Lissa carried feed buckets, topped up with apple slices and carrots, to each animal.

"Enjoy your breakfast, kids." She slid the stall doors closed and secured the horse-proof locks. "You kids could give an escape artist like Houdini a run for his money." She shivered. "The thought of one of you getting struck on the road or roaming the countryside gives me the chills."

She watched them devour their grain, her mind ticking off the daily chores ahead. Muck stalls and paddocks, clean and fill water buckets, sweep the aisle. Bring the horses out to their paddocks and throw a flake of hay to keep them content. Check the grain and hay supply. Set up grain for the night feeding.

Backbreaking work in all kinds of weather to ensure the care and comfort of the animal she loved more than anything in the world. More times than she'd like to admit, she'd come in from the barn with hay sticking out of her hair like a scarecrow, sweat dripping from every pore. Other times she'd staggered through her chores with a raging fever and sore throat.

"Could I imagine my life without horses? Not bloody likely."

She relaxed on a bale of hay and listened to the rhythmic munching of horses enjoying their meal. She almost drifted off to sleep. But a faint rustling woke her.

"Mice? Where's Jesse?"

Keeping the mouse population in check, Jesse James, her beloved tuxedo cat, prowled the barn. Good at his job, he presented her with dead mice at least once a week. She adored Jesse and stretched over the bale to scratch his head and run her hand along his smooth fur. In true cat behavior, Jesse allowed her to fuss over him, fixing her with a try-and-make-me-love-you stare from his green eyes.

"Hey, Andes," she called as Reene's beagle strolled through the barn on his way to breakfast. Andes loved to roam the woods hunting rabbits. Wearing his jaunty red bandanna, he rolled a soulful brown eye in her direction.

After she watched him saunter off, her eyes wandered around the barn. She frowned at the red fire extinguishers clamped onto the wall. Fire extinguishers reminded her of the horse owner's greatest fear. They'd practiced operating those extinguishers till their fingers bled. She was scared to death they'd screw up in a real emergency.

Shaking scary thoughts out of her head, she finished her chores and left by the separate walk-through door on the side of the barn. Bless their contractor for this life-saver. Sliding that heavy main door back and forth lost its charm the second day.

Growling sounds issued from her tummy.

"I wonder what Reene's making for breakfast. I could tuck into some French toast and bacon."

She tugged at the waistband of her jeans.

"Oh, crap. I'll never see size ten again. Whoever said 'Fattening Forties' forgot to mention the 'Flabby Fifties'. On second thought, I'll settle for a granola bar with a side of dried wood chips."

As Lissa washed the dirt from her hands and shook hay from her shirt, her mind drifted back to the hectic days when they'd moved into the farmhouse.

"Six guest bedrooms are more than enough, especially when we're acting as live-in maids. I picked out two rooms on the main floor and four others on the second," Reene had suggested.

"Great minds run on the same channels," Lissa agreed. "Did you check out all those fireplaces? Flames glowing in the firebox are romantic and cozy, but with our luck, we'll land a guest who's decided he's a badge-winning Boy Scout. We'll encourage 'em to cuddle up in the Gathering Room."

"Speaking of the Gathering Room, will you join me in there? There's something that needs doing."

Mystified, Lissa followed her friend. Drink in hand, Reene marched over to the fireplace and placed an ornate pewter urn on the mantle.

"Why on earth are you putting that ugly thing up there?" Lissa asked.

"I'm finally ready to confront what happened to Dan." Reene replied, referring to her late unlamented husband. "When the state police told me he'd been killed in a car wreck, I almost lost it."

She rubbed the urn's pewter handle. "I wish I had lost it. Then I'd have been too numb to realize Dan's arm was draped around his twenty-three year old secretary. A redhead. I thought he'd always go for blondes."

Reene paused to pull her own blonde hair between her fingers.

"Kick off your boots and drink a toast to Dan's memory." She handed a glass of wine to Lissa.

Hesitantly Lissa raised her glass.

"Happy days, you cheater! I wish you were still here so I could kill you myself," Reene railed at the unfeeling urn.

But her choked voice belied her flippant manner. Lissa could see her friend's genuine hurt.

"To happier trails, Reene," Lissa promised.

Fluffing her hair in a vain attempt to achieve the tousled look, Lissa took another trip down memory lane to the mudroom. The space she had convinced Reene was essential when they first discussed renovations for the house.

"Reene, no self-respecting horse person would be caught dead without a mudroom. Rain brings mud. Horseshoe-pulling, boot-stealing mud."

"Muddy boots are definitely not welcome on our gorgeous hardwood floors."

"Let's convert that dead space between the back porch and kitchen into an all-purpose mudroom. I'll pound a few pegs and shelves on the walls for jackets, gloves and wandering bridles."

"Those wooden beams are crying out for decorations," Reene decided when they finally surveyed their handiwork "I dropped into the hardware store last week and bumped into a shelf full of porcelain chamber pots, each one a bit different in design and color. Wouldn't they look cool hanging above the doorway?"

"Chamber pots?" Lissa echoed. "I dunno. Don't you think that's a little tacky?"

"No way! I'll bet our guests will get a kick out of them."

"Go for it. Then we'll be free to tackle the other bedrooms. If we convert the rear wing on the second floor into two suites, we'll have some privacy. We do need a place to lay our weary heads."

For the inn's décor Lissa wanted all horses, all the time, until Reene pointed out one little detail.

"Even though we're catering to the horse-riding crowd, we need to attract skiers." She hesitated a moment, trying to find the right approach to a sensitive subject.

Lissa frowned, thinking of her late husband, Hank, a volunteer ranger who died in an avalanche trying to find a lost skier.

"I'm sorry," Reene said immediately. "I know that's a tough one for you."

"Don't beat yourself up, Reene. I can't avoid skiers or snow or mountains for the rest of my life."

"Both of our husbands let us down, one way or another, didn't they?"

"I'm afraid so. But we're dealing with it. Now what were you saying about attracting skiers?"

"Well, we need to attract skiers and New Yorkers who want to escape from the big city. Let's go with a Country Modern flavor. Indulge yourself with enough horsey stuff to keep you and other horse-mad folks satisfied."

"Count on me to keep horse decorations on simmer." Lissa reached for her jacket. "Come on! Estate sales and second-hand stores are calling our name."

Twenty or so yard sales later, Reene was on board. "You did a fantastic job collecting our treasures. I can picture primitive dolls peeking out of nooks and crannies."

"You were right," Lissa admitted. "Less is more. We knew this ancient house had character. Our personal touch turned it back into a home. Remember your dream? When those guests do gallop up to the door, our inn will finally come to life."

Westbrook, Massachusetts
September, 1865

"Oh, Mother, how could he do this to me? I hate him! I'm ruined! He's disgraced me with his little Negro chit."

In her curtain-darkened bedroom Catherine Thorpe stalked back and forth like a caged wildcat, her long brown hair in disarray. She clutched a worn shawl around her thin shoulders. Peter Williams had broken her heart. She might forgive him for that, but he had wounded her pride. That she could not forgive.

"He had as good as proposed to me, and now I've been cast aside by a darkie! It's disgusting. It's degrading. The whole town is laughing at me!"

"Now, sweetheart," her distraught mother consoled, "he's not worth it! He's proved it by bringing that piece of trash home from the war. And I hear she's with child. I could faint at the thought."

"You needn't remind me, Mother, of my complete and utter ruination by a man I loved so much," she wailed dramatically. Immediately, her mother rushed to her side.

"Darling girl, I'm so sorry for you. Come, sit down on the bed and I'll rub your back."

As her mother kneaded the knots, her body gave into the soothing massage, but her mind still spun like a whirlwind. She must find a way to convince Peter he was making a terrible mistake. Somehow she had

26

to make him listen to reason. Besides, she was meant to reign as mistress of his house, not some trashy Negro!

Later that day when Catherine had shared the news, her sister Deborah had been incensed. "If I were a man, I'd call Peter out to demand satisfaction!"

"Then thank God you're not a man, sister dear. I'll handle this my own way," Catherine told her. "I can't marry a dead man."

Unfortunately, when she confronted Peter a few days later, he was not receptive to her pleas. To her mortification he was a bit puzzled by her assumption they had 'an understanding.'

"Catherine, I had no idea you cared for me. I've always valued your friendship and respected your intelligence."

She shuddered at the dreadful word 'respect', in her mind the universal excuse men always use and women always dread to hear. At his next words, her heart froze.

"I've fallen in love with Josey and plan to marry her. She's everything I've ever wanted in a wife and mother. Please understand and give us your blessing."

"My blessing!" she screeched. "I will never give you my blessing! You are despicable to even suggest such a thing. She's a *Negro*, for God's sake! Peter, how can you even think of marrying somebody who is so obviously beneath you?"

"Catherine, that remark is uncalled for. You know nothing about her! Josey took risks that would've scared off half the men in this town. I thought a young woman of your breeding would be more reasonable and sympathetic. Evidently, I made a mistake."

"You'll be making the biggest mistake of your life if you marry that girl! I intend to let this whole town know the disgrace you're bringing to it. No one will even speak to your 'Josey' when I'm through with her. They'll walk on the other side of the street so they won't be forced to cast their eyes on that trashy Negro! They'll—"

"Catherine! Stop it! That's enough. You can't mean what you just said. You're overreacting."

Catherine watched his face. His patience turned to anger. Peter grasped her shoulders as he tried to steady her.

She shrugged off his steadying hands. "Overreacting! I love you! I won't allow you to marry that good-for-nothing little schemer. She's not fit to make you a suitable wife. One of these days you'll come to your senses and then it will be too late!"

27

"It already is too late, Catherine. I'm sorry you misunderstood my feelings for you."

Catherine felt her face flush and she stood ramrod stiff with rage. She stepped toward Peter who recoiled at the hate blazing from her eyes.

"You will live to regret this day, Peter. I promise you this with every breath I take."

Williams Farm
November 1865

"I'm so cold!" Josey complained. She tried to button the greatcoat over her swollen belly but gave up and left the bottom buttons undone. She shoved her feet into a pair of heavy boots and wiggled her toes as warmth slowly returned. Tucking her hair under a soft wool hat and pulling it down to her ears, she rummaged around in her bureau drawer and found a pair of gloves. Bundled to the eyeballs, she was ready for the long walk into town. She needed more yarn to finish clothes for the baby.

"Just two months to go, thank goodness," she sighed as she clumped into the kitchen, relieved to find the room empty. Peter's mother Harriet was nowhere to be seen. Josey couldn't bear another painful confrontation with the unhappy woman.

Heartbroken over her son's choice to marry a Negro, Harriet pretended Josey didn't even exist whenever the two women were in the same room. Josey had tried to make friends with the older woman who rebuffed her at every turn. Every meal, as Peter's mother sat silently in judgment, felt like a trial. Peter's father, Seth, seated at the head of the dinner table, watched helplessly as his wife carried out her vendetta.

To avoid meeting a resentful Harriet, Josey slipped out of the house and set off along the road. Peter and his father were in the woods cutting firewood for the coming winter. They were so busy she hadn't bothered to ask them to drive her into town.

When she reached Main Street, Josey became aware of the stares and whispers from passersby. Little children pointed to her and laughed. She did not take offense. Instead she smiled at each person with a friendly "Morning!" Some reluctantly responded to her greeting, others did not.

When she arrived at Hill's General Store, smoke from the wood stove inside made her eyes water, but she was grateful for the heat. Her body was still not acclimated to New England weather. Josey wandered around until she discovered a bin of yarn.

Josey felt the storekeeper's eyes on her while she shopped. She smiled at him, but his only response was a deep frown. Other shoppers gave her a wide berth as she gathered skeins of blue yarn. She selected a roll of matching ribbon and some white buttons and carried her goods to the counter.

Edgar Hill, the proprietor, continued to act as if Josey would steal anything not nailed down.

"We don't serve your kind in here," he said coldly.

"I have money," Josey said and placed gold coins in front of him.

"It doesn't matter. I told you I don't serve Negroes."

"But my husband—"

"Don't bother to bring him here. I won't serve him either."

"My husband is Peter Williams," finished Josey, meeting the storekeeper's hard stare.

"My God!" the storekeeper muttered. The whole town talked for months when Peter had returned and a Negro girl soon joined him. "So it's true, then."

Disapproval continued to flood the older man's face.

"I am well acquainted with your husband," Edgar finally said. "It doesn't change my mind. War hero be damned. I don't serve Negroes."

Josey retrieved her coins and cast a despairing look at the yarn. Edgar reached out and pulled the wool closer.

"Good day, sir," she said and quietly left the store.

She walked down the street her back ramrod stiff and eyes fixed straight ahead. But by the time she passed the outskirts of town, her posture had slumped and her eyes filled.

"What am I going to tell Peter?" she cried as tears poured down her cold cheeks. "He'll want to raise a rumpus with that awful man. Why did he act so mean?"

She wiped her face with her glove. *Maybe I won't tell Peter what happened. Our poor baby! How can I make him some warm clothes now?*

Heart aching, she trudged toward the farmhouse, her only safe haven, beckoning from the hill. She had to pull herself together so Peter wouldn't see her tear-swollen face.

"Someday I'll go back to his store and make him wait on me," she declared defiantly. "Someday."

Westbrook, Massachusetts
June 1875

Catherine Thorpe huddled miserably in a stand of trees across from a rushing stream. The day had dawned wet and cold while a thick fog hung over the valley. Steam rose from the stream adding mist to the air.

When she awoke early that morning, the chill in the air darkened her mood. She had struggled to get warm, twisting and turning in her bed, the image of Peter and his darkie gnawing its way into her mind.

"I should be the one lying beside Peter instead of that niggra man-stealer!"

Peter had married Josephine not long after the heated confrontation with Catherine and they christened their son, born four months later, Joseph, after his mother. From all accounts, the child was the apple of Peter's eye. The whole situation was intolerable.

Catherine's mother had harped on her to stop thinking about Peter and go on with her life.

"He's not worth your heartache," she repeated, time and time again. "Besides I already had another match in mind, the nephew of one of my oldest friends."

To stop her mother's badgering, Catherine had given in and was introduced to the young man. Although he was good looking and treated her with courtesy and deference, emotionally she felt nothing. Peter's betrayal left no room in her heart to love another.

Peter's betrayal had also led her to this awful place. Peter's family farm. Her revenge would be complete. She would damn this place forever in Peter's memory.

Catherine shivered as a light breeze swirled around her. She had dressed hurriedly when she decided to put her plan into action and wore no boots to protect her feet from the damp ground. Her thin jacket gave only minimal warmth. If her plan worked, she would not be there long.

Catherine knew that every morning Josey rode her horse along this path; Catherine had hidden in the woods many times to watch. Catherine never cared much for riding, personally, but even she could see Josey was an excellent equestrienne. Making her death appear an accident would not be easy.

But I must go through with this! I cannot endure the torment of watching Peter with his repulsive Negro any longer.

Catherine stamped her feet impatiently. "Where is the little nappy-head? I'm freezing!"

30

She had chosen this place because the trees provided her with a weapon. She bent a young sapling down to the ground and waited. When horse and rider passed by, she would strike.

Faint at first, a sound grew louder.

"Hoof beats! I'll only get one chance! I mustn't fail!"

Josey and Shiloh were cantering along the trail at a steady pace. Catherine knew this was the spot where Josey let him have his head; she saw the horse gather himself in anticipation.

As Shiloh rounded the bend, Catherine released the tree. The trap was sprung. The results were horrific.

When the branch whipped out, the horse shied sideways, his body twisted in fright. He skittered so violently Josey lurched out of the saddle. Somehow she grabbed his mane and clung to his neck. But Shiloh's hooves slipped off the mossy bank of the stream and he stumbled. Unable to regain his balance with Josey hanging on his neck, he crashed heavily onto his side.

Catherine heard Josey's frightened cry and saw the horse thrash as he rolled in the water.

At last the horse struggled upright. He looked down at Josey lying motionless on the rocky stream bed and lowered his head to nose her. There was no response. Shiloh had no way of knowing he had crushed her beneath his body.

Catherine left her hiding place and ran to the edge of the stream. One look at Josey's unseeing eyes and broken body proved her scheme had succeeded.

Shiloh climbed awkwardly out of the water. Catherine regarded him as he stood trembling on the path, holding his right foreleg off the ground to ease the pain.

"Good," she exulted. "Peter will have to shoot you. You killed his beloved Josey. When he puts you out of your misery, the only living thing to remind me of her wretched existence will be the child."

When Josey failed to return from her ride, Peter became worried. He called his father to join him and they hurried off to find her.

Because he knew her daily routine, it didn't take Peter long to discover his wife's lifeless body. Peter, his face white and stoic, carried her in his arms all the way back to the house. His father trailed silently behind leading the injured horse.

Upon closer examination, Peter saw that Shiloh had suffered a deep muscle injury. Peter vowed to tend him until his leg healed. He did not blame the horse, and he knew Josey would have begged him to do everything he could to keep Shiloh alive and sound.

As customary, Josey's coffin lay in the front parlor where Peter sat by her side for three nights with their ten-year old son Joseph. Harriet put in a brief appearance and retreated to her room in silence. Seth took his place for a few hours each night so Peter could tend to the ailing horse.

"Good boy, easy Shiloh," he murmured as he kneaded liniment into the injured leg.

Peter vigorously rubbed the leg muscles until his hands cramped. When he stood up to stretch his aching back, he leaned against the horse and stroked the silky coat. Feeling the warmth of Shiloh's body against his released emotions he had locked inside. He dropped his head on the horse's shoulder and at last, he cried.

On the fourth morning, in a simple ceremony attended by only the immediate family, Josey was laid to rest in the field where she had spent so many happy hours riding her beloved Shiloh. Peter decided no headstone would mark her grave. She would become part of the earth that brought her so much joy.

Catherine had decided to let a decent period of mourning pass before beginning her campaign to win Peter back. Confident he would forgive her for the hateful things she had said when last they met, she planned to make a condolence call.

To her consternation, she learned Peter had left Westbrook with his son a short time after the funeral. If his family knew his destination, they were determined to keep his secret. They claimed that he had gone without a word.

Catherine at last admitted defeat. She had committed murder and although that did not trouble her, she was left alone and thwarted yet again. She lay awake the entire night and made her decision.

"I will encourage the tiresome nephew who is now a widower. He has money and position, which matters a great deal to me. I'll become the mistress of a great house and entertain all the right people. I can survive without love."

Without warning a pang of anguish struck her and her gray eyes filled. She hung her head and sobbed, but only for a moment. She brushed her tears away and pushed back her bedclothes. She must wash and dress. Her decision to marry for convenience gave her the strength to carry on with her deception.

"Mother will be thrilled," Catherine muttered bitterly. "She'd constantly badgered me for not accepting his proposal years ago. Dear uninspiring Clayton. He will never suspect my true feelings."

Eyes dry like a bird of prey, she swept from the room to talk with her mother. "We must make plans if I'm to become a married woman before the end of the year."

Chapter 3

Barn Swallow Inn
Westbrook, Massachusetts
Present Day

"Why doesn't our phone ring? It would be nice if we had some paying guests," Lissa grumped while she and Reene lingered over their morning coffee. "Maybe we're cursed or something. Can't you weave a spell with your Wiccan ways?"

"You know darn well I can't conjure up stuff like that," scoffed Reene. "But if we want guests to sit up and take notice, we'll need a website like every other business. Best way to advertise. I've got some ideas I've been fooling around with. Give me a few days."

Lissa admired her friend's tenacity. Reene spent every spare hour creating their website, tweaking it until it functioned precisely the way she wanted. One hectic morning she struggled with the tricky business of hooking up various links from their site to the local S.P.C.A. and Massachusetts animal shelters.

"Damn, I'm good!" she said triumphantly as everything fell into place. She dragged the mouse to save her work when without warning a small decorative candle on the shelf above the desk pitched directly onto the keyboard.

She jumped as the candle hit with a resounding *thwack*. The heel of her cowboy boot raked the switch on the surge protector under the desk. The results were catastrophic: the computer screen turned black.

For one horrified second, Reene stared at the screen with eyes wide in disbelief. Then she gave vent to her fate. Her anguished wails brought Lissa, carrying a manure fork with a road apple stuck between its tines, running from the paddock.

"What's wrong? What happened?" she panted, out of breath and ready to do battle.

Reene looked up at Lissa's weapon of mass destruction and burst out laughing. But her laughter bordered on hysteria.

"This stupid candle fell off the shelf and landed on the damn keyboard! It blew away my hard work! I lost everything!"

"Oh, my," Lissa gulped. "Lucky for the inn *and* your work the candle wasn't lit. You scared the crap out of me, literally." She lowered her manure fork. "Did you back up your files?"

"Yeah, I can recreate some of it, but all the links I hooked up this morning are gone!" Reene snatched up the offending candle and hurled it into the wastebasket.

"Do you feel better now?"

"Not much. I can't understand it! The stupid thing just jumped off the shelf. Almost as if it were pushed." She scowled at the computer as it took its time rebooting.

Lissa tiptoed from the room and retreated to the safety of the paddock.

"Great recovery after The Attack of the Killer Candle," Lissa approved. "You did an awesome job on our website. Horses dancing across the banner and a swallow darting into the barn. Too good. I noticed you managed to recreate the local S.P.C.A. and animal shelters links."

"The Killer Candle brought out *my* killer instinct. I hooked up the links in a heartbeat. And turnabout is fair play, *chica.* You did an awesome job with your well-chosen words."

"Thank you, ma'am. I am brilliant, aren't I? Between the mouthwatering descriptions of our breakfast menus and the enticing photos of our guest rooms, people should be hooked. When outdoor lovers—especially horse folks—check out our awesome trails, I want them to search no further for another inn."

"I have a good feeling about this," Reene assured her. "Didn't my uncanny dream come true? We'll make a few mistakes, but that's expected. Give it time."

Reene stepped away from the computer. "Back to more mundane stuff. Our website is up and running. Now we need a snazzy sign to advertise the inn."

"Indeed we do. An attention-grabbing image to snag guests before they beat a path to someone else's door. Time for another field trip."

After a bit of searching, they found the right place, a local shop with a beguiling name, *Signs of the Times.* However, when the owner, an artisan named John Fitch, greeted them, Reene and Lissa nearly turned and ran.

35

"Reene," Lissa muttered, "he looks like Grizzly Adams with a ponytail fetish! Those big hands look more suited to an axe than a paintbrush."

But as they bombarded Fitch with their ideas, he casually sketched a rough drawing of the inn, picturing barn swallows flying in and around the barn. Colorful local wild flowers brought the whole picture together. Enchanted, they commissioned him on the spot.

A week later, they hung their handcrafted sign, with its camel-back arch top, pin striping and ornate scroll work, on a wrought iron post at the end of the driveway. Gold leaf lettering on a hunter green background proclaimed 'Barn Swallow Inn'.

Lissa watched the sun playing on the gold letters while she watered impatiens hanging on the farmer's porch.

"Everything's fallen into place", she sighed. "Everything except the folks who'll pay our bills."

Lissa stopped as she passed through the Gathering Room and, for the umpteenth time, straightened the portrait that hung above the massive stone fireplace. When they had looked at the house the first day, the intriguing picture drew their attention like a magnet. According to the realtor, the portrait had hung there for over one hundred years, almost as if it belonged to the house and intended to stay there. As a conversation piece, it complemented the room and consequently it stayed.

Fascinated and troubled by the person staring out at her, she studied the portrait. A young Black soldier wearing the Union Army uniform stood stiffly in front of a tent, his rifle held loosely by his side. Belying the stiff posture, his face wore the hint of a Mona Lisa smile; his eyes had a joyous sparkle.

"What was up with that? In every Civil War photo I've ever seen, the unhappy people looked as if they were facing a firing squad. Oh, well. No one ever found out what Mona Lisa was smiling about either."

She leaned closer. The soldier wore some sort of white cloth around his head. Strange. The picture had darkened with age. Could this be a Matthew Brady? She peered around the frame. No signature. No Matthew Brady in sight.

"Where was I going before I got sidetracked? Oh, yeah, I was headed for my office. I've got a major case of Can't Remember Shit."

She hurried to the office without a backward glance. As the door closed behind her, the picture slipped back to its former lopsided position.

"What the hell?" Reene fumed. The latch on the pantry door had stuck fast. "I oiled the darn thing yesterday and the latch worked fine. Now it won't open."

Reene stamped into the kitchen and wrenched open the drawer under the sink. She grabbed the WD40 and returned to the door. She squirted liquid over the metal and after a bit of yanking and pushing, she freed the latch. Repeatedly she worked the latch, opening and closing the door. Satisfied, she headed for the kitchen and bumped into Lissa.

"What's up, woman?" Lissa asked. "You look a little frustrated."

"I am. I thought I had fixed the latch in the pantry, but I just tried to open it and almost ripped my fingers off."

"Ouch. And I've straightened that picture of the Civil War soldier so many times I do it automatically whenever I go into the Gathering Room. I know houses settle, but you'd think this creaky old ark would've settled after almost two hundred years. Must be gremlins."

Westbrook, Massachusetts
July, 1875

Peter had boarded the southbound train a week after he laid Josey to rest. His leave-taking had been heart-wrenching for him and his young son. Josey's death left him feeling empty and lost.

Now he'd lost his wife and his mother.

Harriet had never forgiven him for marring a Negro. When she had learned Josey was already with child, she had refused to say a word to her and had taken to her bed for two days.

An only son, Peter had always been close to his mother. When he was a boy, Harriet Williams thought the sun rose and set on his head. Not anymore. That had ended when he brought Josey into the family.

"How could my mother claim to love me so much and then all at once withhold her affection? I'll never understand or forgive her change in feelings toward me. Never!"

He glanced down at the sleeping child whose head rested on his lap. The train's motion had rocked Joseph to sleep almost immediately. He had roused his son from his warm bed early so they could take the 8:30 train to New York. From there they would transfer to another train that would take them to Canada.

Sitting alone with his thoughts, Peter noticed other passengers' reaction to his little boy. Some were pretending to ignore a White man and a Negro child traveling together and the obvious affection between the two. One woman sat rigid with disapproval while her husband openly stared.

"Is there a problem, sir?" Peter challenged. The man backed down.

His thoughts returned to the unhappy past. He remembered how worried Josey had been about meeting his parents and how he had soothed her fears. How wrong he had been.

He had hoped the arrival of their child might smooth things over and bring the two women closer. His hope died when Joseph was born. His mother looked at the newborn baby with such loathing that any chance of reconciliation was lost.

Peter recalled the first night he and his father, Seth, had sat up talking after everyone had retired.

"Dad, when you wrote you were involved with the Underground Railroad, I was shocked."

"Son, I couldn't just sit by and let those poor folk get thrown in jail or worse," he said as they relaxed by the fire. "You were risking your life every second and I was so proud of you. I've never even told your mother. She wouldn't have understood. And I wanted to do whatever I could that counted. I wanted to make you proud of me."

"I've always tried to be the kind of man you are. Compassionate, wise and loving. You stood up for your beliefs. What you did for Josey's people meant the world to us. And I don't know if I could have stayed here if you hadn't been so understanding about Josey."

"It wasn't easy at first. I was afraid you had gotten more than you bargained for. Your mother's reaction has hurt you to the core. I've talked to her for hours on end to try to make her see what a terrible mistake she's making. I'm sorry, son."

"I'm sorry too. She's lost me as sure as if a Confederate soldier had cut me down in the field."

His father winced as Peter continued. "I want to ask your advice," Peter said. "I want to tell this town why my wife became a spy for the Union Army. That she risked her life unselfishly time and again. That she died an honored citizen of this country. Couldn't we persuade the town officials to hold a ceremony to recognize her unselfish act?"

Peter saw conflicting emotions playing on his father's face.

"I'm afraid you will be turned down, Peter. Folks around here are still trying to recover from this war. It affected a lot of us in different ways. Some of the free Negroes are good people, but many of them have become Carpetbaggers and are running roughshod over folks who lost everything in the war. I agree with what you want to do, but I don't think others will feel the same. It goes without saying your mother would be horrified."

His father paused to collect his next words. "The North lost good men, thousands of them, in the war. Think on it, son. Have you forgotten why you were so eager to join the army?"

"Of course not, Dad. I only joined up because I didn't believe in slavery; that it was wrong to buy and sell people—" Peter broke off. Before he met Josey, he didn't consider slaves as people who had hopes and dreams just like Whites.

"You're right, son. None of us believed in slavery. But none of us believed Negroes were equal to Whites."

"I've changed!" Peter protested. "So have lots of people!"

"Meeting Josey has changed your opinion, but you're going to have hard work changing other folks' minds after years of fear and distrust."

"I understand what you're saying, Dad, but I want to do *something...*"

"Let it rest for now, son," Seth urged. "Let some years pass and then give it a try. People need time to forget."

Peter turned away from Seth's anxious face. He knew his father was right.

The night before his departure, Peter had sat down with his father again.

"I'll never forget how people in this town acted toward Josey. I'll never forgive Mother's treatment of my wife, either. Some day she may realize the harm she's done, but it will be too late."

Seeing the sorrow in his father's eyes, Peter tried to give him some words of comfort.

"Don't worry too much, Dad. We'll get along, Joseph and I. We need a fresh start, is all."

"So you're leaving us," Seth said sadly. "I can't blame you. Maybe it is for the best. I'll miss you and my grandson more than you'll ever imagine. Where will you go?"

"Canada sounds like as good a place as any. It seems like they truly welcomed the slaves who escaped during the war."

Seth nodded. "You'll keep in touch?"

"I'll do my best, Dad. Besides my son, you're the one person on earth I love."

Seth drew Peter to him in a fierce embrace. "I love you, boy. Remember that. And always remember me to little Joseph. He won't be little much longer, but no matter what happens, I want him to remember his grandfather."

"I give you my word, Dad. He won't forget you and what a good man you are. Who knows? We may come back some day. Oh, and Dad, please take care of Shiloh. You know how much he meant to Josey and me."

Before Seth awoke the next day, Peter and Joseph were gone.

Peter felt the train slowing. It rumbled to a stop and men rushed around picking up mail and loading other packages on board. He peered out the window and could see water being transferred into the tender at the front of the train. Then the conductor signaled and they were moving again. Peter sat back and eventually the motion lulled him to sleep.

Once the train reached New York, his mood had improved. After waking his son and gathering their belongings, he felt more alive than he had since the accident. He gripped Joseph's hand to help him down the steps.

Peter realized this could be a new beginning after all.

Chapter 4

"Lissa, if customers won't come to us, I'm going right onto the streets to charm *them*. With my awesome wagon, Sissy and I'll be irresistible."

Reene waved some papers at Lissa. "I made up some flyers to drop off at local businesses. I'm having smaller versions of our sign made for each side of the wagon. John Fitch is slaving over a hot awl as we speak."

"Wonderful idea! But remember, finesse, woman, finesse. But we should put an announcement in the local paper anyway. I'll do that tomorrow. I've been brainstorming too. We really should have a Grand Opening. How about a High Tea?"

"Hold me back. A High Tea?"

"Precisely. An afternoon tea would fit in with our Country Modern theme. We can invite the town officials and other businesspersons in town, like the grain and tack store owners and local horse owners."

"Good choices. Why don't we create a theme for each month? Maybe a Murder Mystery weekend or a Mother and Daughter Getaway or a Halloween Hoedown..."

"Aha! A hoedown! I wondered where you were going with this. We need to establish ourselves first. Let's concentrate on building up a good client base. And if we make it big time, then we'll definitely do different themes now and then."

"Promise, Mommy?" Reene wheedled.

"Yes, there's a good girl."

"I'll hold you to that promise! I'll check the Internet to see what we should serve. No doubt there's over a million hits for 'English High Tea'. I can make up invitations on our computer."

"Super!" Lissa smiled. "Oh, don't forget to put 'Casual dress' on the invitation."

"That's a relief," Reene said, rolling her eyes. "My tiara and ball gown are at the cleaners."

Lissa pushed open the door of the *Hampshire Times*. The façade looked just like old-fashioned newspaper buildings she'd seen in countless movies and television shows. She half expected to see a balding, wiry man wearing a visor bent over his copy.

"Good morning!"

Instead of a wizened geezer, an attractive petite brunette clad in a beige turtleneck sweater and rust colored riding breeches greeted her. "How can I help you?"

"I'm Lissa Martin. My friend Reene Anderson and I bought the Williams' farmhouse on Breckenridge Road. We've turned it into a bed and breakfast where guests can bring their horses. Now we're planning our Grand Opening. I want to place an ad, but I'm also hoping you could help me with our guest list."

"Oh, how fun! I'm Gina Richards, editor and publisher of the dear old *Times*."

The woman came forward to shake Lissa's hand. "I always knew that old farmhouse had possibilities. You and your friend may have finally picked the right combination for success. More than a few owners have discovered the house too much of a burden for them. You do know its history, right?"

The editor's dark brown eyes suddenly looked darker.

"Nooooo, but I have a feeling you're going to enlighten me. Is there anything we should be worrying about?"

"Nothing worrying in the true sense of the word. Except I've heard rumors swirling around about an accidental death the local people still aren't convinced *was* an accident."

Lissa felt her heart sink. "Oh? When did this accident take place?"

"Actually, the 'accident' happened in 1875. A young woman was killed in a fall from her horse. But stories get passed from generation to generation. In fact, the body count gets higher and the accident gets bloodier with each retelling."

"1875?? Good grief! These folks do have long memories. Reene and I won't get the vapors because someone met an untimely end over a century ago. I suppose there's a card-carrying ghost rattling chains and moaning during the light of the full moon?"

"Not that I'm aware of. But you never can be certain," the editor added, a wicked gleam in her eyes.

"Now that you've scared me to death," Lissa said, eyebrow raised, "shall we come back to the present and the upcoming social event of *this* century? Our High Tea is slated for the first Saturday in June."

"I'll make sure the ad appears in the next edition," the editor promised as they reviewed the copy. "A tour of the house and grounds is a definite selling point. I'll send you a list of names and addresses of local business owners and politicians I'd recommend you invite."

"Ms. Richards, I'm so grateful for your assistance. By the by, I noticed you're wearing breeches and spotted the English riding boots lying under your desk. Are you One of Us?"

The editor pushed back her long hair and looked Lissa squarely in the eye. "I am One of the Many. And please call me Gina. But I just can't find enough time to ride and run this newspaper. My admin went out on maternity leave and won't be back for six weeks."

"In that case, you're going to take some time for yourself because you are cordially invited to the Grand Opening of the Barn Swallow Inn. And you can write it off as work. Besides, you never know what might happen. Maybe a guest will spot a wee ghostie floating through the inn."

"How did it go at the newspaper?" Reene asked when Lissa returned. "Were they helpful?"

"Wonderful. The editor, Gina Richards, and I hit it off right away. Then I found out she's a rider! I invited her to our party. You don't mind, do you?"

"Mind? We need all the help we can get."

"You got that right. She did tell me a spooky story about this place, though. Ancient history, but a young woman was killed in a riding accident somewhere on our property."

"How ironic. A little weird, isn't it?"

"It gets weirder. There were hateful rumors it wasn't an accident."

Reene frowned. "Really? Lissa, you know how gossip gets around in small towns. When did this accident happen?"

"In 1875. Gina hinted some of the old timers carry on as though it were yesterday."

"Don't let warmed-over news worry you. Let's concentrate on making our inn pay its bills. Did she help you with the ad and guest list?"

"In spades. The ad goes in the paper tomorrow and she'll send the guest list later. It'll be interesting to see who she suggested. I trust her judgment though. As the editor of the local newspaper, she's privy to all the comings and goings of the business people. At least we'll get a head's up of Who's Who in Westbrook."

"I'm driving Sissy into town, Lissa. Do you need anything special?"

"Can I tag along? I need to pick up some Ivemectrin. It's time to worm the horses."

"No problem. Could you give me a hand hitching up the wagon?"

"Sure. Hey, did you remember your flyers?"

Reene held up a large manila envelope. "I printed thirty last night. I'm going to cover the town with them after I hang the new signs on the wagon."

Signs hung, the two friends set off via the old carriage road, a hidden gem they'd missed at their first viewing. Reene asked Sissy to set a leisurely pace, but it didn't take them long to roll into town. People emerging from shops and strolling along the sidewalks smiled and waved as they drove by.

After Reene tethered her horse and wagon securely to a railing, she scooped up her flyers and with Lissa in tow headed to the Post Office. To Lissa's surprise, their box was stuffed with mail.

"Awesome," she smiled. "I hope these envelopes are from potential guests."

While picking up their grain order at Baril's Grain & Tack Store, Reene asked the owner to recommend a good farrier.

"You won't find a better man than Ernie Haines," Art Baril said. "He shoes my horses and comes right out when you need him. Just so you know, he's a blacksmith, not a farrier. Some guys are touchy about that. I have his number here somewhere. Hold on, here it is."

"Thanks so much!" Reene held up her flyers. "Art, could you post a few of these in your shop?"

"We'd really appreciate it," Lissa chimed in.

"No problem." Art adjusted his glasses to read the flyer more closely. "What the heck is a High Tea? I'd better ask my wife."

He shook his head and gave her a rueful smile. "Why don't you hand them out at the grocery store and hardware store? Lots of people in and out all day long."

"Thanks for the tip," Lissa said. "Watch for your invitation. We might see you sooner than you think."

To her surprise, Art's eyes turned frosty. "No chance of that happening. Not if our Town Treasurer's going to be there."

"Lissa, you touched a nerve," Reene said when they got outside. "He was not a happy camper. What do you think that was all about?"

"I can't imagine," Lissa replied. "He started out being friendly enough."

While the grain was being loaded, they visited more local shops and dropped off the flyers. When they returned to the wagon, they climbed onto the bench seat and Reene called the blacksmith's number on her cell phone.

Lissa smiled at how incongruous her friend looked, talking on a cell phone while sitting on the seat of a horse-drawn wagon.

"Lissa, I lucked out!" Reene said when she ended the call. "Ernie's coming this afternoon. We'd better knock on it."

She pulled on her driving gloves, gathered her reins and settled comfortably on the seat that Lissa had scorned.

"Let's go, Sissy," Reene commanded and they set off at a brisk trot. The mare knew she was headed home and put some action into her gait. Her legs sprung from the ground. Reene let Sissy have her head and the mare hustled them home.

"I'm cutting it close. We'll barely have enough time to grab a bite to eat before Ernie arrives."

"Reene, the blacksmith is here," Lissa hollered. In the kitchen Reene wolfed down her sandwich and they went out onto the farmer's porch to greet him.

Lissa watched a state-of-the-art half-ton pickup, black with silver anvils stenciled on both doors, maneuver up the driveway. The monster truck was shining like a new dime.

"Afternoon, ladies." Ernie Haines waved a work-swollen hand. "I'm here to look at your horses' feet."

As he lumbered out to meet the two women, Lissa cocked her head to one side. *Where have I seen that walk before? And those clothes: dark grey work pants sagging under a protruding belly and a short-sleeved shirt?*

When Ernie removed his tan Fedora to reveal his almost bald head, she gasped in recognition. Her grandfather! Ernie was the spittin' image, almost. She remembered how her grandfather had been her best pal as she grew up, taking her to movies, giving her an allowance—for doing nothing—and championing her pleas to her parents to provide a sibling. It didn't work, but she always loved him for that. She hated being the Only Child and envied Reene who had two loving sisters.

45

"We spoke on the phone earlier," Reene told him. "With any luck, you'll be the answer to our prayers."

"Hello. Nice to meet you," replied Lissa, jolted out of her nostalgic memories. She extended her hand. "I'll show you the way to the barn. We'll bring the horses one at a time. Reene, will you bring Shenan in first?"

Lissa watched Ernie's eyes wander around the barn, taking in the tack room, grain storage bin and the area that would someday become the warm room.

"Nice," he commented, although Lissa wasn't sure he meant the barn or the horse waiting patiently on the cross ties.

"Have you always been a blacksmith?" Lissa asked.

Ernie picked up Shen's right front leg and tapped her hoof with his hoof knife. "Nope. Worked as a lumberjack once and almost got killed. The wife got worried she'd lose her paycheck. So I became a blacksmith. Learned to forge wrought-iron doo-dads to sell at local gift shops. The wife liked that even better. This animal is fine. Good strong hooves. No cracks. Whoever did 'er before did a good job. Next."

Reene released Shen and walked her back to her paddock. Lissa hustled to fetch Bravo, anxious to hear what this blacksmith-of-few words had to say about her horse's tripping habit. He'd almost landed on his nose one too many times.

Lissa hauled her stubborn horse out of his stall. Food—definitely not her—was the love of Bravo's life and he didn't want to leave his flake of hay. She hooked him onto the cross ties and the blacksmith began his inspection.

"Bravo's good with farriers," she promised. "He's never tried to kick or bite."

"Heard that story more than once. Hmmmm," Ernie muttered and her heart lurched. What had he found?

"Hmmmm?" she repeated. "Is there a problem?"

"I can see he's had his heels lowered. And the toes are rolled. Is he a tripper?"

"The worst. My former farrier said rolling the toes would help."

"It would. Did it?"

"A little. And like me, he's not as young as he used to be."

"Just keep his attention on his job. He's in good shape. He's got that stocky Quarter Horse chest. You're doing things right. Next."

As Reene passed leading Sissy, Lissa whispered "Bravo received Ernie's stamp of approval. Two down, one to go."

Sissy passed with flying colors too. Ernie showed a mild interest when he heard Reene planned to use her exclusively as a driving horse.

"Your horses' feet are in good condition. I'll do my best to keep 'em that way. Give me a call when you need me."

"We appreciate your coming out," Reene said. "How much do we owe you?"

"I'll send you a bill. Take your time paying. You're good horse people. Too bad I can't say the same for some people in this town."

Before Lissa could figure out his cryptic remark, Ernie climbed back into his truck and bumped down the dirt road in a cloud of dust.

The two women exchanged perplexed glances. "I guess we're his new customers," Reene said. "But if there's anything I hate, it's a gabby blacksmith."

Chapter 5

"Lissa, if half these people show up at our fancy High Tea," Reene said when Gina Richards' prospective guest list popped into their email, "our business will take off. Check out these names. The mayor and his wife; the banker who had handled the sale of our inn; police and fire chiefs; tack and grain store owners; and the local vet."

"Mostly the wives will attend. I can't picture some of these guys sipping tea and eating scones and éclairs."

"No doubt you're right, but the political types won't have a problem with tea and crumpets. They're used to the rubber chicken circuit—now let 'em eat cake!"

"What else do we need to think about?"

"Now that you mention it, should we rent a tent or take our chances with the weather?"

"I vote for the tent. If it rains, our Open House may get pretty soggy."

"I'll check with the rental place to see what the drop-dead date is for renting the beast. I'm praying they'll send a couple of strong men to put the darn thing up. Remember what happened when I tried to put up a tent last summer when we took our horses camping? Bravo could have done a better job."

"No kidding. Woodland creatures are still telling stories about you," Reene chuckled.

"Very funny. OMG! I just remembered who we've left off the list! Horse people! What did I do with the phone book? Some clubs and stables should be listed."

"Phone book! This isn't the Dark Ages. Let's check the Internet. We were so busy inviting the butcher, the baker and the candlestick maker we forgot the moneymakers."

A quick Internet search identified three stables and one rent-for-hire place. Most were within an easy drive to the inn.

"Saved by the Net! We almost got caught with our riding pants down," Lissa snickered.

"Next on the agenda is the burning question: what do we serve?"

"Didn't you get any hits on the Net describing High Teas?"

"9,371 hits to be exact. I narrowed the selections down a tad: quiche, deviled eggs, stuffed mushrooms, and finger sandwiches. Nothing we can't handle."

"Stop already! You're making me hungry. What about desserts?" Lissa never met a dessert she didn't like.

"We could do a chocolate or berry trifle, mini éclairs, scones, and cream puffs. Does that satisfy your sweet tooth?"

"I can feel it clamoring for something gooey and fattening. Dare I ask if the invitations are finished?"

"Trot over to the computer and I'll show you."

When she brought up the file, Lissa gasped in delight. Reene had created a charming graphic of a country inn with barn swallows in flight in the background and a grazing horse in the foreground.

"You are amazing! What a gorgeous picture!" She dragged her glasses out of her tangled hair and read through the wording.

"'Please join us on Saturday, June 2nd for the Grand Opening of the Barn Swallow Inn ...one to five p.m., R.S.V.P. to our phone number and email address'. As we say in the old country, spot on! Do you think we can mail them today? We want to make sure the V.I.P.s have enough lead time."

"I'm sure we can. I'll print them out on this cool parchment paper I've been hoarding, address the envelopes and we're golden."

"Why don't we also plan to set up wine, cheese and crackers in the spring house? Offering a surprise treat during the tour of the grounds will keep guests on their toes."

"Whipping up all the food and taking care of the kids will keep *us* on *our* toes," Reene said. "We've got one chance to make a good first impression. Let's not make it our last."

As the days flew by, Reene and Lissa worried there weren't enough hours in the day to prepare all the food, take care of their animals and put finishing touches on the inn. Positive replies to the invitations trickled in each day. Even if most of their invitees were merely curious, the publicity was good for business.

Early Friday morning trucks loaded with tables, chairs, and the tent lined up in front of the inn.

"Hey," asked the burly driver, "where do you want the tent? Over by the barn?"

"No, not there," Reene answered. "On the front lawn on the opposite side of the house. Follow me!"

When the workmen unloaded tables and chairs and set up the tent, Bravo, Shen and Sissy had trotted eagerly to the fence, their ears pricked, their eyes alight with interest. But as the huge yellow and white tent rose to its full height, the horses, blowing and snorting, scattered in fright. After a while their curiosity got the best of them and they were back, acting like sidewalk superintendents.

Blood, sweat and tears were shed until tables, chairs and the enormous tent were at last in position. As the last rental truck drove at warp speed away from the inn, Reene and Lissa surveyed the total effect.

"Well, Reene, we've given the lawns a manicure, planted flowers and pulled weeds. The spring house has been aired and looks spectacular. We're ready for them. I hope they're ready for us."

"Let's hit the hot tub. Whose turn is it to feed? I'm so tired I can't remember."

"I hate to tell you, but it's yours. I'll do it if you're too pooped."

"No, no. I'll never forget: the horse comes first. Only don't be shocked if you discover me face down in the grain bin."

Town Hall
Westbrook, MA

"I understand the Williams' farmhouse has been sold again." Lloyd Collins swirled the last of his brandy before draining the amber liquid.

"Nothing gets by you, does it? It's all over town that Allan Chapman is spending his commission money faster than an F-16." Auburn-haired Andrea Wilson's eyes gleamed with envy.

"The two new owners are ripping up walls and floors and ceilings. They're doing a complete renovation and restoration. I hear they're catering to the horsey set."

"Which means people with money. Aren't you hoping for some new clientele?"

"I'll take them any way I can. My business is thriving, thank you very much. Why don't we discuss the subject dearest to your heart? How is the campaign progressing?"

"I've already made plans with my campaign manager on issues I need to address. You know, the usual bullshit: build better schools, improve roads, and no new taxes. But I've crafted a hot proposal that'll make the rubes sit up and take notice: a new off-ramp from the Mass Pike."

"Aren't you the clever girl? I like it. Nonetheless, I fear some of 'the rubes' as you so condescendingly call them, will not share your enthusiasm."

"And why not? What's the matter with them? Can't they realize the money they can make from tourists who'd be attracted by the new exit?"

"Ahh, She Who Worships the Almighty Dollar. My feeling is the same as the rubes: our modest town will loose its rural atmosphere."

"Don't be so patronizing. You hate the small town attitudes as much as I do."

"Hate is too strong a word. Let me put it another way: I like our bucolic town but not necessarily all the people in it."

"Am I included in the 'like' group?"

"Some days 'yes' and some days 'no'. I should be used to our cat and dog fights from our dear dead college days. This is an I-don't-give-a-crap day."

Her raucous laughter, like fingernails on a blackboard, echoed around the room.

"I'll take that as a 'yes'. You'll be interested to hear, I'm sure, that I received an invitation to the frou-frou High Tea at the farmhouse. Pardon me, Barn Swallow Inn. I'll act the contented guest while I try to find out all the dirt on these two newcomers."

"Try not to piss off anyone in the first five minutes. You can rub people the wrong way by merely saying 'hello'. Remember, you need to win friends and influence people. For your upcoming campaign, this is the perfect opportunity."

"Don't worry your fluffy little head. I'll give you a full report after I've drunk gallons of tea and eaten a shitload of little sandwiches with no crusts."

"Ever the gracious lady. I wasn't invited to the soiree," Collins snapped. "However, I'm positive no one will miss me. Cheers."

He slammed the door behind him and seconds later his car roared down the street.

"Touchy, touchy. So, what do I wear to this freakin' High Tea?"

Chapter 6

"Lissa, everything for our High Tea was spot on. But I'm giving Shen and Sissy a last-minute curry before we put the linens and other stuff on the tables. No one will notice except horse people, but it couldn't hurt."

"Yeah, Brav's probably covered with shavings. I'll pop out to the barn when I've filled my tummy. Speaking of grooming, what are you wearing? I'm dragging out my old faithful beige broomstick skirt and tunic top. Covers a multitude of sins. With my stone necklaces and bracelets, I'll be casually elegant in my Mother Earth duds."

"Sounds good, Mother Earth. I'm wearing gaucho pants, loose white tee shirt and cowboy boots. I want to be comfortable. How's that for a combo?"

"Works for me. By the by, where is your doggie? Andes will bay his head off at the guests if we let him loose."

"I put him in his kennel in my room. Too much excitement. I think he'll do better with a one-on-one situation later on, once we get some customers."

"Excellent plan," agreed Lissa. "It might be bad for business if one of the guests got chomped by your over-protective canine."

Wandering the grounds before the anticipated 1:00 o'clock arrival time, Reene gazed at the inn as if she were seeing it through a stranger's eyes. Antique carriage lampposts dotting the driveway reminded her of old gas lights on Beacon Hill.

She delighted in the large baskets of hot pink and white impatiens that hung from post and rail fences lining the driveway. Purple impatiens repeated the theme on the farmer's porch. Wooden rocking chairs padded with comfy cushions would invite guests to sit and rock their cares away. Poor Lissa mashed her fingers hanging that two-handed saw and wooden sled on the porch, but what's an old inn without them?

In the morning sunshine, the inn gleamed like a snow-capped mountain. Black shutters on the front and sides showcased its historic

New England character. A large black barn star hung above the front door. Inside the farmhouse the scent of fresh wildflowers filled every room. Long white ruffled curtains stirred at the windows.

"Perfect," she approved, soaking up the peaceful setting. She turned her attention back to the inspection of the tables. "We spent hours polishing my silver tea service and washing China cups. If the guests don't notice, they don't deserve us!"

As she concentrated on rearranging a centerpiece of orange and yellow tiger lilies in a tall leaded crystal vase, two cars made their way up the driveway. She hurried over to greet them.

"Well, at least four people showed up. I hope they brought their appetites."

After the first guests arrived, there was a flurry of activity as more cars appeared. Couples wandered among the tables, greeting friends and sampling the pastries. The sides of the tent tugged gently at its moorings as a cooling breeze wafted through.

While Lissa dispensed tea and conversation, Reene joined a couple at a nearby table. A tall man with sandy-colored hair stood talking with an attractive woman. She remembered him from the closing when they passed papers. He was Randal Simms, the loan officer at the bank.

His full beard and mustache gave him a distinct college professor image. The only thing missing was a tweed coat with suede patches at the elbows. He was talking and gesturing so enthusiastically his companion could do little but nod and smile.

"Mrs. Anderson! May I introduce you to Andrea Wilson? She is our Town Treasurer and in the near future may become our new mayor."

"Please call me Reene. Pleased to meet you. How exciting! Lissa and I will register to vote once we've put down roots in Westbrook."

"I will remind you," Andrea smiled. A tall, big boned woman, her auburn hair was styled to frame her open face. Her beige linen pantsuit, obviously cut by an expensive designer, flattered her figure.

Reene took in the moss green and gold silk scarf, held in place by a diamond stickpin, draped around the woman's shoulders. Gold link bracelets gleamed on her right wrist and a ruby and diamond ring on her right hand looked like it had once belonged to the Crown Jewels. Money and good taste. Did she have a personality to match?

"I wish you a lot of luck," Reene said. "Not too long ago I was elected president of a non-profit organization and the infighting almost drove me insane. Friendships were ruined and blows almost exchanged. Some members fought against the mere suggestion of a woman president and others believed only a man could do the job. Power does strange things to some people."

"Surely you wouldn't put *your* experience on the same level as being elected chief executive of a town this size," Andrea responded with a slight edge of sarcasm. "In my opinion, there *is* no comparison."

"Oh, no, of course not! But I promised myself never to discuss or get involved with politics again."

"It's best to accept one's limitations. If you will excuse me," Andrea purred, "there's something I must tell Mayor Stuart." She nodded coolly to Reene and Randal and headed toward the tent.

"I'm afraid I've offended her," Reene worried. "I didn't mean that the way it sounded."

"Between you and me," the banker whispered, "it doesn't take a lot to offend that woman."

"I'll make it up to her. Enjoy the food and drink. And please don't miss our tour of the house and barn."

"I certainly won't. I'm an amateur photographer. I may stumble on some interesting subjects for photo ops as I wander around."

"I'd love to see your work. Maybe you could do some publicity photos for the inn."

"I'd like that very much," he responded. "You and your friend have done a marvelous job on the old place. Good luck."

He shook her hand in parting and left in search of greener pastures.

"Reene?" smiled a brown-haired woman dressed from head to toe in denim. "I'm Linda Baril from the grain store. Art's wife."

"I'm so glad you could come! Your turquoise earrings and cuff bracelet are right out of the Southwest! Where's your husband?"

"Art's holding down the fort at the store. He'd be mighty uncomfortable at a High Tea."

No kidding. He darn near froze Lissa to death when she invited him. "I'm not surprised. I imagine most of the men were dragged here by their wives."

"Between us, that's not the only reason he'd be uncomfortable. I hope you don't mind, we've just met, but I'm in need of a sympathetic ear. He's frustrating me no end."

"What's wrong?" Reene asked. Looked like she'd opened up a can of worms.

"He had a suspicion Andrea Wilson would be here. He's nothing but bad things to say about her since we nearly lost the business a few years ago. We owed four months back taxes. Art's old school. He figured he'd have a grace period to get caught up. But as Treasurer, Ms. Wilson decided that foreclosure was the only option. If it hadn't been for the generosity of friends and family, we'd have lost what we spent a lifetime building. Unlike me, Art won't forgive or forget."

"I'm so sorry, Linda. I had no idea. And I don't mind a bit if you cry on my shoulder."

"Art's been telling everyone who'll listen how unfair Andrea Wilson is and that he wouldn't vote for her if her name was the only one on the ballot." Linda blinked away the tears that threatened. "Now that I've gotten that out of my system, I brought you an inn-warming present." Linda handed a gift bag to Reene.

"How thoughtful of you!" Reene exclaimed. Inside the bag were knitted face cloths each with a different design at the center. She enveloped the woman in a warm hug.

"Thank you Linda! These are fabulous! Lissa will figure out a creative way to display them."

"I'm so glad. By the way, where is your friend?"

"She's passing goodies around at the tables under the tent. I see the mayor is holding her captive."

"I pity her, poor thing. Reene, I'd heard you are Head Chef. In my other life I used to cook for the Salvation Army so I appreciate how difficult it is to come up with different menus. As one old warhorse to another, aren't you tired of cooking the same meals every morning?"

"Not really. I love experimenting with new ways to prepare food and Lissa is very artistic in her presentation."

"If you ever want to swap recipes, give me a call."

"I'll take you up on that. Speaking of recipes, my popovers are scrumptious if I do say so myself. They're my specialty. I'm thinking of serving them every day with breakfast. Imagine the look on people's faces when I tell them they're eating Sally Laplanders. That's what popovers were called during the Civil War and I'm using the recipe I found—"

Andrea, who was hovering nearby, gasped and started to choke. When she tried to clear her throat, her face flushed and her nose ran.

Reene rushed to her aid. "Can you breathe? Should I do the Heimlich?" Reene moved behind the stricken woman but Andrea whirled around.

"Don't touch me!" Andrea rasped. Coughing spasms racked her body. "Some food must have gone down the wrong pipe."

"Would you like a drink of water? Take this," Linda said, handing her a napkin. "Your mascara's running."

"You're too *kind*, Mrs. Baril. I'm fine." Andrea had regained her composure, but a patronizing tone crept into her voice. "Please, Reene, go on with your story."

"Sorry to disappoint you, but there's not much more to my story except I found a fascinating recipe for popovers. Our guests will get a kick out of the name 'Sally Laplanders'."

"Where did you say you found the recipe?" Andrea asked.

"On the Internet. You can look up just about anything on the Net," Reene answered.

"That is so true," Andrea agreed, her voice now cordial. "I'll have to book a room and sample your *famous* Sally Laplanders."

"Please do. We'd be glad to have you. Excuse me, ladies. It's time I kicked off the first tour of the house and grounds."

"I'd love to join your first tour group," Andrea said.

"Absolutely! Maybe the others will follow your lead."

"I'll wait for the next tour," Linda said. "I'd prefer the company of your yummy desserts, Reene."

"Be careful, Mrs. Baril," Andrea cooed. "Cream puffs tend to migrate to one's hips."

"Come along then!" Reene jumped between the two bristling women before a cat fight ensued and led them to the dessert table.

"Afternoon everyone! Thank you all so much for coming. Lissa and I really appreciate your support." A murmur of replies ran through the group. "Now, who can't wait to explore the inn and stables?"

Several women stepped forward eagerly. Reene noted the men were suddenly busy discussing the latest sporting event while helping themselves to goodies. She gathered everyone together like a mother hen with her chicks.

"Follow me, please. We'll start with the barn and outbuildings." She led her group out to the paddocks where the horses were grazing.

"These are our horses: Bravo, Shenan and Sycamore's Folly, better known as Sissy. Bravo and Shen are Quarter Horses and—"

Bravo ambled over at the mention of his name and the mayor's wife gasped when he put his head over the fence.

"Oh, poor thing! Is he blind?"

"No, no, Mrs. Stuart. He's wearing a fly mask. A lot of people make that assumption. It's made of mesh, like the screens on our windows. He can see right through it."

"Oh, dear. I guess I don't know much about horses."

"That's why I'm here. You'll be taking lessons before you know it."

Meanwhile, Lissa was trying to extricate herself from incumbent Mayor Robert Stuart. He had introduced himself and asked a few polite questions concerning her and the inn. Once relieved of his civic duty, he then felt free to launch into a discussion of his views of the world's troubles, large and small.

Trapped, Lissa was delighted when she saw a familiar figure walking along the path.

"Gina!" she hailed a little too loudly. "I'm so glad you to see you!"

"Lissa, it's so nice to see you again too," Gina replied. "Mr. Mayor, it's nice to see you as well. I trust the feeling is mutual?"

Mr. Mayor hesitated a moment before a big smile transformed his face. "Mrs. Richards, it is always a pleasure. Even though we don't always see eye to eye politically is no reason we can't enjoy such a magnificent day. Mrs. Martin has gone to great lengths to provide a congenial atmosphere." He bowed to Lissa. "Such a charming hostess."

"Such a charming guest," Lissa said. One of them was lying and she was pretty sure it wasn't her. Before he could launch into another tirade, she linked her arm with Gina's.

"Please excuse us, Mayor Stuart. I've been anxious to show off our new barn to Gina. She's an accomplished horsewoman, and I'm sure she'll be impressed."

He bowed again and moved off in the direction of the dessert table.

"Thank goodness!" Lissa confided when he strolled out of earshot. "My ear started sprouting a cauliflower."

Gina laughed. "He is a bit much, isn't he? In my opinion, he was *born* the mayor of Westbrook and plays the part well. He's the type who can wear a cutaway coat and top hat to a basketball game and not look ridiculous. But if he's not careful, this year he might find himself out of a job. The woman opposing him has some powerful friends and apparently unlimited funds behind her."

"Gina, there's an old saying, 'Never talk about religion or politics'. Let's talk about our mutual passion: horses."

"Agreed. Horses are much more interesting than politics. Lead me to your barn, woman!"

Lissa brightened as more vehicles pulled into the parking area. A big F-150 truck with Steeple Hill Stables printed on its side rolled up. Two young women and two young girls hopped out. The girls were wearing riding breeches and tall boots.

"Good afternoon," she welcomed. *Be still my heart! Horse people!*

"I'm so glad you could come. I'm Lissa Martin, co-owner of the inn. I'll bet you're in need of a drink and something to munch on."

"Then you'd win the bet," one of the women replied. "It's been a hellacious day. I'm Laurie Hayes, my husband Frank is the local vet. These two young ladies are our daughters Ashley and Emily and this is my friend Allison Hanlon. Ashley and Emmy take lessons at Allison's barn and they've been dying to see your place."

Lissa smiled broadly at the two girls. "Barn brats? I'll bet you'd like to see the horses and barn instead of taking a tour of an old inn, right?"

The two girls grinned back at her and immediately chorused, "YES!"

"Well, come on! We can't keep two demon equestriennes waiting."

"By the way, Mrs. Martin," Laurie said, "Frank received your invitation but as usual, an emergency call came in. So I volunteered to come in his place with Allison and my girls."

"I'm sorry your husband couldn't be here. I'm sure we'll meet him another time and, hopefully, not for another emergency call. Was it anything serious?"

"Serious enough. A mare in labor had a breech presentation and she's a first-time mom. The family is crazy about her and doesn't want to loose her. Fortunately for them, Frank's had plenty of experience with breech births. He's the best."

When Lissa returned from escorting the new arrivals, she excused herself for a quick word with Reene.

"Lissa, the spring house was a big hit. My group got so excited when they discovered the cheese and wine. Too bad the men couldn't drag themselves away from the dessert table. They would have had a pleasant surprise."

"I did notice a general lack of enthusiasm for joining the ladies when you made your offer," Lissa noted. "It's my turn now. I'll try to persuade them to broaden their horizons. I'll dazzle 'em with fascinating tidbits about the coffin door, extra wide planks and buffet closet. If that doesn't work, I'll treat them like a herd of stubborn mules and dangle a carrot in front of them. But instead of a carrot, I'll dangle champagne."

Lissa winked at Reene and walked over to the stragglers. She slipped her arm within the mayor's and smiled her best used-car salesperson's smile.

"I'd like you gentlemen to stop talking shop and get some exercise. Come with me, please. I guarantee you won't be bored and you might even get a pleasant surprise."

Mayor Stuart and his cronies amiably put down their drinks and heaved themselves out of their chairs. They didn't stampede toward her, but at least they didn't act like they were walking to the guillotine.

"Good afternoon, young lady," beamed a walrus-mustachioed man in uniform. "Thank you for inviting me. Fire Chief Ken Bourassa. The mayor filled me in on your new bed and breakfast. In fact, we're predicting it'll be a success. It's just what this town needs."

Lissa shook his hand. "We think so too, Chief. And thank you for your kind words, especially 'young lady'! Shall we go?" Still keeping a firm grip on the mayor's arm, she headed for the inn.

"By your leave, good sirs, we'll enter through the coffin door!"

As she had expected, there were a few murmurs from the group.

"Coffin door? I don't like the sound of that at all," Chief Bourassa remarked.

"Sounds like doom, doesn't it? Sadly, the coffin door was associated with death. The front door was built wider than normal to allow coffins to pass in and out in the event of a death in the family. Funeral parlors were too expensive in the 1800s and most people were waked at home."

"Interesting, young woman," Stuart said. "I do believe I'm going to enjoy this tour."

Lissa led them through the inn and upstairs to the guest rooms. She pointed to the floor in the front bedroom.

"Notice anything unusual?"

"Those floor boards are a mile wide!" Will Jackson, a town selectman who had introduced himself to Lissa earlier exclaimed. "I've never seen any like them before."

"And you probably never will again," Lissa answered. "These boards were cut almost two feet across. Today boards like these cost a fortune, just as they did in pre-Revolutionary days. Evidently our late, unlamented former King, George III, forbade the use of these planks in colonists' houses for a good reason. He wanted them exclusively to build his ships. Did you notice our black-banded chimney? The black band represented loyalty to the King. Quite a few less than loyal colonists laid the planks on the second floor to keep them out of sight of the Tax Man. A hundred years later some people still hide home improvements to avoid paying more taxes. Some things never change, do they?"

Her little group burst into laughter. She knew she wouldn't have much trouble persuading them to finish the tour, since she planned to end at the spring house where the palate-tempting goodies awaited.

She led them down the back stairs, stopping to explain that the current kitchen once contained the blacksmith shop. This discovery brought even more comments from her charges.

"Anyone familiar with the term 'buffet closet'?" Lissa asked as her group walked along the main passage.

No one rose to her challenge. With a mock sigh she ushered them into the former dining room that contained the buffet closet.

"The way to a man's heart is feeding him pastries kept in this closet," she paraphrased. "No self-respecting matron would be caught dead with an empty cupboard. This is where pies, sweet breads and cakes were kept so the hostess could serve her guests at a moment's notice."

Lissa could see the mayor salivating at the mention of all those desserts. She'd found a kindred spirit. His sweet tooth matched hers bite for bite.

"Gentlemen, you have been patient long enough. We'll take a quick spin through the barn and then you'll earn your reward in our spring house. As the name suggests, the building was built over a spring to keep food and drink cool. I'll let you wonder about that as I show off our brand new barn."

Three hectic hours later all the guests were gone. The flowers were wilted and so were Lissa and Reene. They surveyed the empty tables that once had looked so fresh and inviting. A solitary glass of wine and a half-empty platter of limp finger sandwiches were all that was left of the once-appetizing fare.

"Praise the Lord, none of the China cups got smashed," Lissa said. She prowled from table to table inspecting for damage.

"Know what, Lissa? I'm sure all our guests had a blast. Everyone I met showed a genuine interest in our inn. It'll take a little time for them to warm up to us. Don't forget, we're Outsiders. We've got to prove ourselves."

"How much time? Five years? Sorry. Even my eyelashes are tired. Let's clean up the mess and give ourselves a well-deserved night off. If the gossip grapevine is still doing its job, we may have cultivated new friends. And for a refreshing change, we might find ourselves with an inn full of paying guests."

Andrea Wilson raced through a stop sign without slowing down.

"Stupid bitch! Comparing her stint as officer of some asinine little club to my professional career!" she snarled on the way home from the inn. "Little Miss Sunshine probably never worked hard for anything in her life. Her husband conveniently died and left her a fortune. And she probably had the perfect storybook marriage. She and that goody-two-shoes friend paid cash for that overpriced inn!"

"God, that blonde charmer and her damn Sally Laplanders. I've got to be more careful in the future. If I let a slip like that trip me up, I don't deserve to get elected mayor of Westbrook, USA."

Westbrook was only the first step in her climb to the top of the political heap. Before the suckers realize what hit them, she'd be in control.

She had spent a lifetime creating Andrea Wilson. Her parties in New York had all been A-list with the smart set. By guile and judicious flattery, she had managed to keep her friends after her divorce from Stephen, a man with a big wallet but few political ambitions.

Did she have any real friends? Her mind kept pace with her black Lexus. No, she didn't and that's how she wanted it. Close friendships mean sharing and she couldn't risk sharing anything.

Throughout her life everyone knew her, but in fact, no one really knew her. Not even Stephen, though he had tried harder than anyone.

"Poor bastard, he did really love me. Too bad he made the fatal mistake of asking if I wanted to join the ranks of the mother brigade." She could still see wounded bewilderment in his eyes when she had lashed out at him like a shrew.

But that was all in the past. She had made her decision and had rebuilt her life. Her intention never wavered to become as important and well known as her former husband.

She considered stopping to visit Lloyd, her former lover. "He's probably sulking because he wasn't invited to that fancy High Tea. If one of his clients kicked the bucket and entrusted him with a fortune, he'd forget about the tea fast enough."

She gunned the Lexus and it leaped forward in response. Like a moonshiner escaping from the sheriff, she whipped the car along the back roads. Dusk had fallen when the car slid to a stop in front of Lloyd's building.

"If he's still pissed," Andrea snorted, "he'll get over his snit when I tell him a beautiful blonde may need help spending her insurance money."

Chapter 7

Inside the sandstone building that Lloyd Collins Esq., Certified Public Accountant, occupied, Collins had been crunching figures all day. Now his brain needed a rest. He rolled his head back and forth to ease the strain on his neck. His tall angular body protested from being hunched for so long.

Lloyd moved to the black leather sofa and stretched out, his head resting on a throw pillow. His gaze roamed around the room. An Ethan Allen corner table, Chippendale chairs by the used-brick fireplace and a tapestry rug on the hardwood floor screamed a high-end price tag. In the firebox a gas log insert gave an illusion of a carefully laid wood fire. When cooler weather arrived, he kept it lit during business hours. His clients loved the homey touch.

He hadn't appreciated the intrinsic value his expensive belongings brought to his business until Andrea convinced him potential clients would notice his good taste.

"To make money," she'd bitched, "you have to spend some, for God's sake."

"My dear Andrea," Lloyd now muttered from his comfy sofa. "You certainly persuaded me to spend my money."

He settled deeper into the sofa and adjusted the pillow behind his head. When he and Andrea had lived together in college, their décor was Early Yard Sale. Nothing second hand about his Renoir now.

His eyes rested on the exquisite painting. He'd bet his nearest and dearest were salivating to get their hands on it. Greedy vultures!

He gave himself a mental pat on the back. "I deserved a reward after learning the startling details of dear Granny Collins' past."

Shaken by her confession, he had not entirely trusted everything the old girl had said. Still, he had no qualms whatsoever in removing the painting from her house in exchange for keeping the family secret a secret.

He had just begun to relax when a knock at the door roused him from his recollections. Another knock sounded, louder and more insistent.

"Can't I have a moment's peace?"

Lloyd dragged himself upright and went to the door. He glanced into the mirror over the mahogany half table. Snuggling in the pillow had pushed his black hair into spikes while his blue eyes clouded over from eyestrain.

"I look like hell! That won't do. I might scare away a potential customer. Although I'm not sure who needs a CPA at 4:30 on a Saturday." He took a deep breath, straightened his clothes and pasted a smile on his face. When he opened the door, his smile immediately faded.

"I can tell you're thrilled to see me," Andrea said and brushed past him before he could reply. "I thought you'd like to hear about my exciting afternoon in high society."

"I'm all ears. Did you make nice?"

"Butter nearly melted in my mouth. Except I almost lost my temper when that blonde complained about her earth-shattering experience in some rinky-dink organization as a woman president—until these liberated times—that only you men could fill. Or words to that effect."

"Blonde?"

"One of the owners. Reene Anderson. Don't get your knickers in a twist. She's not your type."

"I'll decide what my type is. And I wouldn't cast aspersions on anyone's pedigree if I were you."

For a second, he saw fear in her eyes. Then her face hardened into a mask of hatred.

"I'll match my B.A. against little Missy's presidential peccadilloes," Andrea snapped. "She belongs in the stable with the rest of the servants."

"Beg pardon? Are you sure you aren't imagining this slight on your political acumen?"

"Don't be an ass. And speaking of types, I know her type. Pretty, blonde and thin. Looks forty-three, acts twenty-three. Add that up."

"I already have. Sounds intriguing."

"In case you didn't hear me, she's not your type. I hear her late husband left her a bundle and she and her friend used it to buy the farmhouse. Money, at least to her, seems to be no object."

"Methinks I'll bide my time and make a call on the grieving widow to see if she needs any financial advice."

"Don't say I didn't warn you," Andrea said. She crossed to the wet bar and poured a strong gin and tonic. She sank into the leather sofa, kicked off her shoes and propped her stocking feet on the maple coffee table.

"On the other hand, I do believe I need a break from the rigors of trying to shove tedious Mayor Stuart out of office. And I believe the Barn Swallow Inn is just the place to calm my shattered nerves."

"In other words, you're only staying at their inn to check up on them."

"Damn right. I have too much at stake to let an outsider upset my plans."

Chapter 8

"Reene, I invited Gina to go riding with us this weekend. She's been working too hard at the paper and a long trail ride is just what she needs."

"Awesome! Why don't we explore our property? We've been so busy with the house and barn we haven't had a chance to see what's out there. We'd be riding fence like they did in the Old West. I'll make a picnic lunch," Reene suggested. "We'll stop at the stream. Perfect to cool our drinks."

Saturday morning the three women set out to bushwhack. Each woman also carried a lead rope and had left her horse's halter on under the bridle. Gina's gelding, Sonny, fit right in with Shen and Bravo.

Horses have their own personalities. Like people, they have their likes and dislikes. When they don't play nice together, riding can sometimes turn nasty and dangerous.

"Watch out for woodchuck holes," Reene cautioned as they explored the edge of the fields. Saw grass and wild flowers had taken over the once fertile fields. In some spots wild grass rose higher than their horses' shoulders.

After making two circuits of the perimeter, they found many old stone walls in good shape. Gina explained that New England farmers had found a good use for the endless supply of rocks and built walls to mark their borders.

"Lissa, a few of these stones have come loose, but we can fix the walls ourselves," Reene decided.

"You're too darned energetic, woman," complained Lissa. "Besides we don't have a clue about repairing stone walls. But knowing you, there's probably a recipe for cement in your cookbook."

"Maybe we shouldn't tackle the job right now," Reene laughed, "but I won't totally give up on the idea."

"Lord save us!" Lissa exclaimed dramatically. "Move on, ladies."

"I can see something shining among those trees," Gina said. "Let's investigate."

Emerging from the trees, they found themselves on the edge of a good-sized pond, its glassy surface covered with green algae. Lily pads displaying their daisy-like blossoms dotted the surface.

"You might want to put a few picnic tables here for your guests," Gina suggested. "This is a lovely setting to fish or bird watch."

"What a fantastic idea!" Reene agreed. "We'll bring our weed whackers and rakes and clean out an area. I spotted a trail off to the right. Let's see where it takes us."

They left the pond and followed the trail, no more than a deer track that wound its way into the woods. Maples, oaks and pines vied for growing space and pine needles covered the forest floor.

"Do you think all these maples are sugar maple trees?" Lissa asked. "It would be fun to tap them."

"Fun if we knew what we were doing," Reene replied. "We'll put that on our to-do list after we repair those stone walls. The footing looks good. Want to pick up the pace? Are we ready to canter?"

"Love to! Gina, is that okay with you?"

"Absolutely. Sonny's been ready to move out for some time."

The three riders cantered along the trail until it gradually curved to the right. As they rode out of the deeper woods, the stream unexpectedly appeared to their left.

"Fantastic run!" Lissa exclaimed. She patted Bravo's neck. "Good boy! You gave me a nice controlled canter. Now I'm ready for lunch. Anyone else hungry?"

"Woman, you're always hungry!" Reene accused. "Can you go a little further until we find a nice spot to stop?"

"I suppose I can survive not eating a bit longer, but not the need to pee. Hold on a minute, cowgirls."

Lissa dismounted quickly and hid behind Bravo's left shoulder while she yanked down her riding pants. Gripping the reins in her left hand, she squatted to take care of business. Unfortunately, Brav spotted a clump of grass he couldn't live without. He dragged her forward and she landed on her knees with her lily-white rump sticking up in the air.

"Whoa, Brav! Where are you going? Whoa!" Lissa cried. Desperately she hung onto the reins. If he stepped on them and snapped them, she'd be in big trouble.

Meanwhile, Lissa was grumbling and laughing and peeing and trying to hold her horse all at the same time. She finally got back on her feet and faced her two friends. "All right. You can stop enjoying yourselves at my expense. I feel like an absolute bozo. Okay?"

"Oh my God!" Reene shook so hard with laughter she nearly fell out of her saddle. Gina held a gloved hand to her mouth as she lost the battle to hide her smiles.

"Lissa, we're not laughing at you, we're laughing *with* you," Gina explained.

"Ha! I didn't fall off the turnip truck yesterday. Move on before something else happens." Lissa remounted and they trotted down the trail.

"Upstream by that small spit of land looks like a promising place to stop," Reene suggested. "Ladies, today we dine alfresco!"

Tethering their horses and giving them enough room to graze, they spread out their picnic lunch.

"Honey turkey and cheese sandwiches, carrots and oatmeal raisin cookies! This is wonderful! Thank you so much for inviting me," Gina said, finishing the last bite of her sandwich. "Things are hectic at the paper because I'm short-handed. My mind is in overdrive every day trying to make sure I've covered everything. Did I mention I had a lovely time at your tea? You both did a beautiful job with the food and the tours."

"Our pleasure. And we welcome feedback," Reene responded. "Have you heard anything, good, bad or indifferent, from any of the guests?"

"Not directly. I've picked up some comments as I've been out and about and every one was favorable. Both you and your inn made a good impression."

"That's great to hear," Lissa said. "I was a nervous wreck giving the tour to the mayor and his friends. But they were nice. At least they pretended they were interested in what I had to say."

"Mayor Stuart certainly made the most of this opportunity by his appearance. He's running for re-election and knowing him as I do, he'd show up at the opening of a soup kitchen."

Gina paused, horrified. "Oh, I didn't mean to suggest ..."

Lissa burst out laughing. "Don't be silly. We know what you mean. We learned firsthand about small town politics. We'll stick to horses, thank you very much."

"I met the awfully determined woman who's running against him," Reene said. "Is she a local too?"

"Yes," Gina responded "although she's lived in New York for the last ten years. She moved back to Westbrook to establish her residency so she can run for office. Of course she's already our Treasurer, so she has an advantage. Andrea Wilson is definitely qualified for the job. She earned a business degree from UMass Amherst."

"She's campaigning at every opportunity from what I could see," Reene commented.

"I've heard through the grapevine that she spent a huge amount on ads in the newspaper and on local television," Lissa said. "I imagine that's all part of the process. I wish her luck. I wouldn't run for office for all the money in the world."

"Not everyone is cut out for that sort of thing," agreed Reene. "Throwing the tea wore us to a frazzle. I can't imagine being in the spotlight all the time and having to attend a gazillion functions to keep your face before the public."

"Speaking of faces, I hope she doesn't ask us to post a 'Vote for Me' sign on our property," Lissa griped. "I hate those darn things. They spoil the landscape."

She finished the last bite of her cookie. "Are we ready to head out? Our kids are getting a bit restless."

Quickly they packed their lunch debris into the saddlebags. Back on their horses, they followed the trail as it meandered along the stream before disappearing into the forest.

"Looks like we've gone about as far as we can for today," Reene said. "Lissa and I have a pretty good idea what we need to do to clean up the trails."

"I did notice a lot of blow down, but that's easily fixed," Lissa decided as they retraced their steps. "We could bring Sissy and the wagon out here and pick up the branches. We can use the wood for the fireplace."

"Why don't we go back up the long side? I thought I saw a side trail that looked promising," Gina suggested.

"Sure thing," Reene agreed and turned in that direction. But as Shenan trotted up the long edge toward the inn, without warning she shied and danced off to the side.

"Shenan, behave!" Reene commanded and circled her horse. Again she urged her forward, but Shen wouldn't budge. In protest, she bobbed her head and danced in place.

"What's wrong with her?" Lissa asked.

"She's being a brat," Reene answered, as she fought to make her horse obey. Finally, in frustration, she dismounted.

"I'll try leading her a few feet. She's acted up like this other times." She grabbed Shen's reins and walked her forward. Despite Reene's cajoling, her mare moved forward only a few steps and then planted her feet.

"Shen, you are being a pain! Come on!" But Shen was not giving in. She threw her head high, jerking Reene back.

"Should I try going ahead with Bravo?" Lissa asked. "If he takes the lead, she'll follow him." She lightly kicked Bravo. He never liked being lead horse and moved forward by inches. He too came to a stop and refused to move.

"This is stupid," grumbled Lissa. "What's up with these two? I don't see anything out here that should upset them. Gina, will you hold Brav while I walk up ahead?"

She dismounted and walked to the spot where the horses had refused to go forward. She'd only gone a few yards when she gave a startled cry.

"Oh, no! No wonder they wouldn't go forward! Reene, come here!"

Reene tossed Shen's reins to Gina and ran to join Lissa.

"Reene, take a look at this!"

She pointed to a large round opening partly covered by rotting wooden boards and weeds. "If one of the horses had stepped there, it would've been disaster!"

"Oh my God!" Reene exclaimed. She bent down and cautiously peered into the space between the boards.

"Be careful!" Lissa warned sharply.

"I don't care how this hole got here or how deep it is, but we've got to mark this spot. We don't dare ride out here until it's fixed."

"Ladies, what is going on?" Gina hollered. "I've got my hands full of horses!"

"Sorry!" Reene hustled back and took the reins from Gina. "There's a scary-looking hole up ahead. Do you have anything we could use to flag this spot?"

"Let me look. Here. I always carry a handkerchief in my fanny pack."

They left the delicate hankie to flutter its warning as they headed back to the inn. They rode along quietly, sobered by what could have been a tragic accident.

"Girlfriends," Lissa said, "we owe Shen a big hug, not to mention a bunch of carrots. If she hadn't sensed something wasn't right, we could have ridden into a horrific situation."

"And I got mad at her because she wouldn't move!" Reene replied. "Lately I've been thinking she's lost her sense of direction. Now I'll never doubt her again!"

Long after Gina had loaded Sonny onto her trailer and left for home, Reene and Lissa were still wondering about the strange hole lurking in their overgrown pasture.

"It could be an abandoned well," Reene mused, "or the hole might have been used for an outhouse."

"Yuck. Whatever it is, we need to find out. If it is an old well, we may be able to use the water for emergencies. And if it's dried up, we need to cover the opening properly. Who do we call to fix this?"

"I have no clue. Check the Internet again."

Lissa typed a brief description of their problem into the browser and then turned to her friend. "Guess what? We have to call a 'Well Contractor'. Seriously?"

One call later, Craig Zylak assured her he'd drop by on Tuesday to 'take a look'.

"Cross your fingers this is the end of all these little nuisances," Lissa fretted. "We can't catch a break."

"We have more contractors than guests visiting this place!" Lissa lamented as another pickup truck arrived at the appointed hour on Tuesday. A slender young man with wavy brown hair approached the front door.

"I'd better put on my happy face," she sighed and went out to greet him.

"Hi there. You must be the well man," Lissa said.

"Yep. That's me. I'm Craig. What's up?"

"What's up, Craig, is we discovered what we think is an old abandoned well and can't figure out what to do with it. If possible, we'd like to make use of it again." ·

"Where is the well? Close by?"

"No, it's a distance behind the inn. Do you mind a little walk?"

"Can we take my truck? It's got 4-wheel drive and will plow through anything."

"I guess we can take a chance. But let's be careful."

Moments later, Lissa realized that being careful was not in this young guy's vocabulary. She bounced all over the cab like a rowboat in a hurricane as his truck negotiated the deep field grass.

"See the white hanky on that bush about a hundred yards to the left?" she grunted as the pickup rocked in and out of a hidden rut. "It's right opposite."

"Not a problem." He skillfully manhandled the truck through the grass, brought it to a halt and hopped out.

To Lissa's horror, the young man stomped on the crumbling boards with his work-booted foot. The boards gave way, and she had a dreadful vision of him disappearing into the black hole. She let out a yell and he looked over at her with a grin.

"It's okay. I do this all the time. Now I can see what might be down there. I'll get my tools."

Lissa walked slowly into the inn and headed straight to the kitchen. She heated water for tea and carried her cup into the Gathering Room. She settled onto the couch, her eyes automatically lifting to the portrait. Sure enough, it was tilted in its customary position. She lifted her teacup and saluted the picture.

"Here's to ya. If you want to stay in that spot, be my guest."

"Who *are* you talking to?" Reene asked as she stopped at the doorway.

"No one. I'm in a funk and I'm hiding in here."

"Why are you hiding?"

"In the first place, the well guy just left and according to him, we need an act of Congress to re-dig the damn thing. There are forms and rules and regulations, not to mention a ton of money in fees. I told him we'd get back to him. And in the second place, I'm ready to give up."

"What else did he say? And what's this giving up business?"

"I'm so disappointed! We haven't had a single guest and I foolishly took it for granted our phone would be ringing off the hook right after our High Tea." She slumped back on the couch, the picture of dejection.

"Well, my news may cheer you up," Reene said, sitting down beside her. "While you were busy hiding, I took a reservation for two women for a week's stay and they're bringing their horses."

Lissa regarded her incredulously for a second. Then she whooped with joy and threw her arms around Reene.

"If I may borrow your pet expression, wooo-hooo!"

Her porcelain teacup and its contents hit the floor but she didn't care. "What did they say? When are they coming?"

"Is this the calm, cool businesswoman who acted so professional last week? Looks like a mother and daughter combo. The mother made the reservation. They'll be here at the end of the week."

"Our first official guests! Reene, by the time they leave, we'll be nominated Innkeepers of the Year. Good food, good conversation, perfect guests!"

Chapter 9

"Someone pinched my bottom! I was locking the door to my room and I distinctly felt a pinch."

Lissa had just come around the corner from the kitchen and bumped into her agitated guest. Their first guests! She had so looked forward to impressing them with good food and good conversation. Good conversation was a wash.

"Breathe, breathe," Lissa muttered. Time to put on her game face. The customer might always be right, but this woman and her daughter were certainly putting a damper on her enthusiasm. She was tempted to pinch her guest's ample caboose on general principles.

"Really, Mrs. Jensen? Are you sure your daughter didn't play a joke on you?"

"Don't be ridiculous. My daughter doesn't play practical jokes."

Lissa didn't doubt her. The moment these two had arrived on their doorstep, she sensed tension between them. Mommie Dearest was bold as brass, offspring Pamela quiet as the proverbial mouse.

"Why don't you come out to the porch? I'll bring you some coffee and one of Reene's delicious wild blueberry muffins," she suggested, lightly placing a guiding hand on the woman's shoulder. Alas, the older woman wasn't leaving without the last word.

"Coffee and muffins won't change the fact that someone tried to be funny." With a tightening of her already rigid mouth, she departed for the porch, loath to give up the promised muffin.

Lissa beat a hasty retreat to the pantry where she found Reene whipping batter in a huge earthenware bowl. A Chopin nocturne was playing softly on the CD player. Unfortunately, its soothing effect ricocheted off the grumpy guest.

"Mrs. Crankenstein is on another tirade. She's all bent out of shape because she believes some misguided soul pinched her ass. Wishful thinking on her part, methinks. I promised her coffee and a blueberry muffin to distract her. I'm not sure if she can open her mouth wide enough to enjoy your culinary expertise."

Reene's earthy laughter bounced off the pantry walls. "She's one of those types who's not happy unless she's miserable."

"Miserable is the operative word. I think her sad-eyed daughter chose riding to bond with her mother. But her heart's not in it. She's not feeling the joy she should feel between horse and rider."

"Poor girl. At least she didn't get stuck with piano lessons like you did."

"Don't remind me. My mother made this woman look like Mary Poppins," Lissa grumped. "Fortunately for our sanity, they're leaving day after tomorrow. What are you making now? More muffins?"

"Popovers. I'm serving them with tomorrow's breakfast. Will you check our jam and jelly supply? Gotta keep the paying customers happy."

"Oh, yum," Lissa said as she slid behind Reene. But when she opened the pantry doors, her eyes widened in shock and disbelief. "Ummm, Reene, there's trouble in Paradise."

"What are you talking about?" Reene removed her batter-covered wooden spoon from the bowl and turned around. "Oh my God!"

Uncooked pasta, in all shapes and sizes, from angel hair to farfelle to elbows rained all over the cupboard.

"Damn! How did this happen?" Reene fumed. Her cowboy boots crunched some escaped bow ties. Like Queen Victoria, She was not amused.

"Looks like 5.4 on the Richter scale," Lissa replied. "It's bizarre. The house must be settling again. Come on, I'll help you sweep up our runaway pasta and throw it away."

Once the pasta and Mrs. Jensen's coffee and muffins were dispatched, Reene put her first batch of popovers into the oven. She set the timer and wandered into the office where Lissa kept the books and made reservations.

"Isn't that British couple supposed to arrive today?" she asked.

"Rather," replied Lissa in her best English accent.

"I'm shocked, just shocked! And you, a dyed-in-the-wool Anglophile."

"Guilty as charged. I love to hear the polished tones and clipped phrases of the British. The husband told me he and his wife have been citizens for years, but they haven't lost their accent." She lowered her voice. "They should be a welcome change from the Dragon Lady and her offspring."

As if on cue, the Call to the Post sounded throughout the house. Reene rolled her eyes at her friend's wacky choice of door chime.

"They're off!" she said sarcastically. "Or rather, they're here."

"Don't be cranky. I think it's neat. I heard it at the airport in Kentucky the year I went to the Derby."

"Go answer the door and make nice," said Reene, smiling her most beguiling smile. "I need to listen for the timer. I don't want my popovers to get charcoal-broiled."

Lissa opened the coffin door, adorned with a grapevine wreath and red berries. The new pocket screen door, invisible from a distance, let cooling breezes flow through the maze of rooms.

"Good morning! Welcome to Barn Swallow Inn. Did you have any trouble with the directions?"

"No, indeed. Your directions were brilliant. I'm Nigel Bainbridge and this is my wife, Lorraine." A tall, slender black haired man smiled down at the attractive woman with honey-colored tresses standing at his side. "I believe you have our reservation?"

"Certainly. You'll be in the Nesting Room. It's on the second floor, first door to the right. You'll have a spectacular view of the mountains. You requested box stalls for your two horses. When you're done unloading, I'll show you where everything is."

"Brilliant," Nigel said again. "We'll see you straight away."

Nigel and his wife hurried back to their trailer and busied themselves getting their mounts safely out. Nigel swung the door wide and walked a bay Thoroughbred, 17 hands if he was an inch, down the ramp. Once he moved away, Lorraine backed out her horse, a kind-eyed dappled grey with black mane and tail.

Lissa joined them, her eyes lighting up over their beautiful animals. "We have two paddocks out back with run-ins," she explained. "I don't think they'll need the run-ins, the weather is just awesome."

"Splendid," Nigel said as he loosely held the lead rope, allowing his horse to explore the grounds.

"What's his name?" asked Lissa, running her hand along the silken neck.

"His show name is Botany Bay. However, we call him Billy."

"He's beautiful. Do you hunt or jump him?"

"Billy was an incredible jumper. We even placed high in a few three-day events. I've retired him from the circuit and we're finally having fun together."

"Good for you," Lissa approved. "I hate to see a horse soured or worn out by constant work."

"I agree. Oh, by the way, could you recommend a place for dinner?" Nigel asked. "We didn't even have a moment for lunch. We were in such a hurry to get away."

"No problem. We keep menus for most of the local restaurants."

"That would be lovely," Lorraine replied before Nigel could say "brilliant" again. Her mare was busy foraging through the succulent green grass. Dragging her unwilling horse's head up, she introduced her mount to Lissa.

"This is National Velvet," she said lovingly. "She's a good girl." Lorraine held up a self-deprecating hand as Lissa's eyebrows shot up to her hairline. "You'll have to indulge me. After all, I *am* British."

Lissa laughed so loud Nigel stopped grazing his horse. She managed to pull herself together as he came back dragging a reluctant Billy.

"I say, anything wrong?"

"No, no. Just a tickle in my throat. If you're ready, you can park your truck and trailer in the paved area next to the sheds," explained Lissa. "When your horses are settled, come up to the inn and I'll find those menus. I'll also show you the hot tub. Every rider's cure for aching muscles."

Nigel and Lorraine's eyes lit up at the mention of the hot tub. "Brilliant! We'll be along straight away."

Early next morning Lissa pottered around in the kitchen and put the kettle on to boil when Nigel and Lorraine sauntered in. Both wore breeches and tall boots.

"Good morning," Lissa smiled. "Tea is almost ready. Was your room satisfactory?"

"Our room is spot on," Nigel replied. "Awfully charming."

"I'm so glad you're pleased. Have you fed your horses yet?"

"Yes, we just took care of that," Lorraine answered. "We're really looking forward to a nice long hack this morning."

The kettle howled. Lissa poured hot water into the teapot to let the tea steep. When she brought the teapot to the table, Nigel poured a cup for himself and reached for the sugar basin. He added three heaping teaspoons of the white stuff to his tea. He exchanged a few words with his wife and took a healthy swallow.

"What in bloody hell?" Nigel spluttered as he gagged on the hot liquid. His British reserve disappeared like a Red Sox six game lead in August.

"What's happened?" asked Lissa as she rushed from the pantry.

"This ruddy tea tastes like sea water!"

"Salt water?" Lissa quavered as her toes curled in her sneakers. "That's impossible!"

What had she done? Had she poisoned their guest? Nigel's a little full of himself but she'd never—

She grabbed a teaspoon and dipped its tip into the sugar basin. With foreboding, she raised the spoon to her mouth. The salty taste assaulted her tongue. She shivered and scrunched up her face. Nothing to do but admit her idiot mistake.

"Please forgive me, Nigel," she apologized. Should she try the helpless female routine or just plead insanity? If she couldn't tell salt from sugar, insanity wasn't far off. "I must have mixed up the boxes when I refilled the basins."

Nigel had recovered his stiff but salty upper lip. "I understand. Accidents do happen. Such a nasty shock to my taste buds."

Reene heard the commotion and joined them. "Good morning! Did you sleep well?" she asked. She glanced at Lorraine whose eyes danced at her husband's discomfort.

Lissa held her breath. Would they mention the incident?

"Quite well, thank you," Lorraine answered. "I expect our horses had an equally good night as well."

"Super. We'll fill your tummies and then give you maps of the best trails in the area."

"Brilliant." Nigel really *loved* that word.

Reene followed Lissa into the kitchen to prepare eggs Benedict. Lissa arranged warm-from-the-oven popovers in a wicker basket. Strawberry and grape jam pots were already on the table. She placed sliced cantaloupe on serving plates, added blueberries for a dash of color, and carried them, along with the bread basket, to the table. The coffee maker had finished brewing, but she didn't dare offer Nigel another hot beverage.

"Your popovers taste just like Yorkshire pudding," Lorraine said graciously. "Simply scrumptious."

Two helpings later the sated couple dragged themselves from the table. Lissa piled dishes into the dishwasher and listened from the kitchen as Reene handed out maps and suggested which trails would provide the excitement they craved.

"Thanks so much. We'll follow your advice although first we need to digest your delicious breakfast. I imagine we'll take our time tacking up."

"Well, have a wonderful day! Enjoy yourselves and ride safe!"

Lissa, still a bundle of nerves over her *faux pas* in the kitchen, watched apprehensively from the window as Nigel and his wife departed.

"Reene, I can't believe I mixed up the sugar and salt! What must they think? He took it well, though. The British are always so polite. Should I return their deposit?"

"Lissa, calm down. You just had a minor brain warp. I know! I'll make a picnic lunch for them to take along on their ride. Hurry out and tell them before they ride off."

"You are the best! I owe you big time."

Nigel and Lorraine were delighted with the peace offering.

"They were really surprised when I caught up with them," Reene reported. "I could tell they appreciated our gesture."

"Another day, another snafu headed off at the pass. Thanks again, dear friend." Lissa glanced furtively around as she cleared the dishes. "Those gremlins must be working overtime."

Chapter 10

"Isn't it a hoot how horse people are so secretive about their hay guy?" Lissa asked.

"Too funny," agreed Reene as they drove back from inspecting hay at a farm in Westbrook. "My guess is they're worried he'll get too many customers and won't have enough left for them."

They'd been buying hay in small batches from a local farm, but needed a steady supplier. On her previous trip to town, Reene had grabbed a business card from the grain store bulletin board.

"'O'Brien & Son Farms: Hay for sale. Delivery or pick up. 135 Heron Lane. Ask for Tom.' We'll take a field trip and check out his hay. I've seen some cuts only a scarecrow could love."

After a few wrong turns, they rocked down a dirt road to the farm. A truck loaded with hay bales was parked in front of the barn. The driver had just hopped into the cab when Reene called out.

"Hello! Don't go yet! Can we talk to you?"

The driver opened the door and slid out.

"How can I help you? My name is Tom O'Brien. By the way, I'm the '& Son'."

"Good one!" Reene chuckled. "I'm Reene Anderson and this is my friend, Lissa Martin. We bought the Williams' farmhouse. We're shopping for the best hay for our three horses."

"I heard you turned the old place into a bed and breakfast and fixed it up so folks could bring their horses. Any guests yet?"

"A few. I see the small town grapevine still works," Lissa commented.

"That it does," agreed Tom. "Why don't you come into my barn and have a look around?"

"Lead the way, kind sir," said Reene.

Tom showed them the latest cut of bales stacked to the ceiling. Good green color meant plenty of nutrients. His prices for first and second cut were more than reasonable.

"Can you deliver 150 bales by the end of the week?" Reene asked.

"I can handle that," Tom said.

"We'd like to sign a contract with you to provide hay throughout the year," Lissa said.

"No contract necessary, ma'am. It's a deal." Tom extended his hand and Lissa hesitantly shook it.

"Are you sure you don't want us to sign a contract?"

"No ma'am," Tom repeated. "A man has two things he can call his own: a handshake and his word. You've got both from me."

Reene reached out her hand. "You've definitely got a deal. And you've got our word as well."

Tom grasped her hand and shook it. His eyes kindled as he continued to hold her hand in his.

"Reene? Ready to go? Today?" Lissa asked.

Tom quickly dropped Reene's hand and they exchanged phone numbers. Then he returned to his hay-filled truck and drove out of the yard.

"We should call Tom 'The Shadow' because we know he exists, but we must keep him a Deep Dark Secret!" Lissa chuckled as they headed back to the inn. "Tom O'Brien, Secret Hay Man."

Involuntarily her thoughts flew back to the local farmer who had provided hay at her first barn. He was also a commercial airline pilot. In a cowardly act of terrorism that shook the world, his plane was deliberately brought down after leaving the Boston area. Such a terrible waste. Following his tragic death, she learned he had constantly fought to preserve open land and ensured his family farm would always remain a working farm. Lissa grieved that the world had lost such a caring man.

"Be still my beating heart," Reene said, breaking into Lissa's thoughts. "Did you check out those muscular arms? Those tight jeans and white T-shirt? He's a Sam Adams man if I ever saw one. Do you think I should ask him out for a drink?"

Lissa quickly glanced at her friend. "A little quick on the Trigger, aren't you? It's totally up to you though. Tom seems like a nice guy, but if he ma'amed me one more time, I would've pitched a fit. But I liked what he said about a man and his word."

"Me too. Looks like I … I mean, we have found our hay guy."

Early Friday morning, Tom delivered the hay as promised. Reene dashed out to meet him and supervise the unloading. Lissa glanced at the hay-laden truck as she headed into the tack room.

As the last bale slowly went up the chute, Tom sauntered over.

"All set. One hundred and fifty bales. Want to count 'em?"

80

"No, thanks," Reene chuckled. "I trust you. I'll grab my checkbook."

"No hurry." Tom walked over to the mare paddock and rested his arms on the top rail. "Nice looking horses. All yours?"

"Almost. These two mares are mine. The gelding next door belongs to Lissa."

"Lot of work. From what I can see you never stop."

"We think they're worth it." Reene handed Tom the check and he slipped it into his back pocket. "We can't imagine our lives without horses."

"Do you take time out for some fun once in a while?"

"Why, yes, every now and then Lissa and I help each other out of our rockers and go wild. We might even drive into the big city and stay up till way past 10:00 o'clock."

"Okay, okay. You can quit pulling my leg." He winked at her. "Hey, do you like country music?"

"It's one of my favorites. I listen to country in my truck. I sing along at the top of my voice."

"In that case, I'm inviting you to a concert in the big city next week."

"I'd love to!" she smiled.

Tom returned her smile. A slow dangerous smile. "I'll give you a call later on and we can make plans. I'd better run. I've got another delivery. See you later, Reenie."

Moments later Lissa came out of the tack room. "Did he just call you Reenie?"

"He certainly did. How on earth did he know my special pet name? Damn. He might be too good to be true."

"Lissa, I hate to sound like your mother, but you left the lights on in the barn."

"What? Are you giving me the *Gaslight* treatment?" Lissa peered out her bedroom window. "I could have sworn I turned off those lights after I fed the kiddies." She sighed and reached for her sweats and sneakers. "I'll go shut them off. Again."

"Great. I'm beat. Night, Lissa," Reene yawned and padded down the hall in her stocking feet.

Lissa hurried down the back stairs and out the kitchen door. She shivered as the night air bit through her thin sweatshirt.

"If I had a brain, I'd be dangerous," she muttered as she trudged across the grass. "Why did I... oh my..." Lissa gazed up in wonder. The night sky was putting on a spectacular light show. It looked like

81

thousands of diamonds had been scattered across the heavens. With no artificial light or cloud cover, millions of stars, normally in hiding, were twinkling down at her.

"Amazing! But I'd better pay attention or I'll trip over Jesse—or worse, a skunk. Last time I had a close encounter with a black and white varmint I had to burn one of my favorite outfits. Never again."

When she approached the barn, she could see the overhead light burning brightly. *Why am I such a scatterbrain? I'm losin' it. Might as well tuck the horses in while I'm here.* Soundlessly she opened the side door.

"Good thing I checked in," Lissa muttered. The horses were moving restlessly in their stalls, not the normal motion of settling down for the night. "Something's worrying all of you and I want to know what." She scanned the barn, half afraid something would jump out of the rafters.

"Bravo, is there a predator lurking in the barn?" Her imagination shifted into overdrive. "If I came face-to-fang with a cranky mountain lion, I'd drop dead on the spot."

Quickly she flipped the main switch and the entire barn flooded with light.

The horses stopped circling for a moment and looked anxiously toward her. Bravo blew noisily through his nostrils and arched his neck. She knew his behavior all too well. He only did that when frightened. Sissy swung her head nervously back and forth and Shen kicked her stall door. When they whinnied to each other, Lissa knew they sensed trouble.

"Easy, easy," she comforted in low tones. "It's okay. I'm here. I won't let anything happen to you." She went from stall to stall, patting and stroking heads. Sissy's neck was damp with sweat.

"It's okay, it's okay. There's nothing here to hurt you. Honest."

She walked over to the feed bins where carrots and apples were stored. Trudging back with the treats, an eerie chill encircled her body.

She shivered with sudden fear. The body heat radiating from three big animals couldn't warm her up. Goose bumps prickled on both arms and her heart raced. Afraid to move, she stood clutching the snacks in a death grip.

Bravo snorted and she jumped as if she'd been shot. Carrots and apples flew in every direction.

"Hells bells, Bravo! Knock it off! I almost had a heart attack."

She quickly scooped up the treats and hand-fed each animal. The horses relaxed and dropped their heads in search of hay and spilled grain. But her teeth rattled like castanets.

"I'll be darned. I wonder what made them—and me—so upset." She watched for a few more minutes. "Horses always see and hear things I can't. Except this time I sensed something too."

Lissa warily crossed to the door, but the unnatural feeling that caused her hair to stand on end had vanished. Could she have imagined the whole thing? Hurriedly she turned off the lights and waited a few seconds. When the lights didn't come blazing back on, she didn't hesitate.

"I'm outta here!"

Faster than an Olympic runner, she sprinted the distance back to the inn. Forgotten were the dazzling stars and stinky night critters. She flew into the kitchen, heart pounding, and slammed the door shut.

"I'm getting too old for this shit," Lissa mumbled. Childishly averting her eyes away from the now-dark barn, she double-locked the door.

Chapter 11

"Tom is picking me up in an hour," Reene fretted. "How did I lose track of time? I took too long in the shower. I'd better knock on it!"

Lissa watched from the door as Reene, clutching a towel around her still-wet body, ransacked her closet. "I feel like we're in high school and you're getting ready to impress the football hero," Lissa said snarkily.

"I feel like I'm in high school, I'm so darn shaky. If I want to raise Tom's blood pressure, I'm going with Country Sexy." She pulled on a hot pink clingy tee—her lacy bra accentuated the positive—black jeans and her tooled-leather cowboy boots. She draped a black suede jacket, dripping with fringe, across her shoulders.

"You go, girl!" Lissa applauded as her friend preened in front of the full-length mirror. "I'm heading off to my room and getting comfy."

As Reene slipped on dangly silver and pink quartz earrings, the Call to the Post echoed through the house. Nervous as a cat she almost fell down the stairs in her hurry to open the front door.

"Hello!"

"Hello, yourself. You look like a country queen," Tom approved.

"I'm not sure what a country queen looks like, so I'll take that as a compliment. You haven't seen the renovations, have you? You must have had a previous engagement that kept you from our High Tea," Reene said mischievously.

"Well, now, ma'am, I reckon I was a mite too busy with balin' hay to take tahm to drink tea outa them there China cups."

"You can cut out the naïve country boy impersonation, Mr. O'Brien," Reene laughed. "Come up and say hi to Lissa before we go. Lissa's rooms are through here."

"Time to leave for the concert?" Lissa asked from the comfort of her lounge chair. An unopened paperback lay on her lap.

"This foxy lady is bound to steal the show at the Centrum," Tom replied, encircling Reene's shoulders in a casual yet possessive manner. Reene blushed like a high school teen on her first date.

"Have fun. Be careful now," Lissa patronized. "And drive safely, Thomas."

"Yes, Mother." Reene nearly stuck out her tongue. "What wild and exciting plans do you have for tonight?"

"After I finish this chapter, I'm having a cup of tea. Then I'm watching one of my favorite old movies, *The Philadelphia Story*. Kate, Jimmy and Cary. They had faces then."

"Wasn't that Gloria Swanson?"

"Whoa!! I'm impressed. You're learning from your old buddy."

"Be careful not to watch too much or you'll be carted off to the loony bin like ol' Gloria in *Sunset Boulevard*," Reene warned.

"Run along, children."

"I'll have her home afore midnight, ma'am," Tom promised solemnly. Reene grabbed Tom's arm and they headed downstairs before Lissa could throw her book at them.

Lissa heard Tom's truck making its way slowly down the driveway. She slid the DVD into the player. The day of reckoning finally came when she had to give up her cherished VCR and join the 21st century. A DVD player was still foreign to her, but at least she figured out what buttons to push.

She snuggled deeper into the chair and dragged a shaggy throw across her lap and switched on her gorgeous stained glass lamp.

"From me to me with love," she sighed, admiring the lamp. Its glass shade, a perfect combination of tan, red, and faded green, glowed softly. Native American in design, the bronze base had mellowed with age to a lovely hue. "I told Reene I'd spent all the egg money on that lamp and I wasn't kidding."

She jumped when Jesse leaped into her lap, evidently in the mood for some attention. She stroked his silky fur and he purred like an outboard motor. Lissa knew how he felt. If she were any more relaxed, she would have purred too.

The MGM lion roared as the credits rolled and the movie began. She never tired of old movies. Those beloved stars of the good old days really *did* have faces.

As the familiar dialogue washed over her and carried her back in time, her eyelids drooped.

"You can't be a first class woman, Red, until you've had some regard ..."
tromp, tromp, tromp
"Well, we do get the breezes ..."
tromp, TROMP, **TROMP**

"There's a magnificence in you, Tracy, that comes out of your voice and your eyes ..."

TROMP! TROMP!

"I'll be yar now, Dext, I promise I'll be yar."

CLANK! CLANK!

A splintering crash brought Lissa out of the semi-sleep in which she'd been drifting. Jesse hurtled off her lap. Footsteps echoed along the corridor. She found herself on her feet, eyes wide and heart pumping so hard she thought she might keel over.

Feeling like the ill-fated heroine in a bad slasher movie, she inched toward the doorway. She peeped into the hall. All quiet now. Slowly, Lissa edged down the corridor. The little brass and glass lamps mounted on the walls, lovely to look at, didn't give off much light.

"Hello? Anyone there?" she ventured. "Idiot! If I were watching this in a movie, I'd be screaming, 'Don't go into the hallway, you fool!'"

Fool proved to be a major understatement. When she reached the end of the corridor, she peeped out again, halfway afraid she'd lose her head.

"Bloody hell!" The oversize double-hung window overlooking the back deck was completely shattered. Gingerly she stepped around the jagged glass and peered out the broken window. Nothing moved. Total silence. Not even a howl from Andes, their ever-vigilant protector of the hearth.

With a sigh of resignation, Lissa put on her slippers and cleaned up the mess. "Picking glass shards out of my bare feet was not on my program tonight either," she grumbled.

She swept up all the glass and dragged out the mini-vacuum to remove the last shards. As Lissa straightened her aching back, something scraped and groaned outside. Pulse pounding, she stuck her head out the glass-less window. Her heart skipped a beat before thundering on.

"Is that a *body* swaying from the hay boom?"

The Centrum rocked. Reene hollered as she clapped to the beat of the music reverberating off the walls. Tom had reserved center seats on the floor and they had a perfect view of the well-known musicians who ripped through all their hits. She wanted to dance in the aisle, but figured she'd get in big trouble with the ushers. She was also enjoying the attention from Tom who seemed to be enjoying watching her more than listening to the musicians.

After two encores, the concert finally came to an end.

"Care to stop for a drink?" Tom asked as they jostled their way through the crowd. "There's a nice roadhouse near home called The Golden Horseshoe. They have a great little country band. Like to try it?"

"Love to!" Reene replied, smiling up into his eyes.

In response, Tom stared at her with an intense expression that startled her. Then his eyes softened and he casually entwined his fingers with hers.

As Reene soon learned, The Golden Horseshoe attracted a strictly country and western crowd. Tonight only a handful of couples were performing the latest line dances. Sitting across from Tom at a table for two, Reene listened attentively as he revealed how his life had changed by following his childhood dream.

"Know how grown-ups always ask 'What do you want to be when you grow up?' I always knew. I wanted to be a fireman. That was back-in-the-day before everyone had to be politically correct."

Reene nodded understandingly. She had grown up back-in-the-day too.

"When I was a senior in high school, I saw a movie that made ordinary firefighting seem dull. I decided I wanted to try smoke jumping. My horrified parents couldn't figure out why their son picked such a dangerous profession. Fighting fires on the ground was bad enough. Now I wanted to jump out of airplanes too."

His tone struck a responsive chord with Reene. She knew she must sound the same whenever she spoke of her love affair with horses.

"I had to go to Alaska for my training," Tom said. "There were hours of classroom instruction before I could learn the fun stuff: tree climbing, water landings and mock parachute jumps. I loved it."

"'Course I was a rookie," Tom continued, "but I was cock-sure I could cut it. I couldn't wait for my first fire." He paused for a quick swallow of his beer.

Sam Adams, Reene approved. *Damn, I'm good.*

"I was stationed in Fairbanks with the Forest Service when the call came to jump into a wildfire in Montana. I was first in line waiting for the plane to take off. We flew over the site and the fire was mind-blowing to see. Over ten thousand acres had already burned so we were sent to set a fire break."

Tom took another pull on his longneck.

"We circled the fire waiting for just the right moment to jump. When my turn came, turbulence rocked the plane. I got thrown out. I was falling so fast that I panicked. Before I could remember what to do, I slammed into the guy who had just jumped. Thank God he didn't lose it. He grabbed onto me and jerked my ripcord. I'd drifted a little too low to make a good landing. I crashed and almost burned."

He grinned at the trite expression, but Reene could see the pain in his eyes.

"I broke my leg real bad. The squad leader made it down right behind me and radioed for a chopper. I was airlifted out after the rest of the crew set the fire break."

He shook his head sadly.

"While I was healing, I did a lot of thinking and decided to quit the Service. Maybe I made up my mind too fast. I never did fight any fires. When I came back home, I joined the volunteer fire department. At least I'm a fireman, of sorts. But I'll always wonder what would have happened if I'd stuck it out. I never had the chance to prove myself."

Reene longed to say some words of comfort to ease his torment. But she knew from bitter experience that healing can only come from within one's soul.

While they talked, the band had taken a break. Now they were back, and began the next set with a country ballad Patsy Cline had made famous.

"Let's dance, Reenie." Tom grabbed her hand and pulled her onto the dance floor. Reene fit into his arms as if she'd always belonged there and rested her head against his shoulder. Everything about him was so overwhelmingly masculine. She felt both protected and stimulated. Even as her body melded with his, she held back a little. Tom made her feel she was the most desirable woman he'd ever met. Even if he had unburdened himself to her tonight, she sensed he still had a long way to go.

Could she help him let go of his disappointment? Would he open his heart to her again? And most importantly, did she want to get involved with a man who might be carrying more than he could handle?

When Tom drove up to the inn, Reene was startled to see lights blazing all over the first floor.

"Something's not right, Tom. Hurry!" Reene jumped out of the truck and dashed inside.

"Lissa?" Reene called. "Where are you?" She heard a noise from the second floor and ran upstairs with Tom close behind.

Just as they reached the landing, Lissa came around the corner, looking like death warmed over.

"Oh, Reene! I'm so glad you're back! The fancy window got smashed to pieces and I thought I saw a dead body—oh, hi, Tom—and I had to clean up tons of broken glass and no one was home and—"

"Back up, Lissa! You thought you saw a *dead body*?"

"Is there another kind?" Lissa snapped. "Sorry. When the window shattered, I looked over at the barn and I could have sworn I saw a figure hanging from the ridge beam. Scared the beejezus out of me. After I picked up my teeth, I looked one more time and didn't see a thing. It must have been a trick of the moonlight. Or my overactive imagination."

"Oh my God!" Reene gasped. "Should we see if it's still there?"

Instead of answering her, Lissa gave Reene a look that clearly said, 'Don't ask about anything tonight. We'll talk when we're alone.'

"No. Don't bother. So, how was the concert?" Lissa asked.

"Absolutely awesome. Each band played better than the last. Right, Tom?"

"Damn straight, Reenie. We stopped off at the Shoe on the way back."

"The Shoe? Oh, yes, the Golden Horseshoe. I'll have to try it sometime."

"Do you want me to try to fix the window?" Tom offered.

"No, thanks, Tom. We'll check it out in the morning and see what we need to do. These old sheets I hung up should do it for now," Lissa replied.

"Call me if you need me, Reenie. Night, Lissa. Sorry you had such a rotten night." Tom leaned over and quickly kissed Reene's cheek. "I'll call you tomorrow."

The two women watched him disappear down the stairs. Moments later his truck coasted soundlessly down the driveway.

"Reene, we gotta talk. I didn't want to tell you the whole story in front of Tom."

"I figured that out. What happened?"

"I fell asleep watching my movie. Then these weird noises woke me up. Loud stomping noises overhead. I could have sworn I heard a sound like metal chains clanking across the floor. The stomping got louder and louder as if someone was marching around the room in hobnailed boots. Totally bizarre."

"That is bizarre—especially since the attic ceiling above your room is so low no one can stand up straight, never mind stomp around, dragging stuff."

"Reene, I know you've joked about gremlins, and you're going to think I've gone 'round the bend, but I'm pretty sure I've had a visit from a decidedly mischievous spirit."

Lissa looked at Reene, anxiously hoping she wouldn't laugh in her face. Or have her committed.

"You know, you could be right."

"I could? I was afraid you'd say that."

Reene's laugh brought the color back to Lissa's face. "I didn't say anything to you before because I didn't make the connection until now. Remember the jumping candle and the salt and sugar switch? Mrs. Crankenstein's pinched bottom?"

Lissa nodded. "And I didn't tell you I felt an eerie presence in the barn the other night. The night you said I left the lights on. Our horses were flipping out too. So you think we have a boarder, no pun intended?"

"I wouldn't be surprised. Our spirit doesn't seem dangerous, but it certainly is trying our patience. Not to mention grating on the nerves."

"No kidding," Lissa muttered. "Tonight my patience hit zero tolerance. Should we do anything about this? On second thought, never mind. I don't believe in exorcism or séances."

"Probably not. It mostly seems harmless. We can live with a few practical jokes."

"I guess so. But this could be a publicity nightmare. Let's try to keep our 'friend' a secret from our guests."

"That shouldn't be too hard as long as we keep on good terms with Himself."

"Himself?"

"Why not? We could call him Ezra or Sam or—"

"Enough, woman! Himself it is. What a night! Oh, I never asked *all* about your date. It was so cool though, when the two of you rushed in here to rescue this damsel in distress."

"Tom would have done the saving. He's got something to prove to himself."

"Oh? You learned all that from a first date? Are you going to share any more juicy details?"

"Tomorrow. It's way past my bedtime. We've both had enough excitement for one night."

Reene batted her Scarlett O'Hara-green eyes and drawled, "After all, tomorrow *is* another day."

Like Scarlett O'Hara found out, Fate just didn't give a damn.

Chapter 12

"Barn Swallow Inn. Reene speaking."

"Good morning, Reene. This is Andrea Wilson. I trust you remember me?"

"I certainly do. Please tell me you're not calling to see if we've registered to vote yet."

Andrea's low throaty laugh echoed through the phone. "As a matter of fact, this call does have a little to do with the election. I've decided I need some time away from campaigning and my office. Time for some good old-fashioned rest and relaxation. Do you have room for me this weekend?"

"Hang on a moment, please. Lissa is the keeper of the reservation book and I have to hunt for it. Ahh, here it is. What days do you have in mind?"

"Is Friday through Sunday convenient for you?"

"Absolutely. If you're longing for peace and quiet, I can put you in the Appaloosa Room at the back of the inn."

"Perfect. I'm counting on you to take excellent care of me."

"We will. We'll see you Friday. Check in is at 3:00 pm. Don't forget your bathing suit so you can enjoy a relaxing soak in the hot tub."

"I won't forget. I'm looking forward to exploring your inn. Every inch of it. Until Friday then?"

"Who was on the phone?" Lissa asked as she stuck her head in the office. "Someone wanting to spend money, I trust?"

"As a matter of fact, you're right. Andrea Wilson called. She booked a room for three days. Says she needs to get away from it all."

"Andrea Wilson?"

"She came to the High Tea."

"Reene, I met so many people that day. But you know my memory."

"I keep telling you to take your ginkgo biloba."

"I would, if I could remember where I put the stupid bottle. Menopause is a bitch."

"So you keep telling me. Remember a tall woman with auburn hair in the expensive linen suit?"

"Ms. Mayor Wannabe! I saw her flitting from table to table, giving everyone she met the glad hand. One of the political crowd. That explains why she was turning on the charm. Maybe subconsciously I knew she was a politician and managed to be otherwise engaged."

"Meow! You sound so cynical and you never even said 'hello'."

"Sorry. I just don't trust politicians in general. Most of them turn out to be phonies. When is she coming?"

"Friday. I put her in the Appaloosa Room."

"I'd better make sure everything is up to her standards. Somehow I get the feeling she's used to the best that money can buy."

Andrea arrived late Friday afternoon. Reene showed her the room and Andrea appeared genuinely pleased with her accommodations. Lissa had outdone herself. The room sparkled despite her disdain for politicians.

"I plan to rest a bit and then take a walk around the grounds. Your tour was fascinating but now I'll have time to poke around on my own."

"I'll be out in the barn if you need anything." Reene paused at the door. "I forgot to ask: are you afraid of horses? Some people are terrified by their size. But most horses have no idea of their strength and try their best not to harm anyone on purpose."

"No, of course I'm not afraid of horses!" Andrea answered brusquely. "I've always lived in the city. And I didn't have the time for leisurely rides in Central Park."

Then she smiled, as if to take the sting out of her reply. "They are such beautiful animals. You'll have to show me the ropes."

Reene returned her smile. "I'll do just that. Have fun exploring. See you in a bit."

Yes, dear Reene, Andrea smiled as she closed the door. *You'll see me in a bit. Although I don't think you'll appreciate my kind of exploring.*

She changed into jeans and a cardigan sweater and left her room. She went downstairs, expertly scrutinizing the antiques and furnishings in all the rooms. The towering mahogany grandfather clock in the front entry cost thousands if she were any judge of expensive furniture.

"I told Lloyd money was no object to these women and all these pricey antiques prove it. The old homestead never looked so good."

93

Where to start? She sniffed. She could smell a wood fire and followed the scent to the Gathering Room.

Upon entering the room, her eyes fell on the portrait above the fireplace. Andrea stared at the likeness for a long moment. She walked over to where the picture hung and gripped the frame with both hands.

I hate you! You loathsome little—

"I see you found our Civil War soldier."

"You startled me, Mrs. Martin!" Andrea gasped. "It is striking, isn't it?"

"'Lissa' sounds much better. Yes, he was presiding over the fireplace when we first came to look at this place. We felt he suited this room perfectly so we left him here."

"A part of our history that still fascinates us one hundred and fifty years later. Brother against brother, father against son. Some of the wounds have never healed."

"Sad to say, you're right. Except our friend here had a strong opinion about how we hung his picture."

"I beg your pardon?"

"For a while there, each time I tried to straighten it, the picture drooped back at the corner," Lissa explained. "Vibrations from heavy trucks and planes play havoc with our decor. For whatever reason it's behaving itself now."

"Do you ever wonder about this soldier's identity?"

"I'm afraid not," Lissa replied. "One day we might look into it, but at the moment we have our hands full just running this inn. Are you going on a walkabout?"

"Yes, as a matter of fact, I am. I'd like to browse and see more of the grounds than I saw at your marvelous tea. By the way, the furnishings are delightful. Did you and Reene do all the decorating yourselves?"

"Guilty as charged. I had a ball picking out the furniture and accent pieces. With an amazing house like this, I wanted to make it come alive."

"If you ever decide to give up the bed and breakfast business, I could recommend your expertise to many of my New York acquaintances," Andrea suggested. "You'd actually make money if you utilized your talents."

"Thanks for the kind offer. But I'll stick with our B&B," Lissa responded. "Can I help you with anything?"

"No, thank you. I'll wander around for a while."

"Wander away. I've got twenty bags of shavings to unload. Be careful."

"Excuse me?" Andrea asked curtly.

"Be careful you don't step on any road apples or disappear down our abandoned well. We just discovered it, but we've flagged it to keep our guests safe. Anyway, it's way out in the fields so I don't imagine you'll wander that far today."

"Perhaps not. I'll watch my step."

While she laced up her muck boots in the mudroom, Lissa relived her encounter with Andrea.

"Why was she holding the portrait in a death grip? She jumped a mile when I caught her. She covered up with that dramatic brother-against-brother speech. Ms. Wilson isn't a student of history from what I can see. It seems she majored in political double-speak. Reene said she'll fit right in if she's elected. I wonder why she decided to honor us with a visit, especially as she lives in town. Politicians always have a hidden agenda."

Andrea lingered near the fireplace, giving Lissa time to get well out of sight. Rummaging around, she discovered an open book, *Gone With the Wind*, decorating the mantelpiece. An antique pair of wire-rimmed eyeglasses perched atop the open pages, as if the reader had just laid them down but intended to return.

Charming, Andrea admitted. *Miss Goody-Two-Shoes has taste and originality. I'll give her that.* She looked out the window. Lissa had driven her truck around to the other side of the barn. Reene was carrying hay toward the paddocks.

"Stay right where you are, Reene." Keeping her eyes focused on the paddocks, she slipped out the front door. When she reached her destination, she watched in silence as Reene distributed hay.

"Andrea!" Reene greeted. "What brings you out here?"

"I've been wandering here and there and thought I'd come out to visit the horses. They're lovely. Do they belong to you and Lissa?"

"Actually, they're layovers from some people who are showing in the next town. Our horses are in different paddocks."

"Layovers? Showing?"

"Yes. That's what we call it when people need a one-night stop for their horses. The owners aren't staying at the inn. They have a travel trailer set up at the show grounds. Horse shows can be expensive and most people economize as much as possible. But sometimes it's not practical to sleep with horses."

"I'm certainly getting an education in horse-keeping."

95

"Would you like me to give you a riding lesson?" Reene asked.

"No thank you! I'm one of those people who admire them, but you won't get me on a horse's back."

"It's not for everyone. Excuse me a minute," Reene said as she slipped between the fence rails. "I have to get more flakes of hay."

When Reene disappeared from her sight, Andrea dashed into the barn. Her luck held. She found a bag of apples lying on top of the grain bin. She stuffed two apples in the sweater's pockets and hurried back out. Entering the paddock, she stood facing the horses who were regarding her with interest.

Andrea saw Reene come out of the barn. The innkeeper stopped short.

"Wait for me," she hollered to Andrea and ran to unlatch the gate. "Don't move until I get there!"

"What gorgeous creatures!" Andrea exclaimed. Despite Reene's warning, she walked over to the nearest horse, a big barreled sorrel gelding. Digging in her pockets for apples, she heard the gate clang shut.

"Wait until I give them their hay before you pass out treats."

Lissa was unloading bags of shavings from her truck bed when she heard a short cry of surprise and pain. She looked up and was horrified to see Reene soar through the air and land with a splashing thud in the water trough. All the horses spooked, bucking and kicking.

"Oh my god, oh my god," Lissa choked. Throwing the last bag over the tailgate, she leaped out and ran to the paddock.

"Reene, are you hurt?" she cried. Andrea was already at Reene's side, helping her out of the trough.

"I'm all right," Reene mumbled. Holding her hand over her right eye, she appeared dazed but coherent. She tried to maintain her balance, but her face turned white as a sheet and she swayed against Lissa.

Lissa's stomach rolled as she imagined the worst behind Reene's hand. She turned faint at the chilling image of her dear friend blinded for life.

"Andrea, open the gate and lock it behind us when we're out of the paddock," Lissa barked. She helped Reene to the bench in front of the barn and sat down beside her.

Andrea rejoined them and stood off to one side, murmuring apologies. "I'm terribly sorry! I had no idea they'd react that way. Please forgive me!"

"Not now! My main concern is for Reene."

When Lissa turned to ask Andrea to get some clean towels, she was taken aback by the look of pure maliciousness that darted across the woman's face.

She took a deep breath. *Could I have imagined that look of hatred? Why would Andrea deliberately cause this accident?*

"Run in the tack room and find a few clean cloths," she commanded. Andrea strode into the barn without a word.

"Reene," Lissa implored, "is your eye all right?"

Reene lowered her shaking hand. "Tell me, Lissa."

"Your eye looks unharmed. But I'm no doctor."

Amazingly, it appeared the flying hoof had encircled her eye entirely, leaving a ring of flesh already swelling and turning red.

"I'll drive you to the hospital. An x-ray will tell if there are any broken bones."

"No. No. I'm fine."

"Stubborn. You are not fine. You've just been kicked in the face by a horse, for heavens' sake!" Lissa exploded. "You could have a concussion or internal injuries."

"No bones are sticking out and my eye is still in its socket. You know how I am about doctors and hospitals. I'm just a little dizzy. Give me a few minutes."

"Open your good eye and tell me that fairy story again."

Despite her pain and shock, Reene managed a little smile. "You worry too much. An ice pack will make me as good as new."

Andrea finally emerged with some towels. Ignoring Lissa, she walked over to the trough and soaked the towels in the cold water. She folded one into a square and handed it to Reene. "Hold this on your eye. I'll run up to the house to fetch some ice."

Reene gingerly explored her face. "This feels good. At least she knows a little first aid."

"A regular Florence Nightingale. Let's cut to the chase. How did this happen?"

"The old story. Food fight. I was giving hay to the guest horses and she came in with some apples. Before I could stop her, she got between two horses and tried to hand feed them. One laid his ears back when he didn't get his treat fast enough. I was standing behind him and he lashed out at the nearest body. I never saw it coming. I didn't even realize I'd been kicked until I found myself sitting in the trough."

Then shock set in and she began to shake. Being soaked to the skin intensified her tremors.

"Reene, you're shaking to pieces. I'll bring you a blanket."

Lissa hurried into the tack room, dragged out one of the cleaner horse blankets and draped the blanket around her friend's shoulders.

Andrea had returned with ice wrapped in a cloth. "Here, Reene," she offered, solicitude oozing from every pore. "It will help keep the swelling down."

Lissa stared at Andrea with hostility. She tried not to blame Andrea who obviously knew nothing about horse etiquette, especially where food was concerned. But despite her resolve, she couldn't forget that vindictive look on Andrea's face.

"Andrea, whatever possessed you to get in between those horses? You caused Reene's injury and you could have been hurt or killed yourself!"

Their eyes met and animosity crackled between them. To Lissa's surprise, Andrea gave ground first.

"I'm sorry. I was having a lovely time feeding those horses. They're so beautiful and so friendly. I am shocked they could be so aggressive."

"Horses are notoriously aggressive when food is involved. Now do you understand?"

Lissa exhaled slowly. Maybe she had jumped to the wrong conclusion after all.

"I'm sorry I snapped at you. I realize you had no way of knowing what could happen when you tried to give them treats. It doesn't help matters that you stirred up our guest horses. They've hardly had a chance to settle in yet. But a lecture on horse behavior is beside the point. The bottom line is you overstepped your bounds."

"It was foolish of me, I realize that now. Again, please accept my apologies."

"Apology accepted. Do you have anything to add, Reene?"

"I know you didn't mean any harm. But you didn't listen to my warning."

"You're entirely right. I acted impulsively and stupidly. I don't know what else to say."

"You've said enough," Lissa said. "Reene, will you let me drive you to the emergency room now?"

"No."

"Why did I ask? Run up to the house and put on some dry clothes. I'll finish up here."

"Thanks, girlfriend. A nice hot bath and I'll be good as new by breakfast."

Lissa rolled her eyes. "When pigs fly."

Chapter 13

"Sissy needs some exercise so we're heading for the trails. Want to come along, Lissa?"

"I shouldn't. I have some paperwork to catch up on. Then the laundry basket awaits. Oh joy, oh rapture."

"Poor Cinderella. I'll be back in a couple of hours."

"Need any help?"

"No thanks. I'm getting the hang of this hitching business."

Two weeks had passed since Reene's encounter with the flying hoof. Her eye had swelled shut and her face puffed out as if she'd swallowed a balloon. To her chagrin the swelling was replaced by a spectacular display of vivid colors.

"Reene," Lissa had confessed, tongue planted firmly in cheek, "I've never seen so many beautiful shades on one face. Hey, has Tom seen you yet?"

"No, and he's not going to! He called last night; he wanted to take me to a five-star restaurant back in Worcester. I told him he'd have to wait till I looked human again."

Except, of course, Reene insisted she felt perfectly fit to ride. Almost. Using Sissy's lack of exercise provided her with a perfect excuse. Without much difficulty, Reene harnessed Sissy who stood patiently in the traces.

"Good girl," Reene said as she patted Sissy's neck. "I'm really going to enjoy our drive."

Together they eased down the driveway and Reene turned the wagon onto the carriage road. *We did a good job finding this old carriage road that wound its way from our inn to the Grange Hall. Lissa and I had worked like field hands to clear tons of blow-down and rocks.*

As Sissy trotted along, the sun flashed off the friendly stream where the three friends had picnicked. They enjoyed the cooling shade of the forest as Sissy skimmed over the hard packed dirt.

Suddenly Reene quivered as they passed through an unexpected cold spot, like ones she'd experienced while swimming in a lake. Goose bumps sprouted like mumps.

When Sissy shied violently to the right, goose bumps disappeared in a heartbeat. Reene was nearly jolted off her seat. The cart skewed dangerously and she cried out despite herself.

"Whoa! Whoa now! What's wrong, girl?" Desperately she tried to drag Sissy's head around to the left to counter the skidding cart. Her horse, snorting and blowing, leaped into a canter.

"Easy, easy," she soothed, sawing back and forth on the reins with all her strength. The wagon bumped and shook, rocking for a horrifying moment on one wheel before Sissy began to listen and slowed back to a ragged trot.

"Sissy! Whoa!" she commanded and Sissy finally skidded to a halt.

Gripping the reins, Reene leaped from her seat and cautiously approached the lathered horse. "What happened, sweetie? Did you see a horse-eating lion?" She scanned the woods intently but didn't see anything out of the ordinary.

"Something's out there. Something weird enough to make Sissy react so violently."

Reene ran her hand over the horse's body and felt her muscles trembling. "You're a good girl, aren't you?" she said, murmuring comforting words to her frightened horse. Sissy stopped tossing her head and her breathing returned to normal.

"Time to go home."

Gingerly, she eased back onto the driver's seat. Reene knew Sissy could sense her nervousness through the reins, but to her great relief, Sissy set off at a sedate walk. Her ears, however, were constantly swiveling in every direction as she moved out.

"Easy girl, good job," Reene crooned as they drove on through deep woods into bright sunshine. Despite her earlier fright, she touched up her horse and Sissy willingly picked up the pace. She, too, was anxious to reach the safety of the inn.

They swept up the driveway at a fast clip. Reene pulled Sissy in, walked her to the barn and unhitched her from the wagon. Reene slowly hand-walked her until she had totally cooled down.

The usual routine helped calm Reene's jangled nerves. She threw two succulent flakes of hay into the paddock and Sissy happily trotted in for her afternoon snack. Satisfied all was back to normal, Reene returned to the inn.

"I need a heart-to-heart with Lissa. Now."

Reene slipped in via the back deck. To her relief, none of the guests were there enjoying the late day sun. She was not in the mood for pleasantries.

"Lissa?" she called. "Lissa, where are you? It's important."

"Coming!" Lissa yelled from the second floor. "I'm changing sheets in the Morgan room. Be right down."

Lissa slid the sheets down the laundry chute, the coolest invention since Bell hollered to Watson to come running. Stashing her extra linens in the closet, she hurried to join her friend. Reene's tone of voice sent her warning flags flying.

"What's wrong?" Lissa asked as she rounded the newel post and saw her friend's white face.

"Sissy spooked really bad. I didn't think I could hold her," Reene said. "I could've been hanging from a tree in the next county if she hadn't stopped."

"I'm thankful she did. What do you think spooked her? Did she spot a critter in the woods? A deer or a moose?"

"I didn't see anything. It happened so fast. We were trotting along at a good clip until we reached the stream. Then Sissy went berserk. It's a wonder the wagon and I are still in one piece."

"Thank God you're both all right. When I saw your face, I thought you'd seen a ghost."

"Maybe I did."

"Excuse me?"

"Sissy sensed a presence not from this world. I'd stake my life on it. In fact, I did. Lissa, it's time we find out the whole story about Himself."

Lingering over coffee late next morning, Reene's terrifying incident raised questions they couldn't ignore.

"We might as well face it, Lissa. Our visitor from the Other Side is getting too hard to handle."

"I'm afraid so. Not that there's anything wrong with being a visitor from another world," Lissa added hastily, furtively scanning the room.

Reene chuckled at Lissa's reaction. "I thought you believed in ghosts."

"Yesss... but I don't want to aggravate Himself any further. So, where do we go from here?"

"We should try to learn more about the person who was killed in that riding accident," Reene answered. "We need more details about the accident. It's possible the ill-behaved spirit of the person who died is causing all this trouble. We both know that people killed in accidents or violent crimes before their time haunt the place where they died."

"True," Lissa agreed. "It's what keeps them from passing over."

"Exactly. Did Gina know anything more about this accident?"

"All she knows are the rumors that have been passed down from generation to generation. Why don't we take a field trip to the library? We can hunt through old records of births and deaths. Let's hope their records go back far enough or haven't disintegrated after so many years."

"I had another thought. We could also check old newspaper clippings. Don't they call that a morgue?"

"I wish you hadn't remembered that," Lissa said ruefully. "Come on, Lois Lane, we're off to do some investigative research."

According to the bronze plaque posted beside the front entrance, Westbrook's Public Library, a two-story brick building erected in 1926, had undergone major reconstruction when the Historic Commission took control of it one step ahead of the wrecking ball. The newly landscaped grounds were dotted with wrought-iron benches. A towering red maple shaded the building with its branches. Behind the building, old carriage stalls had been restored to their original glory. A great bronze stag, poised for flight, stood on the front lawn.

Lissa asked the bored young clerk at the main desk for help.

"Reference Section. Second floor, turn right at the top of the stairs."

"Geez, someone needs an attitude adjustment," Reene muttered.

Reaching the top of the stairs, an attractive older woman with shoulder length black hair and eyes like Hershey's chocolate greeted them.

"Good morning. My name is Donna Palermo. May I help you?"

"Good morning," Lissa smiled. "Yes, we're trying to find some information about an old family from this town. We recently bought their house. Their name is Williams."

"Oh, yes, I heard the property is now a productive bed and breakfast. I'm delighted to meet the new owners. Are there any specific areas you'd like to explore?"

"We'd just like to learn a bit more family history in general," Lissa said.

"And an accident that happened a long time ago in particular," Reene added.

"I'm afraid I can't be much help with family history unless a book has been written about them. Is that a possibility?"

"We don't have any idea," Reene replied. "We've only lived in Westbrook for three months. From what we've learned, we're pretty sure the accident happened around 1875."

"Our library maintains records of births, deaths and marriages dating back to that time period. With a little digging, we might come upon a clue as to where we go from here."

Donna stood and beckoned them to follow her. She led them to a bookcase filled with volumes of thick books in faded yellow bindings. She ran a practiced hand along the rows and stopped at 'Vital Records: January 1874 – December 1880'.

"Why don't you start with this volume and see what you come up with? If you have any other questions, I'll be right around the corner."

"Thanks so much. We probably will pester you with more questions," Lissa promised.

Reene opened the book and flipped through it until she found the section on marriages. She scanned page after page. Finally she stabbed an entry with her finger.

"'Williams, Peter, 22 and Taylor, Josephine, 19, married September 16, 1865.' I'll keep looking—"

A few moments later, Reene closed the book dejectedly. "Damn. Only one entry with the family name of Williams."

"Then we'll go on the assumption we've located a family member, probably a son. Let's ask the librarian if she has any other ideas."

"You're back already. Didn't that volume help?"

"Most certainly," Lissa answered. "We're on the right track. We were wondering if there were any other old records we could look at."

"As a matter of fact, there are, except they won't be hard copies," Donna replied. "We recently received a grant from the state and were able to put hundreds of old newspaper articles on microfilm. I believe you'll find them beneficial. We have a new microfilm reader as well. Come with me and I'll set you up."

Donna opened a sliding drawer in an enormous filing cabinet. "The tapes are labeled according to month and year. Were you able to narrow your search any?"

"Yes. Please try June of 1865 to 1900," Reene replied. "We should be able to locate other entries within that time frame."

"No problem," Donna replied. She located the reel that contained the dates Reene had suggested and brought it over to the reader. Skillfully she set up the film for viewing.

"If you're not familiar with the newer readers, just push the bar back and forth to scroll through the articles. See these wheels underneath? Use them to fine-tune the focus. You'll notice the print on old newspapers is incredibly small. Excuse me. I have people waiting."

Reene lugged over a chair. "Lissa, this could be like looking for the proverbial needle in a haystack. We don't have time to sit here all day and scroll through every reel."

"I'm sure we'll locate the information we're seeking," Lissa said stubbornly. "I'll make a deal with you: if it turns out our whole afternoon is wasted, I'll cook dinner for the next month!"

"An offer I can't refuse! You're on!"

But as they scrolled through a number of articles, straining to read the tiny print, even Lissa's high spirits flagged. An hour passed, their eyes ached and the boring search aggravated them. To relieve the tension, they read ads from the thrilling days of yesteryear.

"'Got Worms? If your child is ailing, check for worms. Buy True's Pin Worm Elixir,'" Reene quoted dramatically. "Check out this picture of a chicken. What's this one about? 'Don't blame the hen: if she doesn't lay when egg prices are high, coax her with Sheridan's Conditioning Powder.' Hold me back!"

Reene giggled and Lissa clamped a hand over her own mouth to keep from laughing out loud. Trying to regain her composure, she pushed the bar further over to the right and frowned.

"A Morris chair for only $4.98. Now that's a bargain! Must have been high end furniture of the day."

"Woman, don't you know what those chairs were used for?"

"No, I've heard of them but I thought they were a fancy chair, like a Chippendale."

Reene looked at her with a lopsided grin.

Lissa regarded her stonily. "What is so funny?"

"Funny, no. Painful, yes. Those chairs were used for giving birth."

Lissa's horrified expression was hilarious. But she recovered instantly. "Ah guess ah doan' no nothin' bout birthin' no babies, Miz Reene."

Both of them dissolved into near-hysterical giggles. Heads turned and dirty looks flew in their direction. Even Donna gave them the evil eye.

"We'd better behave, or we'll get tossed out the door and banned for life."

"Okay. I'll be good," Reene promised. "Let's keep scrolling."

"Here's another knee slapper: 'World Soap: No Naptha or Kerosene. Beach Soap Co.' Well, *there's* a ringing endorsement. No wonder so many women aged before their time," Lissa criticized.

"No kidding. Maybe we need some Beecham's Pills. It says here they cure biliousness and sick headache. I'm starting to get a sick headache myself."

"Hang on just a little longer," Lissa sighed and settled more comfortably in her chair. As the minutes crawled by, their frustration mounted. And because they were so frustrated, they almost missed it. Lissa pushed the button for the next page and her tired eyes roamed over the text. Suddenly, she jerked upright.

"Reene, this might be it! I think I found what we've been looking for."

They crowded closer to the microfilm reader and strained their eyes to read the minuscule print.

Local Wife and Mother Killed in Riding Accident

June 5, 1875
Westbrook, Massachusetts

The young wife of a local man, Peter Williams, was killed today in a riding accident. She was riding alone at her husband's farm when the incident took place. It is assumed she may have been riding through a stream where her horse slipped and fell. It is also believed she was killed instantly.

Per the wishes of her husband, she will be buried on their family farm. Her young son, Joseph Williams, also survives her.

"This must be the accident Gina told me about," Lissa said. "And the name is 'Williams'. This article is awfully short on details. Evidently it wasn't considered serious enough for an investigation."

"I guess people of that era were realists who didn't have the time or energy to examine every detail the way we do today. They simply accepted their fate and went on with their lives."

Reene paused to reread the short article. Then she grabbed Lissa's arm.

"Lissa, don't you realize what this means? Our He is a She!"

"You're right! We were wrongly assuming that our visitor is male. It must be Peter's wife. And if it *is* Peter's wife, do you suppose that's what spooked Sissy the day you drove by the water? Maybe She waits by the stream sometimes because that's where She was killed."

"Sissy definitely sensed her presence," Reene agreed. "Horses and dogs are especially intuitive about that sort of thing."

"Another thought just occurred to me. Did you notice that she wasn't mentioned by name, only referred to as a 'wife and mother' of the former owner of our inn? Do you think that was standard for the time?"

"I'm not sure. It does seem odd, though, doesn't it? You'd think that the wife of a prominent farmer at least deserved to have her name printed in the paper."

"I'm sure there's more to this story but, unfortunately, we're not going to find out anything more from this piece. Curioser and curioser. Let's call it a day."

Moments later, Reene dropped off the reel on the Reference Desk.

"Thanks for your assistance, Donna. We couldn't have done this without you."

"I'm pleased you had good hunting. You were fortunate those old records had been restored on film. Did you find everything you wanted?"

"No, not really," Lissa replied. "We've cleared up one mystery, but we need to do a lot more research. Something doesn't ring true in this article we found and we won't be satisfied until we figure it out. I can't imagine how we're going to do it 'cause right now our brains have turned to mush. But don't be surprised if we're back to pester you."

"You aren't pestering me. I love a mystery," Donna answered. "If we all put our heads together, maybe we can solve this puzzle."

From a study table in an alcove by the stairway, Lloyd Collins had been quietly watching the two women. Without calling attention to himself, he had listened intently to their conversation but couldn't piece things together. As the women headed down the stairs, he cast an appreciative eye in Reene's direction.

Must be the blonde who got Andrea's knickers in a twist. This could be my chance to untwist them. I'm positive the black-haired woman at the desk knows what's going on.

Lloyd had only exchanged pleasantries with her in the past. Perhaps now was an opportune moment to start a new friendship. Wearing his most charming smile, he approached the desk.

"Good morning, Mrs. Palermo, Donna, if I may? I'm in dire need of assistance. Could you answer a few questions for me?"

Chapter 14

"Any inspiring ideas how to help our resident spirit cross over, Lissa?" Reene asked as she measured milk to make chocolate pudding. "Now we know why she's here, we've got to make her understand it's time to leave."

"We'll have to return to the scene of the crime, figuratively. If she's still hanging about the inn, there must be something else that's keeping her here. Except I really don't want to go around knocking on walls and digging up bricks in the fireplace."

"We can save that plan as a last resort. Let's think about this. Who else would know of or have old records?"

"Other than the library or newspaper, the only other place I can think of is a historical society. Most towns have one to preserve old documents and artifacts. I'll give our new friend Donna a call," Lissa said, reaching for her cell phone.

"Reference Desk, Donna Palermo speaking."

"Hello, Donna. Lissa Martin of the Barn Swallow Inn. My friend Reene and I descended on you yesterday. You helped us research some information concerning our inn."

"The Williams family and 'the accident', correct? You both had me awfully excited with your venture. Almost like a treasure hunt. Did you and your friend come up with a new angle?"

"Yes and no. We were wondering if Westbrook has a historical society that keeps old records and maintains the town's history."

"Actually the Westbrook Historical Society has been active for over a hundred years in such projects. Because of their efforts a number of artifacts and buildings have not been lost. I should have mentioned them yesterday. Do you have a pen handy for the contact information?"

"Hang on!" Lissa replied. She balanced the cell phone on her shoulder and whispered to Reene. "She's found a lead for us. What? Oh, yes, sorry Donna. Got it. I can't thank you enough."

"You're welcome. I'm enjoying your search vicariously." Donna paused and the pause turned pregnant.

"Donna? Is there something else?"

"I'm not sure. It's just a feeling I have. Consider it woman's intuition. Have either of you met Lloyd Collins?"

"Lloyd Collins?" Lissa echoed. "I'm afraid I've never heard of him. Reene is right here and she's shaking her head 'no'. Why?"

"When you left the library yesterday, Lloyd popped up at my desk. He and I have known each other off and on over the years, but we're not best friends, if you get my drift," Donna said.

"I get your drift. What did he want?"

"He asked me to search for some technical information. He's an accountant, so outwardly his questions were not out of the ordinary. In between my attempts to look up what he wanted, he managed to ask more than a few questions about you, your friend, and the inn."

"Just being a little nosy, I'll bet. I'm sure you've met people who can't stand it if someone knows gossip they don't."

"He acted more than a little nosy. The questions he asked were innocent enough, but I felt like he put me under a microscope."

"Interesting. Thank you for telling me. If we run into this Lloyd Collins, we'll see if our intuition matches yours. I'll keep you posted on the latest developments when I speak to Mrs. Long," Lissa promised.

"Mrs. Long?" Reene asked as Lissa disconnected the call. "Who is she?"

"Mrs. Ruby Chapman Long is President of the Westbrook Historical Society. She's 85, sharp as a tack, and for the last forty years has made sure Westbrook's priceless goodies don't disappear into some rich person's collection."

"Good for her. We've found the next link in our chain."

"Without a doubt. I'll call her," Lissa volunteered. "I've always had a way with the older crowd, just like you're so good with the kiddies."

Mrs. Long sounded interested when Lissa called with her request for an interview and invited her to come for afternoon tea.

"You work fast," Reene commented as Lissa, wearing a black blazer, a cream colored chemise, and her best dress jeans, came into the breakfast room.

"Am I appropriately turned out for a visit with one of the town's respected senior citizens? And she invited me to afternoon tea."

She turned slowly and struck a pose like a professional model.

"Nice. She'll be impressed. How are you going to get the information we want without telling her about you-know-who?"

"I've been thinking about that too. I'll just tell her we're interested in the history of the old place, and I dabble in genealogy. I could say we're planning to include a detailed history of the inn on our website."

"That'll work. Go with it."

"So, what's on your schedule?"

"I'm going for another drive with Sissy. I don't want to give her time to think about our last adventure. I should pick up some more shavings. Two couples are due in next week so I want to make sure we have enough of everything."

"Good thinking. See you in a bit. Hopefully I'll return filled with lots of tea, cookies and information about our not-so-friendly visitor."

Lissa pulled up in front of a small Cape set back from the road. The house was painted a soft gray with mulberry-colored shutters adding a touch of color. Long muslin ball fringe curtains hung in the windows. Fuscia petunias and lavender asters lined the brick walkway.

She rang the front door bell and waited an eon or two until she detected movement at the long window that flanked the door. *I know she's expecting me. I hope she doesn't think I'm an axe murderer.* She could see the older woman peering at her from behind the curtains.

"Good morning!" Lissa greeted, pitching her voice so the woman could hear her. "I'm Lissa Martin. I called you earlier today."

"Oh, yes! Please come in." The elderly woman's face visibly relaxed as she stepped aside to let Lissa pass.

"I appreciate your seeing me on such short notice," Lissa smiled. "I'm sure you were a little apprehensive about meeting with a total stranger. Especially in this day and age."

"I must confess I was a bit nervous but now that I've met you, I don't suppose I have anything to worry about," Mrs. Long declared.

"Thank you."

Mrs. Long's youthful appearance was amazing. The older woman's short hair, a soft, natural-looking honey blonde, complemented her nearly flawless complexion. Lissa surreptitiously touched her own face with its crow's feet and wrinkles and wondered where she'd gone wrong.

Mrs. Long was dressed smartly in a chocolate brown and white color block sweater, a pale blue silk blouse and wool slacks. Two wedding rings soldered together hung from a gold chain around her neck.

Leaning on her cane, she led the way to the front room where a teapot encased in a tea cozy and two China cups sat in the middle of a maple coffee table. Cera linen napkins lay next to a plate of chocolate chip cookies.

Mrs. Long sank into a burnt orange velvet wing chair. "Before we begin, I'd like a cup of tea. Would you mind pouring?"

"Not at all. How do you take it?"

"Black, thank you." She accepted the cup Lissa handed her. Lissa fixed her own brew and placed two cookies on her napkin.

"Now, how precisely can I help you?" her hostess asked as she sipped her tea. "Will you refresh my memory?"

"Certainly, Mrs. Long—"

"Ruby, please. That's what everyone calls me."

"Well, Ruby, as I explained to you over the phone, my friend Reene and I bought the Williams' farmhouse. We've turned it into a bed and breakfast."

"My brother informed me about the nice young women who bought the farmhouse from him," Ruby commented.

"Your brother!" exclaimed Lissa.

"Yes, Allan Chapman is my little brother." Ruby's eyes twinkled like her brother's. "He is so proud of his second career as a realtor. He is a former Mountie, you know."

"I had no idea!" Lissa smiled at the fond reference. "A Mountie! How exciting!"

"I emigrated from Nova Scotia to Massachusetts over sixty years ago and Allan stayed in Canada to become a Mountie. Now he's joined me here. You must meet his wife, Joan. She's lovely."

"Why, yes, that would be nice."

Lissa stumbled over the detour in the conversation. "Where was I? Oh, I remember. You're aware that our inn is geared for guests with horses? My friend Reene Anderson designed our website to advertise the inn. Our problem is we haven't been overwhelmed with guests. We thought if we put some intriguing history on our website we might attract a different clientele."

"Yes, that's understandable. Do you have the period of time that you're trying to cover? Do you want details or just a brief overview?" Ruby asked.

"I'd like to know as much detail as possible and then I'll choose what I need. We were thinking of starting around 1875 to present."

"Very sensible. That should make our task easy. May we take your car?"

"My car? Why?"

"Because the information you seek isn't here. We store our records at Town Hall. We hold our monthly meetings in a suite of rooms on the upper floor. But, ah, perhaps you don't have time to go there today?"

"That's not a problem! I can spend all afternoon with you."

"All right, then. We should go. Leave the tea things. I'll attend to them later."

Ruby wiggled forward to extricate herself from the deep chair. Lissa leaped up to help her.

"Don't you bother with this mess," Lissa said. She gathered the cups and saucers and carted them into the pantry.

"Thank you. Now that we're ready, I'll just take your arm, Lissa."

Lissa slowly drove through town with Ruby riding shotgun. The talkative woman regaled her with stories of various and sundry denizens of Westbrook in general and her brother in particular.

By nightfall Lissa returned the older woman to her house. After lugging volumes of dusty books, looking at pictures from the past, and pouring over old records, she was too worn out to turn down Ruby's invitation to dinner. She spent hours listening to more stories over chicken divan and then bade her hostess good night. She'd discovered some fascinating information, but at the moment, her tired brain couldn't process all she'd learned. Her head full of facts and her stomach full of food, she headed home.

"I'll talk with Reene in the morning. I hope I won't burn in Hell from lying to a nice old lady," she groaned. She dragged her tired body upstairs to her room. "With a bit more brainstorming we can sort everything out. Our dear old inn may have a few skeletons rattling around in its closets."

"Good morning!" Reene greeted in a tone that shook the windows. "You must have had a late night. I didn't even hear you come in."

"Woman, you are so darned cheerful in the morning!" Lissa groused. "No, I wasn't out too late. But I was so dog-tired I couldn't even dredge up enough energy to tell you about my visit with Ruby."

"Ruby?" Reene echoed.

"Mrs. Long to you. Actually I can't get used to calling her 'Ruby' either. A child of the 50s, I am."

"Do you think she figured out what we're up to?"

"A regular Miss Marple I was. Mrs. Long had endless stories at her command, right down to the last detail. She filled me with such niceties as to who died when and where, what they died from, and who married their fourth cousin twice removed. My head was spinning when I left her house. She insisted on giving me her recipe for chicken divan. I sort of promised her we'd use it for our guests."

"For *breakfast*?" Reene gasped. "Sounds like you had a workout. Time to feed the hungry critters. Then I'll make you a yummy bacon and cheese omelet and we can figure out if we're any further along in our Great Whodunit."

Chapter 15

Back in the breakfast room after feeding all creatures large and small, Reene cleared the dirty dishes and placed a plate of fresh cut fruit on the table.

"What did you find out?" Reene asked.

"According to the Society's accounts," Lissa began, "Peter Williams served as a lieutenant in the Union Army. He was decorated for gallantry in the field. When the war ended he returned home to Westbrook. Following his wife's death he left New England with his son and never returned. There's no documentation that he ever remarried or where he eventually settled. I couldn't find a record of the child returning to Westbrook either. He vanished along with his father."

"Then we're at a dead end."

"Not necessarily," Lissa continued. "Mrs. Long also told me there's a list of all the furnishings in this house dating back to day one. Fortunately for us, she kept an inventory for the Historical Society. I wouldn't be surprised if an old Bible is stored away somewhere. People of that era were always recording important milestones in their family Bibles."

"That's true. If only there were easier ways to find all the answers to our questions. Let's give it a shot. It may be fun following clues and trying to piece things together."

"Reminds me of the Nancy Drew detective novels I read back in the Dark Ages. I hung onto one or two of them and put them in the Gathering Room. Those old books might bring back some pleasant memories."

"So where's this inventory?" Reene prodded.

"Right here in glorious black and white. Mrs. Long was efficient. She had typed and dated the inventory. I'm glad that most of the furnishings were included when we bought the house."

As they scanned the items, Lissa exclaimed "My desk! It's described as a slant-front Queen Anne Chippendale! It's a genuine antique, circa

1760, and in beautiful condition. What else is on that list? Mahogany highboy, dry sink, pedestal dining table and matching chairs..."

"Let's go back to your office and look up this desk on the web. A desk is a perfect hiding place."

Three web sites later they found the details on the Queen Anne.

"'Small cherry slant front desk," Lissa read. "'Desk top has a central (prospect) door with small drawers and pigeon holes. There is a secret compartment below the removable floor behind the prospect door.'"

She turned to Reene. "Why is it called a prospect door?"

"Whatever it's called, I'm dying to see if there really is a secret compartment," said Reene eagerly. She opened the ornate door, reaching inside and tapping at each corner until her fingers found a small metal ring. With a bit of tugging, she triumphantly removed the square piece of wood.

"*Voila!*" she cried, reaching into the small opening and exploring the compartment. "I've snagged something! Definitely papers."

Carefully she drew out the document, afraid it might rip on the corner of the compartment.

"Lissa, look at this! It must be a hundred years old. It's awfully wrinkled but it's still legible. We need more light." She jumped up and switched on the overhead fixture.

"Oh my God! I can't wait to see what it says. Spread it out on the desk."

Heads bent over the yellowed parchment-like paper, they struggled to decipher the faded but distinctive handwriting.

July 18th, 1865
Regimental Headquarters

My dear Miss Taylor,

Your contribution ⋯ victory has not gone unnoticed. Your gallant actions in the field ... carrying messages to the North ⋯ great personal risk, saved hundreds of lives.

I have been authorized ⋯ Federal government to provide you with payment for services rendered. A money

116

*order is enclosed· If I may, I wish ··· increased by a thousand
fold·*

From a grateful Nation,
Yours sincerely,
Captain Richard Ellsworth
37th Massachusetts Infantry Regiment

"1865! The year the Civil War ended," Lissa exclaimed. "'Gallant actions carrying messages to the North saved lives.' Miss Taylor. That must be Josephine Taylor who married Peter Williams. Evidently Peter's wife was a soldier for the North. What's this business about carrying messages? That doesn't make sense unless—"

"Unless she was a courier," Reene finished the thought for her. "Or a spy. Gallant actions, saving lives. What else could it mean?"

"Let's not jump to the obvious conclusion. We just don't have enough information about her to say for sure. Fish around in that compartment and see if there are any other papers."

"No luck, Lissa," Reene said a moment later. "My search came up empty. If we keep hunting, we may find more letters in other hidey-holes in this ginormous house. There are only a thousand spots they could be."

"Don't get discouraged. Remember how we found 'our' Josephine in the first place."

"Wait a minute!" Reene exclaimed. "Didn't you mention a Bible on the list of possessions? If we can find that, we may get some answers."

"You're on the right track now. Do you remember seeing a Bible in the attic or in any other piece of furniture?"

"No, I don't and if I did, I didn't pay much attention, I'm afraid."

"I just had the craziest thought. You remember the book I put on the mantel as a conversation piece?"

"Yes, but what... No! *Gone With the Wind*! It couldn't be that easy, could it?" Reene asked.

Like two kids on a scavenger hunt, they dashed into the Gathering Room and scooped the book from its resting place. Eagerly they checked the inside front cover.

"'To Lillian, with affection, Alfred. December 25, 1940'," Reene deciphered. "Must have been a Christmas present." She turned the book to the back cover. "Nothing here."

"Well, it was a long shot at best." Lissa glanced up at the crooked portrait. "Do you suppose the person in this portrait is Josephine Taylor? Why else would it have remained in the family homestead so long? And that little hint of a smile on her face? Now I'm certain a secret is hiding behind that smile. Help me get it down!"

Reene dragged a chair away from the game table and climbed on. Lissa steadied the chair to keep it from tipping. Reene eased the portrait off the wall and handed it down.

"Well, well, Ms. Taylor or should I say, Mrs. Peter Williams? What do you think? This young soldier could be either gender, but I'm ready to bet the farm this is a woman."

Reene studied the portrait intently. "Even though the face *is* androgynous, I'd bet the farm too it's a woman. Help me turn it over. I don't remember any writing on the back, but it's worth a look."

The back of the portrait was made of cardboard, rippled and stained with age and moisture. "Try the lower right hand corner. That's where artists always sign paintings."

Reene tilted the portrait to examine it more closely. "You're right! There *is* printing! It's faded but if I squint hard enough, I can read it. 'J. Taylor from R.E., 1865'."

"'R.E.' must be the captain in the letter. He must have been her commanding officer. Or Peter's. And she's wearing that ghost of a smile, no pun intended, because she was a success at her job. Courier *or* spy."

"A lady or a tiger? I sense you're caving to the spy theory. Can you imagine, Lissa? She was barely into her teens! She had a lot of courage to take such dangerous risks. I definitely want to learn more about her."

"Then we've got to find that Bible or anything else that might give us more clues to her history. There's much more to this story than what we've found. And where have the rest of the Williams' relatives gone? Everyone seems to have vanished into the Bermuda Triangle."

Reene carefully rehung the portrait. "I'm all for another treasure hunt, but not today. We've got stalls to muck out."

"I suppose I can hang on a few more days before playing girl detective again."

The insistent ringing of the phone sounded from the office. Reene dashed up the back stairs as Lissa ran to answer the call. Neither glanced at the portrait that had stubbornly stayed crooked for months.

Now it hung perfectly straight and true above the fireplace.

"If I were a Bible, where would I hide?" Lissa muttered. She wandered from room to room peering up in the rafters and groping under the furniture. "It's probably right under my nose and I'm too dumb to figure it out."

She yanked out the desk drawers for the zillionth time hoping the Bible would magically appear. Nothing. She and Reene had searched every bookcase in the house. Strike two.

"Where else should I try?" On her hands and knees, she crawled around the hearth poking and prodding the bricks.

"What the heck are you doing down there?" Reene demanded. She stopped dead at the doorway when she saw Lissa crawling around the floor. "You're obsessed with finding that Bible."

"No kidding. It's driving me crazy! Where could it be?"

"I hate to bring this up, but it could have been sold, thrown out, or fallen apart from old age."

"Humor me. I may be in denial but I know it's here somewhere!"

"We've turned every piece of furniture inside out, searched all the closets and drawers—"

"Wait. Did we check the drawers under the buffet closet in the dining room?"

"Yep. Nothing except silverware and a few odds and ends. If I remember correctly, that's where we found all those beautiful old tablecloths. We planned to use them for the tea and then decided they might get ruined."

"I'd forgotten about that. Let's have a quick rummage around so we're satisfied we've tried every nook and cranny in this place," Lissa insisted.

Lissa opened the top drawer and carefully removed the first lace tablecloth. It was in amazingly good condition. Tissue paper between each cloth rustled as they removed another layer. Matching napkins were neatly folded and held in place by ribbons. A dozen lace doilies wrapped in more tissue paper joined the growing pile.

She removed the last tablecloth and caught her breath. A leather bound book emerged from its lacy nest. Embossed on the cover were the words Holy Bible.

"Wooo-hooo!" Reene yelled. "Here it is!"

"I just knew we'd find it!" Lissa exulted. She lifted the book from the drawer as if it were a newborn.

"It's in fantastic shape even though it's been hidden away for years. The leather cover is awfully dry so we'd better be careful."

"Don't fret, I'll treat it kindly. Cross your fingers a long-forgotten relative made a record of the family's comings and goings."

"Try the inside covers first," Reene suggested. "That's the usual place for writing all that stuff."

"You're spot on!" The Williams' family history was written in a fine hand in pencil. "It's gonna be hard to read this," Lissa grimaced as she strained to read the washed out writing. "Do we have a magnifying glass?"

"No, we don't. Let me try. Here's Peter's son Joseph. He was born in January of 1866. Something's off. Do you remember the date on that letter we found? I think it was July of 1865."

Lissa flew into her office and snatched up a manila folder.

"Your memory is too good! Guess you aren't ready for my ginkgo biloba yet."

"Guess what else I found? If you do the math, Josephine was already pregnant."

"Whoa! That must have been a major scandal! A Black girl married to a White man? And pregnant?"

"No kidding. Maybe that's why their son vanished from the family history after his mother was killed. No, wait, I see another entry for him. He married in 1891 and had two children, Maddie in 1893 and Joshua in 1895. Evidently he must have kept in touch despite moving away."

Lissa turned the book toward the light for a better look. "Maddie married Andrew Carson and Joshua...oh, dear. He died in 1918. I wonder if he joined the Cavalry. Perhaps he shared the same love of horses as his grandmother and grandfather."

"Perhaps. That's something we'll probably never find out."

"Reene, it breaks my heart to watch those old documentary films of World War I that show horses in battle," Lissa shuddered. "Imagine the terror those beautiful animals suffered. Shells exploding and planes flying overhead. It's beyond my comprehension why horses were still used to fight in wars in the 1900s. 'The War to End All Wars'. What a joke. A horrible waste of human and equine lives."

She paused and took a deep breath. "Sorry I got on my soapbox. Back to the book. Maddie Williams married in 1922 and had two children, Elaine, born in 1926 and Robert in 1929."

Lissa turned the Bible over to the back covers.

"Only two more entries on this cover: Robert married Mary Ann Keddy in 1955. Elaine married George Watson, Wilton—I can't make it out—in 1958. No more entries. Either whoever kept these records passed away or the tradition of writing family histories died out."

Reene shrugged. "I don't see how these old notations are going to solve the puzzle. Can you put sleuthing to rest for just a few days? We *do* have a business to run."

"No argument this time. I'm more than ready for a break from the whole crazy, confusing story. If I put it out of my feeble brain for a while, things might make sense.

Then she sighed. "Right. When we win the lottery."

Chapter 16

"Lyme disease! Oh, no, Reene. Not Shen!"

"Don't be frightened Lissa," Reene said. "It's not fatal, but no fun for my poor horse. All I have to do is buy four bottles of this ridiculously expensive medicine and give it to her twice a day."

With sleuthing on the back burner, she'd gone out to the barn to hang out with her second best friend. But she had run to get Lissa when she realized Shen wasn't acting like her normal self.

"Hey, pretty girl!" she had called when they had returned to the barn. But Shen's only response was pawing and shifting in her stall.

"Stop begging, Shen," Reene had warned. Reene had groomed her and spent time with her which seemed to calm her. But when Shen wouldn't eat her grain that night, the women agreed that the horse might be in trouble. Colic? Reene had phoned the vet immediately.

Frank Hayes had come early the next day. He ran a thorough check on the mare and drew blood to test for Lyme. An anxious week passed before the results showed that indeed Shen had contracted the dreaded disease.

"Rotten good-for-nothing ticks!" raged Lissa. "The creepy things serve no purpose other than to bite people and animals and carry disease. I'd like to burn every single one of them with a flame thrower."

Reene smiled in appreciation. "I'm all over that. The worst of it is the disgusting things won't die until the first frost. Poor Shen. She doesn't deserve this."

She sighed and snatched up her pocketbook. "I need to make another trip to the vet's for medication. Keep an eye on her, will you? I won't be long."

"No worries. I'll run out and talk to her. Shen could use some extra TLC even if it's not from her mom."

Reene gave Shen her daily dose of medication hidden in her food, but the molasses and applesauce that unexpectedly appeared in her grain bucket did not fool her. Her delicate nose detected the medicinal smell and she wanted nothing to do with it. Reene mixed different combinations for every feeding and finally managed to get most of the stuff down her throat.

Late one evening Reene stayed with Shen, talking to her and letting her know she was the center of attention. As a gesture of moral support, Lissa grabbed a lawn chair and kept her friend company. Satisfied the mare at last seemed comfortable, the weary women headed off to bed.

Giving their support, Bravo and Sissy hung over their stall doors, watching and listening. Their instinct told them something wasn't right with their barn mate.

The night dragged on. The horses slept off and on, lying down in their warm beds of shavings, only to lurch back up after a twenty-minute nap. Thousands of years of domestication had not changed their prey animal sleep habits. As far as they were concerned, enemies lurked behind every rock and they intended to be ready for flight if necessary.

Although Reene had settled Shen in for the night, the mare again became restless. She shifted from foot to foot, unable to find her comfort zone. Without warning, she sensed an unknown energy in her stall.

Shen stood immobile, her eyes wide, ears flicking back and forth, desperately trying to understand the unnatural force she felt swirling around her. Bravo spun in his stall and faced Shen across the aisle. Sissy followed his lead a second later. Both horses whickered softly to Shen, but she did not respond.

Now the barn turned eerily quiet. No rustling of night creatures disturbed the stillness. Bravo and Sissy crowded close to their stall doors as they watched and waited.

Shen's head bobbed in confusion. The horse's mane ruffled gently as if a feather-light touch was traveling down her spine and over her rump. Her nostrils flared as she detected the scent of one of her own. A low nicker rumbled in her throat. Eagerly she blew out her breath in greeting and felt an answering rush of warm air.

As Shen relaxed, her eyes grew soft, as if something had washed all her fear and discomfort away. The nervous shifting of her weight eased, and she sighed in contentment.

All at once the night came alive again. Noisy crickets chirped and an owl added its call. Jesse James' hunting cry slashed the air. The horses settled in their stalls, adding their normal blows, snorts and grunts to the cacophony of sound. A soothing calm descended over the barn.

Bravo and Sissy intuitively realized the crisis was over and relaxed their vigil. They pulled hay from the hay racks and drank deeply from their water buckets.

At that same instant, the mysterious healing presence had vanished. But it would never be forgotten.

Chapter 17

Wall Street
New York City

Stephen Marshall leaned back in his leather chair and tossed a letter onto the mahogany desk. Sunlight beamed into the office of his Wall Street high-rise building. It did not help lighten his mood. He sat in silence for a moment and then snatched the letter up again. His friend and college classmate, Randy Simms, kept him informed of his former wife's comings and goings.

> *Andrea's running for mayor, Stephen, and I'd say she has a pretty good shot at dethroning Bob Stuart. Her name is plastered all over town and signs are staked in everyone's yard. She's promoting some interesting ideas about how the town should be run. She puts in appearances everywhere and hasn't missed a supermarket or day care center opening. Last month, she went to a tea given at a new bed and breakfast that just opened for the horsey set. During the short time I spent there, I watched Andrea working the crowd. She was dressed to kill too.*

Stephen sighed. He knew it was only a matter of time before Andrea sought a career in politics. One of the many things about which they had disagreed during their five-year marriage.

He had presumed his profession, a stockbroker in one of New York's tonier establishments, would satisfy her craving for power, money and position. His six-figure salary, not to mention hefty bonuses, put them in the upper tax bracket. To his deep regret, he soon discovered her happiness demanded constant attention. Not content to act as hostess for his parties and entertain his clients, she wanted her own place in the spotlight. And she did not intend to share that spotlight with a child.

He could still remember her violent outburst the first time he broached the subject. They had discussed having a family before their marriage and she'd always evaded a direct commitment with answers like "We'll see how things work out." After traveling abroad several times and tiring of entertaining all the 'right' people, he yearned to have a son or daughter to make his life complete.

"Stephen, how can you suggest such a thing?" she had blazed. "I have no intention of having a child, now or ever! If we had a baby, I'd be trapped at home while you were out enjoying a career. Changing shitty diapers and washing grubby little hands is not my idea of fulfillment."

"I can well afford a live-in nanny and a cleaning person," he reminded.

"You don't want me to have a life of my own! Nanny or no nanny, I'd still be chained to your house! What's the problem? Are you afraid I'll eclipse you in your world of high finance?"

"Of course not, darling," he reassured her. "I've always been proud of you and your business acumen."

He tried to take her in his arms, but she stiffened and glared at him in defiance.

"Don't patronize me," she hissed. "And don't insult me by thinking a roll in the hay is going to make it all better."

He never brought the subject up again but knew their relationship had suffered damage beyond repair. Andrea remained constantly on guard and her manner toward him cooled even further. On the surface, she remained an impeccable hostess and they appeared in public together as a happily married couple. Only he knew the truth. His heart ached because he truly loved her. He tried over and over to show Andrea that he wanted her to share his life. The more he persisted, the more she hardened. With no more options open to him, he gave up.

Within a year of this episode, she announced she wanted a divorce. He pleaded with her to give their marriage one last chance, but she remained adamant.

"I want more than you can give me, Stephen, and I intend to get it."

"As you wish, Andrea. I can't hold you to your vows since you feel this strongly. If you ever need anything…"

She laughed at the old platitude and Stephen's face whitened in response.

"Don't lose any sleep over me, Stephen. There's nothing you can give me I won't already have."

Now she was close to accomplishing her goal. She kept her word. She didn't need him.

Not altogether true, he conceded. Clearly, she had needed every penny she'd received in the divorce settlement.

Ironically, he was proud of her accomplishments. If only he could convince Andrea he was still in love with her.

"I'll remain in the background until I see how things develop," he decided. The timing must be just right. "I'll take a trip down to Westbrook. I can stay at that inn Randy mentioned." He quickly scanned the letter. Unfortunately, Randy hadn't named it. He leaned over and pressed a buzzer.

"Sandra, please try to find a new listing for a bed and breakfast in Westbrook, Massachusetts. I'd like you to check their availability for the next few months. You might try searching for inns catering to horse owners."

"Horses?" she repeated. "That should narrow the choices down. I'll check the Net as well."

"Good idea. Please keep me advised." He hung up the phone, refolded the letter and tucked it into his private drawer.

He'd wait a little longer before taking a well-earned vacation at this quiet country inn.

The dog days of August had descended upon New England. Almost every day the air turned hazy, hot and humid. Lissa hated the three H's with a passion. Uncomfortable weather for people and animals. She rushed to finish her barn chores so she could escape to the coolness of the inn. At the beginning of summer, both women had loaded up their trucks with air conditioners from the enormous home improvement store. They didn't want to discourage guests from coming because they didn't have air conditioning.

Summer was the worst season for riding. If she and Bravo ventured into the woods, deer flies made a meal of them.

Fortunately, non-horse clients had finally discovered their inn. Families with young children were a welcome change of pace. Reene delighted in giving the kids a ride around the paddock on Shen or Bravo. Much to the chagrin of their parents, the horse bug bit many of them, the girls in particular. Now their parents would have no peace. They'd be

127

bombarded daily by tearful pleas for lessons—or worse, the dreaded "Daddy, buy me a pony!"

Lissa, pouring over the monthly bills, started when the phone rang.

"Barn Swallow Inn, Lissa speaking. How may I help you?"

"Good morning. My name is Sandra Wamboldt and I'm calling to make a reservation."

"Wonderful! How long will you be staying with us?"

"The reservation isn't for myself. It's for my employer," Ms. Wamboldt explained. "He plans to arrive next Saturday if that is convenient. He also asked that I make the reservation open-ended."

"Open-ended?" Lissa echoed.

"Yes. Is that a problem?"

"No, no. We've never had a request like this before. Will he prefer a double room or a single?"

The details finalized, Stephen Marshall would be arriving next Saturday for an indefinite stay.

"Reene, wait till I tell you the latest! We're going to have *another* guest hanging around the place. Only this one's from New York and it sounds like he's got money he hasn't counted yet. He made an open-ended reservation. Actually, his secretary did."

"That's awesome! I knew we'd get the New York trade sooner or later. I wonder why he made an open-ended reservation."

"Beats me. No doubt he has a stressful job and needs some quiet time."

"We'll make sure he gets that here. Which room did you give him?"

"The Morgan Room. It's the quietest. Speaking of quiet, I hope Josephine behaves."

"I hope she does too," Reene replied. "She hasn't been too active lately. Maybe she's pleased we've been trying to find out more about her accident."

"Good point. With any kind of luck, we'll solve this mystery. Reene, I've been thinking a lot about this. Of course it's way too late to figure out if she actually was murdered. Even if it wasn't an accident, we've discovered a long-overlooked part of our history. Why don't we come up with a plan to honor Josephine Williams' sacrifice for her country?"

"What a super idea! I absolutely agree. If we could include the whole town, their involvement would make a perfect ending to her story."

"Know who else may be interested? Hizonner the Mayor. It would be a feather in his cap if he could play a part in this commemoration."

"Ahh, yes, politics make strange bedfellows, or so I've heard. Mr. Mayor might have a heart attack if he knew he was getting entangled with a ghost. We need to come up with some way to explain the whole scenario without mentioning, shall we say, Josephine's current address."

Lissa sighed. "Yeah, that's not going to be easy. Heck, we've already told a few white lies already. What's a few more if they help her to pass over?"

"Exactly. Once we get all the facts, we can plan our next move. In the meantime, I'd better start planning menus and laying in enough enticing foods for our New Yorker. He probably eats snails and fancy French food three times a day."

"Ugh! Snails!" Lissa wrinkled her nose in distaste. "There's not enough garlic in the world to force one past my tonsils. With any luck, he'll surprise us and be like us common folk."

"Let's assume he's one of us. Of course, you know that old saying about assuming. I'll bet you a new silver show halter he'll show up in a red Mercedes convertible and have $5,000 worth of golf clubs in the trunk."

"You're on! If he's got that kind of money, you'd better start cooking that fancy French food."

"He'll have to settle for my garden quiche recipe. I've been saving it for a special occasion. The eggs come out sooo thick and creamy. I use green onions and cover the whole mixture with thin slices of tomato. It is scrumptious."

Lissa's mouth began to water. "In the interest of pleasing our important New York guest, I volunteer to taste-test this concoction. Why don't you make a batch for supper tonight?"

"I can tell by your puppy-dog eyes you won't be your cheery self unless I do."

"Correct. I'll let you know if it's worthy of an upscale business person who drives a red Mercedes."

Stephen Marshall put his car, a two year old silver Prius, on cruise control as he tooled along the Mass Pike. Traffic had thinned once he left New York. Seeming puzzled by his abrupt departure, his partners nonetheless assured him they would keep the office running smoothly. He offered no reason other than he had put off taking a vacation far too long.

The trunk held his luggage and tennis rackets. He did play golf with business colleagues who loved the game, but tennis better suited his lifestyle. He could play indoors or outdoors. No water hazards to drive him crazy. He had the build of an athlete and walked with an easy grace.

His mind drifted back ten years, and he recalled meeting Andrea during her time as an intern in his office. The red-haired girl had proven to be intelligent and efficient. He'd been impressed by both her body and her mind.

Before the month was over, they had dined and danced several times at exclusive restaurants and clubs. They saw the latest hit Broadway plays. When he proposed, he was surprised she insisted on a small, quiet wedding. Then they had honeymooned for a month in Europe.

As soon as I'm settled, Stephen decided, *I'll map out a strategy to win Andrea back. I'll promise to do everything in my considerable power to help her to win the election.*

He wondered if she would be receptive. He hoped the passage of time had softened Andrea's memories of him and their life together.

Following commands from his GPS, he drove directly to the inn and parked his car in front. He climbed out and stretched his legs. The quiet country setting enveloped him like an old friend. No screaming sirens, no taxis honking, no people yelling at the top of their lungs.

When a flaxen-haired horse whinnied at him, he walked over to the paddock.

"Hello, yourself," he smiled. But when he reached out and tried to stroke the horse's velvet nose, she jerked her head up.

"Fair enough," he chuckled. "After all, we haven't been formally introduced." He stepped out of her personal space.

"I don't understand what I did wrong," he told the animal, "but I can learn."

He patted her neck and this time she allowed the caress. Stephen smiled again. Evidently there were rules about equestrian etiquette he didn't quite fathom. His mood lightened. He no longer felt tired and whistled a few notes of a popular song from the Big Band era as he climbed the steps to the farmer's porch.

"Welcome!" Reene greeted as he approached the desk. She noted his beautifully styled brown hair liberally sprinkled with grey that complemented his moss green short-sleeved shirt and tan Dockers.

"Good day," he responded. "I believe you have a reservation for me? Stephen Marshall."

"Oh, yes. You'll be with us for a while, I gather."

"Yes, I will. I've only been here a few moments and I already feel at home. I even tried to make friends with one of your horses."

"Oh? Which one?"

"The one with the blonde mane and tail. She gave me a bit of a hard time at first, I'm afraid."

"I'm Reene and that's my mare, Shenan," She gave him an encouraging wink. "Don't take it personally. I'll take you out later to see her, if you'd like. Follow me. You'll be in the Morgan room."

He was impressed by the spacious guest room. The walls were painted the lightest shade of green, suggesting new shoots of grass. Louvered doors concealed the clothes closet. Two windows opened onto the fields. The window opposite held an air conditioner.

Like a kid, he bounced on the cannonball style queen-sized bed to test its mattress. Which caused an avalanche of pillows.

"Lord, why do women insist on frilly throw pillows!" He lobbed two of them onto a cherry hope chest at the foot of the bed.

He inspected the bathroom, still talking to himself. "Shower stall's quite roomy. Not the usual broom closet."

He placed his laptop on the maple secretary desk near the window. Force of habit had made him bring it.

"I don't want to stay entirely out of touch with the office, but I'll be damned if I'll log on the first day," Stephen decided. He had no desire to spoil his mellow mood by checking emails.

His eyes were drawn to a large picture of a beautiful black horse, a young blond woman holding a huge trophy, standing by its side. A large rosette with red, yellow and blue streamers flowed from the horse's bridle. He looked at the frame and read the inscription on the brass plate: 'Motion Maker, Reserve Champion, New England Morgan Division – 1995'.

"So that's a Morgan horse. Magnificent animal. The Morgan room has a solitary picture of a champion Morgan horse. Very subtle. At least they don't hit you over the head with equestrian *objects d' art.*"

Tossing his suitcase onto the bed, he began to unpack. "L.L. Bean's finest hiking boots. The Berkshires aren't far away. Perhaps I'll get an opportunity to break them in. Maybe I should start my fitness regimen this afternoon. Or read the latest thriller on the bestseller list. I might try to make friends with that horse again."

Stephen shook his head in disbelief. "I don't know what to do with my down time! Is that pathetic or what? I'll take a quick walk around the property and then ask my innkeepers to recommend the best place for dinner. Tomorrow I will begin making plans for my own campaign. And why do I keep talking to myself?"

Chapter 18

"Andrea, you have a call on line two."

Andrea looked up brusquely from the spreadsheet on her computer and frowned. Janice Navin, Andrea's administrative assistant, was standing in the door to Andrea's office.

"It's Michael Gibbs. Something about the off ramp he's designing for you. He said it was urgent."

"Every damn thing is urgent as far as he's concerned. Close the door."

Andrea wrapped up her conversation with Michael Gibbs and asked Janice to retrieve a file folder regarding the off ramp project. Lately her assistant had been really getting on her nerves. It didn't help that the woman was still pining after Lloyd Collins, either. From what Andrea could gather, they had dated for a while, but Lloyd, in his typical fashion, had simply walked away. The time of the breakup had coincided with Andrea's return to town, and she was pretty sure her annoying assistant probably blamed her for that, too.

When Janice returned, she told her to set up another meeting with her campaign manager, Grady Ferguson. As she reviewed the file, she could hear her assistant's voice from the outer room.

"Mr. Ferguson, Janice Navin calling. Yes, I'm fine, thank you. Ms. Wilson is requesting a meeting with you tomorrow morning at 10:00. Is that convenient? Yes, I'll tell her."

Andrea made a note on her desk calendar. There was still a lot to accomplish between now and the election. When she had announced her campaign for mayor, her proposal for a new off-ramp had set off a chain reaction. Half the town had cheered for it even as the other half fought against it. Dust from that bombshell still hadn't settled.

"Odds are I'll win November's election," Andrea gloated. "Mayor Stuart certainly has nothing exciting to offer."

Janice knocked softly on her door and entered the office. "Excuse me. Mr. Ferguson will be here tomorrow promptly at ten o'clock."

"Promptly? He's never been on time yet. Make sure you order coffee and Danish. Lots of coffee. We may even work through lunch."

"Yes, Ms. Wilson," Janice said.

"'Ms. Wilson'? Aren't we a little formal today?"

"No, Ms. Wilson. I'm merely familiarizing myself with your new position, if you *are* elected. But then of course I'll have to address you as 'Madam Mayor'," Janice said, honey dripping from every syllable.

"Don't bother about what to call me. I have to get elected first," Andrea snapped, slightly disconcerted by Janice's tone.

"I have every confidence you'll be voted our first woman mayor. If I may say so, you have all the qualifications and the experience. Especially the experience of an *older* woman."

Before Andrea could process what Janice had said, Janice had quietly left the room. Again Andrea felt disconcerted and off balance. She shook her head impatiently. She had to review notes from her conversation with the engineer regarding the off ramp project. She had more important things to worry about than the off-center comments from her secretary. If things went as planned, Janice would no longer be working for her. She wondered if Janice suspected the change in her future. She reached for the buzzer.

"Janice, please hold all my calls until three o'clock."

"Yes, Ms. Wilson. Don't concern yourself. I'll let everyone know you cannot be disturbed. Perhaps you'd like to take a little cat nap? Campaigning can be *so* tiring."

Andrea swore under her breath and slammed down the phone.

"Michael Gibbs did an excellent job with the initial estimate on the off ramp," Andrea informed Grady Ferguson during their meeting. "He put all the details in layman's terms so at least I'll sound like I know what I'm talking about. The burning question is: what is the best way to present my brainchild to the voters?"

Grady reached across her desk and snatched up the paperwork. As he read, he scribbled a few notes in his Tablet. He slurped the last drop of his cold coffee. Andrea watched him in revulsion as he wolfed down one pastry after another. His waistline had rapidly expanded since their partnership began. Repulsive eating habits aside, she respected his opinions regarding her campaign.

"We," he replied with a slight accent on 'we', "are going for the jugular. Tell them straight out this is the only way for this town to grow, to develop into more than just a whistle stop on the way to New York. Make it sound so attractive, so appealing, they'll trample each other to vote for you. Even if they are cutting their own throats."

"Cutting their own throats?"

"Don't play innocent. And don't tell me you haven't thought of this. More accessibility brings more tourism and more businesses may be attracted to this corner of the world. Property values will go up and, of course, taxes will go up. It's the domino effect."

"That's why I hired you. You've got to cover all the angles and make this proposal sound like the greatest thing since sliced bread. That dates me, doesn't it? How about the greatest thing since the computer?"

Grady chuckled in response. "Don't worry. I'll come up with a way to sugarcoat everything and give you an answer for any question that could be asked." He paused and gave her an admiring look.

"You're a born politician, Andrea. You'll handle yourself like a pro once you're used to fielding uncomfortable questions. With my coaching, by the time election rolls around you'll convince everyone a new off ramp *is* the best idea since sliced bread. Stick with that simile. If ever it fit a town, it fits this one."

"You're good. We're going to make a first-rate team."

"Damn straight. I think so too. But before we go any further, I need to ask you a question."

"Be my guest."

"You don't have any illegitimate children or a prison record, do you? No drug abuse?"

"Last time I checked, I was totally free of children and I have never 'done,' I believe that is the expression drugs. But why this sudden interest in my morals?"

"Glad to hear you're as pure as the driven snow. Bigger people than you have seen their campaigns torpedoed for less. I want to make sure you're not hiding anything from me. Not a day goes by without some celebrity getting busted for drug possession. Especially those overpaid, whining Black athletes. My God, Blacks think they're entitled to riches and fame even if they don't deserve it. Half of them were so piss-poor they should be grateful for anything we give them."

He lowered his voice ominously. "Remember, Andrea, as your campaign manager, I need to be prepared for any unforeseen problems. If you blindside me, I'll quit."

"Message understood, Mr. Ferguson," she snapped. Her aversion to him had crept back. "Now can we get to work?"

"Yes, ma'am. I'll clear this junk away." Grady scooped up empty cups and discarded napkins. "I understand the opposition doesn't have any tricks up his sleeve yet. You dropped your little bolt from the blue at just the right moment. His Honor got caught with his pants down and didn't have any new ideas to counter your attack."

"Bob Stuart with his pants down?" Andrea snickered. "I don't think I can ever look him in the eye again."

Grady finally took his leave, his tirade against 'whining Black athletes' echoing in Andrea's mind.

Why can't I let it go? Why can't I acknowledge the truth? Because I'd lose everything! And if I'd shown my fear, he'd be on me like a hunting dog. He'd better do himself a favor and concentrate on his job. It's all about me, Mr. Racist Ferguson. That's the name of the game.

As Lloyd entered a New York style-deli, tucked inside a two-story bookstore, he almost collided with a patron who was leaving. He immediately recognized the man as Andrea's ex-husband.

"Pardon me!" exclaimed Stephen. Lloyd started to apologize, but startled by Stephen's apperearance, he lost his bearings for a moment.

"No problem. After you." Lloyd stepped aside and Stephen nodded on his way out.

Lloyd entered the restaurant and casually looked out the front window. He watched as Stephen strode down the sidewalk toward the town square.

"The plot thickens," he muttered as he proceeded to the deli counter.

"Good day, my good serving woman! What dost thou recommend to tempt my palate today?"

"Lloyd, you always make me smile!" the matron giggled. "I don't know what your palate is hankering for, but our special today is a tuna salad roll-up with Romaine lettuce, tomato and cheese, and cucumber dill dressing. We have homemade turkey soup with wild rice or corn chowder."

"Zounds, that sounds fit for a king! Be good enough to prepare two specials with turkey soup and I shall be on my way."

Shaking her head at his foolishness, the server bustled into the kitchen. Lloyd sat down at one of the round marble-topped tables and thought about his near collision with Stephen. He didn't believe the older man had recognized him. They'd only met once or twice and had barely exchanged greetings.

"I wonder how the former Mrs. Stephen Marshall will react when I break this news."

Minutes later, Lloyd paid the smiling woman and left a generous tip.

Brown bags in hand, he arrived at Andrea's outer office. He scanned the room. Janice must have gone to lunch. Ever since their breakup, he'd felt uncomfortable in her presence.

"Knock, knock," he called as he entered Andrea's office.

"I didn't think you'd ever get here! I'm starving!" She pushed back her chair and joined him at the conference table in the corner. "What did you bring me?"

"For your discerning palate, food-wise, I brought tuna roll-ups and turkey rice soup. News-wise, I don't think you are going to be pleased."

Andrea paused as she took the food from the bags. "Good food first, bad news second."

While they ate, Lloyd asked about her campaign and how she was dealing with Grady Ferguson. "I'd heard he was a bit coarse around the edges," Lloyd said as he sipped his steaming turkey soup.

"*Coarse* is a gross understatement. He's the original diamond in the rough," Andrea agreed. "At first his personality irked me but we've come to an 'understanding'. Lloyd, I must complement you on your choice of *haute cuisine*. Excellent. Where did you get these?"

"I thought you'd never ask." He intended to enjoy the moment even if she threw one of her famous temper tantrums.

"I picked them up at the little deli inside Books & Bagels. I nearly had a head-on collision with a gentleman coming out as I was going in. I believe you know him. It was your ex-husband."

He never saw a face change so drastically. Her eyes went blank and all color drained from her cheeks. To his horror, he thought she might faint and he tensed to catch her if she fell. All of the potential humor had gone out of the situation.

"Stephen is here? Are you sure?"

"Dead sure. It's been a few years since we bumped into each other, but I'd know him anywhere. He looked healthy and tanned. Which is more than I can say for you at the moment."

"I haven't the time or the inclination to lie around in the sun or work out in the gym. And I don't care how he looked. What is he doing here?"

"Well, we didn't have time for a chat. Maybe just passing through our quaint burg on his way back to New York. It is a free country, I believe."

"Stephen never does anything spontaneously. He's not just passing through. Hell!"

Color had returned to her face and she pushed back her chair impatiently. "I need a drink. Preferably a scotch and soda."

"Scotch and tuna salad?" Lloyd arched his eyebrows in mock surprise. "You really are in a snit. I could make inquiries if you're that concerned. However, I'm not sure I understand why his sudden appearance has caused such a reaction. I assumed you two had a highly civilized and amicable divorce."

"Oh, yes, I could always depend on Stephen to remain civilized." She hesitated a moment. "Lloyd, will you use your considerable connections and charm to see if his visit is just temporary? I don't want him upsetting my life again."

"I'll do my best. However, my lady doth protest too much, methinks."

"If you're trying to play games, remember, two can play at that game. Shall I ring for Janice?"

"Touché." Lloyd bowed to her, but his eyes had lost some of their devilry. "If there's anything pertinent to report, I'll get back to you. Cheerio. I enjoyed our little *tête-à-tête* luncheon as usual."

Andrea's mind was in turmoil once Lloyd had left. The combination of her bigoted campaign manager and her former husband's unexpected appearance lit the fuse to her short temper.

"Why did Stephen come back here?" she fumed. "Maybe Lloyd is right. Maybe he's just passing through on his way back to the city. Only I'll feel a whole lot happier when I know he's back where he belongs."

Chapter 19

"Know what we need to do, Lissa?" Reene asked as they mucked out stalls.

"Work out a plan for world peace? Cure the common cold? Don't we have enough on our plate?" Lissa grumbled as she dug out a nasty wet patch of bedding.

"Don't get cranky. I mean for the inn. We should do something about the draftiness. Winter isn't far off. I'm thinking we should have some insulation installed."

"Damn. You're right. We did talk about that when we first bought this place."

"I'm thinking blown-in insulation is the way to go," Reene offered.

"I don't know if that'll be practical in this old barn, pun intended. Call Contractors R Us. I'm putting you in charge of this project. Whoever you get is just ducky with me." Lissa threw a last forkful of manure into the wheelbarrow and went to the next stall.

"Since I'm in charge, I'll get at least three estimates and ask the winner to start work as soon as possible," Reene promised. "As you said, there's a lot going on, and it would be great if this project could be finished before Yankee Homecoming Days. We've taken a lot of reservations for that week."

"Sounds like a plan. I'm so looking forward to the Homecoming. We'd better find out who we should talk to about riding in the parade. What are the dates again?"

"Second weekend in September. It starts Friday and runs 'till Sunday. The parade is held on Saturday."

"We definitely can squeeze the parade into our schedule. Are you riding Shen or using Sissy and your million dollar wagon?"

"Excuse me? It only cost *half* a million. I'm definitely going to drive."

"We'll keep you company. I'll dress Brav up in his best silver tack."

"Perfect. Once we're finished here, I'll make some phone calls about the insulation."

Lissa sighed as she pushed the loaded wheelbarrow out to the manure pile. "We've been responsible for half the contractors in this area making big bucks. I'll bet they all have our phone number on speed dial."

"Speaking of contractors, we still haven't decided what to do about the well," Reene said. "At first I thought we could do the job, but I've changed my mind. Too much darn work."

"If you hadn't changed your mind, I would have changed it for you. We're up to our eyeballs in projects. Let the experts handle this one. I'll bite that bullet and call 'our' well contractor back."

"You're a saint," Reene said gratefully. "Maybe it won't be as bad as you think."

It was worse. Lissa almost burst into flames filling out the necessary dozens of multiple-page forms before the contractor could start digging. Turning a blind eye to their present bank balance, she sent $500 to cover fees for the work to begin.

The nano-second their check cleared, the ground breaking started. Loads of debris were hauled out as clear water filled the shaft. Then the diggers hit a snag. Despite repeated efforts, their equipment could go no further.

"My guess is that a buildup of sand and mud is causing the problem," the foreman who took Lissa on the wild ride informed her. "We'll need special tools to take care of it. Then we'll have to do a static water level test once we get the blockage cleared up."

The project again got put on hold.

As a precaution, Lissa asked the contractor to put up a sturdy chain link fence a few feet back from the well and box it in. She didn't want to take the chance of any critters—or guests—falling in.

"Is this place cursed or what?" Lissa grumbled.

"Hello! Anyone home?" a voice called through the screen door.

Lissa, who was helping Reene chop mushrooms for her mushroom and cheese omelets, quickly excused herself.

"Yes? Can I help you?" She noticed the white van parked out front. "Oh, I'm sorry, Lee, I didn't recognize you. Come on in."

Lee Bowden's company won the job to put in their insulation. As Reene had pointed out, his price sounded reasonable and his company had been in business for over thirty years.

"We're starting at the back of the inn today. We should finish by the end of the week," Lee promised.

139

"That is definitely good news. I'll be in the kitchen if you need me or Lissa can answer any questions."

"Fine. I'll give you a holler if we run into problems." Lee left to unload the equipment.

Two noisy days passed as the workers marched in and out of the house, lugging hoses and cords as they hunted for electrical outlets.

Just when they figured they were home free, they heard the words every homeowner dreads.

"Excuse me, ladies, I need to speak with you," Lee said.

As if they were walking the Last Mile, Reene and Lissa followed him down the hallway through the kitchen into the pantry.

"What's wrong?" asked Reene.

"Nothing's wrong, but we found something we didn't expect. When we drilled a hole into the outside wall, we found a big opening. I'm betting there's another room or closet on the other side of this wall."

When Lee tapped the pantry wall with his hammer, a hollow sound echoed.

"What should we do about this?" asked Lissa. "Will it stop you from finishing the insulation?"

"You really should find out how large this opening is. Do you have any blueprints for this place?" Lee asked.

"I'm afraid not," Reene responded. "This house was built almost two hundred years ago. We have no clue what's behind these walls."

"We're almost done here anyway," Lee said. "I'll give you a few days to decide what you want to do. Actually, this'll work out good for me. I've got to hire a new man. One of my guys just quit. He came roaring out a bedroom, his face white as a sheet. I asked him what the hell happened. He yelled 'I'm never coming back!' and took off. Your dog didn't try to bite him, did he?"

"Of course not!" Reene was indignant. "Andes is a perfect gentleman. I always put him in his crate when workmen are around."

"Sorry. I can't figure out why my guy lost it. Let me know how you make out. I'll call on Monday and we'll take it from there."

"We appreciate your suggestion. It's really nice of you," Lissa replied.

Lee's workmen packed up their tools and hoses and left the place cleaner than when they arrived. The van departed in a cloud of insulation dust.

"We know why this guy acted as if he'd seen a ghost," Lissa sighed. "Poor man. She must have given him the fright of his life."

"We're so lucky she hasn't tried to hurt anyone," Reene said. "Maybe she just didn't like him. Remember the spirit at your aunt's house that only liked women?"

"I certainly do. So do the women he scared half to death. And now we have another problem. If this doesn't sound like a Sherlock Holmes mystery, *The Case of the Hidden Room*, I'll eat my saddle blanket."

"I suppose we shouldn't be so surprised. A lot of these old places had rooms boarded over for one reason or another. And maybe we'll find more of the information we still need."

"That's true. Now we've got to investigate. Feel like playing detective one more time?"

"Why not? This hollow space might be a secret room or just a closet someone walled off. We might as well check it out. Lead on, Sherlock."

"Elementary, my dear Reene. We shall endeavor to start in the pantry. Is that ol' Sherlock, or what? There's probably a secret panel behind the cupboards," Lissa said gleefully.

Reene rolled her eyes. "You're a hopeless Anglophile. But wouldn't it be a hoot if you were right?"

"Indubitably, Watson. I believe the correct procedure is to tap on the walls," Lissa decided as they stood in the middle of the pantry. "At least that's how it's done in all the best mystery novels."

Reene opened the deep drawer where she kept the cooking implements. "Here's a wooden meat tenderizer for you. I'll use this wooden spoon. We don't want to whack *another* big hole in our walls."

Eons passed while they lightly tapped over and around the cupboards and shelves.

"Damn. We can hear the difference in the sound of the walls, but there's no way in from this side," Lissa grumbled.

"Don't give up yet. Remember those mystery novels. Maybe there's a trap door or sliding panel." Reene ran her fingers over and under the shelves once more.

"Owww." Reene pulled a painful sliver from her finger. "No hidden buttons or switches. No sliding panel. Guess it's a dead end."

Lissa searched the shelves from floor to ceiling. If ever there was a textbook spot for a hidden door, she'd found it. Tempted to kick the bottom shelf in frustration, she held back. In her present state of mind, she'd break her foot. Back to square one. She looked more closely around the bottom shelf. Gouges on the floor. She crouched down for a better look.

"What did you find?" Reene asked.

"I'm not sure. Look at all these deep scratches! As if a heavy object had been dragged across the floor. You don't think?"

"I do think! Quick, take all the dishes and plates out. Then we'll use our muscles."

Eager to find the secret opening, they stacked dishes and plates on the opposite counter. Then they confronted the shelves. Nothing jumped out to give them clues of what, if anything, was behind the wall.

"What now, Sherlock? I don't believe we're doing this," Reene griped. "But we've come this far. Try feeling around for buttons or levers."

Nothing.

"Let's try pushing on the middle shelf," Lissa encouraged.

Both women took an extra lungful of air and pushed. A slight cracking noise made them stop.

"Was that your rib or mine?" gasped Lissa.

"Sounds like the old wood is protesting. One more try and if nothing happens, we'll quit."

Together they pushed with all their strength against the immovable wall. Lissa's arms started to tremble and she was just about to collapse into a quivering heap when the shelving slowly and agonizingly moved back.

"Again!" cried Reene and they renewed their attack. With a terrible creaking and rendering of wood, the entire wall swung inward.

"Oh my God! This is incredible! I can't wait to see what's in there." Lissa could barely hold back her excitement. "I can't believe we moved that wall! Wait. I think I'm having a stroke."

"You can't stroke out now. I'll get a couple of flashlights."

"I'll be right here hyperventilating," Lissa puffed.

When Reene returned, she handed a heavy-duty flashlight to Lissa. "Let's see what's behind door number one," she laughed.

"If a skeleton is hanging behind door number one, I am not going to be a happy camper," Lissa groused as they approached the opening. Hearts thumping, they shone their lights into the room. No skeletons, hanging or otherwise.

"Ready to go exploring?" Reene asked.

"Yes. No, stop! We should put a wedge between the door and the wall. I have a terrible vision of us getting trapped in here like those poor wretches in an Edgar Allan Poe horror story."

"We almost burst a blood vessel opening this door! I can't imagine that it could close—" Her voice trailed off as Lissa gave her the evil eye.

"Okay! Okay! I give in. We shouldn't take a chance. Can you go grab a kitchen chair?"

With the solid maple chair jammed between the door and wall, they felt safer. Gingerly they went forward. The flashlights revealed plenty of headroom. "At least we can walk around without knocking our heads," Lissa said.

The room echoed with their footsteps. Cracks in the walls had allowed air, now musty and stale, to seep in. A dust-laden wooden trunk rested in the corner and a cobweb-covered table and chair sagged against the far wall.

Two cracked, dirty plates lay on the table. A few battered tin cups, covered in cobwebs, sat next to them. Dead insects were trapped in the webs. The spiders were busy here.

"It's so eerie in here," Reene whispered. "The hair on my neck just stood up. Do you feel it too?"

"Yes," Lissa breathed. "This place is spooky. Why are we whispering?" she asked as they tiptoed around the room.

"Somehow I felt it was the right thing to do," Reene answered in her normal voice. "There is a terrible feeling of sadness as well as despair in this room."

"Claustrophobic and no escape. Like prisoners who've lost hope."

"Not prisoners, Lissa. A holding place for human traffic. Runaway slaves? Gives me the shivers. I'll bet that's why this room was built and why it was kept hidden."

A faint smell she couldn't identify assailed her nostrils. Shining her light on the floor, she found dark stains embedded in the wooden floor. Kneeling to investigate, she touched the stains with her fingertips. "Someone shed blood here."

"What did you say?" Lissa asked. "Blood? Are you sure?"

"Almost. We've seen enough dried blood in our barns to know the difference."

"If escaping slaves *were* kept here, we were naïve to think they would escape uninjured. I only hope someone showed them compassion."

Lissa played her light on the sagging table. "And I wonder how much food and drink these plates and cups held. Enough to help them get away? Look, wisps of ancient straw scattered on the floor. Bedding, do you think?"

"No doubt. Someone cared. Lissa, that trunk looks definitely promising. But it's padlocked."

"Oh, crap. We might have trouble cutting that lock off. We should drag it into the main house so we can examine what's inside."

"Good idea. I don't fancy coming back here for any reason. Grab the other handle. Heave ho!"

"If we do much more heave-hoeing, my muscles are going on strike."

"Oh my god," Reene groaned, "this thing weighs a ton. Hurry! My hand is slipping!"

They staggered into the pantry just as the trunk crashed to the floor.

"No damage, thank goodness!" Lissa exclaimed. "I wonder who left it there. No markings, no nameplate. Could belong to anyone."

"Anyone named Josephine Taylor? I'm hoping it'll be full of papers that will answer all our questions," Reene said as she massaged her hand. "Then we can get back to normal, whatever the hell that means."

"Nothing is normal around here. Okay, I'm ready to call it quits. Give me a hand closing this door."

But closing the hidden door proved harder than opening it. No handle or knob they could grip to pull it shut. When they tried to find a purchase, their fingers slipped off the shelves.

"Well, this isn't working," Lissa complained. "How does this tricky thing operate anyway?"

"Hand me your flashlight," Reene demanded. She peered around the door's edge.

"Piano hinges! The oil on the hinges has all dried up. No wonder we had such a hard time moving this wall. Better the hinges squeaking and not our bones breaking. The only way we can close this stubborn door is to lubricate those hinges. Right now, I don't have the strength to even think about it. And don't forget. Ernie's coming early tomorrow to shoe the horses."

"Fine. Leave it open for now. We'll fix it once we've opened the treasure trunk—which will also have to wait for another day. If it's empty, I'm gonna be one pissed off woman."

Chapter 20

Right on schedule Ernie's truck rumbled up to the inn. Lissa could hardly wait to tell him about their discovery.

"Morning, Ernie," Lissa greeted as Ernie banged a few nails into Sissy's off fore. "Almost done? Is Bravo good to go?"

"Yep. Your friend do much driving with her?"

"Not as much as she'd like. But if things work out, she's driving her in the Yankee Homecoming Parade."

"Glad to hear it. I might even come to see that."

"I have some *other* news I'm sure will interest you. You may not believe this, but Reene and I discovered a hidden room in our house. We didn't find much in there except for a small table, a few chairs and a trunk. It's a mystery we haven't solved yet."

"Is that a fact?" Ernie said as he moved around Sissy to trim her hoof with his file. He didn't seem too surprised.

He picked up a hoof and said "I suppose you're wondering what it's doing there."

"As a matter of fact, yes, we are. We thought we'd ask around in case someone kept a record."

"Won't be any records. They didn't want anyone to know such a room existed." He put Sissy's hoof down. "There, she's all set now."

"Ernie, you know why that room was built?"

"'Course I do."

Lissa felt like screaming. Dragging information out of Ernie was harder than losing twenty pounds.

"Then please tell me!" she begged.

For a moment, Ernie's face almost broke into a smile.

"Just waiting for you to ask. Now, back in the days when the Williams' family settled here, this place was a working farm. A year after the Civil War broke out, Seth Williams, the father, got himself involved in the war. You've heard of the Underground Railroad?"

"Yes, of course," Lissa nodded.

"Well, 'round about 1862 or so, this place became one of the 'stations'. A station acted as a rest spot where slaves could eat and sleep before they moved out during the night. They'd walk ten to twenty miles a night and take different routes to throw off anyone coming after them. The owner of the house was called a 'stationmaster'. Sometimes a stationmaster sent a message ahead that a bunch of slaves was on their way. More often than not, those people had nothing to eat except whatever the stationmasters would give them. Some were real good to them, others not. Slaves ate leaves or grass or, if they were lucky enough, they might catch a fish or a rabbit. Those poor folks had to hide in swamps, cross rivers and beg rides in hay wagons."

Lissa listened in amazement to his fascinating story. She had a passing knowledge of the Underground Railroad, but never gave much thought to how the system worked. Her romanticized version was a far cry from the truth.

"Do you think a lot of them got away?"

"Most of 'em, I've heard. Over thirty thousand Blacks made it to Canada. Some escaped to Free states. They had special code words so they wouldn't get caught. Some clever ladies wove symbols into quilts and hung 'em out on the line. If the slaves saw those symbols, they knew it was a safe house. The code words for Canada were 'Heaven' or "Promised Land'. I really liked that because I was born in Canada."

A look of sadness spread over his face. "Know what else happened to them?"

"No. And it doesn't sound good from the way you say that."

"It wasn't. Those greedy slave-loving Southerners were all upset when the slaves got away. So a law got passed that let slave owners hire people to catch their runaways and arrest 'em. That meant legally freed slaves got arrested too. Bounty hunters captured free Blacks and sold them back into slavery."

Lissa's mind raced, astounded at the mind-boggling information Ernie had told her. Now she understood the significance of the hidden room.

"How terrible! I can't even imagine what those poor people went through to gain their freedom."

"Yep. That law woke up a lot of folks here in the North. Many used their houses or farms as part of the Underground Railroad. Guess that's one thing we can be proud of."

"Yes, I guess we can. So the Williams' family aided the slaves during the war. That explains a lot of things."

146

Ernie cast a quick look at her. Before he could ask what she meant, Lissa hurriedly asked him another question.

"Do you know any history of the Williams' family? Reene and I found an old Bible and we thought it would be fun to trace the family through the years."

"Not too much. I did hear one of the descendants got killed in the First World War. If I'm not mistaken, one of the grandsons lived somewhere in Massachusetts. Sorry, that's the best I can do."

"Ernie, you've been a great help and solved a mystery for us! You've given me a history lesson I won't forget. Here's your check. I can't wait to tell Reene!"

"Glad I could help. Tell your friend I'll be watching for her in the parade."

"I will. I'll be there too. I'm Reene's outrider."

Ernie nodded and ambled out to his truck. Lissa, thoughtfully watching his truck disappear down the driveway, returned Sissy to her paddock.

"Well, missy, you've got nice new shoes for the parade. Wait till I tell your mother what I found out!"

"Reene, where have you been? I've been dying to tell you the latest." Lissa nearly danced with anticipation when her friend slid open the pocket door.

"I had lunch with Tom after my hair appointment. He surprised me at the salon."

"How sweet," Lissa sighed. "Nice cut by the way."

"What's up? You look like the cat that swallowed the canary."

"A very *big* canary! You know, Ernie was here shoeing the kids—the receipt is in my office—and we got to talking."

Reene raised an eyebrow.

"Yes, Ernie and I actually had a lengthy conversation. Anyway, I was telling him we were going to ride in the parade, and he was so happy to hear you'd be driving Sissy, and—"

"Woman, can you cut to the chase?"

"You're spoiling my fun! Turns out our Ernie is a Civil War buff. When I told him about our secret room, he knew just what it was!"

"Sooo, are you going to tell *me* why it's there?" Reene asked in exasperation.

"Drum roll, please. Evidently this farm was one of the stops—Ernie said it was called a station—on the Underground Railroad. That room

147

was used to hide slaves during the day so they could eat and rest. That is, if the stationmaster gave them any food. It was awful, Reene, what those desperate people were forced to go through. They had to walk miles during the night with empty stomachs and hide from bounty hunters who could be chasing them. From what Ernie said, the Railroad was pretty successful because over thirty thousand slaves made it to Canada."

"That's mind-boggling! I had no idea." Reene drew a shaky breath and shuddered. "Those poor souls trapped in that cramped room. Injured or wounded. That's why we saw those bits of straw. They did use straw for bedding. So our innocent-looking inn played an important role in the Civil War. Unbelievable. Did you ask Ernie if he knew anything about the missing relatives?"

"Yes, he confirmed what I thought about Joshua Williams. He did die in World War I. Ernie believes a grandson might have lived in Massachusetts, but he isn't sure."

"Another dead end. I'd hoped we could find out if there were any living relatives we could contact. If we could locate them, they may be interested in seeing Josephine's portrait."

Reene kicked off her boots, but as she laid them on the rubber mat, she whirled to face Lissa.

"The portrait!" she exclaimed. "I don't know why we didn't think of this before. Shouldn't we donate it to the Historical Society? After all, it's invaluable, historically."

"I agree, but I believe she belongs here. This was her home if even for a short time."

"You're right. I'd hate to take it away from here too. There must be another way. Could we have the photo copied?"

"Great suggestion! I'll go fetch her." Lissa scurried into the Gathering Room and returned with the portrait.

"Lissa, I'm afraid if we tried to take the picture out, it might get torn. It's probably so brittle the slightest move the wrong way will ruin it. We can't risk that."

"No, we can't. That eliminates taking it to a photo shop."

Reene's eyes brightened. "We can bring the photo shop here! Remember Randal Simms, our banker? He told me at the tea that he's an amateur photographer. He also takes pictures of the Yankee Homecoming events for the town's website. I'll bet he'd love to make a print from it."

"By Jove, I think you've got it, girl! Perfect solution!" Lissa exclaimed.

"We'll give him a call tomorrow morning. It's past three o'clock. Bankers' hours. Too late in the day to push our grand inspiration."

"Well then, let's go for a ride. It's never too late to ride."

"Reene, I've done this procedure many times," Randal Simms explained, "and have obtained excellent results. Today I have two closings; however, I'll drop by the day after, early morning, if that's convenient?"

Punctual to the minute, the banker arrived at the inn. Reene and Lissa ushered him into the Gathering Room.

"Mr. Simms, we are so pleased you could help us out with our request," Lissa said.

"Randy, please. I'm delighted you thought of me. I can see why you didn't want to take a chance removing the portrait from its frame," he said as he studied Josephine Williams' picture. "An old print like that is so delicate it would rip no matter how careful you were. I'll bring in my equipment and get started. I won't be in the way here, will I?"

"Not at all, Randy," Reene assured him. "We don't have any guests arriving today so take all the time you need."

"Superb. Before I start, I'd like to tell you what I propose to do. Since the original is in black and white, I'll use black and white film. When the negative is printed, it should come out as an exact reproduction of the original."

"Wonderful! We're so grateful you can do this for us."

Once he set all his equipment in place, Simms thoroughly inspected the portrait for dust or dirt and placed it on the easel. He took a number of shots from different angles, using various light settings.

Reene hung around in the kitchen so she could sneak a few peeks. Lissa tried to catch up on office work but, like a little kid, she too couldn't resist watching.

"Finished!" he called. Eagerly both of them abandoned their chores to join him. "I'll develop these negatives and then make a print. What size did you have in mind?"

"We figured an eight-by-ten would work best," Reene replied. "We'd better check to see how much space is allotted in the display case. Can we get back to you tomorrow?"

"Take as long as you need, ladies. It will take me a day or two to create the negative. I'll crop out any extraneous furniture or knickknacks. I tried to focus on the portrait, but when taking a picture of a picture, it's not easy to eliminate everything in the background."

"To show our appreciation, I'm having a brass plate made that reads 'Josephine Taylor Williams, 1844 – 1875. Photograph by C. Randal Simms'," Lissa promised.

Randy swelled with pride. Photography was his life's passion and he was touched by their generous gesture. "Thank you," he said sincerely. "It will be a thrill to exhibit my work under my own nameplate. I'm anxious to get to my darkroom to develop the negative. I'll wait for your call with regard to the size of the photograph."

Once he departed, Reene and Lissa relaxed in front of the fireplace. "Another job well done, if we do say so ourselves," Lissa sighed as she sipped her iced tea.

"I can't wait to see how the photo comes out," Reene said.

"I've been so wrapped up with all this photography stuff I forgot to tell you! We've got another guest, Misty O'Connor, coming this weekend," Lissa said. "Actually she's arriving on Thursday and staying for four days. I'm putting her in the Chickadee room. You'll love this! She's an equine massage therapist! I have a suspicion she's trying to drum up a little business, but that's okay with me. What do you think?"

"Sounds good. We could invite a few people over if we can persuade her to put on a clinic."

"I don't think she'll take much persuading, but those were my feelings too. I've attended clinics for equine massage and the results are amazing."

"We keep forgetting we're literally sitting on their backs when we ride. No wonder they get aches and pains. I pity the poor horses that have to carry the heavyweights," Reene sympathized.

"A clinic could be interesting and different," Lissa agreed. "A guest is a guest. I just hope she's not afraid of ghosts."

"Well, Stephen Marshall hasn't reported that anyone's pinched *his* bottom. Yet."

Chapter 21

"Oh, my aching body!" groaned Lissa. "Over these last two days, I've swallowed a dozen pain tablets just to take the edge off and I'm still walking like Gabby Hayes."

"Gabby who?"

"I keep forgetting you're a mere child. He was one of the greatest Western movie sidekicks ever!"

"I stand corrected. That heavy door really gave us a workout. But it was worth all that trouble. Between Ernie and Randy's visits, we haven't had a second to ourselves. Are you ready to tackle the trunk?"

"Ready as I'll ever be. What time is it? Will we have time before we feed?"

"Not to worry. It's only 4:30. Why, are you hungry already?" Reene scoffed.

"In case you haven't noticed, I'm always hungry. I'll grab crackers and cheese to keep us from fainting. I'll bring some wine too. We might want to celebrate. Don't start without me."

Fortified by their snack and a bottle of merlot, they confronted the locked trunk. The old padlock resisted repeated whacks from a hammer. They didn't want to destroy the trunk so Reene fetched the bolt cutter from her toolbox.

"Hold it steady, woman, so I can line up the jaws!"

"Have you used this tool before?" Lissa asked nervously. "I don't fancy losing a finger."

"I've been a jack of all trades since Dan went to Cheater's Heaven. Don't you trust me?"

"Sort of. But be careful! Make it quick."

Reene applied pressure on the arms of the cutter. Gritting her teeth, she squeezed a bit harder. With a nasty snap, the padlock broke. Lissa toppled involuntarily onto the floor.

"Open it!" Lissa exclaimed as she scrambled to her feet. She rubbed her hands – digits intact - with glee. "I can't stand any more suspense."

"You're worse than a kid at Christmas," Reene chided. "Cross your fingers." And she lifted the heavy lid.

Lissa peered over her shoulder. As treasure trunks go, it was a major disappointment. No glittering jewelry or long-lost Confederate gold. At first glance it appeared to contain the meager belongings of a foot soldier. But each article they removed began to piece together parts of a story nearly one hundred and fifty years old.

"Here's an outfit of sorts," Reene said, removing a pair of faded brown trousers, a ragged shirt, a tattered vest, and the familiar blue cap of the Union Army. "My goodness, these clothes are so small! They look like they'd fit a slender teen-aged boy."

Lissa held the trousers up to her waist for comparison. "I'd have to lose fifty pounds to squeeze into these pants." She laid the clothes and cap on the floor. "Do you suppose these clothes belonged to Josephine?"

"They must be hers. Remember how tiny she looks in the portrait? She probably wore this outfit as part of her disguise."

"No doubt. What else is in there?"

"Something we're familiar with," Reene said, taking out a headstall with attached reins. The leather reins were stiff and dry with age. The snaffle bit, now rusted beyond redemption, drooped in place. A small pair of shabby leather shoes and a cloth cap were tucked in beside the bridle.

"This is amazing! I feel like we're getting to know Josephine Taylor as a rider and a woman before she married Peter Williams. Anything else?"

"There's a saddle pad of sorts. It's just about falling to pieces." Reene lifted it out and examined it. "Compared to the thick pads our horses wear, this thing is a horror. The poor horse wouldn't have any cushion from the weight of the saddle or the rider. Look! More goodies. Brushes and curries!"

Lissa bent down to help. When they removed the grooming implements, a rectangular metal box lay underneath.

"Please tell me this is what we've been looking for," Lissa said as Reene drew it out. The box had a simple twist latch to hold the cover in place. Happily for Lissa's fingers, the bolt cutters wouldn't be needed.

"Only one way to answer that question." Reene released the latch. Letters and other documents still in their original envelopes lay in a neat pile.

"Look at these addresses, Reene! 'Lt. Peter Williams, 37th Massachusetts Infantry Regiment, Manassas, Virginia', 'Miss Josephine

Taylor, c/o Captain Richard Ellsworth'. There must be ten or fifteen letters. We've found the treasure!"

"Wooo-hooo!" yelled Reene. "This is awesome! I can't wait to read these letters!"

"Let's bring the box into the office," Lissa said excitedly. "We can examine them on the desk."

"Good idea. Here, you take the letters. I'll repack the trunk and put away the munchies and wine. We don't want to spill wine all over our prizes."

Lissa took the letters and looked at the clock. "Wait. It's nearly time to feed and my tummy is starting to growl."

"Mine too. We lost track of time. You feed and I'll throw together some angel hair pasta and chicken."

"Works for me! I'll make a salad when I get back. Then we'll tackle the letters after dinner."

Lissa hurried through the Gathering Room but stopped as she passed Josephine Taylor's portrait and studied her youthful face under the Union Army cap. She seemed so young, so innocent yet so knowing. What a tragedy her life was cut so short.

"Ms. Taylor, we're getting closer and closer," she said, "to figuring everything out. I have a feeling you understand what we're trying to do. It won't be long now."

Lissa soon learned she shouldn't make promises she couldn't keep.

Hours later, the two friends rubbed their tired eyes, astounded by what they had learned from the letters. Peter Williams, a Union Army officer from Massachusetts, and Josephine Taylor, a former runaway slave from Virginia, had begun a clandestine romance during the most turbulent and controversial war in American history. The young lovers wrote of shared danger, pride in their duties and joy in their blossoming love.

"Oh my," Lissa said, visibly moved by Josephine's terrifying accounts of her desperate rides through enemy lines. "Reene, you're too quiet over there. What are you thinking?"

"I'm trying to take it all in. A young slave becomes a spy for the North. While she's spying on the enemy, she falls in love with an officer in the Union Army. If that's not improbable enough, she's an honest-to-goodness hero! Not only that, we're living in their house. Just like a plot from those bodice-rippers I used to read."

"I know what you mean; I read those rippers too. In the meantime, Peter's father was using this place to help Blacks escape slavery. Peter mentions it in one of his letters." Lissa fished through the pile. She put her reading glasses back on. "Here it is. I'll read you the highlights."

'Dearest Josey, I hope this letter reaches you before your next assignment ... I fear for your safety, my love ... war almost over ... Don't worry, my father will be on your side ... he's using our farm as a station to help your people get away to Canada ... he's already helped dozens of slaves to escape ... take care, sweetheart·

All my love,
Peter'

"Peter's letter confirms everything Ernie told me about Seth and the Underground Railroad. This is incredible!"

"It is incredible." Reene picked up another letter and skimmed the now-familiar writing. "You know, this was not a normal love letter. They faced a lot more than the dangers of the war."

Struck by her friend's serious tone, Lissa took the paper she held out.

'Regimental Headquarters
May 1865

My dearest Peter,
The courier just brought me your letter· I was so excited I threw my arms around him and hugged him! I don't think he liked that too much, but I didn't care· It's been such a long time since I've heard from you· I was afraid something bad had happened or you had changed your mind·

Please forgive me for thinking that way, my darling· But I was scared that you were writing to say we couldn't

154

get married. Since you went home, I've been so worried I could hardly sleep at night. When you asked me to marry you, I knew we'd have no end of trouble because I'm a Negro and you are White. Here in the South it's still against the law for us to marry. We could be jailed, or worse, if we asked a parson to perform the ceremony. But I felt so much better when you told me we could be married in Massachusetts. I suppose it's too much to hope we could marry in a church, but wherever you and I are together is all I can ask for.

I am counting the days until I join you up North. I know we'll be happy in our new home. I want your friends to visit us often and will try hard to make them like me too.

I wish I had my arms around you right now, but your letter is the next best thing. I keep it under my pillow so I can dream about you every night.

Goodnight, sweetheart,
I love you so,
Josey

P.S. How is my sweet Shiloh? Do you think he misses me? I miss him almost as much as I miss you! Give him a kiss and an apple from me.'

"Poor innocent Josephine," Lissa sighed. "Did she think Northerners would welcome her with open arms?"

"I can't imagine she was *that* naïve," Reene answered. "But I'd forgotten how difficult it would be for them to marry in those days."

"So did I. I was so caught up in their love affair I didn't give those details a moment's thought."

"No doubt, Peter and Josey, as Peter calls her, must have given those details more than a moment's thought. But they were young, in love and invincible. After the war there were still such hard feelings toward the

155

Blacks. Probably they hoped people would treat them differently in the North. I can't imagine how Peter's parents must have reacted when he brought her home."

"Reene, did you notice the 'P.S'? Unless I miss my guess, 'Shiloh' must have been her horse. The horse that carried her to safety through all those dangerous missions."

"Yes, I did. And unless I miss *my* guess, he must have been involved in Josey's 'riding accident'."

"How tragic! Especially as she loved him so. This letter has opened my eyes to another side to their story. It's doubly important now that we safeguard these papers so we can tell the world, or at least Westbrook, about their unsung hero. Or should I say our heroine, *Josey*."

"Definitely," Reene agreed.

"We found all the proof we need and can make plans to honor her. Any suggestions?"

"Yes. Why don't you call Gina to see if she'll run a story in the paper about our spirit? Of course, we'll leave out the part of her being of the Other World. We'll donate these letters, along with Josey's clothes and portrait, to the Historical Society. None of this belongs to us and these discoveries would give the people of our adopted town something to take pride in. We can keep copies of the letters to put on display in the inn."

"What a wonderful idea! I love it! I'll contact Gina tomorrow," Lissa promised. "Then I'll give Mrs. Long a jingle. She'll be ecstatic. This will be a major coup for her. Speaking of publicity, I wonder if there'll be some sort of ceremony when we hand over the documents and other stuff."

"I'm sure of it! Doubtless our pictures will be in the paper."

"Oh the horror! I'll have to dress up and wear real shoes," groaned Lissa. "Do you suppose I can lose twenty pounds before we become celebrities?"

"I know a good way to start," Reene promised. "By playing detective, we've been neglecting our horses. Let's hit the trails. I'll let you groom Shen for me; you'll burn off a ton of calories."

Randy Simms busied himself in his darkroom, visions of the new project whirling through his brain like a dust storm. Not only would he be part of his town's history, his contribution would be recorded for posterity. No more flowers or covered bridges on greeting cards. This time his work would be taken seriously.

In the darkness, he set his enlarger to eight-by-ten and inserted the negative. He placed a piece of photo paper underneath, exposing the negative and paper to the enlarger's light.

With rubber-gloved hands, he placed the exposed piece of paper into a developer tray. Waiting a sufficient time, he removed the print and placed it in the stop bath for its final soaking stage. Using plastic tongs he gently swished the print back and forth in the tank.

Randy snapped on the overhead lights. The image, invisible at first, began to appear. His smile of satisfaction broadened as the Civil War picture fully developed. The soldier's face, uniform, and background details emerged with amazing clarity.

He continued to study the enlargement, but his smile faded and he frowned.

"Something's wrong with this negative!" he complained. "There's a smudge hovering over the soldier's rifle. Is it dirt?" Grasping the print with the tongs, he hung it up to inspect it more closely.

"What *is* that?" he demanded in frustration. He scrutinized the dripping print. "That's not a smudge!"

He peered closer. "It's taking shape. It looks like a woman! Her face is somewhat familiar. Then who...Good God! It's an image of the young woman in the portrait!"

"Barn Swallow Inn, Lissa speaking."

"Good day, Lissa. Randy Simms here."

"Randy! How are you? I hope you have good news for us."

"Well, I do have news, but I'm not sure if it's good or bad."

"Should I ask for the bad news first?"

"It's not bad, I'm just a bit baffled. I promised you and Reene that the enlargement would be ready by the end of the week. But the strangest thing happened."

"Strange?"

"Yes. While the picture was developing, an unexpected image appeared. At first I thought I'd put my finger on the lens," he admitted. "But the shape was different. It was a bit hazy, but I'll swear the image was that of a young woman."

"A young woman! Are you positive?" Lissa clutched the phone in a white-knuckled hand.

"The original photograph doesn't show the image, but it appears on the negative I'd created," Randy said. "It's bizarre."

"That *is* bizarre! I'm sure you took additional photos?"

157

"Why, yes, I always do. But don't you think—"

"That you'll have the same problem again? Of course not! I'm sure your weird shape was a trick of the light."

"I doubt that," he argued. "I took every precaution. This image looked so much like the woman in the photograph that—"

"You thought it was a double exposure!" Lissa gushed. "I wouldn't worry about it, Randy. We have every confidence in you that one of the other photos will turn out perfectly."

"Thank you. I *am* a bit of a perfectionist. I'll develop the remaining negatives and make the final print. Did you determine the size you'll require?"

"Yes, we're only allowed an eight-by-ten. The display case isn't high enough for anything larger."

"Excellent. I'll contact you as soon as the enlargement is finished. Sorry to have bothered you."

"No bother at all!"

Lissa dropped the phone and rubbed the back of her neck. Her shoulders were threatening to push up into her eyeballs.

"Lissa, why do you look like you're going to keel over?" Reene demanded, arms full of folded bath and hand towels fresh from the laundry.

"Randy Simms just phoned. He's having a little problem with the enlargement. Guess whose face turned up on his reproduction?"

"What do you mean? Another face? His film was probably old or bad or ... oh, no! Josey!"

"Oh, yes. Josey."

"If she weren't dead already, I'd kill her myself," Reene fumed. "What did you say to him? Does he suspect?"

"I hope not. I double-talked faster than a carnival pitchman. After I soothed his ego, he seemed happy. He'll contact us by the end of the week."

"Lissa, sit and relax. I'll mix us a drink. Girlfriend, we're getting too old for this shit."

Chapter 22

"Misty O'Connor, I presume?" Lissa greeted. "Welcome to the Barn Swallow Inn."

"Thank you!" replied a petite blonde who dragged in assorted bags and carry-alls. "You presume correctly."

"Let me take you to your room. You're in the Chickadee room on the first floor."

"It's beautiful!" she exclaimed as Lissa opened the door and adjusted the shades. "I love the double-globe Victorian lamp and wicker fan back chair."

"I must've had a premonition when I selected this room for you. Let me know if you need anything. We'll see you at breakfast."

But next morning Misty picked at the dropped eggs on toast Reene had placed in front of her. As Lissa poured coffee, she noticed their guest's preoccupied air.

"What's wrong?" Reene asked. "Aren't you hungry?"

"Yes, yes, your food tastes wonderful," Misty answered. "I had a terribly restless night. I couldn't sleep. There's something I need to discuss with both of you."

Reene sat down abruptly, and Lissa rolled her eyes skyward. Did Josey aggravate their guest?

"I've been trying to establish equine massage therapy with the horse community, but so far my clients have been few and far between," Misty said. "Owners appreciate the results, but they're still reluctant to hire me on a steady basis. It's all so frustrating!"

"We can certainly empathize," Reene agreed. *We lucked out. We don't have to explain Josey's antics. This time.* "Some people hate change."

"If I offered to hold an equine massage clinic for free, would you be interested?" Misty asked.

"We would love that!" Lissa answered. "Reene and I will volunteer our horses for your demonstration."

"That's what I was counting on!" she smiled. "When can we set this up?"

159

"How about Saturday morning around ten o'clock?" Lissa suggested. "That will give us plenty of time to get chores done and set up space for your demonstration."

"It's short notice but with luck I can round up enough curious horse people," Reene promised. "I'll make some calls right after breakfast."

"Perfect," Misty responded. "I noticed you don't have a riding ring, but I can give the demo in front of the barn."

Lissa rose earlier than usual Saturday morning. Preparations for the clinic would start as soon as breakfast was out of the way. Stephen Marshall had decided to opt for an early breakfast so he wouldn't be 'in the way', as he graciously put it. When she came down to the breakfast room, she found Misty engrossed in a magazine. She noticed its pages were yellowed with age and ragged around the edges.

"Mrs. Martin, I just love this interesting article. Thanks for leaving it on my bed!" Misty exclaimed.

Lissa paused as she poured a glass of orange juice. "Article?" she echoed blankly.

"Yes. Even though it was written in 1921, it's timeless."

Misty handed the ancient periodical to Lissa. "'Always Listen to Your Horse'. Isn't that a wonderful title? I'm using this article as the theme for my demo."

"Oh, of *course*! You're welcome!" Lissa managed. "We just thought…it's been lying around for years … What a coincidence! I'll check on your breakfast."

She escaped to the kitchen, where Reene was stirring ham and egg scramble in one frying pan and seasoning home fries in another.

"Reene!" she hissed. "Did you leave an old magazine on horsemanship in Misty's room?"

Reene felt a quiver of anxiety. "No, I didn't."

"Well, neither did I! I let her think we left it to help her with the clinic."

"Oh my God. Josey! Our little horse lover thought she'd do us a good deed."

"Good deed or not, this is a new one," Lissa muttered in exasperation. "If she starts floating candles all over the joint, I'm leaving!"

Reene laughed and turned off the burners. "Don't fret. Floating candles aren't her style. Come on, help me serve my latest masterpiece."

"Looks yum as always." She grabbed a plate from the cupboard and Reene scooped out two portions of the steaming food. Lissa added a bunch of red grapes and slices of orange to the plate.

"Before I scoot upstairs I'll check with Misty just in case something else has materialized out of the Great Beyond," Lissa said. "Josey's worse than a two-year old!"

By gentle persuasion, Reene's last-minute invitation had convinced many of the locals to watch the demo. Jill Stanton, their nearest neighbor, rode over on her buckskin horse, Dakoda. If she were sold on massage therapy, her horse would be close at hand.

Misty addressed the group with a bright smile. "Good morning! Thank you all for coming on such short notice! You won't be disappointed. Now you've all heard the expression 'always listen to your horse'," Misty continued. She paused to wink at Lissa who smiled brightly in return, but behind her back her fingers were crossed.

"Your horse will tell you when something's wrong. Often the symptoms exhibited are caused by pain. I'll help you recognize the difference between pain and bad habits. An ill-fitting saddle or worn out saddle pad can cause major discomfort."

Bobbing heads confirmed her words.

"Perhaps your horse exhibits odd behavior when asked to perform. Bucking at the canter is a common indication of back pain. Can you imagine how *your* sore back would feel if you were asked to carry over 150 pounds at the walk, trot and canter?"

Lissa saw sheepish looks were exchanged all around. She knew that most riders rarely gave that notion a second thought. How many times had they heard the expression 'strong as a horse'? Her experience had shown that this expression is almost an oxymoron.

"I'm certain a few of you have had at least a back massage if not a full body massage," Misty continued. Many nodded and smiled.

"With that in mind, I apply the same technique with a horse. I use deep muscle massage to soothe aches and pains. Imagine painful knots in your neck and shoulders. Horses get them too only they can't reach up to work out those knots."

She walked over to Reene who was holding Sissy. Since Sissy was their working horse, they had decided she would benefit most from the free rubdown.

Misty ran her fingers lightly on each side of Sissy's spine. Then she slid her hands under Sissy's mane and massaged her neck vigorously.

161

At first, Sissy resisted and showed the white of her eye. She wasn't altogether happy with the actions this stranger was performing on her.

"As you can see, the horse is resisting me a bit," Misty said as she continued with a gentler motion. "She will eventually give in and her head will drop slightly." Misty's hands worked further down the horse's neck.

"Good girl," she said softly. "Feels nice, doesn't it? I've found a few knots by her withers so I'll use the heel of my hand to knead those out."

Just as Misty predicted, Sissy stopped resisting as the knots loosened.

"Reene, I'm almost finished with her. I'll stretch her front legs and give her tail a bit of a stretch too." She pulled Sissy's legs forward and then moved around to the hind end to give the tail a gentle tug.

"Done! Walk her around in a wide circle for a few minutes. Once her muscles are warmed up, the blood flow is increased and any toxins are released."

"How often should horses be massaged?" Laurie Hayes piped up. "And a full body massage sure would get my blood flowing!"

"Sorry, I don't do two-legged clients!" Misty laughed. "I recommend a full massage once a month. That way you can keep your horse in excellent condition and fix any trouble spots."

"Can I ride my horse soon after a massage?" Jill asked.

"Give your horse at least an hour to recover. If you've had a full body massage, you'll remember feeling a little lightheaded when you first tried to move. Your horse will feel the same."

"I hate to ask this question, but I'm sure a lot of us are thinking the same thing: how much do you charge?" Laurie asked.

"Before I answer that question, please let me explain. The first thing I like to do is evaluate the animal. Once I see how much work I need to do, I'm able to give an estimate and can make arrangements with the owner."

Murmurs ran through the crowd. Horse lovers spared no expense for their best buddy but were notoriously skeptical about trying something new.

"Come on, give it a try!" Reene exclaimed. "You saw the results with Sissy. You'll have a happier horse who'll give you happier rides."

"Personally, I think massage therapy is worth twice the price," Lissa chimed in. "Misty deserves combat pay! Think of the stepped-on toes, not to mention getting nipped by some of the more, shall we say, playful horses?"

162

"Not my horse!" Jill laughed. "He only steps on *my* feet!"

"I can't help you with that, Jill," Misty smiled, "but I hope you've all enjoyed my clinic and learned more about a beneficial way to increase your horse's conditioning."

A scattering of applause followed.

"Bravo!" Lissa said. "Pun intended. Please drop by the breakfast room before you leave for a cool drink and some of my world famous chocolate chip cookies. You're welcome to ask Misty any further questions. Thank you all again for coming!"

Within the hour, the demonstration concluded and Misty headed into town to shop. Lissa retreated to her office to catch up on paperwork. Intent on her task she didn't hear the phone ringing until Reene hollered from the kitchen.

"Lissa, this call is for you. It's John McDermot. He says he used to work with you."

"Wonderful! A blast from the past!"

"John, how are you?"

"I'm fine, Lissa. I have a favor to ask. I was wondering if it would be possible for me to bring my son's Boy Scout troop out there to camp for a few nights." He paused to give Lissa time to respond. "We'd make our own breakfast. The leaders and I want to take them on nature hikes. Practice setting up tents. That sort of thing. Maybe they could meet your horses. There's only thirteen boys in the group."

Thirteen boys? Lissa pinched her nose til it hurt. "That's a lovely idea, John, but I'll have to check with my colleague. Hold on a sec." She slapped the phone against her hip and sprinted into the kitchen.

"Reene, my old workmate wants to bring his Boy Scout troop out here and asked if we'd let them camp out for two nights in one of the fields."

"Ordinarily I'd say yes, but it sounds like too much to handle right now. Tell him we'll definitely do it next year."

"My sentiments as well," she whispered. She raised the phone up to her ear and walked back into her office.

"Hi, John. Listen, we'd love to invite you and the scouts out here sometime next year. We're up to our fetlocks in some special projects. We've even found stuff from the Civil War. I promise I'll send you a reminder in the spring."

"Brilliantly done, Lissa."

163

"Man, I don't think I could have survived a tribe of Boy Scouts even if they are brave, trustworthy, and true blue," Lissa groaned. "Can you imagine if the Scouts were camped out in their tents telling ghost stories in the wee dark hours and Josey sent them screaming into the woods? Anyway, John said he'll keep in touch. Let's hope the dust will have settled by then."

Chapter 23

"Lissa, Gina's story about us is in today's paper. She did a great job."

Lissa, who'd been stripping upstairs beds, joined Reene in the kitchen. She popped an English muffin into the toaster, poured a cup of tea, and read the article.

Historical Discovery at Local Inn
Letters Date Back to Civil War
By Gina Richards
Managing Editor

WESTBROOK. A local farmhouse dating back to the early 1800's recently gave up its fascinating secrets. Earlier this year new owners Reene Anderson and Lissa Martin purchased the old Williams' farmhouse and transformed it into a thriving bed and breakfast catering to the equestrian-loving crowd. Recently they discovered a hidden room containing letters and clothing from the Civil War era.

"A contractor we hired found a hollow space between the walls," Anderson said, "so we decided to check it out ourselves. We were completely surprised when we found a concealed door. The door led into a secret room where all the items were stored in an old wooden trunk."

Anderson and Martin are graciously donating the letters and articles of clothing to Westbrook's Historical Society.

Chairperson Ruby Chapman Long was thrilled by their generous gesture.

"I am very excited these artifacts will be added to our collection," Mrs. Long said. "Of course, everything will have to be authenticated. I'm confident, however, they will be proved genuine. The Society is grateful to these young women for their unselfish generosity."

Significantly, one letter contained proof that a young Black woman, Josephine Taylor, acted as a spy for the North during the Civil War. When the war ended, she married Peter Williams, son of Seth Williams, who originally built the farmhouse in 1830. Other correspondence confirmed that Seth Williams became involved in the Underground Railroad. He used his farmhouse as a station where slaves could stop to rest before traveling north.

Once the articles are authenticated, the Society plans to display them for public viewing in their museum. This important piece of history is a welcome addition to the town of Westbrook.

"'Thriving bed and breakfast!' Isn't she sweet? She's so generous. Let's see, what else does the article say?" Lissa reread the article. "'Civil War spy ... Underground Railroad ... secret room ...' Nice work."

"Speaking of things long-undiscovered," Reene said, "we may hear from Peter and Josey's relatives now. These letters could close a link to their history."

"Good point. Gina's article might help if anyone still lives in the area. We need to talk with her about our next step in paying tribute to Josey's long-unsung accomplishments."

"One issue at a time, Ms. Martin. Think of the publicity we're getting from this story! Our discovery brought us the big break we'd been hoping for."

"I'll bet our phone rings off the hook and the website will be smokin' with people checking us out," Lissa declared.

Their phone did ring off the hook but not quite the way they wished. Friends called to congratulate them. But unfortunately, so did people with too much time on their hands. Some calls were harmless. Others were not.

"You should have minded your own business," a deep male voice snapped when Reene answered the phone. "No one gives a damn about some little Black bitch from the Civil War. Leave it alone."

Reene gasped and slammed the phone. Lissa looked at her curiously but before she could question her, the phone rang again.

"I'll handle this one. Barn Swallow Inn, how may I help you?" Lissa said in her perkiest voice.

"Did she wear a feather in her cap like Yankee Doodle?" a young voice asked.

"Yes, and she called it macaroni," Lissa retorted. Tempted to use stronger language, she smiled despite herself as she hung up. Kids fooling around. "What happened with that first call?"

"Nasty jerk made racist comments. I should have told him to stick it where the sun don't shine," Reene fumed. "I hope we don't get a lot of calls like these."

"It's sad, isn't it, that people still behave this way? Just when I think we've gotten past the color of a person's skin, racism rears its ugly head again." Lissa shook her head.

"Let's ignore these idiots. And to change the subject, we're all hot to ride in the Homecoming parade, but haven't found out yet if we're welcome. I haven't the faintest notion who to contact. We'll be all dressed up with nowhere to go."

"Don't worry, Reene. I'm sure there'll be room for us in the parade. I'll call the Clerk at town hall. He or she should be able to point us in the right direction."

When she reached the town hall, she was redirected to Peggy Simms, who for the past ten years had been in charge of organizing the parade. Peggy was very gracious about their last-minute call.

"Due to other commitments, our regulars had to cancel this year," Peggy replied. "You are welcome to join the festivities. Everyone loves to see the horses,"

"Reene and I will do our best to make up for the other riders," Lissa promised. "You won't be disappointed."

"I'm sure you'll be fabulous," Peggy said. "Lissa, horses always come at the tail end, if you'll pardon the expression, of the parade. As the date gets closer, we can finalize the details."

167

"Wonderful! My friend is really looking forward to participating. By the way, your last name is Simms. Are you related to Randal Simms?"

"Only by marriage," Peggy laughed. "When did you meet Randy?"

"He handled the sale of our inn. Then I had a few words with him at the tea. That's when he told me he's an amateur photographer."

"A few words? You got off lucky. I'm sorry I missed meeting you. Randy was impressed with you and your friend. He had a wonderful time. I heard all about it when he came home. And I've heard all about his pet project that he's undertaking for you and Reene. He's happier than a pig in shit. Why don't you give me your number? I'll be in touch."

Lissa hung up, a big smile on her face. "We're in! I just talked to Peggy Simms, the chairperson of the parade committee. She's excited we want to ride 'cause the regulars had to bag out this year."

Reene's face lit up at the news. "We're in like Flynn! You'd better pull Brav's breastplate and silver headstall out of storage. By now, they'll be tarnished to a fare-thee-well. You should wear a spiffy outfit too. You always were a Zorro freak. Would that work?"

"I dunno. I should be more dignified. Besides, Zorro should be saved for Costume Class at a horse show or Halloween." Lissa switched gears. "On the romantic front, what's up with Tom? Is he coming to watch his favorite cowgirl, or is he in the parade too?"

"I forgot to tell you! Tom told me, he and the other volunteer fireman dress up in clown makeup and ride in an old open fire truck. The guys jump on and off the truck, squirt kids with water and throw confetti into the crowd. They have a blast."

"We'll all be in the parade, then. I can't wait! I wonder what other stuff goes on during the Yankee Homecoming Days?"

"Tom says we should check out Westbrook's Home page. All the events are listed. Hey, did I hear you right?" Reene asked. "Peggy Simms? Is she any relation to …?"

"'Only by marriage', quoth Mrs. Simms," Lissa laughed. "Why don't you link the information to our website so we can snag a few more guests? I have a feeling this'll turn out to be our best weekend ever."

Chapter 24

Streetlights blinked on when Andrea parked her Lexus in front of the converted Victorian mansion she called home. Her apartment on the second floor included a turret that she used as her home office. The view usually put her in a mellow mood.

"Tonight I have no intention of working on the campaign, writing memos or paying bills," Andrea decided. "I'm fixing a large and powerful drink and chilling out."

She clicked the car's remote, picked up mail and the newspaper from her front hall box and climbed the stairs. Living on the second floor had its benefits, but tonight she wished the antiquated Victorian building had an elevator.

"Damned Hysterical Commission and their rules! One of these days one of the old biddies who live above me will break a hip," she griped. "Then an elevator will appear in a heartbeat."

As she entered her apartment, two glass and brass table lamps set on timers glowed brightly to welcome her. She tossed the mail and newspaper on the granite counter top. She could hardly wait to get undressed and into a dry martini.

Another hellacious day spent playing phone tag in between a budget meeting and yet another committee meeting. Andrea kicked off her high heels and wiggled her toes in relief. She padded across the deep pile carpet into the galley kitchen.

Should I forage in the refrigerator for dinner or call my favorite takeout joint? She made a face at the bowl of congealed pasta next to the week old pizza. *Ugh! What did I do with that takeout menu? Vegetable lo mein with sweet and sour chicken sounds a lot more appetizing than this crap.*

She placed her order and told them in language that would make a longshoreman blush that her food had better be delivered on time.

"Your last delivery took so long, the food was stone cold. If you don't shape up, a food inspector will be at your door tomorrow."

Satisfied she'd intimidated the hapless person on the phone, she changed into one of her designer sweat suits from her New York days.

Martini in hand, she stretched out on her sofa and adjusted her glasses. She'd have plenty of time to read the paper before her food arrived. If Grady had done his job, there should be a nice article extolling her qualifications.

Nothing exciting on the front page. "Gambling during the college basketball finals! Scandalous, just scandalous. Where the hell is my endorsement?" she grumbled aloud.

She continued to scan each page. "He promised he'd get that thing in this week."

The next page brought more than she bargained for. "'Historical Discovery at Local Inn'! Son of a bitch!"

Andrea's heart thumped painfully and her hands turned to ice as the words jumped out at her. "'Young Black woman…Underground Railroad…Williams farmhouse where slaves could…' Damn those nosy bitches!" Reene freakin' Anderson and Lissa Do-Gooder Martin kept digging until they found something she'd hoped was lost forever! Her biggest fear finally come true.

"Oh my God!"

Her doorbell jangled, jerking her attention away from the article.

"Shit! The damn food's here!"

She buzzed the delivery person in and waited impatiently as he climbed the stairs to her floor. As the young man approached with the brown paper bag, Andrea vented her frustration.

"Your cook must have been out killing the chicken," she hissed. "This is the last time I'm ordering anything from your joint."

She jammed money into his hesitant hand. "Keep the change. Now you can retire." She slammed the door in his face but she heard his response.

"Bitch," grumbled the delivery boy. "I hope this stuff makes her hurl."

Her appetite now gone, she contemplated flinging the food into the wastebasket. Instead she yanked open the fridge and shoved the cartons onto the bottom shelf. Impatiently she grabbed her drink and downed it in one gulp. The alcohol added its sting to her already churning insides. Too upset for useless tears, she paced around her apartment. She stopped and stared pensively out the front window.

The workday had ended, and the flow of traffic on Main Street dissipated. From her vantage point she could see the Town Hall and noted the midnight oil burning in the mayor's office.

170

For years she'd pictured herself presiding in that office. *Her* office. The election was only a few months away. Her plans could come crashing down because those two pains in the ass stumbled onto those damning letters. She mustn't overreact. Just stay in control.

With her confidence somewhat restored, hunger pangs rumbled insistently. She strode over to the fridge, retrieved her food and reheated it in the microwave. Rotten news always went down better on a full tummy.

"Why I am worrying? 'Historical Discovery' my ass! If the worst happens, I intend to have a backup plan. And I don't care who gets ruined in the process."

"Can you recommend a nice restaurant nearby? I want to impress a lady."

Stephen, their long-term guest, settled in his usual spot for breakfast and buttered toast in anticipation of his soft-boiled eggs.

"Ohhh!" Lissa breathed as she set the timer on the stove. "How romantic!"

"You mustn't mind her, Steve," Reene counseled. "She is, hands down, the most romantic woman on the planet."

Lissa ignored her friend's jibe. "Stephen, in my humble opinion, the restaurant that has everything you desire is my absolute favorite: The 1761 Old Mill. It's in Westminster, a bit of a drive from here but worth it. First time I went there, I was smitten on sight. At night the lights from the carriage lamps along the walkways give the whole place a soft glow. Their pond is chock full of every species of duck and geese. You can sit on a wooden bench on the porch and feed the birds. Or hold hands!"

She laughed mischievously and Stephen responded in kind.

"Now for the educational segment of our program," she continued in a singsong monotone. "The restaurant was originally a saw mill built in 1761 and it provided wood for most of the homes in the neighborhood. It fell into disrepair until 1946 when new owners bought it. It's been owned by the same family for three generations. With its post and beam ceilings, aforementioned duck pond and walk-through waterfalls, this converted saw mill provides a unique dining experience for the discerning patron."

"Bravo! Bravo!" applauded Stephen while Lissa, coffee pot in hand, bowed in acknowledgment. "You have sold me. We'll go there."

"Anyone we know?" asked Reene, placing two soft-boiled eggs in their porcelain eggcups. She added a rasher of bacon and pineapple rings to his plate.

"Most probably. But I won't risk my luck by telling you who she is or talking about her."

Seeing Lissa's dejected face, he relented. "If all goes as planned, I will give you a full report tomorrow morning. Will that satisfy your curiosity until then?"

"Yes, indeed! When you're gazing into each other's eyes in the candlelight, your mystery lady won't be able to resist you."

"Don't say I didn't warn you, Steve," Reene reminded sarcastically as she washed the cooking pans.

"I'm flattered Lissa's so concerned about my love life." Then he hesitated. "Because you've both been so accommodating, I hate to even mention this, but odd things have been happening lately in my room."

Reene nearly dropped her washcloth and Lissa's body tensed.

"Really?" Lissa managed.

"Yes. I found my toiletries scattered around the sink and yesterday when I came in late, the bed was unmade."

"Oh, dear. I'm terribly sorry," Lissa apologized. She looked over at Reene who was now vigorously scrubbing a suspiciously clean saucepan. "I must have forgotten to make your bed and straighten up. It won't happen again."

She emphasized her last words, trusting *other* ears were listening.

"No harm done. I realize how busy you are running this place and taking care of your animals."

Fortunately the phone rang. Lissa escaped to her office. Stephen was such a sweet man. She hated lying to him. But if he had caught Josey bouncing his belongings around his room in one of her playful moods, she'd help him pack his bags. That is, if he stayed around long enough.

"It's not easy running this inn, Miss Josey, and you aren't making things any easier!" she grumbled, shaking a fist at the ceiling. "Give it a rest, will you?"

"Reene, after the bank closes today Randy's dropping by with the enlargement. Let's hope he doesn't mention the late unpleasantness with his developing horror."

"If wishes were horses, beggars would ride," Reene said wickedly. "Randy'll be all over us with a blow-by-blow description of the figment of his imagination."

172

"We'll have to baffle him with our bullshit and dazzle him with our double-talk. It worked before when he phoned all in a dither, but I don't think lightening will strike twice in the same place."

Later that afternoon Simms, a manila package under his arm, stood expectantly on their front porch ringing the doorbell.

"Randy! Come on in!" Lissa greeted. "We can't wait to see your work of art. I'll call Reene. She's whipping up another culinary masterpiece in the kitchen."

"With pleasure," Simms beamed and opened the envelope. Between two pieces of cardboard lay the enlargement. Reverently he removed it, and grasping the picture by the edges, he laid it on the table.

"Excellent job!" Reene said, joining them. "The photo is clear and sharp."

"I have the perfect antique brass frame to set it off," Lissa said. "Mrs. Long will be so pleased."

"Considering the trouble I had during the development stage, I'm extremely proud of the results," Simms stated.

"We knew you'd persevere, Randy," Reene said.

But the banker's expression turned somber, and he cleared his throat. "I'm still a bit concerned about the mysterious figure I imagined I saw on the first negative. Its appearance gave me quite a shock."

"I can imagine," Lissa agreed. "Almost as if you'd had a paranormal experience. You don't believe in that ridiculous sort of thing, do you?"

Reene suddenly began coughing uncontrollably. Lissa bent and pounded her solicitously on the back. "Follow my lead," she whispered. "Best offense is a good defense."

"Paranormal?" Randy echoed. "Why, no, I don't put much credence in that, but I've heard that reputable photographers spend hours setting up their cameras trying to capture such images."

"Isn't it amazing what some people believe?" Lissa remarked. "Stuff and nonsense, of course, but it takes all kinds."

"Exactly," Reene said, her coughing fit miraculously cured. "You are so well respected in Westbrook your reputation has preceded you. That's why we chose you for this special project."

"Let me say again, Randy, that we are thrilled with your work and I'm positive this will put the finishing touch on the dedication ceremony," Lissa said.

Randy's face beamed once more and he squared his shoulders. "Thank you both for giving me this opportunity even though I gained a few gray hairs in the process."

"Would you care for a slice of my warm-from-the-oven sour cream coffee cake to celebrate?" Reene asked, ignoring his comment. "A pot of Earl Grey tea to wash it down?"

Simms salivated at the mere mention of warm coffee cake, but declined. "May I take a rain check? There's a board meeting tonight and Peg is preparing an early dinner for me."

"No problem. You are welcome any time," Lissa assured. "Don't forget, the dedication of the letters and the print will be set soon. We'll keep you posted."

"Nothing could keep me from attending," Randy promised and took his leave.

Sagging against each other, Reene and Lissa burst into nervous laughter.

"You were right on the money, girlfriend," Reene approved. "The best offense *is* a good defense."

"You should watch more football, you'll learn lots of cool stuff. I'll stash Josey's picture in my office safe until we hand it over to Mrs. Long. I don't trust Miss Josey an inch. She's liable to cart the thing around trying to scare the guests."

Lissa's tummy spoke to her. "Hey, did you really make coffee cake and a pot of Earl Grey?"

"Most definitely. Want some?"

"You have to ask? Only, put a double shot of whiskey in the tea pot."

Chapter 25

When Stephen and Andrea returned to Andrea's apartment, Stephen was exhilarated. It was now close to midnight. Not only had Andrea accepted his invitation to dinner, somewhat reluctantly, but the evening had gone favorably. She had been reserved, but kept the conversation non-confrontational. The food proved exceptional and the restaurant had impressed him with its rustic ambiance. His new friends at the inn had advised him well.

"May I come up for a night cap like the good old days?" he asked.

"What 'good old days'? They're gone forever."

"I won't stay long, Andrea," he promised. He'd blundered by bringing up the past. If he weren't careful, she would show him the door in short order.

"Fair enough, Stephen. You've been a good boy."

Standing in the foyer, his eyes wandered around the room, noting the touches she had once incorporated into their penthouse decor. "You haven't lost your sense of style," he approved.

"Thank you. I'm glad you noticed." She moved to her wet bar. "What would you like? Brandy? Gin and tonic?"

"Have you forgotten my favorite drink already?" he asked playfully. "Scotch on the rocks, please."

Andrea did not respond to his good-natured banter. She expertly fixed his drink and handed him an exquisitely cut tumbler.

"To a beautiful day and a marvelous dinner," Stephen toasted.

Andrea kept her distance. She did not join him in clinking glasses, instead she moved restlessly around the apartment, fussing with the drapes and emptying the dishwasher.

"What's wrong? You're behaving like we've never shared dinner or enjoyed being in each other's company."

"I made a mistake. I shouldn't have agreed to have dinner with you."

"Why, Andrea? We had an exceedingly pleasant day and the food was superb."

"It has nothing to do with the day or the food. Knowing you as I do, I'm positive you have your own agenda. And I'm afraid you want more than I'm willing to give."

"What have I said or done to give you that impression?"

"Nothing. It's a strong feeling I've had ever since you dropped out of the everywhere and landed in Westbrook."

"You're acting as if I were singing love songs outside your window," he jested. "I didn't think you'd object to a quiet dinner in the country."

"Just because you weren't singing outside my doorstep doesn't mean you haven't bothered me."

"Bothered you?"

Andrea lifted the dish garden that had arrived a few days earlier. "At least you didn't send roses. This shows a little originality, even though you know damn well I have a black thumb."

"I found it in one of the quaint shops in town. I've become quite the gentleman farmer. I believe that's the correct term," Stephen smiled.

"'Gentleman farmer'? Get real, Stephen," she snapped. "I know you've been staying at that new inn."

"Then my appearance out of the everywhere, as you put it, isn't as surprising as you'd have me believe."

"Don't get the wrong idea. A friend of mine informed me he saw you in town and asked a few questions."

"He must be a very good friend. Is it serious?"

"Even if it were, it's none of your business."

"Sorry. I shouldn't have asked. By the way, how is the campaign coming? I've seen your banners all over town, and I read the flattering article about you in the local paper last week. Brilliantly presented and unbiased."

Despite his promise not to linger, he walked over to the bar and freshened his drink. Discussing the campaign was safe ground, the one subject he knew she could talk about for hours.

"Things are going well. My manager knows when to push and when to back off. No doubt you've heard of my proposed plan for the new off ramp. Stodgy old Bob Stuart is scrambling desperately to come up with a new ploy of his own to offset it, but so far his camp has been quiet."

"Too quiet, as they used to say in the old movies."

"What do you mean? What is he saying about me?" she asked sharply.

"Nothing. Just a figure of speech. But I wouldn't count him out. He's a seasoned campaigner and may yet surprise you. My innkeeper friends told me he's getting involved with their discovery of the Civil War letters and their generous decision to pay tribute to the late Mrs. Peter Williams by donating the letters to the Historical Society."

"Do you mean those two broads who bought that broken-down farm? You hardly know them!" For a moment, she knew she sounded like a jealous fishwife. "Those are your *friends*?"

"Mrs. Anderson and Mrs. Martin have been wonderful to me during my stay. If it's possible to become friends in such a short time, then yes, I believe we have."

Stephen hesitated. "Does that mean you still care?"

"Damn you, Stephen! I knew that's what you were leading up to. You don't give a shit about my campaign. You just used it as an excuse to keep me talking. I'm asking you to leave."

"Don't turn me away, Andrea. I care a great deal about you and your political aspirations. If I didn't I wouldn't have written that letter of recommendation when you were appointed Treasurer."

Andrea's face turned to stone. "What letter, Stephen?" she asked, her voice flat and expressionless.

"I'm afraid I've let the cat out of the bag. I knew you were anxious to secure this job as Treasurer," he explained. "So I wrote to Bob Stuart who was impressed with your qualifications."

"And how did you know he was impressed with my qualifications?" she asked.

Her calm demeanor gave Stephen pause. He had good reason to fear her violent mood swings.

"Why, I," he stumbled, "that is, he informed me as a matter of courtesy."

"So I owe you my job, is that it?"

"Of course not! I simply sent a letter of reference, as any friend would do in that situation."

"Friend! You are not my friend, now or ever!"

Her words flicked him like a lash. "Andrea, you don't mean that!"

"Damn right I mean it! I don't believe this! I thought I'd come into my own without needing a big, strong man to take care of me. We've been divorced all these years and yet you're still helping me."

"I never intended you should know. Moreover, the position was already yours. I only added a little embellishment. Why can't you believe that?"

"Stephen, get the hell out. Now."

"Andrea, please. I can't leave you like this. The day started out so wonderfully, with such promise. I didn't mean to spoil it."

"Such promise? For who?" she yelled. "If you've convinced yourself we'd get back together, you'll be sorely disappointed. That will never happen."

"Our situations have changed over the years. You have come into your own through your talent alone. I'm positive you'll be elected mayor in a few months. Can't you give me one more chance?"

Moving over to the picture window, Andrea stared unseeingly into the night. Her head ached from tension and she rubbed her temples to ease the pressure. Stephen came up behind her and lightly placed his hands on her shoulders. He took it as a good sign that she relaxed against him.

"I give you my word things will be different this time," he promised. "We can establish a new life here. I have come to love your town. I could even commute back and forth to New York. We can make it work, darling."

For a brief instant, she appeared to consider it. Then, to his dismay, she stiffened her resolve.

"Stephen, it's no good. We can't go back. I want to go forward but not with you."

"Andrea, I don't want to go back either! And if you want to know the truth, I've never understood what really ruined our marriage. You fed me a song and dance about not wanting children because of your great future and I accepted it. I let you go. But I never believed that was the real reason."

Andrea whirled out of his grasp. Fury burned in her eyes.

"You want the real reason? I'll give you the best damn reason I didn't want your child, then or ever! I'm Black! Is that reason enough for you?"

Chapter 26

Color drained from Stephen's face as he struggled to comprehend Andrea' startling announcement. He was stunned. He tried to speak, but could not collect the thoughts that stampeded through his mind.

"How does it feel to know you've slept with a Black woman before it was politically correct? To know you've been duped all these years?" Andrea said bitingly. "Have you changed your mind now? Do you still want to get back together?"

Stephen continued to stare at her in stunned silence. "Black? That's impossible!" he blurted. "You're as white as—"

"The driven snow? Get a grip, Stephen."

"Why didn't you tell me? I don't understand."

"I've had to live with this secret since I was a little girl," she said bitterly. "What would your classy New York friends say now if they knew? Or are they sophisticated enough to ignore the truth?"

"Andrea, this is not about my friends. It's about us. The truth is you obviously refuse to accept who you are. The woman I loved."

"You wouldn't have loved me if you'd known! No one would have!"

"Listen to yourself, Andrea! You're speaking nonsense. And why do you consider yourself Black? The lineage must be too old, too watered down—"

"Stephen, you're insulting! 'Too watered down'? Isn't that like being 'only a little bit pregnant'? Did you think the marches on Washington in the sixties changed everything? 'We Shall Overcome', 'I have a dream' and all that bullshit! For God's sake, have you been living in a cave for the last few decades?"

"New York City is hardly a cave. I deserve some credit. Andrea, your fears are absurd! No one will care about your ancestry."

"I don't want my reputation or career ruined because of this. My run for mayor would be finished if the news leaked out! Are you blind? Nothing has changed. Racial slurs erupt daily from drunken actors and dumb ass sports commentators. Do you think they woke up one day with those outrageous opinions in their heads? Give me a break! Those opinions were put in their pointy little heads by their parents who heard them from *their* parents!"

"Those people are the exceptions, not the rule. Consider the source, Andrea! Not everyone feels that way. Why, there are hundreds of Blacks who are professors, doctors, lawyers—"

Andrea cut him off. "Black is Black! I won't have friends scrutinizing me for telltale signs that I'm a Black woman. I won't stand for it! If anyone tries, I'll kill them!"

Stephen was frightened. He had witnessed her towering rages in the past, but she had never threatened to harm anyone.

"Andrea, please listen. I won't insult you by saying 'I know how you feel' because obviously I cannot even imagine the torment you have imposed upon yourself. However, you are underestimating your friends' capacity for tolerance and acceptance."

"You know damn well our parents' generation wouldn't tolerate any minority. My ancestor was a slave on a Southern plantation! When she married a White boy from Massachusetts, the state almost declared war again! Admit I was Black? I hate my Black ancestry!"

She watched him like a cat watches a mouse. "Where do you stand on tolerance and acceptance, Stephen?"

"My beliefs have not changed. However, I admit I'm a little shaken by the news. But now that I finally know the truth, I'm still willing to go forward. I still love you."

He regarded Andrea warily, waiting to see her response.

"You don't love me. You can't. Swear to me you won't reveal my secret. I want your word."

"I wish you would believe me. But I know what this campaign means to you. You have my word."

Finally, he looked away and slowly walked toward the door. As he gripped the doorknob, he turned to regard her once more.

"Good night, Andrea. You aren't rid of me yet. I will keep your confidence. Remember, we're not teens fighting parental opposition. You need help dealing with your issues. I'm willing to help you if you'll let me."

Deep into the early hours Stephen returned to his room, his only safe haven after his nightmarish evening. He lay on his bed listening to the soothing night sounds.

I've always prided myself on my tolerance for others. It's Andrea who is no longer tolerant.

By first light, he couldn't stand his thoughts another moment. He dressed and soundlessly slipped out of the inn.

I can't face the questions those two lovely women are bound to ask about my evening out. I need space to think how to handle this situation.

His car coasted silently down the driveway and he drove aimlessly through the breaking dawn.

Disappointed Stephen did not come down to breakfast, Lissa listened for his footsteps on the stairs. Then she found a note on the kitchen table that said 'Please don't cook breakfast. I'll see you both later.'

His note troubled her. Evidently the evening had not gone as well as he had anticipated.

"Why the frown?" Reene asked as she came into the kitchen. Shaking off a pink Boston Red Sox cap, she raked her fingers through her hair to cure a major case of hat head.

"Stephen left us a note that he didn't want breakfast," Lissa replied. "I hoped he'd be all smiles and blushes this morning. I'm assuming his romantic evening did not go as planned."

"I noticed his car was gone. Maybe he had an early appointment," Reene ventured.

"Could be. But I don't have a good feeling about this. He was so excited and confident when he left yesterday."

"I know. But there's nothing we can do about it right now. We'll have to play this by ear when he returns," Reene advised. "I wonder what I should plan for tomorrow's breakfast. I'm running out of ideas."

"Make it easy on yourself: English muffins with cheese, aka McReenies, and oatmeal." Lissa made a face. "Ugh. Maybe not oatmeal. It looks like wallpaper paste. If I poured a couple of gallons of maple syrup on the stuff, I'd still have a hard time swallowing it."

"I'll remember your disparaging remarks next time you want me to cook something special," Reene chided. "Besides, oatmeal is for winter. I haven't tried crepes yet. Where's my cookbook?"

As Lissa pulled a raisin bagel from the freezer, Stephen's silver Prius slid past the kitchen window.

"Reene, he's back! I'm dying to know what happened to make him leave without his breakfast."

181

"Remember what I said. Play it by ear. Let him come to us when he's ready."

Chapter 27

"Barn Swallow Inn, Lissa speaking. May I help you?"

"Yes, you may, dear friend. Are you ready for another trail ride?"

"Gina! How are you? I wanted to call to thank you for your wonderful article. Reene and I were really pleased."

"Lissa, I enjoyed writing it," Gina responded. "What a fascinating story! You both went through a lot to find all that information."

"You got that right. My muscles still haven't recovered. Speaking of muscles, are you serious about riding again?"

"I'm more than serious," Gina answered. "I haven't ridden much since I went out with you and Reene. It's definitely time."

"Super! But we have an ulterior motive. We'd appreciate your advice about the next step in our Master Plan."

"Master Plan? Sounds intriguing."

"Spoken like a true newshound. What day did you have in mind?"

Saturday morning, Gina's truck and trailer pulled into the guests' parking area. She'd tacked up before loading her horse onto the trailer, so she was ready for the trail.

"Thanks for coming early," Lissa said. "We want to hit the trails before the sun gets too hot."

"Ready in a minute," Reene promised and tightened Shen's girth.

Their woods offered some shade but after a few spirited runs, they stopped to give their horses a drink. Gina's horse Sonny moved a bit deeper into the stream and lowered his head into the water.

Suddenly Sonny's head snapped up, water dripping from his muzzle. His ears were pricked forward while he scented the air. Snorting and nervously tossing his head, he whirled around and splashed back and forth.

"Gina, what's up with Sonny?" Reene asked.

"Something's upsetting him." Quickly Gina shortened her reins and pulled Sonny's head toward the bank. Sonny needed no urging to leave.

He launched himself out of the stream, slamming Lissa's leg hard as he rushed by.

"Lissa, are you hurt? I'm so sorry!"

"Not to worry, Gina. Nothing's broken," Lissa grunted, rubbing her smarting leg. "You're lucky he didn't go down with you."

"Let's keep moving," Reene suggested, "I think they need to stretch their legs."

Lissa threw Reene a grateful look as she hurried them away from the water.

If only Gina knew the truth about this stream! Did Sonny sense Shiloh and Josey's presence too? I wish our horses could talk. We'd understand more than we do now.

The rush and gurgle of the stream seemed to mock her. Lissa shivered as she turned her horse to follow the others.

After trotting, cantering and exploring new trails all morning, both horses and riders were ready to call it a day. Reene invited Gina to lunch and she readily accepted. Once the horses were munching hay in their respective paddocks, their riders adjourned to the deck.

"Luncheon is served," Lissa announced. She set plates laden with sandwiches, garnished with pickles and olives, on the picnic table. "Reene, is the sun tea ready?"

"It should be. I'll put some in a pitcher and bring the glasses and ice bucket. Do we need anything else?"

"Everything is here and looks wonderful. Can I do anything to help?" Gina asked.

"No way. Just sit and act like a contented guest," Lissa ordered.

"This is delicious!" exclaimed Gina, savoring an overstuffed sandwich quarter. "What a treat. I usually eat at my desk so I never get the chance to enjoy my food. These past few weeks I've been existing on coffee, bagels and more coffee."

"Are things always this crazy-busy at the paper?" Reene asked as she stabbed a gherkin with her fork.

"Some days are worse than others, but it's a challenge every day to meet my deadline. I'm dreading the upcoming election. Full-page ads with color photos of candidates complete with more and more stories about promises they don't intend to keep. Demands for retractions. Threatened lawsuits. The gods be thanked, this circus only happens once every three years."

"I don't envy you. I had delusions of being a journalist when I was a naïve child in high school," Lissa said. "In fact, it says so right under my extremely hideous yearbook picture."

"Speaking of elections," Reene said, "we thought now would be a good time to run our plan by you, especially since we were hoping you'd give it a big write-up in your paper."

"Not to mention our plan may affect the outcome," Lissa added.

Gina placed her partially eaten sandwich on the plate and regarded the two women. "That's a strong statement. I trust you have good information to back it up?"

"We do." Lissa took a deep breath. "Remember you told me about the accident that happened here back in 1875? The day I came to your office to place the ad for the High Tea?"

"Of course I remember. But how does that tie into present day?"

"Bear with me for a moment, Gina. Finding the letters confirms Josephine Taylor led a double life: a Civil War spy masquerading as a stable boy. Taylor married Peter Williams when the war ended. After she died in that accident, Peter Williams left his home, this farmhouse, and never returned. Reene and I feel very strongly that Josephine should be recognized for what she accomplished. We couldn't find any evidence that her part in the Civil War ever came to light. She risked her life carrying messages through enemy lines. She could have been killed or taken prisoner. Or had her horse shot out from under her."

The shattering image her words conjured up surged in her voice. "You finish, Reene."

"We've given this a lot of thought and we want her memory honored in some way. We've decided a bronze plaque cast with her likeness including a description of her service to our country would be in order."

"I totally agree and I think it's heart-warming you wish to pay tribute to this young woman, but I still don't understand what it has to do with the election."

Reene and Lissa exchanged glances. "Did we mention that Josephine Taylor was Black?"

"*Black*? No, you didn't. That makes it even more newsworthy. When did you plan on telling me?"

"Please don't be upset, Gina. We wanted to take this slowly and weigh the town's reaction. And your reaction as well. We still haven't gotten the official word that the letters are authentic."

"We have our own reasons to believe they are," Reene said. "We thought if we invited Mayor Stuart to dedicate the plaque, it would give him some needed publicity. Josephine Taylor was Black. Racism is very much alive and well in this country. By getting involved with this project, our mayor could definitely earn some respect with the minorities by supporting our proposal."

"Speaking of minorities, if you've done your research, now you both understand why her contribution was never acknowledged. So I assume you would like me to support this plan? Give it coverage in my paper?"

"Since you asked, yes," Reene replied.

They held their breath, worried they had overstepped their bounds with Gina and presumed on their new friendship.

"I'm impressed with the way you've thought this all out," Gina replied. "In fact, I was saving my surprise until after dessert. We *are* having dessert, aren't we?" she grinned. "But you've beaten me to the draw, if you'll excuse the expression from an English rider."

"Don't keep us in suspense! What is your surprise?" asked Lissa.

"You'll be pleased to hear I've received a great number of phone calls and emails regarding your discovery of the Civil War articles. Many people I talked with felt this breakthrough will give the town a much-needed shot in the arm. In fact, I took it upon myself to call Mrs. Long, partly out of curiosity and partly because of the newswoman in me. She confirmed that the letters and articles of clothing are indeed authentic."

"Yes!" cried Reene. "I would have bet the farm they were the real thing."

"Fortunately, you didn't have to!" Gina said. "I suggest we wait until after the official dedication to the Historical Society. Once that is out of the way, we can concentrate on enticing the mayor to champion your proposal for a plaque in honor of Josephine Williams. We can sow the seeds in that direction at the ceremony and then follow up with some well-timed articles. I've already written a rough draft of an editorial that will appeal to his politician's need for good public relations."

"Gina, that is perfect!" Reene exclaimed. "It's almost as if you've read our minds."

"Not exactly. I've been through similar situations before, but now the circumstances are different. I'm working with you on a personal level. Normally, it's not good business to become personally involved. Let's keep this strictly between us. If you want my advice, contact Mrs. Long. Explain that you spoke to me and I confirmed the letters are authentic. You may want to ask about the dedication, but I have a notion it will already be in the planning stages. Mrs. Long is very efficient."

"You don't have to tell me," Lissa said. "She had all the information available at her fingertips when I went on a field trip with her to the Historical Society. Together we researched the Williams' family history."

"Do you think the dedication of the letters and portrait should take place right away?" Reene asked. "The mayor needs time to clear his calendar."

"I would say the sooner the better. Mayor Stuart hasn't done much strenuous campaigning because he feels his record speaks for itself. To his credit, he has achieved many accomplishments during his tenure. But you know people: a new face, new ideas. They're fed up with the same old, same old. Andrea Wilson is proposing a new project that has the whole town buzzing. As we say in the newspaper biz, 'I don't care what you say about me, just spell my name right'!"

"And as we say in the horse biz," Lissa laughed, "always end on a good note. Are you ready for dessert? Today, Madame, we are serving French silk chocolate mousse with real whipped cream and a strawberry garnish. May I interest Madame in a cup of coffee or perhaps a spot of tea?"

"Madame desires a cup of coffee, the stronger the better. I love chocolate mousse. If it's as yummy as it sounds, you both will be handsomely rewarded. I'm a big tipper."

"Hear that, Reene? Let us serve Madame right away. We can use the extra cash."

Sunday morning Lissa was surprised to find Stephen relaxing in the Gathering Room. He was reading her conversation piece, *Gone With the Wind*. From the expression on his face, he was thoughtfully devouring every word.

"Well, good morning!" she said cheerfully.

Instantly, she regretted her exuberant greeting as Stephen's face turned somber. He quietly closed the book.

"Good morning, Lissa," he replied.

"I see you're enjoying my favorite book. Are you reading the part where Scarlett stays in Atlanta when Melanie has her baby? Or the chapter where poor Frank Kennedy is killed and Rhett takes all the men to Belle Watling's whorehouse for an alibi?" she babbled, alarmed by his haggard look.

Reene came to her rescue. "Steve, we've missed you. I'm just starting breakfast. Won't you join us?"

"I'd like that," Stephen replied.

Both women fussed around him, bringing the paper and a cup of freshly brewed coffee. They chatted about all sorts of general subjects, determined not to ask what had driven him out without a word of explanation.

"You have been so kind by not asking what went wrong the other night," Stephen said finally as he finished his second cup. "I feel terrible that I deserted you."

"Not a problem, Steve," Reene reassured him. "We understand. We respect your privacy."

"I appreciate that."

"If and when you ever want to talk about it, we'll listen," Lissa said. "And I swear on my horse's life not to recommend any more restaurants."

"It wasn't the restaurant," he smiled.

"I feel so much better now!" Lissa grinned. "Stephen, this weekend is Yankee Homecoming Days. Reene is driving Sissy in the parade and I'll be riding shotgun beside her on Bravo. We'd love it if you came to watch."

"I second that motion," Reene added. "You'll have a blast."

He seemed touched by their eagerness to help him through his crisis, even though they still had no inkling of what had happened.

"An enticing offer I dare not refuse," he replied. "When is the parade?"

"Saturday afternoon at two o'clock," Lissa answered.

"There are lots of activities on the common," Reene added, "although our little tent sales can't compare to the Great White Way."

"Trust me, neither of you would trade what you have for New York's fast lane. Oh, it has its perks. Some people couldn't live any other way. But I'm going to enjoy watching you both doing something you love. Well, dear friends, you can count on me as part of your cheering section."

Stephen raised his cup.

"To us and to Yankee Homecoming Days!"

Chapter 28

'Yankee Homecoming Days are a New England tradition.'

Lissa read the *Homecoming Days* newsletter as she walked toward the green. "'To keep their small town atmosphere alive, state governors decreed days be set aside for festivities to entice friends and family to return to their hometowns. From mid-summer to late fall, small towns in all six states put on a two or three-day celebration. These festivals typically took place in late August or early September when farmers were between harvests.'"

"Who knew?" she muttered. "We city girls don't have a clue."

She wrinkled her nose with displeasure. Now so many towns have been taken over by housing developments and strip malls. Most of the original farmers were taxed out of business and the surviving farmhouses are surrounded by modern McMansions. They were lucky their inn was still intact.

"Let's see what this year's Days has to offer," Lissa murmured as she continued on to check out events on the common. A Doll Carriage Stroll was scheduled for ten a.m. But as she watched little girls proudly wheeling their carriages, she heard an auction in progress on the other side of the common. Her heartbeat quickened at the prospect of acquiring another piece of antique furniture for the inn. Daydreaming about turning trash to treasure, she started to cross the road to her Promised Land.

Suddenly, a hard shove to her back sent her sprawling toward the pavement. Before her head could strike the ground, strong arms hauled her to safety.

"Easy does it, ma'am," Lissa's rescuer warned.

"Thank you so much! Serves me right for not paying attention!"

Red-faced and shaking her head to clear the cobwebs, she slipped among the people watching the auction. *Did I imagine a hand at my back? Was that really a deliberate attack?* She couldn't concentrate. When the auctioneer yelled "Sold!" for the third time, she left.

In frustration she headed toward the tents set up along the length of the common. Lissa stopped at the local animal rescue league's booth, where a rescued collie lay at the feet of one of the workers. He looked peaceful and content. As she scoped out the jumble of tents, she spotted a familiar face. Linda Baril was busy displaying her knitted creations.

"Good morning, Miss Linda," Lissa greeted. "I figured I'd find you here somewhere. How's business?"

"Lots of lookers so far, but no takers. It's still early and I haven't put everything out yet. I've also made up some mini bags of horse cookies with peppermint chunks from our store."

"Our horses have a sweet tooth. I'll take a couple of bags."

"Awesome. You're my first sale. Poke around some more while I put out all the stuff Art asked me to bring. He gave me samples of the new halters and brushes we just got in."

"Are you staying for the parade?" she asked. "Reene is home decorating her wagon and I'm riding my horse. His silver tack is shined to within an inch of its life. You'll see us coming a mile away."

"I'll hang an 'Out to Lunch' sign so I can watch. I'll need a break by then anyway."

Lissa set off to explore other venues. She admired a pendant in the jewelry tent, but the line of shoppers was long and she decided to come back later.

As she walked around, she cordially greeted people she'd met in her short time in Westbrook. She saw Donna Palermo browsing along the used book table. Always on the hunt for out of print books by her favorite authors, Lissa joined her.

"Find any bargains?" Lissa asked.

Donna looked up from the hard cover she was skimming. "Hello, Lissa! Nothing earth-shaking yet, but this one could have possibilities for my personal library. And may I add my congratulations on your exciting news? You've only been in town a few months and already you and your friend are celebrities."

"No autographs, please!" Lissa replied with a wave of her hand. "I wouldn't lump us in the celebrity category just yet. You were a great help when we drove you crazy at the library. We've certainly received our share of publicity though, good and bad."

"Oh?"

"The usual crank calls. One guy was really nasty. I hate to say it, but he made a racist remark."

Donna shook her head sadly. "I believe it. I'm afraid not everyone will be thrilled that a lot of attention is being paid to a Black girl even if she was a Civil War hero."

"We're finding out the hard way, I'm afraid, but we're not letting anything stop us. We're going to ignore these stupid people. We won't let them win."

"Good for you! You've got my support. Keep me posted."

Lissa rejoined the throng of shoppers and did a double take when she wandered into the last tent next to the public benches.

"Oh, boy! Penny candy!!! I haven't seen this stuff in years!" Lissa grinned at the woman behind the table laden with Necco wafers, chocolate babies, licorice whips, spearmint leaves, and candy cigarettes. In a flash, she was transported back to her childhood when she had pressed her face against the glass that held the precious candy.

"So, how much for penny candy these days?"

"Only five cents apiece. Or you could fill this bag for a dollar," the woman suggested, bending to dig out snack-sized brown bags.

"Sold!" She handed over her dollar and picked out her favorite pieces. She could hardly wait to sink her teeth into the long-forgotten sugary treats.

"I've got to boogie! I want to grab lunch before I head back. And pick up a pendant that's been calling my name."

Lissa scurried back to the jewelry tent. "Happy Unbirthday to me!" she exclaimed.

The square malachite pendant set in silver wire peeked from under a bracelet, just where she'd hidden it. Definitely a Sign from Above that she should buy it.

"Wrap it up, please."

She tucked her new pendant securely into her fanny pack and set off in search of the mouthwatering smells wafting her way. Her nose led her to a grill where sausages were cooking, mountains of peppers and onions keeping them company.

"Good thing Reene isn't here to see me devouring this sandwich," Lissa muttered. Reene avoided red meat as much as possible and this concoction would give her fits. She squirted yellow mustard over the sausage and grabbed an order of French fries and a soda. "My conscience is clear."

The picnic tables were all occupied by wiggling children, harried parents and grandparents, so she plopped down at the base of a towering oak. Using the tree trunk as a backrest, she ate her tasty but messy sandwich. Between rescuing escaped vegetables and wiping mustard off her chin, she indulged in people watching.

Lissa jerked upright when she saw Stephen wandering in and out of the booths and tents, talking with many of the vendors and indulging in some free samples.

"He looks a lot happier since the morning he *didn't* tell us about his disappointing date. Today's outing will do him a world of good."

She was even more surprised to see Stephen hail Randy Simms who had just arrived on the common. From her out-of-sight vantage point, she watched the two men shake hands and pat each other on the shoulder. They moved off together talking and laughing.

"I wonder how they know each other," Lissa mumbled between mouthfuls. "Obviously they're friends. Good grief, Randy looks like a tourist with all those expensive cameras hanging around his neck."

Lissa lifted her face to the sun as a strong breeze ruffled her short hair. *Reene's long skirt and jacket are just right for this weather. It's not usually this cool and breezy for early September. At least I don't have to worry about either of us fainting from the heat.*

As she swallowed the last bite, she heard the church steeple clock chime the hour.

"I'd better get a move on! Reene and I were supposed to meet at the high school for instructions with the rest of the troops by one o'clock."

Lissa gathered her purchases and headed for her truck. As she maneuvered out of the tight parking space, she nearly collided with a black Lexus that came roaring out of nowhere. The driver, unrecognizable behind the tinted windshield, threw her the one finger salute out the window and sped off.

"Jerk!" Lissa hollered. "You're an idiot!"

Two nasty incidents in one day. Trouble always came in threes. She might not survive number three.

When she swung up the inn's driveway, Lissa could see Reene's wagon already parked in front of the barn. Sissy's tack, cleaned and polished, hung on the fence post. Reene looked up as she threaded the last roll of crepe paper through the front wheel.

"You had a good time! From the mustard all over your face, I'd say that you indulged yourself royally," Reene accused.

"Be nice to me. A stupid jerk almost clobbered me when I pulled into traffic. A big bad Lexus. It would've smushed my truck like an accordion. And I struck out at the auction. Never got there. I almost did a two-point landing on the pavement. Don't quote me, but I think someone accidentally-on-purpose gave me a nasty shove."

"Oh my God! Lissa, you're sure?"

"Not sure enough. Maybe someone's not-so-nice reaction to our recent discovery." She shrugged. "Or parade nerves. Let's forget it." Lissa walked over to the wagon for inspection.

"Your wagon looks fantastic," Lissa praised. "Crepe paper in all four wheels. White bunting and American flags go nicely with the harvest theme."

Reene had set up corn stalks, a bale of hay and a bushel basket full of pumpkins and gourds in the bed. A scarecrow perched in one corner.

"A big contrast with your outfit but it works," Lissa commented.

"That's what I thought too. Did you make up your mind for your costume? We're leaving in twenty minutes!"

"O ye of little faith," Lissa scolded. "I'm going with my Frontier Scout motif. Besides, I'm a quick-change artist. I'll wear my Western leather tunic trimmed with fringe, cowboy hat and trusty six guns. The heck with dignity. I'd better scoot! Coming?"

"Almost ready. I want to polish the brass a bit more before we head out."

When they finally headed down Breckenridge Road, Reene presented an impression of a proper English governess, who just happened to pick up a scruffy Frontier Scout as her escort, driving her colorful wagon to town.

"Lissa, we'd better take the carriage road. Roads near the center of town have already been blocked off."

"I totally agree. Besides, we don't want parade-goers to see us in our finery too soon."

When they reached the big parking lot at the high school, participants were starting to form in order of step off. The color guard, Westbrook High's marching band, cheerleaders, and Cub Scouts made up the first group. Town officials and V.I.P.'s, and floats sponsored by local businessmen, came next. Noisy fire engines and the volunteer firemen would join them near the back of the parade.

Waiting for their cue, Lissa dismounted and watched the cheerleaders as the girls collected their pompoms and formed two lines. After nearly thirty years, she still felt a pang of envy that she hadn't been chosen as a cheerleader in high school. Not for lack of trying. She practiced cheers until she lost her voice, cart wheeled all over her father's precious lawn and pasted a smile on her face while she marched in front of the judges. In the end she missed the cut by two lousy points.

But horses, bless their hearts, had saved her self-esteem. Now there was something special she could do. She patted Bravo's neck.

"I learned to ride and love horses more than life, and that's all that counts," she murmured.

Bravo turned his head to look at her as if he understood, but Lissa wasn't fooled. He was nosing her, hoping she had some treats hidden in her leather tunic.

A piercing whistle sounded. Peggy Simms, clipboard in hand, signaled the groups to start. Lissa could hear the band begin the drum cadence and a few moments later, "Stars and Stripes Forever" resounded loud and clear. One by one the groups left the parking lot until it was almost their time to step off.

"Wait until the fire engines have moved far enough ahead before you follow," Peggy cautioned. "If the air horns start blasting, your horses might go into flight mode."

Lissa nodded and walked her horse over to where Reene waited. "Not words we like to hear. How's Sissy doing? Is she getting antsy?"

"The blinders she's wearing are helping, but I'll feel more comfortable knowing you're right next to me. How are your parade nerves?"

"Never better," Lissa assured. "We'd better head out or we'll get left at the post!" Quickly she mounted and settled in her saddle, giving her horse encouraging pats.

Reene lightly touched Sissy with the reins and she stepped off smartly. Lissa allowed plenty of space between her horse and the gaily decorated wagon.

Along the parade route, young voices called "Horsey! Horsey!" Parents held children on their shoulders so they could get a better look. A scattering of applause greeted them as they walked on. Reene and Lissa waved and smiled. Lissa was so pleased at the response. She wanted people to remember the days when horsepower meant the norm and not the exception.

"I wonder if Ernie is watching," Lissa wondered. She knew the blacksmith shared her feelings.

She tried to scan the faces in the crowd, but she had her hands full with Bravo who was reacting to the noisy onlookers. He'd been in parades in the past, but he was still a horse. Anything could happen.

Especially as the guys on the fire truck were tossing candy into the crowd and kids were darting onto the road to pick up the treats.

"Hey, kids! Watch out!"

A tall clown in a red checked shirt and baggy pants held up by loud plaid suspenders swaggered over to the boisterous kids who'd scooped up most of the candy. Carrying a red metal bucket with FIRE printed on it in big white letters, he held the bucket high over the kids' heads.

"Get ready to get wet!"

The kids screamed and tried to back away, but they were too late. The clown hurled the contents of the bucket directly at them. Instead of soaking water, colored confetti rained down on their heads.

"Afraid of a little paper?" the clown jeered while he scampered down the road in search of new victims.

Across the street, another clown was working the crowd. Short and stout, his trousers fit tightly across his belly. Purple fright wig askew, sweat running down his cheeks, he dashed back and forth squirting seltzer water at unsuspecting spectators.

An old red fire truck rolled down the street, an Emmett Kelly look-alike at the wheel. He wore a straw hat with a huge sunflower pasted on the front. His over-sized gloves made driving difficult. Other clowns leaped on and off the truck when they needed more supplies or a breather.

As the fire truck moved farther down the road, Stephen Marshall watched from the sidelines. A psychedelic clown wearing white face, a huge bulbous nose and painted on eyebrows, burst out of the onlookers and headed toward him. The clown slithered in and around floats and marchers, honking a horn strapped to a box around his waist. He dug into his box and threw candy to the crowd while he capered up and down the street.

An orange wig, complete with wings and a little derby hat, perched on top of his head. He wore a wild orange and yellow plaid suit, a large green bow at his neck and a matching green cummerbund around his middle. Large white gloves and floppy white shoes completed his costume.

"Over here! Over here!" someone yelled. The clown made a face and wagged his index finger back and forth. Then he continued moving in Stephen's direction. The little girl in front of Stephen became frightened as the clown advanced purposefully toward her. She clung to her mother's leg and ducked her head.

Stephen felt sorry for the young child. Clowns were scary to many children. He leaned down and whispered to her. "Don't be scared. I'll bet he has a treat for you."

When he straightened up, the clown almost loomed in his face. Startled, Stephen stepped back and looked directly into the clown's eyes. Surprisingly, the clown winked at him. He decided to join in the fun.

"Do you have a piece of candy for me?" he wheedled in his best little boy voice.

In response, the clown honked his horn and shook his head back and forth. With a great flourish, he waved his arm and a bunch of flowers popped dramatically out of his sleeve. He gave the flowers to the little girl who was still hiding behind her mother. The girl snatched the flowers and stuck her nose into them.

"No fair!" she yelled. "They're plastic!" Disgusted, she shoved them into her mother's hands.

In mock horror, the clown's eyes grew wide and his jaw dropped. Hands on hips, he stared at the child. Then he fished in his huge pockets and dug out a colorful beaded necklace. Gently, he placed the necklace over the little girl's head.

"Oh, it's beautiful!" she cried. "Thank you! Look, Mummy!"

Now the clown turned his attention back to Stephen who was enjoying the byplay. The clown reached into his box and presented Stephen with the requested candy.

"Almond Joy! My favorite! I'll enjoy this. Thank you."

Stephen bowed ceremoniously and the clown returned his bow. The clown winked again. As Stephen unwrapped the chocolate and popped it into his mouth, the clown honked his horn loudly again and skipped off through the crowd.

To the crowd's delight, Bravo pranced like he'd performed in parades every week. In between prances, Lissa waved a small American flag.

"Look! There's Tom!" Reene pointed excitedly.

"Which one is he? I see a bunch of guys dressed as clowns, but with those white faces and wild clothes I can't tell who's who."

"The one in the red checked shirt."

"Uh-oh. He's coming this way. I wonder what he's up to."

Tom jogged up to the horse and wagon. He patted Sissy's neck and crooned, "Nice horsey, nice horsey," loud enough for everyone to hear. Then he jumped on the side of the wagon, his right foot balanced precariously on the hub of the wheel, and grabbed the back of the seat.

"Hey, lady! Can you spare a kiss?"

Reene turned to speak to him but before she could get a word out, Tom kissed her slowly on the lips. Then he leaped off the wagon leaving her open-mouthed and blushing.

"Thanks, lady. I might be back!" Then he ran to catch up with his buddies.

Amid the laughter, Reene, her face redder than the stripes on Lissa's flag, tried to regain her composure. The crowd ate it up and hollered for more.

Lissa prayed her mortified friend wouldn't glance her way or she'd fall off her horse in hysterics. Lissa cheered Tom's sweet, romantic gesture. She was a sucker for romance.

"Dang!" she sighed, "Like those movie cowboys of yesteryear, the only one I'm kissing is my horse!"

They had barely progressed a few yards when the parade abruptly came to a halt. The band stopped playing and the flatbed truck carrying the Boy Scouts and their leader idled behind the contingent of cheerleaders.

Probably some minor snafu ahead. Lissa relaxed in her saddle. Suddenly she saw one of the emergency vehicles pull out of line. With its siren wailing and lights flashing, it snaked its way down the street.

"What's happened?" Reene asked, struggling to keep her horse calm. The siren had spooked Sissy who was now jigging in the traces.

"I can't tell. People are milling around so I can't see. Oh, wait! Firemen have jumped out of their truck and are running over to the side of the road. Something's happened to a spectator!"

"Can you see Tom? Is he with them?"

"No...yes!" Lissa stood in her stirrups. "All the firemen are clustered around. Maybe someone's had a heart attack."

All at once things started happening. The parade began moving again. The band hurriedly launched into a rousing march and the majorettes twirled their batons. But Lissa could see a police officer directing the parade. He wore a grim expression and obviously wanted to get the marchers on their way as quickly as possible.

Lissa leaned over to Reene. "It doesn't look good. I think the chief of police is involved and I can see someone being loaded into the ambulance."

"Oh, no! I hope it's no one we know."

From the safety of a narrow alleyway between two buildings, the clown stood trembling with fear and exhilaration at the commotion she had caused. She listened to the siren's wail as it grew faint. Everything had worked out perfectly. Her disguise had been a masterstroke. No face or voice for anyone to identify.

"What does the well-dressed murderer wear these days?" she smirked. "A cropped white tee and Capri pants. *Tres chic.*" She stripped off the clown garb and hurriedly stuffed the clothes into a trash bag hidden underneath some boards. Wrenching a nondescript straw carryall from the trash bag, she pulled out sanitary wipes.

"Shit, this white face makeup is creepy," she muttered. "No wonder kids are scared of clowns."

A pair of straw sandals replaced the floppy shoes. Transformation accomplished, the fright-wigged clown ceased to exist.

After a cautious check to ensure there were no passersby, she emerged from the alley as a confident, glowing woman and sauntered down the sidewalk. She paused before a few storefronts and casually purchased a cup of hazelnut coffee with whipped cream at Books 'n Bagels.

Sipping her coffee, she thought of the man she had just poisoned. By the time the ambulance reached the hospital, all the medicine in the world would not save Stephen. She was finally free.

Free! Free at last!

Then she remembered the man who had uttered those impassioned words. "His idiotic rhetoric didn't change a thing! Gunned down by a racist of another color." For a moment, her face darkened.

"I've eliminated Stephen from my life. All I have to do now is show the proper amount of sympathy while agreeing 'Isn't it a shame'?"

With each passing moment, her mood brightened. She couldn't believe how easy it was. He was so pathetic. 'Have you got a candy for me?'

She took a final sip of her coffee. *Stupid bastard. And no one can prove a thing.*

Chapter 29

'Tragedy at Yankee Homecoming Day Parade', Lloyd read as he sipped his morning coffee. "Didn't a would-be Julia Child win the best apple pie contest?" He had heard murmurs about this in the coffee shop, but wasn't sure what had happened. His eyes widened in disbelief when he read the next paragraph.

Prominent businessman Stephen Marshall, 58, of New York collapsed yesterday while watching the Yankee Homecoming parade. Paramedics responded to the scene and tried unsuccessfully to resuscitate him. Marshall was transported to Houston-Adams Memorial Hospital, where he was pronounced dead on arrival. Pending an autopsy, cause of death has not yet been determined.

"Too bad. He was a decent guy. I wonder how the heartbroken widow, or should I say former grass widow, is holding up?"

Lloyd reached for his phone and called her private number, but she didn't pick up. Minutes later he locked his office door and headed toward Andrea's apartment. He didn't believe in coincidences and Stephen's death was too coincidental.

"Morning, Andrea. Taking the day off, I see. Are condolences or congratulations in order?"

Lloyd raised an eyebrow at the sight of Andrea curled on the love seat, feet tucked under her, a notepad balanced easily on her legs. "Evidently I don't need to console you too much, do I? Hard at work on Stephen's eulogy?"

She slammed the notepad down on the glass top coffee table. "You are an insensitive ass. You know I cared about him."

"Don't perjure yourself, Andrea. This is me you're talking to."

"Cut me some slack, Lloyd. If you remember our days together, I'm not *that* cold-blooded," she reminded. "I always had warm feelings for Stephen—if you remember."

"And if I remember, you nearly had a meltdown when I told you he was staying in town." Lloyd poured a glass of sparkling water from her wet bar.

"This damn campaign has me on edge. Purely a case of nerves. And I did care about him," Andrea insisted. "I don't appreciate your cross-examining me."

"Interesting choice of words. Like you are rehearsing for the witness stand."

"You definitely have an overactive imagination, Lloyd. Do you have to take everything I say so literally?"

"Ordinarily, no. But your ire was roused whenever Stephen's name was mentioned. You didn't have anything to do with his, shall we say, dispatch, did you?"

"What a rotten thing to say! Of course not!"

Lloyd lowered his glass and watched her intently. He knew Andrea's penchant for twisting the truth if it were to her benefit.

"I did love the man. We were married for five years."

"Andrea, me darlin', is it a little bit of the Blarney you're feedin' me?"

"All right, all right! You can drop the damn brogue. So I'm not totally devastated he's dead. So what?"

He was certain she was lying. But he decided to play his full hand.

"And how would you be feelin' about the famous Civil War letters being discovered at the 'thriving bed and breakfast'?"

"Why would I give a damn about some old love letters?"

"Love letters, is it? And how would you be knowin' that?"

"I must have heard that old harpy, Mrs. Long, talking about it. She's been bragging all over town that these insipid letters are priceless historic finds. Priceless? They're disgusting!"

"I suppose, from your perspective, you would call them disgusting. As the love letters were from your great-great grandmother to the man she eventually married, I abhor your lack of sentiment. The fact that she was Black and he was White complicated matters quite a bit, I'd say. I imagine you've been terrified all these years someone would connect the dots. Like I did."

He could see her mind racing. She turned to face him, her face gray with fear and resignation.

"Clever boy. How long have you known?"

"Not as long as you might think. But an elderly aunt helped piece it together. If truth be told, it's a fascinating saga when you come right down to it."

"Fascinating!" she cried. "I told you it's disgusting! I've spent a lifetime denying what I am."

"Did Stephen guess the truth too? Is that why you did him in?"

"I told you I had nothing to do with that!" Now her face was white as the walls. "Tell me everything!"

"My great aunt Alda is spending her last days at the Whispering Pines nursing home in Southwick. Actually, I am quite fond of the old girl. She's one of the few relatives whose company I can stand. Anyway, the dear lady was in a reminiscing mood the last time I visited. She recounted an intriguing tale. I was astounded to hear we have a link that neither of us ever dreamed. If memory serves me correctly, it involves a killing that's gone unsolved for over one hundred years."

"I can't wait to hear your aunt's version of this fairy tale."

"As you wish, Madame Mayor." He saw her face flame with anger and he softened his tone. "Andrea, I don't really care what you've done. But if we handle this situation correctly, we both will get what we want." Seeing her puzzled look, he continued before she could speak.

"According to Auntie Alda, her mother's sister, who is not so fondly remembered as Mad Catherine, was insanely jealous of Josephine Taylor. Rightly or wrongly, Mad Catherine convinced herself that Josephine stole her lover. To exact her revenge she came up with the perfect solution: she murdered your great-great grandmother and made it look like an accident. No one ever suspected or questioned the accident. So my sweet, we are almost related in a perverse sort of way. What do you think of my fairy tale now?"

"It's outrageous! That's what I think! What a crock!" Andrea raged. "You actually believe this cock and bull story told by your ancient aunt? No wonder she's in a nursing home!"

"I realize you'd like to believe these are the rantings of an old woman not playing with a full deck. Nonetheless, Auntie Alda is in full possession of her faculties. To use another cliché, she has a mind like a steel trap. She may have embellished the story a bit over time, but she showed me proof positive that she spoke the truth."

"Show me this alleged proof," she snapped.

"If I may borrow your favorite phrase, 'don't be an ass'. Obviously, I don't carry it with me. Besides, I wouldn't want anything to happen to it. It might accidentally get destroyed or stolen."

"You don't trust me too much, do you?"

"In a word? No." He softened his voice. "What really happened with Stephen? Why did you kill him? Tell me the truth for once."

Her face crumpled and her body sagged with resignation. "Not too long ago he insisted on taking me out to dinner. When he came in for a nightcap, I found out the real reason he'd been camped on my trail. Stubborn bastard wanted us to get back together again. I refused. He kept badgering me to tell him why we broke up. He wouldn't let it go. Finally I lost my temper and blurted out the truth."

"I gather he didn't take the news too well?"

"He tried to convince me I was overwrought. That no one would care that I'm Black. When I told him how wrong he was, he backed off."

"Stephen was an honorable man, Andrea. I'm sure he would have respected your wishes."

"I couldn't take the chance! I've worked too hard to get where I am."

"Didn't you stop to think that committing homicide might put your political plans on hold? By hanging onto your past, you have painted yourself into a corner."

"You don't understand any more than he did! And I'll ask you the same question. How do you feel knowing you've slept with a Black woman? That I never told you the truth either?"

"Actually, I don't care. We were speaking of telling the truth, weren't we?"

"You shit, you have all the answers," Andrea growled. "Now what? Do you intend to turn me in? March me off to the police station like a bounty hunter with his fugitive?"

"Although that does have a certain cachet, I have another plan in mind. I want you to marry me, Andrea," Lloyd said.

"Marry you? Are you out of your mind?" she demanded.

"Actually, I'm reasonably sane. This is the best solution for both of us. If it should come to it, I can't testify against you and vice versa. Marital privilege, I believe it's called."

"I know what it's called," she snapped. "I have no intention of marrying anyone. Tell me. What's in it for you?"

"After the election, First Husband has a decided flow to it. Consider the publicity. Separated lovers reunite after so many years. Think of it as a marriage of convenience if it makes it more palatable for you," Lloyd said casually. "We may rekindle an old flame."

Conflicting emotions flew across Andrea's face. She knew she was caught like a fly in a web. But sometimes the clever fly could outwit the spider.

"Don't get your hopes up. Say whatever you like. I'll agree with any scenario you dream up."

"I can see we're going to make a beautiful couple," Lloyd said sarcastically. "In the meantime, I will procure a flashy engagement ring. I can't compete with the rock Stephen gave you. However, I *can* provide you with an alibi."

Lloyd opened his wall safe and removed his current will. He set it aside with the letter he had just finished. In a separate envelope he inserted a photocopy of a tattered newspaper clipping his aunt had given him. The clipping, Josephine Williams' obituary, had vile comments and rambling insults scrawled in the margins. His aunt had found it among her mother's private papers and kept it all these years. Reading between the lines, it was Mad Catherine's declaration of murder.

After rereading the will and letter for changes or errors, he put both in a manila folder. Next week, he'd have them notarized. He planned to leave specific instructions with his lawyer just in case anything happened to him,

"I may find it expedient to drop a few hints during future conversations with Andrea. It may keep her from killing me like she did poor Stephen." He tucked the folder into the safe, closed the door and spun the dial.

"Perhaps I should hire a bodyguard. Or a food taster."

Chapter 30

Police Chief Paul Frechette was not a happy man. He had just received the Medical Examiner's report concerning Stephen Marshall's cause of death. He had expected the results to show heart failure or a blood clot, typical of an older man who led a sedentary lifestyle. He never anticipated this verdict: 'Cause of death: cyanide poisoning'.

Stephen Marshall had been murdered.

Chief Frechette frowned as he read further. Method of ingestion: cyanide contained in a mixture of chocolate and coconut. Almonds were also present in the stomach contents.

"Good God! This poor bastard died eating a piece of candy! Either the candy itself became poisoned at the factory or the poison was somehow injected into the candy."

He remembered horror stories of children dying from eating tainted candy on Halloween. Many of the stories were urban legends, but much to his disgust some parents had actually poisoned their own kids.

Paul shook his head. *I'll never understand that kind of sick killing.* Now he was dealing with a case of premeditated murder. Westbrook was hardly a high crime area. This town had seen homicides in the past, but not on his watch.

He reached for the phone and dialed State Trooper Sergeant David Edmondson. Time to delegate his authority. Dave, who had grown up in Westbrook, still lived in town. Paul had known him for over ten years and they'd worked well together.

"Hey, Dave. How you doin' these days?"

"Protecting and serving. You?"

"Can't complain. Only seven years before I can retire. Listen, this isn't a social call. I've got a nasty murder case."

"Aren't they all?"

"Yeah, but not like this one. Poisoned. Figured it for a heart attack. Just my luck," he snorted, cradling the receiver against his shoulder.

"More like the vic's bad luck."

"Yeah, poor choice of words. *His* bad luck." He picked up the ME's report and read high points to the trooper.

"Be there in about an hour," Dave said.

Chief Frechette broke the connection and tossed the file into his in-basket. Dave was a good man and had that state cop mentality that irritated the rank and file. People were intimidated by his over six-foot height and presence. If anyone could solve this case in a hurry, it would be Dave.

Chief Frechette conducted his department, as well as his personal life, on a no-nonsense basis. His hero was Joe Friday, but he'd never admit it under pain of torture.

"I want this case wrapped up, and fast," Paul growled. "I won't stand for any wacko putting my town on the map and getting off on an insanity defense."

"A clown at the Homecoming parade gave the vic a piece of candy and two minutes later the victim collapsed. Have you any idea who this clown might be?" Dave asked. He was slouched in a leather swivel chair in Paul's private office, his long legs casually stretched out.

"None. The guy disguised himself so well that no one I spoke with could even tell if it was a man *or* a woman," Paul replied.

Dave read the report to the end. "There were two main witnesses, a mother and her little girl. Do you have their address? Did you get a statement?"

"Yeah, I got a damn statement! It's all here in the file. They thought it was all part of the act. You can read what they said, but I'm sure you'll want to talk to them. The name's Carson."

"They're first on my list. Have your boys taped off the scene?"

"Damn right we did!" Paul snapped.

"Temper, temper," the trooper replied with a slight smile. "I'll mosey out to the site before I call on the mother and daughter."

"Those two women who run the new B&B knew the guy pretty well. He's been staying there for over a month. Add them to your list. Give them a call to expect your visit. And keep me posted," Paul said.

"Yes, Father," the trooper said. As he went out, he threw the chief a mock salute.

"Pain in the ass Staties!" Paul hollered. "You think you're God's gift to law enforcement!"

Edmondson glanced down at the directions to the Carson's home and then checked his wristwatch. *Too early for the daughter to be home from school. I'll give the crime scene the once-over.*

When he arrived at the common, he parked his blue and gray Crown Vic and walked over to the section cordoned off by yellow and black crime scene tape. Too many footprints—nearly impossible to get a good match. The black and whites had gone over this small patch of ground and found nothing. He canvassed the grounds, running a practiced eye over every tree stump and blade of grass. He saw nothing that suggested a crime had taken place.

He checked his watch again. It was time to go. He hated this part of the job. Kids either refused to talk or babbled like brooks.

When he pulled up in front of the small ranch, Dave saw a young girl playing in the front yard. She stopped and pelted into the house as he emerged from the police car.

"Good God," he muttered. "From the look on her face, she's telling her mother that a big, scary giant is coming to crunch her bones."

He knocked on the front door, and a young woman greeted him.

"Mrs. Carson? I'm Sgt. David Edmondson of the State Police," he said, producing his ID and badge for inspection. "I believe Chief Frechette informed you I'd be interviewing you and your daughter."

"Yes, of course. Please come in."

He followed her into the living room. Mrs. Carson sat down on the sofa and he perched uncomfortably opposite her on a ladder-back chair.

"I'd like to discuss what you saw the day of the parade. Then I'd like to talk to your daughter to get her impression of what happened."

"Heather is locked in her bedroom at the moment," she said ruefully. "Don't worry, I'll convince her to talk to you. I read in the paper that the police are looking for someone dressed as a clown."

"That's correct. Can you give me a description of the person you saw?"

"I would say he—well, I'm only assuming it was a he. All the clowns I've ever seen were men. Actually, the clown dressed in such a way I couldn't be sure of the gender."

"Did the clown speak to you?"

"No. He just honked a horn on a box around his waist. He used hand gestures, but never spoke."

"Probably why he chose that disguise. Could you estimate height and build?"

"I'd say five-foot-eight or five-foot-nine. With the baggy clothes, I couldn't tell the build. Wait. I did notice that the wrists were small."

"You couldn't see any distinguishing features? Color of eyes or hair?"

"I think the eyes were hazel. He wore a fright wig that completely covered his hair. He wore white face paint so I couldn't see if he had any scars or moles."

"Let's move on then. Can you tell me exactly what happened that day?"

"Heather and I were watching the parade. We had found a good spot on the edge of the road. The parade had stopped and we noticed this clown come through the crowd. He pointed at someone behind us, a nice looking older man. The man asked the clown if he had any candy for him, but the clown ignored him and came over to us. He performed the flowers-out-of-the sleeve trick, but Heather wasn't impressed. Then he dug into his box and pulled out a plastic beaded necklace. He put it on Heather and then he reached in the box again and took out a piece of candy. A bite size Almond Joy like the ones I give out at Halloween."

"The clown didn't offer this candy to you or your daughter?"

"No, he gave it to the man, honked his horn a couple of times and ran back into the parade. I could see him dancing in and out of the floats. Then he disappeared. I didn't think a thing of it as other clowns in the parade were playing to the crowd."

"Did the victim say anything?"

"Yes, he did. He said 'My favorite candy. I'm going to enjoy this'. I guess he ate it right away. The parade had started moving again and I turned to watch."

"Did he say anything else?"

"No." She nervously rubbed her arms before continuing. "I heard him grunt as if he'd been hit in the stomach. Then his arm bumped me. When I turned around, his face had turned white. He put his hands to his throat. I realized he was choking."

The trooper could see she was close to tears. He gave her a moment to compose herself. "Anyone else see that he was in trouble?"

"Yes, a few other people on either side of us tried to help. One of them tried CPR."

"Do you know these people?"

"I'm afraid not. Haven't they come forward?"

"Not yet. Can you think of anything else you saw or heard that might be helpful?"

"Something about that clown is bothering me. Why don't you talk to Heather now? My memory might get a wake-up call."

"Yes, please," Dave smiled. "You might tell her that I'm not as bad as I look,"

"I'll be back with Heather if I have to break down her bedroom door."

Minutes later he wondered if the girl's mother could coax her out of her safe place. He'd had a few shouting matches on the wrong side of a door with his pre-teen daughter. At that instant, Mrs. Carson appeared with her hands firmly placed on her daughter's shoulders. The bedroom door had escaped destruction – this time.

"Heather, Sgt. Edmondson would like to speak to you for a little bit," she said, guiding her reluctant child into the room.

"Hi, Heather," he said in his friendliest tone. He remained seated so his height wouldn't further intimidate the young girl.

"Hello. I didn't see anything except the clown who gave me the necklace," she said breathlessly. "Can I go now?"

"You just got here! We've hardly had a chance to talk. Will you answer a few questions for me?"

"I guess so," she said resignedly and flung herself onto the sofa.

"I won't keep you too long. Did the clown talk to you or make any noises?"

"No, he honked his silly horn and made funny faces."

"Did you speak to the man standing behind you and your mother?"

"No. I was watching the parade all the time."

"Did you keep the necklace the clown gave you?"

"Yes, it's in my bedroom. Do you want to see it?"

"Yes, please, Heather."

The youngster leaped off the sofa, glad to escape to her bedroom once more. Dave could hear drawers opening and slamming. Then Heather ran back into the room and thrust the necklace into his hands.

"Here. I don't want it anymore. You can keep it."

"Why don't you want it anymore, Heather?"

"Because the clown who gave it to me killed that man."

"Thanks to you, Heather, this necklace might help me find out who did kill that man. I'll take it with me."

"That's good. Can I go now?" she asked again.

"Yes, you can. Will you tell your mother if you remember anything more?"

"Yes, I will," she said, edging toward the doorway. "Cross my heart. Good-bye." She scooted out of the room so fast she nearly left skid marks on the floor.

"Mrs. Carson, I've noticed you watching me closely while I interviewed Heather. I hope you weren't afraid I'd upset her."

"Of course not. But I'm embarrassed to ask this. Do only men have an Adam's apple?"

"Actually, men *and* women have them. It just sticks out a bit too much in our throats. Not too attractive," he replied lightly. "Please don't feel embarrassed. Most people would never notice a detail like that."

"Despite what you've just told me, I'm quite certain, sergeant, that your murderer is a woman. Her throat was smooth as a baby's bottom, even under the greasepaint. And she forgot to cover her earlobes. I could see holes where the lobes had been pierced."

Trooper Edmondson sat in his car for a few moments examining the cheap plastic necklace he had placed in a baggie. The necklace, twenty inches long, was made of small colored beads strung on nylon thread. Anyone could pick up this kind of thing at any novelty shop or discount department store.

"Not much chance a decent fingerprint could be lifted off those beads. But the guys in Forensics wet their pants over a challenge like this. I can narrow my search to a woman, if Mrs. Carson is right and I'm sure she is. Women pick up on that stuff. A woman who bought a cheap necklace and a bag of Almond Joys. And keeps a clown suit in her closet. No pressure."

He grabbed his cell and punched in a familiar number. Time to drop by the fire station for a little chat. He wheeled the Crown Vic away from the curb and headed back to town.

The local firefighters gave him nothing new to go on. They didn't have a clue who the extra clown might be.

"At first we were a bit pissed off to think someone else was stealing our thunder," said an older grizzled veteran. "But hell, it was all in fun. We've done this routine at dozens of parades and picnics. We never imagined anything could go wrong."

"We did wonder why the guy never said a word to us the whole time," one man offered. "I gave him a shout, but he ran off honking that stupid horn."

"If we remember anything new that might help, Dave," promised the older man, "we'll definitely give you a call."

209

Lissa disconsolately shuffled around the kitchen. "I'm in total shock. What a terrible thing to happen! And it's our fault! We encouraged him to go to that parade! 'Come watch us, Stephen. It'll cheer you up, Stephen!' Dear God! If only we'd seen something!"

"I understand how you feel, but we're not at fault," Reene insisted.

Lissa grabbed a bunch of Kleenex and wiped her eyes. "You're right," she choked. "I just feel so helpless. Do you think he had a heart attack or stroke? I can't stand the thought of him suffering."

Two days had passed since Stephen Marshall had been stricken. From what Tom told them, the firemen, two of whom were paramedics, had doggedly worked on him until the ambulance arrived to transport him to the hospital.

"I wish I could tell you what you want to hear. But Tom doesn't know any more information than we do."

"He was such a nice man!" Lissa cried. "He so enjoyed his stay here! He loved taking long walks in the woods and exploring the local shops. Just the other day I noticed him hanging out by the paddocks, watching the horses. Stephen told me he hadn't felt so relaxed in years."

"Try to hold onto those thoughts." Reene walked over to her friend and put her arm around Lissa's shoulders. "I wish we could help to ease his passing. We don't have a clue whether he had any family or where he lived."

Lissa sighed heavily. "Chief Frechette phoned about an hour ago that he'd gotten in touch with Stephen's secretary. I gather she was distraught and wasn't able to help much. Evidently he didn't have any children, but he does have a younger brother who's coming to claim the body."

Tears spilled down her face. "I don't know what's wrong with me!" she sobbed. "I hardly knew this man, yet I'm devastated."

"You're reacting this way because you've suffered a previous loss. We both have. Our husbands and your beloved horse Indy. It's only been a few years. This dear man touched our lives in a special way and now he's gone. We can take comfort in knowing his last few weeks were happy ones."

Lissa snuffled into her tissue. "You're right. That's some consolation. Not only is it a new shock, but it brings back the grief as well."

The persistent ringing of the phone interrupted them. "Let the machine pick up," Lissa mumbled.

"No, you stay here and have a good cry. I'll answer it."

Given permission to bawl her head off, Lissa's tears dried up. Frustrated, she yanked open cupboard doors in search of something fattening.

"If only we had some sticky buns! Darn Reene and her healthy oat bran muffins!" She started to fill the kettle when Reene returned.

"Officer David Edmondson—actually, he's a State Trooper—wanted to make sure we'd be home. He needs to talk with us about our 'relationship' with Steve this afternoon."

"Oh, Lord. When will this ever end?"

"I'm sure it's the usual procedure. He's going to take our statement and then search Stephen's room."

Arms full of wildflowers and cattails, Lissa spotted the cruiser marked State Police as she was returning from the fields. A law-abiding citizen all her life, she always felt guilty, no matter what she was doing, whenever a police officer appeared. Involuntarily she felt a quiver of fear. She dreaded meeting him face to face. After her meltdown that morning, she still had the shakes.

She flew into the house. "Reene, that State Trooper is here! Put that dust mop down and get over here before I confess I shot JFK."

When Lissa opened the coffin door, that guilty feeling rose up in her throat as she gaped at the police officer who filled the entire doorway.

"Good afternoon, ma'am," he greeted, flashing his badge. "My name is Sgt. David Edmondson of the State Police. I believe you were expecting me."

"Yes, please come in."

Lissa smothered a laugh when he almost knocked his police cap off on the low door frame. He had the good grace to laugh out loud. That small gesture put her at ease.

Reene appeared at her side a moment later. "Shall we sit in the Gathering Room?" she suggested. "It's much more comfy in there."

Sgt. Edmondson followed them through the dining room. He glanced around the room for a few moments before asking his first question.

"Did you know the deceased for very long?"

Lissa winced before she answered. "Not long at all. A little over three weeks. Right, Reene?"

"Yes. He arrived here on August seventeenth with an open-ended reservation."

"Didn't that strike you as odd?"

"Yes, it did, but it's not unheard of," Reene replied. "We were so thrilled to have a paying guest who wanted an extended stay."

"Did you ask for references?" he continued.

"References?" Both women looked puzzled. "No, we didn't feel references were necessary. That's not our policy," Reene stated firmly.

"Did he ever tell you why he made such a reservation?"

"He said he needed a break from work," Lissa replied. "And it seemed to help. We noticed how much more relaxed Mr. Marshall became the longer he stayed. Mostly he kept to himself. It wasn't until recently that he mentioned his private life."

"In what way?"

"He told us at breakfast one day that he wanted to impress a lady," Reene said. "Lissa recommended a restaurant, but he wouldn't tell us the identity of the 'lady'. He didn't want to risk his luck by telling us any more about her."

"Which restaurant did you recommend?"

"The 1761 Old Mill in Westminster," Lissa answered. "Evidently my recommendation didn't help because he came in late that night and left us a note the next morning not to expect him for breakfast. That was so unusual for him, we knew something went wrong."

"Did he confirm your suspicion?"

"Not in so many words. He begged off, saying only that it was a disappointing evening and he'd rather not talk about it. We respected his privacy so we didn't push it," Lissa said.

Lissa decided to confront the officer. "Sergeant, Reene and I are overwhelmed by this horrible crime. Can you tell us how Stephen, that is, Mr. Marshall died? Not knowing is causing us great grief."

"I'm sorry, it's against procedure to give out that information. If you don't mind, I'd like to inspect his room now," the sergeant said, closing his notebook.

"Not a problem. I'll take you up," Reene volunteered.

Upstairs, Reene opened the door to Stephen's room. However, she definitely wasn't prepared for what she found.

The room looked as though a cyclone had passed through. Clothes were tossed on the floor, bed linens were ripped off the bed, bureau drawers hung open and toilet articles were strewn all around the room.

Reene gasped and the sergeant muttered something under his breath.

"I assumed you knew enough not to disturb this room," he snapped.

"I beg your pardon, Officer, but we had nothing to do with this mess," she snapped back. "We didn't touch anything in his room since he was killed. He must have left it in this condition."

The trooper's body language warned her he didn't believe her explanation. Reene stood her ground. Without another word, he began examining Stephen's clothing and personal articles.

"If you'll excuse me, Officer, I have horses to bring in."

Edmondson nodded and continued his search. As Reene closed the door, she saw him putting car keys, a hairbrush and a Swiss Army knife into an evidence bag.

She almost ran down the stairs, shaken by her encounter with the officer and the chaotic condition of the bedroom. But if she'd told him the truth, he'd lock them both up and throw away the key.

Trooper Edmondson was not amused. After thoroughly searching the room, he had a few parting words with Lissa who continued to insist they had touched nothing in the victim's room. The slight quaver in her voice told him she was holding something back.

"I'm not satisfied with my search. Or your answers," he finally grunted. "I may come back. Do *not* to touch anything else!"

With a curt nod, he strode out of the inn. Looking back at her anxious face, he knew she had gotten his message.

Before Edmondson returned to his office, he stopped at Forensics to drop off Marshall's hairbrush. He was assured of results within a day.

Sitting at the computer in his cubbyhole, Edmondson hunted and pecked as he searched for answers. "Now let's see what this guy's background looks like. Was this guy worth a fortune someone couldn't wait to inherit?" Money and sex were the most common reasons to kill. Maybe he had a girlfriend stashed somewhere and she had another guy on the side.

"Interesting. Ms. Mayor-wannabe, Andrea Wilson, is the vic's ex. No children salivating to collect their inheritance, so that angle is a wash. She's definitely next on my list. God, I love this job."

"Ms. Wilson, Sgt. David Edmondson of the State Police is here to see you."

Janice Navin's professional voice intruded on Andrea's busy morning.

Andrea's hand tensed on the receiver, but she forced her voice to sound warm and natural.

"Please tell him to come in, Janice. I'll be in conference until further notice."

With a professional model's smile, Janice escorted the trooper into Andrea's office. Her manner clearly showed she wished she could linger in the hallway and listen in.

"Janice, I'd appreciate your running the errands we talked about," Andrea said pointedly.

"Yes, of course, Ms. Wilson."

The sergeant took a seat across from her desk. "Ms. Wilson, I need to ask you a few questions regarding your ex-husband's murder."

"Of course," she said graciously. "It was such a shock to hear that news. I'm ready to answer your questions as best I can."

She forced herself to relax into her high backed leather chair and smiled at the officer.

"Did you have a cordial relationship with Mr. Marshall?"

"Yes, I did. We had an amicable divorce and we've corresponded from time to time."

"When did you see him last?"

"About a week before his death. Stephen took me to dinner. We had a pleasant evening. He came back to my place for a drink and left around two a.m."

"That's pretty late for one drink."

Andrea laughed lightly. "We talked about the old days and lost track of time."

"So you parted that night on friendly terms? Either of you stir up any bad memories?"

"Most assuredly, we did not. Stephen was a fine man. Unfortunately, things didn't work out between us."

"Can you tell me where you were on the day he was killed?"

"My fiancé, Lloyd Collins, and I spent the day in the Berkshires. We're both into outdoor fitness like many people these days."

"I will need to talk to him to confirm you story."

"That won't be a problem. I'll give you his number." She scribbled Lloyd's number on her business card and handed it to him.

"Regarding your relationship with your former husband, did you receive a large settlement at the time of the divorce?"

"More than adequate. Stephen's generous settlement enabled me to finance my mayoral campaign."

"Do you know if he had any enemies? Did he ever mention anyone threatening him?"

"Everyone makes enemies, Officer," she replied. "As a high profile Wall Street broker, he dealt with transactions involving thousands of dollars on a daily basis. Not all those dealings were successful. Naturally I'd assume some clients felt, shall we say, disgruntled."

"Could you think of any names? Anyone who might have had a grudge against him?"

"Not offhand. Stephen never mentioned any problems."

"Ms. Wilson, did you have any reason to wish him harm?"

"No officer, I didn't," Andrea answered levelly. "As I stated, Stephen and I had an amicable divorce. I held no animosity toward him."

Sgt. Edmondson's face remained impassive, giving her no clue as to what he might be thinking.

"Did either of you have any children from former relationships?"

"No, we did not. And when we were married, we decided not to have children due to our careers."

Her tone of voice suggested the meeting was over. He accepted the hint, closed his notebook and rose to leave.

"If you think of anything else that might help in my investigation, please don't hesitate to call," he advised as he handed her his card.

"I certainly will, Officer. As I said, I had no ill will toward Stephen and I want to see his killer brought to justice."

"Lord, deliver me from politicians," Edmondson muttered as he left her office. "And if she expects me to believe she likes to hike in the Berkshires and check out little birdies, I'm quitting the force tomorrow for my new career at McDonald's."

He slid into his cruiser. "Looks like I need to do some more digging. Time to take a field trip to New York. A little grunt work could bring some interesting results from Marshall's coworkers and acquaintances."

He placed a courtesy call to the New York State Police to let them know he would be in their jurisdiction and headed for the Great White Way.

From her office window, Andrea watched the trooper pull out of the parking lot. *I handled myself extremely well under his questioning,* she thought. Unfortunately, she couldn't read his official cop's interrogation face. Her smugness faded.

Should she call Lloyd and warn him to expect a visit from the trooper? She decided against it. Phone calls could be traced so easily. She didn't want that pompous cop delving into her records.

215

She and Lloyd had rehearsed their stories, and she was confident no incriminating discrepancies would screw them up. Andrea had no qualms her ever-lovin' fiancé could take care of himself.

"Too bad Lloyd had no reason to kill Stephen," Andrea muttered as she logged back onto her computer. "If Lloyd were languishing behind bars, I wouldn't have to marry him." *What rotten luck!*

"Lloyd, me darlin'," she mimicked, "you'd better watch your ass. There are other ways to break an engagement."

Chapter 31

To keep her mind off the terrible tragedy that had befallen Stephen, Lissa threw herself into preparations for the next phase of their plan. She was determined to haul the bronze marker idea out of limbo before their good intentions could get sidetracked again.

"I've just finished the first draft of the wording for our marker," Lissa said when Reene strolled into her office. "Want to give it the once-over?"

"I'd love to, but I'm sure it'll be letter perfect," Reene smiled, peeking over Lissa's shoulder to read the rough copy.

Historic Marker

Built in 1830 by Seth Williams, this farmhouse is important historically for two related reasons. In 1862, during the height of the Civil War, the Williams' farmhouse was used as a station to help Black slaves escape via the Underground Railroad. Recently discovered evidence confirms that Seth Williams' future daughter-in-law, former slave Josephine Taylor, acted as a spy for the Union Army. Ms. Taylor risked her life to bring vital information to the North. Mrs. Williams lived at the family homestead with her husband and son until her untimely death in 1875.

"Just right! You don't need to change any of the words. I do have a suggestion though. I'd put a Civil War cap with the crossed swords emblem and an American flag at opposite corners."

"Perfect! Those little touches will add a bit of patriotic charm. The marker does look a bit boring."

"Do we have a date for the official dedication?"

"No. I'm still waiting for the mayor's office to get back to me. In the meantime, I figured we could work together on the marker with John Fitch who's done such a fabulous job on all our signs."

"Did you call him?" Reene asked. "He may be too busy to finish the sign in time for the mayor to break open the champagne."

"I'm way ahead of you. I faxed a rough drawing to him yesterday. I wanted your verdict before I gave him the go-ahead. I'll call him today to make sure these additions won't cause a problem."

"I have the perfect spot for it," Reene said, "next to the coffin door on the farmer's porch. I'm sure Josey would prefer we put it on the barn, but the most logical spot is the house. And God forbid the mayor steps in horse poop."

"I'm leaning in that direction too. The plaque, not the horse poop. Speaking of the mayor, do we have to feed him again?"

Reene laughed from the bottom of her toes. "You are too funny! Lissa, can we forget about food for the moment? I've had this fantastic idea brewing to go along with the plaque dedication and I'm sure you'll want to do it too."

"Uh-oh! Why do I feel like Ethel Mertz trying to talk Lucy Ricardo out of another wacky stunt? What are you up to now?" Lissa demanded.

"We know from those letters Josey was a fantastic rider. As part of her job she often rode great distances to carry her messages. She wrote lovingly of her horse, Shiloh, and of the strong bond they shared. She was thrilled when Peter sent him home to Massachusetts after the war ended. I'd like us to recreate a ride like hers. We'd finish here at the inn just in time for Mayor Stuart to do his thing."

"It's the craziest idea I've ever heard of—and I love it!"

"I knew I could count on your sense of adventure. Here's my plan. We could do a five-mile loop using the carriage road and Main Street. For a big finish, we'll gallop the last few hundred yards up our driveway."

"That's perfect! If we rode any longer than five miles, we'd be too pooped to enjoy the ceremony. Should we wear costumes?"

"My thoughts: we could wear Union blue to represent the North. Or since this is all about Josey, maybe we should wear clothes similar to what she wore when she posed as a stable boy. Makes it more personal."

218

"I like your last idea better. I'd feel really stupid in a Union Army jacket and striped trousers. Not to mention that cap. We'll go with the stable boy motif. When the mayor's staff returns my call, I'll explain the details of our latest brilliant scheme. Hope the mayor will think we're helping instead of causing him aggravation. After all, he is in the midst of a campaign for reelection," Lissa reminded.

"The poor man hasn't had a minute's peace since we moved here. Cheer up! Remember, he's a politician. He's probably spent half his life smiling and schmoozing at parties, rallies and High Teas."

Lissa laughed in spite of Reene's reference to her High Tea. "I suppose we should check with Chief Frechette about us romping down the middle of town. If *you* ask nice, he might block off a few roads for us."

"I'm sure the Chief will welcome a happy distraction," Reene said. "The latest crazy rumor making the rounds speculated that Stephen had been whacked by the Mob. Maybe the ceremony will help the town return to normalcy."

"Lissa, good news," Reene said as she met Lissa in the kitchen. "Chief Frechette was kinda cranky, but gave us the go-ahead for the ride, once we set a date. I think he agreed so I'd go away. Isn't that great?"

One look at Lissa's face told Reene that nothing was great at the moment.

"What's wrong?" she asked sharply.

"Mrs. Long called me shortly after you left. I thought she called to let us know the date and time of the dedication. She told me someone tried to steal the letters."

"What? Is she sure?" Reene nearly dropped the olives she was putting in the cupboard.

"Mrs. Long is sure. Trust me. She put the letters under lock and key at the Town Hall and she has the only key. She went to remove them so they could be framed under glass and found the door to the office had been forced. Thankfully, the letters were still there. Something or someone must've interrupted the thief."

"Thank God she's okay. Are the police investigating?"

"She said they took a quick look around but they aren't too optimistic. No fingerprints or clues were found. In the meantime, she's going to figure out a better security system."

"No wonder the chief was preoccupied when I asked him if he could block off the streets for us. First the murder and now a break-in. Do you think there's any connection?"

Lissa nodded. "No doubt in my mind."

"What about the dedication? Is it still on?"

"I think so. But Mrs. Long was all shook up so I didn't press the point. I'll give her a few days and then call back. Gina has agreed to get us some publicity and John Fitch assured me the marker will be done by the end of the week. We're set for the Great Ride. And speaking of riding, I'd better get Brav in condition. I'll trot his fat fanny off every day. I haven't ridden as much as I'd like and we're both out of shape!"

"We'll train together. It'll be more fun for both the horses and us. Can we start tomorrow morning?"

"You've got a date, so long as we're back in time to greet our new guests. Thank God no reservations have been cancelled."

"Exactly. I feel awful about what happened to Steve, but our business has to survive."

"You know, Reene, we may have caused a domino effect by finding those long lost letters. If we'd known then what we know now..."

Lissa waited two days and contacted Mrs. Long. Much to her relief, the older woman had calmed down considerably since the break-in. In fact, she was eager to get the dedication underway before another attempted theft. She had locked the enlargement in a safe and had the door lock changed.

"I've decided the ceremony will take place on October the eleventh at the Historical Society," Mrs. Long declared. "I'm not comfortable waiting any longer."

"I still don't understand why anyone would want to steal those letters," Lissa said.

"Possibly someone had a secret to protect," she retorted. "Setting aside the monetary value of these papers, I'm not giving this disturbed person a second chance." She ended the call.

Lissa called Gina Richards next. "Gina, did you hear anything more about the attempted theft?"

"No, at the moment you know as much as I do. My police reporter hasn't filed anything new. Strange, isn't it?"

"*Strange* is the operative word these days. To drag out an old cliché, I think we've stirred up a hornet's nest."

"Don't worry too much about it. Let the police do their job," Gina advised. "Hopefully the would-be thief won't try again."

"Speaking of trying again, I just learned the dedication will take place at the Historical Society next week on the eleventh," Lissa said. "Mrs. Long wants to have the letters officially blessed and put under tighter security."

"That is good news. I'll put the date on my calendar and assign my feature person to cover it."

"Gina, I'd so hoped you'd join us! We couldn't have done it without you!" Lissa exclaimed.

"In that case, I believe my feature person will be reassigned."

"Wonderful! Just one more thing. Could you squeeze in a paragraph or two in your paper about your new best friends' latest escapade?"

"What on earth are you up to now?"

"Well, Reene had this fantastic idea that on the day of the marker dedication we'd ride hell-bent-for-leather, sort of, through town … only five miles really… to honor Josey in her role as a Civil War heroine. We're going to wear old clothes and everything, and so we thought … a little publicity never hurt anyone … if you could mention our jaunt in the *Times*, we'd be eternally grateful!" Lissa gabbled.

"Take a breath, for Heaven's sake! What a fabulous idea! Do you have a date for this hell-bent ride?"

"Not yet. I'm waiting for a call from the mayor's office. And I still have to convince him our plan will help him win re-election. I'll keep you posted."

"Mayor Stuart may not be thrilled, but he does need extra publicity. Don't worry. I'm sure I can find you some room in *my* inn. I'll see you both on the eleventh for the dedication of the letters and photograph."

Lissa slouched back in her chair. They could rely on Gina to play up their role in the discovery of the letters and champion their wild ride. But she wished she could tell Gina the real reason behind their hurry.

She longed to share their conviction that Josey's spirit was present at their inn. She knew Gina would keep an open mind. Unfortunately, there were too many skeptics who would either make morbid jokes or deride the notion altogether.

Like the thief, they too had a secret to protect.

On the morning after the long-awaited dedication ceremony, Reene turned to the Local News section of the *Hampshire Times*. The event had come and gone in a dizzying blur. Now she intently studied the colorful

221

photo above the headline. Gina's staff photographer had taken numerous shots, positioning the three women to their best advantage.

Civil War Artifacts Come Home

"'Reene Anderson and Lissa Martin, co-owners of the Barn Swallow Inn, present authentic Civil War letters and accompanying reproduction of Josephine Taylor Williams' portrait to Mrs. Ruby Long of Westbrook's Historical Society. The letters and picture will be available for viewing by the general public next week.'"

In the newspaper photo, she and Lissa had flanked Mrs. Long who grasped the precious letters as if afraid someone would take them from her. The framed photograph of Josey's portrait stood on a table in front of them. The dedication had lasted only a short time. They then adjourned to an adjacent room for a small reception.

"Lissa, did you see this?" Reene asked as Lissa returned from giving the horses their morning feed.

"Is that the paper? Are we on the front page in all our glory?" Lissa asked excitedly. Wisps of hay floating from her clothing and drifting around the room, she peered over Reene's shoulder,

"Well, the letters and Josey's picture are finally safe," Reene replied.

"Just shoot me already!" wailed Lissa. "I look ninety years old and fifty pounds overweight! Thank God this hideous photo—no offense—is buried on page ten."

"That's ridiculous," Reene said. "And you looked wonderful."

"I'm glad you think so. I am the most unphotogenic person on the face of the earth."

"You're impossible! By the way, I was a wreck the letters might disappear at the last minute. I didn't read any more stories in the *Times* about the theft, did you?"

"Only a little paragraph that the police are still investigating and a rehash of the attempt."

"Why do you suppose someone wanted to destroy the letters before they became public knowledge?"

"Because someone was afraid those letters would connect him, or her, to Stephen's murder?"

"Exactly. Too bad the cops didn't use the letters to set a trap. The thief would've snapped up the cheese."

"Brilliantly reasoned, Ms. Columbo. I wish we had taken notes when we had the chance. I remember the night we read each letter word for word. We were so entranced with the romantic story of the two young lovers. Who knew?"

"I wonder if Sgt. Edmondson has considered this angle."

"I have no idea. We should notify him. He did say to contact him if we remembered anything. Didn't he?"

"But we didn't actually remember this. We came to our own conclusion," Reene said coyly.

Lissa folded her arms across her chest as she regarded her friend. "So what you're saying is we can start investigating on our own without bothering to inform him of this pesky little detail?"

"I knew I could count on you."

"Don't count on me just yet. Look, if this escapade turns dangerous, I'm pulling the plug. Don't forget that Stephen is dead and we're not sure if it's connected or not. According to every detective novel I've ever read, amateur women sleuths end up on the wrong side of a gun."

"Not if we get the drop on them first. We've got a few days off between guests. Let's pore over those letters again, in detail this time. See if Mrs. Long will give us a private showing. We can spend more time hunting for clues."

"You know, Reene, if we had used our heads, we would've made copies of *all* the letters we've found. Then we'd have them at our fingertips."

"Excellent idea! But better late than never. After the dust has settled, we will get our own copies and put them in an embossed binder for guests to check out. Our personal Civil War exhibit."

"I know the perfect spot too," Lissa said. "Let's put it in the Gathering Room next to *Gone With the Wind*. An ideal complement to that famous book."

"Meanwhile, we're on a hunt for clues."

"Do we have to?" Lissa sighed. "I'm still basking in the glow of our latest accomplishment."

"Come on, don't wimp out on me now."

"Us wimps have our uses. But I'll call her. She'll either hang up in my face or promise to make us tea and cookies."

Chapter 32

Gina Richards studied the words on the screen in front of her. She had finished the first editorial draft on the merits of acknowledging Josephine Williams' heroic contributions to her country.

"Reene and Lissa will be extremely pleased. I believe I've captured Josephine's story. It reads lovely."

A Deserving Honor Finally Recognized

Over one hundred and fifty years ago, an unforgettable war divided this nation as never before, ending after four years of bloody conflict. In the South it was known as 'The War Between the States' while the North preferred the designation 'The War of the Rebellion'. Most of us simply call it the Civil War. No matter what the label, this terrible human tragedy evokes strong feelings to this day. Others rally with the stirring cry "The South will Rise Again!" Some say the South never recovered.

Slavery split our country apart. There were heroes and villains on both sides, but one fact continues unchallenged: selling people into slavery remains morally and legally wrong.

Recent evidence had been discovered that brought the personal side of the war to light. Long-forgotten letters proved one of Westbrook's residents, Josephine Taylor Williams, a former slave from a Southern plantation, had been recruited as a spy for the North. At great personal risk, she infiltrated Confederate ranks and carried messages to the Union Army.

Disguised as a stable boy, Josephine Taylor spent three harrowing years running enemy lines to deliver messages to her Union contact.

Our town also found itself involved in the war on another front. Local farmer Seth Williams used his farmhouse as a station on the Underground Railroad. However, this incredible story has a twist: Williams' involvement came about because Taylor's Union contact was his only son Peter. When the war ended, Peter Williams brought this courageous young woman home to become his bride.

In the aftermath of the war, mixed marriages met with great disapproval. Despite Josephine's heroic deeds, neither she nor her deeds were ever publicly acknowledged. Clearly, race was the principal reason. Even in the North, attitudes had not changed. Sadly, her efforts and efforts of countless others like her were reduced to a few lines in a history book.

Due to the tireless efforts of two newcomers to Westbrook, Josephine's story has finally emerged. To honor this young woman, Reene Anderson and Lissa Martin, current owners of the Williams' homestead, offered to place a bronze plaque on their farmhouse so that all who come to visit will be conscious of Josephine Taylor's sacrifice for her country. On a more personal note, Anderson and Martin are planning a spirited ride on horseback through town to recreate Taylor's exploits.

It is this publication's opinion that this acknowledgment is long overdue. In addition, *Hampshire Times* whole-heartedly supports this opportunity to bring closure and enlightenment to one of our own.

Am I stirring up controversy or inspiring people to think in a positive way? Looks like a little of both. Generally, Gina found it hard to set the right tone regarding editorials. Some readers felt an editorial provided the newspaper with a subtle way to slant a story.

How small-minded! I always present both sides, fairly and objectively.

Gina prepared other articles for printing, pondering the cause and effect of events that had taken place these last few months. An innocent man had been murdered. A missing part of the town's history had been uncovered. Could there be any relationship between the two?

"I may have just found the subject for my next editorial."

"Grady Ferguson to see you, Ms. Wilson," Janice announced, quietly entering Andrea's office with the morning mail.

"Does he have an appointment?" Andrea asked peevishly. "Mayor Stuart has called a last-minute all-hands meeting."

"No, but he said it won't take long," Janice answered.

"Show him in then. But make it clear I don't have much time."

The words were barely out of Andrea's mouth when Grady strode into the office and sank into the low-slung chair opposite her.

"Were you invited to this asinine dedication?" he asked, tossing the morning edition of the *Hampshire Times* on her desk.

"I'm sorry? Has the time for courting manners passed?"

"Don't go there, Andrea. When I read this article, I couldn't believe it. Then I realized you might have to make an appearance to support this fiasco."

Andrea picked up the paper and skimmed the article. "Fiasco? What's got your nose out of joint?"

"All this publicity because one Black girl became a spy during the Civil War. Who cares? Patriotism? I don't think so. She was sleeping with the guy she reported to."

"Calm yourself, Grady, the war is over."

Hell, Stephen never would have acted this way. And she'd killed him. If she didn't need this jerk, she'd kill him too.

"To answer your question, no, I wasn't invited. Only our beloved mayor received this distinction. He's so desperate for votes he'd attend a sixth grade dance recital."

Grady threw back his head and laughed, unaware of Andrea's grim expression.

"Thank God for small favors," he said. "Bob Stuart is one of the good ol' boys. Let him pretend that he's delighted to pay tribute to a nig—"

"I prefer not to hear that word in this office," Andrea snapped, rising from her chair to face him. "If you say it again, you're fired. Are you trying to lose this election by using such a politically incorrect slur? I thought I'd picked the right man for this job. Perhaps I was wrong."

Grady's face flushed at her rebuke. "I apologize. And you did pick the right man. I'll be more careful in the future. It's just when I think of *those* people getting so much publicity, I blow a gasket."

"Now that we understand each other, would you mind getting the hell out of here? My meeting with Mayor Stuart starts in ten minutes."

"I just wanted to make sure we're on the same page regarding the long-lost 'hero'. Pardon me, heroine."

"You made your point," she snapped and returned to her desk, dismissing him without a glance.

"Well, Mr. Ferguson, your true colors are beginning to show. If you cross the line one more time, you will find yourself on the outside looking in."

Despite her brave words, she was shaken by his vehemence.

"But if he knew my secret, he'd despise me. Just like he despises Josephine. God! Could my life get any more complicated? Walking a tightrope with Lloyd and tiptoeing around that bigoted asshole. One more misstep could send me tumbling into an abyss."

Chapter 33

The *Hampshire Times'* editorial brought unexpected results. Letters to the editor poured in via email and snail mail. Most responses contained positive feedback. But letters filled with hateful comments and thinly disguised threats arrived as well.

"Gina, the editorial is wonderful!" Lissa exclaimed when she heard the familiar voice on the phone.

"I'm so glad you're pleased. But I wanted to warn you both to be careful. It doesn't take much to push an unstable person over the edge."

"What do you mean?" Lissa asked.

"I thought I'd seen it all during my career in journalism. Disgusting innuendo and filthy language found their way to my door."

"I'm afraid you're a bit late with your head's up," Lissa said. "We've gotten nasty phone calls again, but Reene and I deleted the degrading messages before we were forced to listen to the hostile words again."

"What a shame," Gina said. "You'd think that in this day and age, racism would be a thing of the past."

"Apparently, not for everyone," Lissa muttered. "To get off this unwelcome subject, Gina, I finally heard from the mayor's office. According to his staff, he can only squeeze us—and himself—in the last week of the month. Suggested date is October twenty-eighth for the plaque ceremony. And our wild ride."

"Actually, Lissa, that is very timely. Right before election. I'll mention it in the paper in time, I promise."

"Excellent point. Thanks, Gina. I just hope we haven't opened a Pandora's Box."

"If I heard you correctly, I'm afraid we have." Reene had slipped in the front door. "Look at the envelope that came in today's mail. We've seen it a hundred times in the movies: words clipped out of magazines pasted on a piece of paper. Only this time it's real, not a movie script."

Lissa read the crude message. "'Keep that Black bitch in the stables where she belongs. Mind your own business or you'll regret it.' Can you imagine the mentality of the person who sent this? If one more person dares tell me animals are dumb, I'll shove this in his face. Who's the higher and lower animal here?"

"This message is a little stronger than those phone calls. Do you want to back off and skip the ride through town?" Reene asked as she reread the note.

"Hell, no! If we do, then this jerk will have won."

"I was hoping you'd say that. I don't want to give this idiot the satisfaction of thinking he's scared us away."

"Damn right. We'll ride our horses through town like modern day Lady Godivas..."

"Excuse me? Lady Godiva rode naked through town!"

"Oh yeah, she did, didn't she?" Lissa said sheepishly. "I guess I got carried away."

"I guess you did. Hang on to your pantyhose, Lady G. You told me our mayor only has a free day on the twenty-eighth. And it's mid-week. I hope enough people come out to watch us. If we get any more nasty grams before the plaque ceremony, we should notify the police."

"Agreed. Our innocent little B&B is attracting too much notoriety. And speaking of the plaque, I picked it up today. It's a work of art. I'll fetch it." Lissa hustled to her office and returned with a huge rectangular box. She flipped the lid up for Reene's inspection.

"You were right. This is a masterpiece. The polished bronze around all four sides is spectacular. The cap and swords standing out in relief are amazing. Josey will love it!"

A few hours later Reene and Lissa were pouring through Josey's letters again, sitting in the Historical Society's anteroom, as stone-faced autocrats in gold-framed portraits frowned over them.

"Lissa, we must have missed a clue in one of these letters. Something that would have raised a red flag to show why someone wanted to steal them. Or murder Stephen. Or both."

"You're right, but what? Let's try process of elimination first. We'll look for any letters we tossed aside because they weren't connected with Josey."

Carefully they separated the letters into two piles. One pile held correspondence between Peter and Josey, the second a mixture of letters and a few clippings from ancient newspapers. They concentrated on the more recent documents in the second pile.

"Reene, this letter is from Peter to his dad, dated 1888. He says he and Joseph are happy living in Canada and they miss him very much.

Joseph has met a nice girl and they plan to marry when Joseph completes his education. Peter goes on to say that he'd just as soon not hear any more news about Catherine Thorpe. He didn't care that Catherine had married into money; she'd hated his wife so much she treated her as if she weren't even human."

"I don't think I like Catherine Thorpe," said Reene. "I wonder if she had a relationship with Peter? Sounds like a former girlfriend. You've heard that old saying, 'a woman scorned'."

"Indeed I have. I want to investigate Catherine Thorpe's involvement a bit more. And you may be right. If she despised Josey that much and treated her like dirt, I'll bet it wasn't only because Josey was Black."

"Here's a clipping about Joseph's marriage, dated 1891. Evidently Joseph and his bride moved to New Brunswick. Look, I found a birth announcement: Joseph's first child, Maddie, born in 1893 and his next one, Joshua, born in 1895..." Reene's voice trailed off. "Nothing new here. We found this same information in the Bible. We didn't pay much attention because we were concentrating so hard on Josey's history."

"Then we need to check those names in the Bible more closely."

"I wish we'd found more clues though. I have the nagging feeling we're overlooking a piece of the puzzle that's staring us in the face."

"Barn Swallow Inn, one moment please." Lissa switched off the noisy washing machine. Stuffed with sheets and towels, it was groaning like it was about to give birth. "May I help you?"

"Lissa, it's Donna. You were asking about Catherine Thorpe. Well, I just remembered why her name sounded so familiar. We have a book called *Catherine Thorpe: From Heiress to Madness* by Leonard Rogers. I can hold it for you if you'd like to borrow it."

"Wonderful! We'll drop by later today."

Lissa scurried out to the barn. Reene was unloading grain and needed her help. Together they hoisted the fifty-pound bags of grain and dumped their contents into the bin. Bravo's special Senior Feed went into a separate barrel.

"Reene, guess what?" Lissa puffed. "There's a book in the library about the late unlamented Catherine Thorpe. Listen to this title: *Catherine Thorpe: From Heiress to Madness*. Sounds like a bitch on wheels. One of us should run into town to pick it up."

231

Reene folded the sturdy grain bags, keeping one for waste, and stored the rest in the tack room. As she set up a bag next to the walk-through door, she had a mysterious twinkle in her eyes.

"Why don't we both go? It's about time you had a ride on my million-dollar wagon. If you'll lend a hand, we can hitch up Sissy and we'll be good to go."

"My hitching skills need updating so you've got a willing helper. While we're in town, I'll run in and pick up the book. Speaking of Sissy, you can't double-park in the middle of the street. I don't think there's even a hitching post left since the old stables were chopped into firewood."

"Good point. Why don't I hang out at Baril's while you're at the library? No doubt I'll have plenty of visitors to keep me from getting bored."

When they finally skirted the Grange Hall and stopped at Baril's Tack Store, Lissa was almost sorry their ride had ended.

"Reene, that was awesome! You and Sissy make a great team. I can't wait for the return trip."

"We'll be 'ere waitin' on you, Marm," Reene said in her best Cockney accent.

"See that you are, Missy! I'll hurry over to the library and pick up the book," Lissa promised. "Maybe I'll pick up a little gossip while I'm there."

"When you come back, I want to run into the tack store. There might be some new stuff I can't live without."

Lissa quickened her steps to the library. "I don't like leaving Reene and Sissy by themselves if only for a short time. If this were the Wild West, the whole street would have teemed with horses, carriages and buckboards. Then Ah'd have stopped off at the ol' saloon to hoist a few, Ah reckon," she drawled.

Donna, assigning computer time to an attractive young woman, nodded when Lissa approached her desk. As the woman turned, Lissa was struck by the expression on her face. Her eyes were bleak and her mouth was held in a grim line. She acknowledged Lissa with a curt nod.

"Good grief, Donna! She looked mad enough to chew nails," Lissa said as she watched the young woman walk away.

"You can't blame her. That's Janice Navin, Andrea Wilson's admin. I feel sorry for her. Earlier this year she had an unhappy love affair with

Lloyd Collins. Remember him? He's the guy I warned you about; he'd been asking questions about you and Reene."

"So that's Lloyd Collins. Do go on."

"He and Andrea recently became engaged. Between you and me, Janice plans to resign if Andrea is elected mayor. She's trying to find a new job so obviously she doesn't want her boss to know."

"Andrea is engaged?" Lissa momentarily forgot all about Janice Navin's romantic problems. "I had no idea."

"You're the only one in town who didn't know. She's been waving her splashy engagement ring under everyone's nose."

"Well, Reene hasn't a clue either, so that makes us the last to hear the glad tidings. Not that I care. She's rubbed me the wrong way ever since she caused Reene grief when she stayed with us."

"Between you and me, I'd say she rubs a lot of people the wrong way. I have to give her credit though. She's accomplished quite a bit in this town. I wouldn't underestimate her until the last vote is cast. Here's your book."

Lissa studied its jacket. A photograph of Catherine Thorpe's unattractive face, devoid of any emotion, stared back at her. She and Josey were contemporaries, but Catherine Thorpe gave every appearance of a woman twice her age. Lissa had known people who were born old and evidently Ms. Thorpe fell into that sad category. Still, she must have been important to have a book written about her.

"*From Heiress to Madness*," she read as she handed her library card to Donna. "Intriguing title, isn't it? I can't wait to read this woman's life story. Who is Leonard Rogers? Is he a local author?"

"I can look him up for you if you can wait just a little longer."

"I've been gone too long already, Donna. My friend is parked out front of the tack store with her horse and wagon. I don't want her horse to get antsy. Can I call you later?"

"Of course! Best of luck with the book. Have a safe trip home."

Clutching the book, Lissa hurried back to the store. To her great relief, Reene was enchanting a few youngsters by letting them pat Sissy while their mothers hovered protectively in the background.

"Guess what?" Reene greeted. "I lucked out big time! Art Baril volunteered to stay with Sissy. Of course, he talked my face off! Art regaled me with the story of his life, telling me he ran a boarding stable in Westbrook before he bought the grain store. He's one of the last of the old-time horsemen, like Ernie. After I escaped, I picked up some awesome bargains at the tack shop. Three pairs of riding gloves for ten dollars! And I've become the Pied Piper of Westbrook. These cuties followed me around and kept me company. Did you get the book?"

"Yes, I did Ms. Pied Piper." Lissa smiled at the little group. "I hate to tear you away from your fan club, but I think Sissy has been patient long enough."

With a wave to the kids, Reene cued Sissy and they trotted off toward home. Lissa was amazed at how easily her friend handled the reins. She exuded a confidence that put her horse at ease.

Sissy may have been at ease, but Lissa wished the bench seat had a higher back. Sitting up straight as a poker made her tailbone throb with every bump. She couldn't wait for *this?*

"Did you get a chance to thumb through the book?" Reene asked, as they clip-clopped along the road.

"No, I'm afraid not. I didn't want to leave you stranded while I sat around reading. Let's save the book about Ms. Thorpe for tonight. I don't feel like cooking. Why don't we order some fattening pizzas and indulge ourselves royally?"

"Girl, you have the best ideas! Pizzas and a mystery! I'll bring up wine from the spring house."

Lissa looked over her shoulder. "You might want to wave on that pickup truck. It's been following us for some time."

Reene gestured to the driver. But the truck didn't swing out to pass. Instead, it edged a few feet closer.

"Reene, what's with that guy? He's getting awfully close."

"I know! I waved at him to go by." Reene repeated the gesture, but the pickup's engine only revved in response.

Suddenly the truck accelerated and bumped the back of the wagon. Both women screamed in fright. Sissy jumped in her traces, and Reene lurched forward from the pull on the reins. Lissa grabbed her to keep her from pitching off the seat onto Sissy's rear legs. As Reene fought for control, the truck bumped the wagon again with such force that the wagon jolted sideways.

"Stop it! Stop it!" Lissa shouted at the driver. "What the hell is the matter with you? Get away from us!"

In answer, the driver wrenched the pickup around the wildly rocking wagon. "Black-loving bitches!" he bellowed as he drew alongside. "You're nothin' but white trash! Go to Hell!"

"You lunatic! Keep away!" Lissa yelled. "You've scared our horse!!"

"I'll do more than that, you damn jigaboo lovers! Stupid pieces of shit!" He floored the powerful truck and peeled away.

"Bastard!" Reene screamed.

The confusion and noise were too much for Sissy. Terrified, she exploded into a gallop. Her flight response kicked in and she desperately wanted to rid herself of the wagon.

"Hang on, Lissa! I'll never be able to hold her back! I've got to let her run!" Reene hollered, bracing herself against the backboard. She let Sissy have her head and fought for control as the wagon barreled down the road.

Lissa grabbed the side of the wagon and hung on so hard her fingers almost dug holes in the wood. If she cried out, she'd only add to Sissy's fear.

"Please, please," Reene whimpered, "don't let any cars pull out in front of us! I can't stop her!"

Reene worked the reins and talked to Sissy as she desperately tried to prevent all of them from being smashed to pieces.

"Lissa, look for an open area where I can turn her!"

"I'll try!" Dense woods and rocks lined the road. "Not a damn driveway anywhere!" Lissa cried as Sissy sped along.

"I can't take much more!" Reene gasped. "My arms are giving out!"

Just when she thought Sissy would never come back into her hands, she felt a change in her horse's gait. With Reene talking to her and seesawing on the reins with all her strength, the wagon somehow survived the turn toward the inn.

Even in her panic, Sissy knew the way home and wasn't stopping until she got there. Lissa felt the blood drain from her face as she leaned away from the turn to keep the wagon balanced.

"Whoa, sweetie, easy," Reene soothed. "Good girl, come back now. Easy. Easy."

Sissy's ears moved in her direction and Reene knew she'd finally gotten her attention. Sissy's gait slowed even more until she returned to the trot. The speed of her trot, still a bit too fast, was controlled at last.

With the inn in sight, Sissy made a beeline for the barn and slammed on her brakes inches from the door. When the wagon shuddered to a stop, Lissa toppled out like a sack of potatoes. Stones scraped her face and hands, but she was so grateful to be alive she didn't care. A wave of dizziness washed over her. She hugged the ground until it passed.

"Reene," she croaked, "are you all right?"

There was no answer.

"Reene?" Lissa cried anxiously. She dragged her quaking body off the ground and forced her jelly legs to move.

She found her friend slumped on the seat, taking huge gulping breaths, with her head resting on her knees.

"Are you all right?" she repeated.

Hands trembling, Reene picked up the reins. Thankfully Sissy was spent. Lissa knew that if she acted up in the slightest, the wagon and Reene would be scattered over the landscape.

"Talk to me!" Lissa implored.

Reene lifted her head, her face deathly white and eyes burning like coals. "This is the second time I've experienced a runaway horse that almost killed me. I don't know if I'll ever drive again. Poor Sissy. It wasn't her fault. That man was freakin' deranged. How about you?"

"I'm still in one piece too, thanks to you." Lissa shook her head in disbelief. "How you kept us from getting killed is beyond me!" She threw her arms around her overwhelmed friend and hugged her.

"I don't know how I did it! I was so scared!" Reene choked. "At least we're still in one piece. I could kill that son of a bitch! Never mind me. We'd better check on Sissy! She may have hurt herself in her mad run."

Sissy was lathered and breathing heavily. It would take a long time to cool her out. In Sissy's frantic efforts to escape, her metal shoes had made neat slices on her legs.

"Poor sweetie!" Reene exclaimed. "She's cut herself on the inside of her left foreleg. There's a slashing cut down her right rear leg too. Thankfully, the cuts don't appear deep."

Lissa made eye contact with Reene. Unspoken between them was the reality. If she suffered any tendon damage, her life could be in danger.

"Hook up the hose while I get some clean rags," Lissa said. "Cold water will keep the swelling down."

After spraying Sissy's legs for twenty minutes, Reene applied antiseptic ointment to her cuts and left her safe and comfortable in a run-in shed. Then she went into the house to phone Frank Hayes. The vet promised he'd come over later that night.

"Lissa, did you get a good look at that truck? We need to call the police right away. I want to nail him if we can."

"I can describe it pretty well but damn it, I didn't get his license plate. Wait, I remember! I spotted a NASCAR logo on the back window! That's pretty common, but it's one thing the cops can use. I want to nail his hide to the wall too. That guy must be insane to do what he did. Did you hear what he hollered out the window?"

"I only heard the part about damning us to Hell. Then I had my hands full."

"He said some pretty nasty stuff. Racial slurs. Don't be surprised if he is the lowlife who sent us those weird letters."

Reene punched in the number of the police department. As she waited for the call to go through, she snapped, "When we're finished with him, he'll be the one damned to Hell."

Chapter 34

"Can either of you give me any details about this vehicle? Make, model, and color? I don't suppose you remembered the license plate?"

Realizing these stubborn women were getting into deeper trouble than they knew, Chief Frechette drove out to take their statement.

"Chief, there was no way we had time to check the plate number! When he took off like a bat out of hell, he scared our horse and she bolted. It's a miracle we weren't killed or seriously injured," Lissa snapped. "Look for an older model GM pickup. Dark green or black. I did notice a NASCAR decal on the rear window."

"Would either of you recognize the driver if you saw him again?" Chief Frechette asked.

"I didn't see his face. I was trying to keep my wagon on four wheels," Reene answered.

"I'd say he was late twenties or early thirties," Lissa said. "When he pulled alongside us, I got a pretty good look at him. Dark hair and clean-shaven. No glasses. His ugly face was contorted with rage."

The police chief paused before writing that last statement in his notebook. "Do you know of any reason why he would attack you?"

"Other than the fact he's a total asshole, no, I don't," Reene growled.

"He swore at us and yelled some racial comments," Lissa added. "My guess is he's not happy about our discovery of a Black Civil War hero."

"Doesn't take much to push some people over the edge," the chief responded.

"Especially when some people have zero tolerance and zero mentality," Reene snapped.

"I agree one hundred percent, but let's keep to the subject if you don't mind," Chief Frechette snapped back. Frustrated by the murder on his watch, he felt his Gallic temper flaring. Murder and mayhem somehow followed these women and now they were in danger as well.

"Have you had any other trouble?"

"As a matter of fact, we recently received crude letters with threatening messages. We've also had a few phone calls that were not very pleasant," Lissa answered. "We decided to ignore them. Why give these idiots the attention they crave? Or let them know we were frightened?"

He glared at both women in frustration but neither one dropped their gaze.

"Can I see these letters?"

"Of course. I'll get them," Reene said.

"I understand your reasoning," Frechette grudgingly admitted, reading the child-like pastings Reene handed him. "This situation has gotten out of control. I'm certain these incidents are related. You remember Trooper Edmondson? He left for New York City shortly after he interviewed you to follow up on some leads. Unfortunately, he didn't learn anything pertinent to this case."

The chief ran his hand through his thick silver hair. "So I'd like you both to come down to the station to look through mug shots. You may be able to identify the man who did this."

"Fine," Reene replied. "We'll be there. But it will have to wait until the morning. I'm expecting a visit from the vet. My horse was injured when that damn truck rammed the wagon. When you arrest the guy who tried to kill us, I want to confront him."

The police chief held up a hand as a caution. "I realize how upset you are, ladies, and I'm sorry the horse was injured, but I suggest you leave the confronting to us."

After they ushered Chief Frechette out the door, Lissa checked their messages.

"We've got company coming, Reene," Lissa said. "Four people, two bringing their horses, for an extended weekend."

"At least our hard-earned reputation is still intact. Not that the phone is ringing off the hook," Reene remarked gloomily.

Since the murder, people had reacted in one of two ways: some wouldn't come near the place, while others had a macabre fascination with all the gory details.

"You got that right," Lissa agreed. "I'm gonna get really creative for the newcomers. I need a break from crazed drivers and runaway horses."

"I'll second that. Instead of contractors, we now have Westbrook's finest on speed dial. This is definitely not part of that great dream I had."

"If only your dream had predicted this awful tragedy, we might have saved Stephen's life."

Later that night, Dr. Hayes stopped by to check on Sissy. As the two women watched anxiously, Hayes examined her legs and praised Reene's first aid technique.

"Your prompt action has made my job easier. Those cuts don't require stitches. Keep cold water on her legs for another day. I'll prescribe an antibiotic to prevent infection."

As they watched the vet drive away, Reene suddenly grabbed Lissa's arm.

"What's up, cowgirl? Sissy's okay, but your hair is on fire."

"My hair's on fire because I remembered something important about the truck that rammed us. It had farm plates, just like the vet's truck. I'm sure of it."

"Farm plates? That narrows things down a bit. Do you remember any numbers or letters?"

"No, damn it," Reene answered. "I only remember seeing 'Farm' on the bottom of the plate."

"Well, at least we can tell our new best friend, Chief Frechette, when we look at mug shots in the morning."

Reene smiled grimly. "I'm sure he'll be thrilled to see us. Between you and me and the fence post, we're the bane of his existence." Then she yawned so loudly, her jaw cracked in protest. "See you at breakfast."

"Nighty night," Lissa said. "I'm hunkering down to read Catherine Thorpe's biography. In all the excitement, I kinda shoved her on the back burner." She ran down the stairs to her office.

A perfect opportunity to dig into the book!

When she flipped the light switch, her eyes roamed across the desk for the book. They didn't have too far to roam. Lissa sucked in her breath and held it. The book lay in the center of her desk, her pewter letter opener thrust into the cover. Its point pierced the picture of Catherine Thorpe directly at the base of her throat.

Lissa, knowing full well who had staged this theatrical display, still moved cautiously around the desk. As if on cue, the old house creaked and groaned.

"The only thing missing is creepy organ music and an owl hooting in the belfry," she muttered, gingerly picking up the book and removing the mangled opener. "Lucky thing for me, we don't *have* a belfry."

240

She'd never look at her letter opener again without remembering the chilling image of its blade stabbing Catherine's throat.

"Josey, your method is a bit over the top," Lissa said softly. "But message understood. From what I've read in Peter's letters, Catherine had a hatred for you that bordered on obsession. I'll read this book from cover to cover to see if there are any clues that demented Miss C may have caused your fatal accident. This is one promise I intend to keep."

Chapter 35

Lissa parked her truck beside the front porch and unloaded pumpkins, corn stalks, fake black crows and straw bales. The calendar said October 16th but Lissa's favorite holiday couldn't get there soon enough.

If we weren't running this inn, I'd put up skeletons and witches all year.

Decorating for Halloween usually filled both women with excitement, but their pleasure was subdued this year. The dark cloud caused by the ongoing investigation into Stephen's death hung directly over their inn. For purely selfish reasons, they would be extremely happy when his murder was solved.

On top of that, there was still the unsolved incident with the truck. The mug shots had not proved useful, and the case was still open. Fortunately, Sissy's injuries were healing nicely, and the threatening letters had stopped.

We've got to get our enjoyment of the holiday back, Lissa decided. *We'll transform the inn into a Halloween lover's delight.*

With an enormous farmer's porch, to say nothing of the driveway, she intended to create the ultimate spooky display filled with Frankenstein monsters, witches, black cats, and scarecrows.

Before Lissa could put up a single cornstalk, Reene joined her on the porch.

"Lissa, remember the promise you made in the spring? You agreed we could put on another function geared more toward fun. Why don't we throw a Halloween Hoedown? Costumes, a square dance on horseback? The works!"

"A Halloween Hoedown!" Lissa exclaimed. "You come up with the darnedest ideas!"

"Well, I've seen square dancing done in the movies and I've been dying to give it a try."

Lissa smiled. It was nice to see Reene excited about something again.

"I guess we can give it a shot. And you *did* graciously suffer through our High Tea."

"Let's go inside and pick a date for *your* Hoedown."

Back in her office, Lissa snatched up her desk calendar. "Would the Saturday before Halloween work? That way parents can go trick or treating with their kids on the Official Day. Can you put a blurb out on our website? I'll run another ad in the *Times*. We'll advertise only to horse folks. I'm sure they'd love a hoedown."

"Most definitely. This is going to be a blast. We'll need to pick up a bunch of country music CDs. I'll have to hunt around for my stereo system and speakers."

"Can we keep it simple this time? We'll serve drinks and munchies. Some apple cider donuts? A chicken wing or two? Agreed?"

"Agreed. We'll post some flyers in local stables and the tack store. This is starting to sound familiar," smiled Reene. "Where should we set up our do-si-do?"

"I suppose we could use one of the fields if we mowed it really short and put up temporary fencing. We should hold the party during the day so we won't have to worry about lighting."

"Perfect. I can ask Tom to mow one of the fields," Reene said quickly. "I'm sure he won't mind. Maybe he'll help us get started."

"Maybe he will, especially if he knows you'd be bringing him a thermos of hot coffee. Wearing your skin-tight jeans, of course."

"Okay, I'm bagged," Reene laughed again. "You caught me. By the way, he's coming over for dinner tonight. Could you do us a favor and make yourself scarce?"

Lissa slumped dejectedly and batted her soulful brown eyes at Reene. "I suppose so. I only hope there's a bowl of soup or crust of bread to eat, all alone in my room."

"Martyr!" Reene exploded as Lissa burst out laughing. "If you don't behave, I might not save any jambalaya for you!"

"Ha! You won't be worrying about me for a second and you know it! But listen, our new guests are arriving tomorrow. Before you seduce Tom with your jambalaya, we'll need to get the stalls ready for two horses."

"I totally forgot them! I got so excited about my brainchild. *And* seducing Tom. I'll stock the stalls with the usual goodies. Two men and two women, right?"

"That's them. Only two rooms though. They'll be here for four days. Good thing they aren't coming in late. You might be caught in a compromising position in the hot tub," Lissa warned.

"You took the words right out of my mouth."

243

"Good morning, Missy. Did you have a good time last night?" Lissa asked. "I mean, did Tom like your cooking?"

"Yes, and yes, he did. He said he'd hay the field for us. He'll bring over his big haying machine. It shouldn't take more than a few hours."

"Super! I don't imagine you had to work awfully hard to persuade him to help us?"

"I was a perfect lady," Reene said with a straight face. "When we finally came up for air, I asked him again if he'd do it. I've been wondering if he was good at everything he did. And he *was*."

"Oh, my God! Why did I even ask?"

As the late afternoon shadows crept over the farmer's porch, Lissa plumped and turned cushions on the rockers. Her thoughts drifted to Reene and her date with Tom. Intimate details aside, it was great to see her friend happy again, especially after the enormous fallout of Dan's affair.

Even so, Lissa wasn't sure she would ever be ready for dating. She and Hank had always been happy, and she missed him dearly, but she was also enjoying this time to make her own plans and stand on her own two feet. During their marriage, she had always supported his plans and his dreams. She wondered what he'd think of her venture with Reene.

Her thoughts were interrupted by tires crunching on gravel. A pickup towing a three-horse trailer pulled up next to the porch. A small passenger car followed closely behind.

"Hello there!" Lissa called as she walked down the stairs to greet the newcomers.

"Hi, I'm Aericka and this is Bob. Where should I park?"

"Right beside the barn on the left. See where it's paved?"

"Yep. Thanks," Aericka smiled and put her truck in gear. Lissa had trailed along and watched with admiration. By deft twists and turns, she expertly parked the rig and hopped out of the cab to unload.

Lissa shook her head. She could never, ever drive a truck pulling a horse trailer, much less park one. The whole concept of backing a truck while steering in the opposite direction scared her to death. If Reene weren't so expert at hauling, she'd never leave the property.

The passenger car crept alongside. "Excuse me. Should I park over here too?" asked the driver. "I'm Hilary and this is Matt."

"Hi, Hilary. Yes, park next to your friend. We keep that space for our guests. Come up to the house when you're ready."

Lissa watched them unload and explained which stalls were set aside for their horses, who exchanged snorts and whinnies with the other horses.

"All set?" Lissa asked when the foursome trooped into the house.

"Yes. Our horses love it here already," Hilary replied. "We can't wait to get out on the trails."

"I noticed the barrel racer stencil on your truck, Aericka. I assume you ladies are barrel racers? That's so cool! I tried it a couple of times, but I was always afraid either my horse or I would topple right over."

"All you need to do is practice a couple hundred runs," Aericka grinned, "Then you'll get the hang of it."

"Thanks, but no thanks," Lissa laughed. "Please fill out these cards for my records. Aericka, you and Bob will be in the Standardbred Room. I've put Hilary and Matt across the hall in the Barn Swallow Room. The hot tub is on the deck outside the Gathering Room. Breakfast is served from seven to nine. We have menus for all the local eateries and for restaurants a bit further away. Any questions?"

"Is there a pond or lake nearby?" Matt asked. "I'd love to go fishing while Hil is out riding."

"You're in luck," Lissa replied. "We have a nice pond out back in the north forty. Give me an hour or so and I'll show you where it is."

"Great. I'd really appreciate that," said Matt.

"Help me carry all this stuff to our room, Aericka," Bob said. "I'd like to soak in the hot tub."

"You're strong enough to lug a couple of bags. Then you can soak. I'll join you after I check on my horse."

Bob rolled his eyes. "Always the horse comes first."

He picked up two soft-sided pieces of luggage and clattered up the stairs. Matt and Hilary trudged after him as Aericka headed for the barn.

"Barrel racers! Be still my heart!" Lissa gloated. "No question about their riding skills, but I'd better tread slowly before I ask them to participate in the horsey hoedown. If one of them falls off and breaks all her bones, we might get slapped with a lawsuit. They don't look like the Trigger-happy type, but these days you never can tell."

"What's on the menu this morning?" Lissa asked. "My nose detects something yummy."

"Your bloodhound nose is working overtime," Reene teased. "Blueberry pancakes with Vermont maple syrup and bacon."

Reene poured dripping batter thick with blueberries onto the black wrought-iron gridle. Hurriedly she turned the spitting bacon before it curled into inedible crisps.

"I love that combination." Lissa reached in the cupboard for corn flakes, Cheerios and raisin bran to make sure the guests had plenty of options.

"Reene, hear me out on my brainstorm. Our new guests are barrel racers. If we can get them to do-si-do, other riders will follow. Think it over while I set the table."

Lissa set up plastic containers of cereal in the antique dry sink and added a big bowl of fresh fruit. Coffee was perking and the kettle was on simmer. She filled a ceramic blueberry motif vase with flowers and placed it in the center of the table.

As Lissa took plates off the shelves, Reene asked, "Did you feed yet?"

"On my way. So are we on the same page? Could you drop a few hints about our hoedown to see if the two women are interested? From what I've seen, their significant others would rather cheer them on from the sidelines."

"I'll try. I don't want to scare them off. Is everything all set in the breakfast room?"

"Yes, ma'am. I'm off to feed our starving critters."

As Lissa left the kitchen, she heard voices in the hallway. The smell of bacon cooking must have wafted upstairs and roused their guests. No one could resist that aroma. She suspected the cereal would go untouched.

"Good morning," she greeted when the foursome arrived in the breakfast room. "Reene's ready for you with a mouth-watering meal."

Aericka and Hilary, dressed for the trail in long-sleeved turtleneck jerseys under quilted vests and sturdy jeans, returned to the table with bowls of fruit.

"Morning," Reene greeted. "If you'll pass me your plates, I'll serve from the kitchen."

"These pancakes are the best!" Bob said, generously pouring more maple syrup. "I could eat a dozen." He caught Reene's attention and winked.

She returned his wink and mixed another batch. "What are your plans for today, ladies?" Reene asked.

"Aericka and I were hoping you'd recommend good trails," Hilary replied. "We're giving our horses a break from the barrel racing circuit. We thought they'd enjoy some quiet trail riding. No pressure."

"Good for you. Horses *and* riders need a little variety," Reene smiled. "Speaking of variety, barrel horses are so quick and agile, they could tackle different disciplines. Like polo? Or riding to music?"

"Polo is beyond my skills, but riding to music sounds interesting," Hilary said.

"Yeah, my gelding Red isn't a polo-type guy either," Aericka said. "Dancing? He probably has four left hooves."

"Who's ready for more flapjacks?" Reene asked. Unless they were too stuffed to care, the barrel racers would think about her comments on their ride.

Guests fed and happy, Lissa went out on the deck after lunch to check the hot tub. Time to put a few bromine tablets in the water. She scooped up the tube floating in the water and took out the tablets. If not done regularly, the water would turn as green as the tub's shamrock-green liner.

As the tablets dissolved, she watched a figure trudging through the fields. She recognized Matt by the fishing pole slung over his shoulder. But as he came closer, she was shocked to see he was dripping wet.

"What happened? Are you okay?"

"Yeah, I'm just dandy. I started out fishing in your pond. After two hours of not getting a single bite, I headed over to the stream. I found a nice deep pool upstream. I cast my line out in the middle of the pool and got a strike. I was standing on a big rock and the fish was putting up a great fight. Just when I landed him, I lost my balance and pitched in headfirst."

"How awful," Lissa said sympathetically. "It could've been worse. You could've bashed your head on that rock. Well, at least you caught your fish."

"Yeah, and I caught a few more too. What the hell, I was already soaked." He shook his head. "I've never taken a header like that before. But tonight we'll eat like kings. If I can borrow your grill, I'll make us a feast to remember."

"No problem! Reene and I will bring a salad and some potatoes to bake on the grill. Is 6:30 good for you?"

"Sounds great to me. The girls will be ready to devour these snappers, bones and all, after their long ride. See you at dinner."

Lissa watched Matt squishing his way back to the inn. She wondered if his drenching was 'accidental'.

Her heart ached for Josey, but she still wished their resident spirit would stop playing tricks on their unsuspecting guests.

"The fish was delicious!" Reene smiled, finishing the last morsel on her plate. "Matt, you did a great job of cooking the fish *and* catching it."

"Thanks. I went through a lot to catch the darn things."

Enjoying the nippy fall air on the back deck, they were full of good food and drink. Bob lit a fire in the chimenea and they lounged in front of the flames.

"How was your outing today, ladies?" Lissa asked. "Where did you ride?"

"We stuck to your maps which led to some really nice trails," Aericka replied. "The footing was so good we were able to lope for long stretches. Red was rarin' to go. We had a blast."

"Gracie did her flighty mare routine," Hilary chimed in, "but once she got that out of her system, she gave me a great ride. I can hardly wait to go out again tomorrow."

Lissa noticed the silver belt buckle Aericka wore. She knew a rider didn't win a buckle like that riding push-button horses. She decided the time was right to spring her surprise.

"Would you daredevils like to try something different? Something you've never tried before? You'll have fun, but it will take a bit of practice."

Aericka and Hilary exchanged glances. Even in the firelight Lissa could see the wary expressions on their faces.

"What are you talking about?" Aericka asked. "Something to do with riding?"

"Yes ma'am. Reene has been dying to have a hoedown on the property and we need riders to make it work," Lissa explained. "I figured if you could handle barrel racing, then square dancing on horseback would be easy as falling off the proverbial log."

"Square dancing on our horses? Are you two feeling all right?"

"I know it sounds crazy, Aericka, but I think it will be a lot of fun," Reene said. "I've got books on it and with a little practice, we should be able to pull it off."

"Wait a minute. I smell a rat. 'Polo anyone?' 'Riding to music'?" Aericka mimicked.

"Guilty as charged," Reene admitted.

248

"Are you and Lissa square dancing too?" asked Hilary.

"You bet. And a couple of riders down the road have already shown some interest," Reene answered.

"When is this hoedown taking place?" asked Bob. "We're only staying until Monday."

"Funny you should ask," Lissa said. "This coming Saturday! Since Halloween is right around the corner, we thought we'd combine the two. You can wear costumes if you'd like."

"Now I'm sure you two are nuts," Aericka scoffed.

"Come on, Aericka. You didn't get that silver buckle by being afraid to go fast," Bob reminded. "Give it a try. You too, Hil."

"It's easy for you to say," Hilary jeered, "you'll be sitting on the sidelines putting away a few beers with Matt."

"Please try do-si-doing a few times with us," Lissa asked. "If you hate it, we won't bug you anymore."

Aericka leaned forward, scooped up some dip with a tortilla chip and popped it into her mouth.

"Okay, I'm game," she said between munches. "I'll have to fight with Red to go slow enough once he gets into the ring...wait, you don't *have* a ring! Where are we doing all this square dancing?"

"We're haying one of the fields out back and putting up temporary fencing," Reene explained.

"What do you think, Hil? I mean, we've only just got here and these two crazy ladies want us to teach our horses to square dance!"

"Crazy ladies or not," Hilary replied, "it does sound like fun. Like Lissa said, if we hate it, we can quit."

"Yeah, okay," Aericka said. "I'm still not totally won over but with everyone gung ho, I give in. With reservations." Aericka tossed a twig into the flames. "I'll go along with this nutty scheme for now. Until we all crash into each other."

"Did you call Tom?" Lissa asked while they flipped mattresses and made the upstairs beds. To save time, they'd come up with a system that'd make a Marine top sergeant cry for *his* momma.

"Yes. He'll drop by later today. The way our luck's been running, we might have a hurricane. So he wants to start cutting right away."

"What about fencing? Can he give us a hand with that? We need stakes, a lot of yellow nylon rope and red flags to hang on the rope. We don't want the horses thinking they can get out."

"He'll help us put it up when we pick up the supplies," Reene said as she bundled up the dirty linen.

"Then we'd better scoot to the hardware store, I beg pardon, home improvement store. We need a GPS to find a screwdriver in those cavernous places."

Once Tom arrived they followed him out to the field and kibitzed as he hooked up the hay tedder to his tractor. After haying the field, he switched to the bailer. In amazingly short time, the overgrown field was reduced to a workable length. Heavy rectangular bales lay on the ground ready for pickup.

"I'll leave the bales out overnight. They'll dry quicker," Tom told them when he switched off the noisy tractor. "If you'll lend a hand tomorrow, we'll store them in the barn. Now let's figure out where to set the stakes and rope off the field."

Working like Trojans, Reene and Lissa prepared the field, dragging the heavy bales out of harm's way, but Lissa had to admit no one worked harder than Tom.

To show her appreciation, Reene invited him to supper. She also promised him a few beers at The Golden Horseshoe.

Lissa decided she was terribly busy and couldn't possibly join them.

"Bless you, Lissa," Reene whispered, "you're a real friend."

Chapter 36

"Reene, I had an epiphany last night," Lissa said the next day. "Ashley and Emily Hayes are a bit too young for square dancing on horseback, but I'll bet they'd love to help out with the hoedown. What do you think?"

"I think they'll be over here in a heartbeat. They'll love it. Why don't we let them try running, or should I say trotting, the barrels on one of our horses? It'll be a new experience for them and a lot more fun than going round and round in an indoor."

Both girls were delighted, promising to come over after school and help set up. Lissa figured that splitting their duties between grooming horses and serving refreshments would keep them hopping.

Somehow Reene and Lissa found time to finish their decorations before the hoedown. Cornstalks were tied to fence posts the entire length of the driveway. Pumpkins and gourds were piled high in a wheelbarrow on the porch. Everything in sight was covered with fake cobwebs where poisonous-looking rubber spiders clung to long narrow strands. Ceramic jack-o'-lanterns cast an eerie light from the first floor windows.

"Let's leave just one or two lights on in the driveway," Lissa said as they anchored big black crows into straw bales. "It'll make a real spook walk."

"Awesome idea!" Reene responded. "I bought CDs with scary moans, shrieks, and blood-curdling screams. I'll set up some speakers so everyone will get the full effect."

"Where are my tombstones?" Lissa grumbled as she rummaged through the boxes. "Aha, here they are! The last perfect touch! Reene, help me with these skeletons. Should we hang them from the lamp post or lay them around the tombstones?"

"Looks like we have enough to do both. Doesn't everything look perfectly creepy?"

"We done good. We're too far out of town for regular trick-or-treaters. Too bad. I think any kid would get a kick out of our display."

Suddenly Lissa was struck with another idea. "Know what else would scare the beejeezus out of the kids? The Headless Horsewoman and her fiery steed Bravo! I'd hide around the corner and at just the right moment, I'd come galloping up and rear Bravo up and hurl a flaming jack-o'-lantern and..."

"And trample one of the kids and fall off your fiery steed and cause a parent to keel over in a dead faint!" Reene exclaimed. "I don't think so!"

"Party pooper!" Lissa pouted. "I guess my brilliant idea needs work."

"I guess. Next year why don't we open a Spook Walk to the public? Or a Haunted Hayride? Damn. I just realized what I said."

"Reene, we can't worry every time we make that kind of reference. I'm sure she understands we mean no disrespect. And if anyone has a sense of humor, Josey certainly does! Let's just hope she doesn't decide to do any more haunting on Halloween. Don't forget, All Saint's Day *is* the day dedicated to the dead."

In preparation for the hoedown, Reene and Lissa read all the how-to books, watched several videos and practiced do-si-doing with Aericka, Hilary, neighbor Jill Stanton and Jill's teenage daughter Sarah. Allison Hanlon's husband Cory and Jill's significant other Travis rounded out the group.

"Sarah is an absolute phenom in the ring," Lissa declared. "She's picked up the patterns and timing like she's done it for years. Youth is *so* wasted on the young."

Bravo, who hated going round and round in circles, actually put a little spirit into his trot and canter once he got the hang of changes in direction and patterns. All the horses were learning together and figuring things out by themselves. Playing the same tune repeatedly made it easier for them and they began to anticipate the next move when they heard the music. Like school horses, they understood certain inflections and tones of voice.

Before long, all the riders were performing simple figure eight outlines and knew their allemande left from their allemande right. During practice, they used poles and barrels to follow the patterns. But one small detail had been overlooked. They had no one to call the dances.

"Aericka, do you think Bob would do the calling?" Reene asked as they cooled out the sweaty horses. "He'd just have to read the calls and try to sound Western."

"Are you kidding?" She winked at Reene. "Not a problem. What the hell, he's got nothing else to do."

Lissa ran up the front steps, intent on finishing her housekeeping chores before more do-si-do practice got underway. She stopped short when she saw a small box lying on one of the rockers.

"What's up with our mailman? He never leaves packages without telling us." She scooped up the box but was startled by its weight and odd clinking noises from inside.

When she reached her office, she noted the grubby condition of the brown wrapping paper. The words scrawled on the paper shocked her into immobility: 'Black-loving bitch women'.

"Reene!" she yelled. "Reene!"

"What is the matter?" Reene asked as she hurriedly joined her. "I heard you all the way in the mudroom."

"A package arrived for us," Lissa answered. "I'm afraid to open it. Look who it's addressed to."

"Not very original, is he? It's from our friendly neighborhood asshole."

"Who else? Something metallic was rattling around in there. Listen." She shook the box. Metal banged against metal.

"Open it, Lissa," Reene urged. "He's not smart enough to make a bomb."

"Don't be funny," Lissa snapped. She grabbed her scissors, cut through the tape down the center of the box and yanked it open.

"What on earth...?" she said, dragging out wads of tattered newspaper. Then her heart nearly stopped.

Lying on the bottom were four horseshoes. Four horseshoes covered in blood.

"Oh dear God!" Reene cried in horror.

"How despicable! He's demented!" Lissa gasped. "I don't even want to touch them!"

"We don't dare! We'd ruin any fingerprints this sick bastard may have left."

"Maybe he's done something already! Good God! We've got to check the horses!"

"We will. Take a deep breath, Lissa."

"What are we going to do? We can't ignore this warning! He obviously timed it right before the hoedown."

"Before we call the police, we'll call an emergency meeting with all the riders," Reene said. "We'll let them decide if they want to continue."

Reene, Lissa and their riders met after lunch in the Gathering Room. Matt and Bob hung at the back of the group uncertain as to what was happening.

"We have something important to tell you. Something serious," Lissa said.

"How serious?" Aericka asked. "You sound like it's a matter of life or death."

Reene placed her arm on Aericka's shoulder. "Almost. It's bad. We hate that you're involved in our mess."

"What mess?" Bob demanded.

"A few hours ago Reene and I received an unexpected threat," Lissa said. "A horrible threat. It may be another scare tactic, but we couldn't in good conscience let you ride tomorrow until we told you."

"Another?" Allison Hanlon asked.

"Someone's been harassing us ever since we found some old Civil War letters," Reene explained. "Today he sent us a box of bloody horseshoes."

"Son of a bitch!" Matt exclaimed.

"That's horrible! Are you saying he means to harm one of us?" Jill asked. Her daughter Sarah, hands on hips, looked ready for a fight.

"We believe this threat was aimed at Lissa and me," Reene said, "but we can't rule out an attack on any one of you."

"Not while I have my two fists," Matt growled.

"We don't want this creep to dictate our actions, but we won't risk you getting hurt," Reene said. "We're not giving in, but we'll understand if you want to quit."

"Hell, no! I'm not letting some sleazeball intimidate me," Aericka declared.

"If he tries anything, he won't live to see another day," Bob promised.

"Aericka, if you're willing, so am I," Hilary said. The others nodded in agreement.

"You all are the best!" exclaimed Reene. "We can't thank you enough."

"Save that for later," Aericka retorted. "This isn't over yet."

254

Saturday morning Griffin McGuire thrashed through the woods behind the inn like a bull in a china shop. He hardly noticed the autumn sunshine or the canopy of oak and maple leaves above him, which had turned the woods into a kaleidoscope of color. He didn't care how much noise he made while he searched for the perfect spot, close, but not close enough, for anyone to catch a glimpse of him.

But he couldn't know that other eyes tracked his every move. Or that other ears listened to his every footstep. Focused on his mission, he plowed ahead.

"'Let's go to that new B&B', she said. 'You'll have fun,' she said," Bob growled, climbing up to his perch on a stepladder. Black Stetson on his head, he clutched a microphone in one hand and a list of calls in the other. He was not overly pleased by the way he'd been suckered into this job. After the meeting yesterday, he was uneasy as well as confused.

"Hell," he decided, "I'll make it up as I go along. I'll try to make it fun. As much fun as I can while watching for a homicidal maniac."

Matt, moving among the crowd and acting as a spotter if anything went wrong, nodded to Bob and gave him a thumb's up.

Bob reviewed his notes again and repeated the calls until they rolled off his tongue. He looked back. Riders were queued up at the entrance, ready to go. He had to admit the women looked great in their colorful Western regalia. Each horse wore splashy silver-studded headstalls and saddles. The men wore Western jackets over their jeans. Bolo ties with silver and turquoise accents made a splash of color against white shirts.

"Might as well git this shebang motorin'," Bob muttered. "If we survive this Hoedown from Hell, we'll need beer. Large quantities of beer."

"I changed my mind about wearing Halloween costumes," Lissa confided to Reene as they checked their tack. "If everyone dressed as ghouls and monsters, I'd be more of a wreck than I am now."

"Try not to worry, Lissa," Reene reassured her. "If all goes according to plan, I'll wear my good witch outfit on Halloween and we'll take Shen and Brav for a night ride."

"Let's hope we're all alive and well enough for a night ride," Lissa said. Mounted and waiting for their cue, she nervously checked out the crowd. A familiar face was missing.

"Reene, where's Tom? After all the work he did to help jump-start this hoedown, I'm surprised he's not here to watch his favorite cowgirl. Or didn't you tell him about the latest development?"

"He got a call for an emergency hay delivery," Reene evaded. "A good friend of his who lives over an hour away lost his barn in a fire. Don't worry, the guy didn't lose any horses. Tom promised to deliver 200 bales as quick as he could. He should be back in plenty of time to join us for a couple of Sam Adams' pale ales."

"In other words, you didn't tell him about the package."

"His buddy needs his help more than we do. Come on, girlfriend. We'd better line up with the others."

Griffin McGuire found the perfect spot for his ambush. He broke off a few small branches on a gnarled maple tree to create a better gun site. From his vantage point, he had a clear view of the improvised ring.

"That hard-nosed bitch'll show her gratitude by paying me top dollar for this job," he growled. "She paid me to try to run those broads off the road. But I deserved more. And she owes me for my new BB gun. It can fire off a hundred rounds a second. Those nags'll freak out and dump those meddling women on their heads."

He loaded his gun and tested the mechanism. Slouching uncomfortably against the deeply grooved tree trunk, he waited. Before long, he saw horses and riders approaching the gate. He steadied his arm in the crook of a branch and took aim.

As Reene and Lissa walked their horses through the field toward the ring, they spotted Gina sitting along the sidelines, her digital camera ready to record the event for the paper's Entertainment section. When they took their places, Aericka gestured to Bob they were ready.

"Welcome to the Barn Swallow Inn's First Annual Halloween Hoedown!" Bob announced. "Riders, you may enter the ring."

He quickly signaled Ashley and Emily to start the music. Then he nodded to Matt to open the gate.

The riders split left and right as they entered. Halfway down the long side, they stopped and turned to face each other across the ring.

"Salute your partners!" Bob commanded in his best down-home twang. The riders bowed their heads to each other.

"All couples out to the center of the ring! Ladies circle left, gents circle right!" Bob sing-songed and the riders trotted in a wide circle.

As Lissa trotted along, she scanned the crowd clustered along the ring. Matt caught her eye and mouthed 'okay'.

Lissa circled Brav behind Allison, but above the music and Bob's calls, her heart lurched when she heard the excited howling of a dog.

Oh no! It's Andes! He's caught or treed something.

Lissa saw Reene's face as she trotted toward her. Her strained expression belied the joyous whoops around her.

Another long-drawn out howl greeted their ears. As Reene's head swiveled in the direction of the woods, she nearly rode up Sarah's horse's fanny. She jerked Shen's head around and sat ramrod-straight in the saddle, her attention fixed on the trees.

Had Andes found something—or someone—he couldn't handle?

"Like shootin' horses in a barrel!" Griffin chuckled.

Suddenly a low, menacing growl widened Griffin's eyes in fear. His heart thumped and he whipped around, gun in hand.

A small dog, eyes darkened with anger and fangs bared, stared back at him.

"A freakin' beagle!" he sneered. "Get the hell away from me, little man!" He waved the gun menacinglyin Andes' face.

With his hunting instinct sharpened by this threat to his territory, the dog leaped forward and attacked Griffin's right leg, sinking his teeth into the fleshy area just above the ankle.

Griffin yelled in surprise and pain. The dog worried Griffin's leg a moment before renewing his attack. Griffin desperately tried to keep his balance, but the beagle clung to his leg. He crashed to the ground and the Bee Bee gun bounced under some low bushes.

"Let go of me, you rotten cur!" Griffin snarled.

His awkward kick at Andes' head glanced off the dog's shoulder and the beagle briefly lost his grip on McGuire's ankle. Then the dog growled and rushed in again, snagging Griffin's pants.

Frantically Griffin scrabbled on all fours as he struggled to regain his feet. Pain stabbed through his leg. Finally, his pant leg tore free, and he lurched up, his wound forgotten.

Pursued by his assailant's deep baying cries, Griffin crashed frantically through the trees.

"Hurry up boys and don't be slow, there's chicken in the bread pan pickin' up dough!" Bob trouped on.

Lissa finally relaxed. Except for the dog's howls, everything was going well and the riders kept perfect time.

"All join hands with the lady in the lead! Find your honey and waltz the floor."

She joined in as the riders' laughter floated back to the onlookers. Bob was really getting into his role.

"Line up and face your partners! Meet your lady and promenade home!"

With the spectators adding a rhythmic clap, the pairs cantered down the center of the ring. Greeted by enthusiastic applause, the riders exited single file as Matt swung the gate wide.

"All you cowboys and cowgals," Lissa shouted. "Refreshments are available outside the ring. Thanks for coming and we hoped you've enjoyed our square dance."

At her announcement, Bob climbed down his ladder faster than a fireman rescuing a cat.

"Man, am I glad that's over!" Matt exclaimed.

"Nothing happened, thank God," Lissa agreed. "Matt and Bob, you did a mighty fine job. Reene and I owe you one."

The barn was a madhouse of activity as horses were untacked and riders shed their fancy outfits. Reene put Bravo and Shen in the outside paddocks to make room for the guests.

"Well, friends, we survived," Reene said, heaving Shen's heavy leather saddle onto her saddle stand. "I couldn't get those bloody horseshoes out of my head. Lissa and I will always be in your debt."

"Put it on my bill," Jill said. "I haven't done this in years and I'll probably be sore tomorrow. But right now, all I want is a cold beer!"

"Cold beer? We'll all need some extra-strength liniment," Allison Hanlon groaned. "Reene, may Cory and I take you up on your long-standing offer to use the hot tub?"

Suddenly the barn fell silent. Trooper David Edmondson loomed in the doorway. Frightened looks replaced the laughter and chatter.

"Good evening, everyone. There's no emergency. Please don't be concerned."

Jill laughed gruffly. "You don't know the half of it, Dave. We're glad you showed up."

"In an official capacity, Jill?"

"You'd better ask our hosts."

He walked over to Reene and Lissa. "Would you ladies please come with me? I need to speak to you in private."

"Give us a few minutes to help our riders," Reene replied. "We need a word with you too. We'll meet you in the tack room. Last door on the left."

"The sergeant will not be pleased when he hears how we handled the latest threat," Lissa muttered. She folded Bravo's sweaty saddle pad wrong side out and hung it over his stall door to dry.

"Reene! Lissa! You were both wonderful!" exclaimed Gina, who was now standing in front of Shen's stall. "I could never have done that in a thousand years!"

Her exuberant praise was lost on both women who felt as deflated as two-day old balloons.

"Thanks so much, Gina," replied Reene, "but the long arm of the law is here. Again. The sergeant is waiting for us."

"Do you have any idea what he wants? Is this visit about the murder?"

"We have no clue," Lissa replied, "but we're about to find out. Gina, we've had another incident. It's worse than last time if that's possible. Wait for us. Please."

Reene grabbed her arm. "Come on, Lissa, we gotta face the music. I'll get the box of shoes. This time it won't be pleasant."

In the tack room Officer Edmondson was studying Sissy's harness pegged on the walls. As they came in, he examined the brasses and handled the leathers.

"Soft as a baby's bottom, isn't it?" Reene asked. *He must have been impressed. He almost smiled.* "I've worked hard on that harness with neet's foot oil to keep it supple."

His official policeman look returned. "Before I explain why I'm here, what do you want to tell me?"

"Sergeant, this morning a box was delivered to our doorstep," Lissa replied. "When we opened it, this is what we found."

Reene handed the box to the trooper.

When he looked inside, a muscle on his cheek twitched. "Did either of you touch these shoes?"

"No, sir," Lissa answered. "We were afraid to mess up any fingerprints. We were horrified."

"Not horrified enough to cancel your hoedown," Sgt. Edmondson snapped.

Reene's face flamed. "We realize it looks like we acted irresponsibly, but we had a meeting with all our friends who were involved in the hoedown. No one wanted to back down."

"That's no excuse for endangering innocent people," the trooper admonished. "Or endangering your animals. Did any of you notice anything unusual during the performance?"

Lissa hesitated. Should she tell him about Andes' barking frenzy? If she did, would she look even more foolish than she felt?

"Just after the hoedown began," Lissa said, "I heard Reene's dog barking and baying in the woods. He was howling like he does while hunting. It sounded like he was chasing something."

"Has the dog returned?"

"Not yet. He often stays out for hours," Reene said.

"No other unusual occurrences? No uninvited guests?"

"No, we didn't notice any strangers. We posted a friend on watch. Everything went off as planned," added Lissa.

The trooper gazed out the window at people still milling around the makeshift ring. Dusk had settled over the fields.

"It'll be dark soon. Too late to search the woods. But I'll be back first thing tomorrow," the sergeant promised.

"Of course. We're so sorry we didn't call you," Lissa apologized.

The trooper ignored Lissa's apology. "During my previous interview with both of you, I suspected then that you were holding back important information." His hard glance shifted between the two women. "If you know something pertinent, I advise you to tell me. Otherwise, your interference with this official investigation could land you in more trouble."

Both women could only nod dumbly at his harsh words.

Sensing his message had hit home, Edmondson continued to admonish them. "Chief Frechette delegated authority to me on this case. And I believe I have a lead on the person who has caused all this mayhem. Someone has a vendetta against you. Your reckless behavior drew him out again. By good fortune none of you were harmed."

The sergeant regarded them with unconcealed anger.

"Contact me immediately if you receive any more unexpected packages. In the future, perhaps you'll remember we're here to protect you. I'll leave you to your guests." With a curt nod, he picked up the box and left the tack room.

The barn was now deserted except for Gina who was feeding carrots to the horses.

"Good evening, Mrs. Richards," the trooper said.

"Good evening, sergeant. Lovely performance, wasn't it?"

"I wasn't here to enjoy the performance. And unfortunately, I didn't get here in time to exercise my authority. If you have any influence with those women, I advise you to use it." Without a backward glance, he stalked out.

Mystified, Gina watched his tall figure disappear. Reene and Lissa came up behind her.

"Dear friends, I'm afraid to ask, but what was this visit all about?" Gina asked. "When he left, he appeared angry."

"I'm afraid he has good reason. You may agree when we tell you the latest," Reene admitted. "He came out to warn us about interfering with police work. And that we should mind our own business and be careful."

"I'm assuming he was referring to the terrible day your wagon was rammed," Gina said. "However, that's not the impression I got. What happened today, Lissa?"

"I found a package on our front porch. A package meant as a warning."

"A warning? What kind of warning?"

Lissa hesitated. "Gina, the box contained four bloody horseshoes."

"My God!" Gina gasped. "This monster is insane! I give you both a lot of credit for carrying on. But you took a terrible chance. I gather that's why Sgt. Edmondson is not pleased by your action."

"The good sergeant is totally browned off at us. We told him we didn't want that bastard to think we would give up," Reene said. "We didn't mention we were shaking in our riding boots from start to finish."

Gina put an arm around each woman. "Try to forget this cruel person for the time being. Let the sergeant do his job. We should join the rest of the crowd. Ladies, your public awaits."

Outside the roped-off ring, Aericka, holding her relaxed horse, flashed them a broad smile and winked. She and Hilary had become the center of attention. Other riders crowded around, asking if they could help teach their horses to dance.

Bob dispensed beer and explained the intricacies of calling a square dance to anyone who'd listen. Matt stood by his friend and rolled his eyes.

"Despite looking over my shoulder the whole time, our hoedown went off without a disaster," declared Reene. "I still think we did the right thing."

261

"We squeaked by, but if things had turned out differently...," Lissa replied. "I need a drink."

"Hey, Bob, how about moving a little faster?" Reene demanded. "Three gorgeous, thirsty women are clamoring for your services."

"Don't say that too loud," Bob said as he furtively looked over his shoulder. "Aericka will kill me. Man, I didn't mean to say that," he added guiltily.

"We've had enough murder and chaos around here," Reene said. "Hand over those drinks, Bob. We're celebrating a victory today."

Hours dragged by as Reene and Lissa watched anxiously for Andes' return. His suppertime was long past, and usually he was as punctual as the horses when it came to feeding. Reene paced back and forth in the kitchen and opened the door time after time to call him. Finally just as Reene was near tears, Lissa heard a familiar scratching on the door frame.

"Andes! Thank goodness! You had us worried to death!" Reene drew him into her arms to hug him, but he yelped from her embrace.

"What's wrong, honey?" she crooned while she explored the dog's body for an injury. When she touched his shoulder, he flinched in pain.

"My poor Andes! You have a lump as big as a goose egg! I'll make it better." She crushed an aspirin and sprinkled it in with Andes' supper. She sat on the floor and stroked him as he wolfed his dinner.

"So that's why he was baying his head off," Lissa said. "No four-legged animal gave him this bump. Andes, I have a feeling you are our little knight in shining armor."

Chapter 37

With Catherine Thorpe's biography parked on her lap, Lissa made herself comfortable on her chaise lounge. Preparing for the hoedown—and *surviving* the hoedown—had pushed reading Catherine's life story on the back burner. It was her turn to feed so she gave the horses an early dinner. Now she could enjoy, if that was the word, delving into Catherine's life story.

She flipped the pages, grimacing at the damage done by Josey's vengeful letter opener stunt. Fortunately, the blade hadn't penetrated too deeply.

"Darn you, Josey. I'll owe the library a new copy."

She intently studied photographs in between the chapters. None of the names or faces looked familiar.

Out of the corner of her eye, she noticed an upraised tail. Jesse hopped onto the chaise and she made room for him, absently stroking his head.

As Lissa continued to read, she acquired a good grasp of Catherine's personality traits. Definitely Type A. Ambition and a thirst for money had driven her to become one of the wealthiest women of her generation. Catherine had bought the majority of shares in her husband's company and therefore held a controlling interest.

"Methinks 'control' was the key word in Ms. Thorpe's vocabulary. I wonder if she wore the pants in the family? Silly question. Of course she did."

Several years after the Civil War ended, Catherine had married the son of a wealthy railroad baron and produced two children in a relatively short time: a boy and a girl.

"No doubt Catherine had planned their sex. Now, that's a control freak," she muttered. "Let's see, when did this marriage take place? 1875, the same year Josey was killed. Interesting."

Shadows crept into her room while she continued to delve into the life of this morbidly fascinating woman. Engrossed in the book, Lissa vaguely heard Reene holler.

"I'm running over to Tom's, so don't wait up for me."

"No problem, whatever," Lissa mumbled in reply. Skipping forward a couple of chapters, she found things heating up.

Approaching middle age Catherine had shown signs of erratic behavior and an increasingly violent temper. From all accounts, Catherine's husband had tried to remain supportive, but had fought a losing battle. The pressure of maintaining her business holdings increased, causing Catherine to become more and more irrational. Her descent into madness took its toll on her immediate family. Both children married young and immediately moved as far away from their mother as possible.

"This woman practically invented the dysfunctional family," Lissa decided, turning the pages. "I can't wait to see what happened to her."

The next chapter held the answer. Due to her unreasonable demands, she was removed from many of the Boards on which she sat. Eventually she became delusional, and her mind retreated to the days when she had been a vital, young woman. She spent hours endlessly pacing the rooms and corridors of her empty mansion.

According to the author, before her confinement she constantly called out to her long lost love, a man named Peter. She vacillated between piteous sobs for him to come back and maniacal outbursts of terror. Her servants could hear her scream 'Go away! I killed you! Leave me alone!'

"Holy crap! If that isn't an admission of guilt, I'll give up riding."

It was now the turn of the twentieth century, where insane asylums and madhouses were the norm. Her family reluctantly stepped in and finally had her committed. Catherine Thorpe spent the rest of her life in an asylum for the insane.

Lissa felt a twinge of horror and revulsion as she imagined what life must have been like for those 'patients'. But she found it hard to work up any sympathy for this murderer.

"Reading between the lines," she decided, "Catherine had fallen in love with Peter. But when he came back from the war in love with a Black girl, Catherine went crazy with jealousy. Hell hath no fury like a crazed woman scorned. In revenge, she murdered Josey."

Subdued by the realization of Josey's murder, Lissa read the last few chapters. Catherine died in 1915, a few years after her husband, and was mourned by virtually no one. No surprise there. Her children made an appearance, took charge of the funeral arrangements and departed at the earliest opportunity. Her mansion, sold almost immediately, was demolished and an office complex built in its place. Nothing remained of Catherine's accomplishments but her name on a few old buildings.

Lissa closed the book and rested her throbbing head on the chaise. "Well, Josey my girl, now I know why you haven't crossed over. We've solved this part of the puzzle. Is that good enough to help you find peace?"

No response. Josey must be playing hard to get.

I'll try one more thing, Lissa decided as she dragged her tired body off the chaise lounge. A cozy chat with the author. *I'll call Donna in the morning. She promised me she'd run a search on his name. I'm sure he knows more than what he revealed in his book.*

"Good night, Josephine, wherever the heck you are."

"Reference Desk. This is Donna."

"Good morning, Donna. It's Lissa from the Barn Swallow Inn."

"Lissa, I have that information you requested about the author of *Heiress to Madness.*"

"That's why I'm calling," Lissa replied. "But you gotta excuse me. I've been incredibly busy escaping certain death and destruction."

"I heard you and Reene had a frightening adventure recently," Donna said.

"Bad news still travels fast, doesn't it? Luckily none of us were seriously hurt. The police are investigating. Enough said. Donna, what's the scoop on Leonard Rogers?"

"Leonard Rogers is the pseudonym for Scott Collins, a local author who has published a few books. Mostly reference material. He's a lawyer with a practice in Westbrook. Got a pen?"

Back at her cluttered desk, Lissa frowned at the number she had written on her notepad.

"Will a visit to Scott Collins do me any good? Would he reveal anything new about Catherine Thorpe? If he's a typical lawyer, he can talk through my allotted hour and say absolutely nothing. Same as a politician. "

Lissa called the number and a pleasant-voiced woman took her name and information and scheduled an appointment for the following week. Scratching the appointment on her calendar, she heard the back door slam.

"Helllooooooo!!!! Is that you, Reene?" Lissa hollered.

"Yeah, it's me," Reene replied.

Lissa walked into the kitchen where Reene was dumping bags of groceries on the counter. When she began slamming cans and boxes into the cupboards and muttering, Lissa could stand it no longer.

"Reene, what is the matter? You're making enough racket to raise the dead."

"Nothing's the matter except I've fallen in love with a male chauvinistic jerk!"

"Oho, we're using the L-word now? What horrible thing has Tom said or done to put you into such a temper?"

"Silly me! Last night I failed to apologize on bended knee for not running to him like a damsel in distress. He was not too polite, and a team of wild horses couldn't drag two words out of him. Idiot!" She slammed the cabinet door so hard it popped back open, making her even angrier.

"My, my, love does strange things to people." Lissa quietly closed the swinging door. "Reene, don't you realize how much Tom cares for you? That's why he's so angry. When a man is frightened for the woman he loves, he usually stomps around and growls and acts like a grizzly bear with four sore paws."

"You think?" Reene snapped. She scuffed the floor with her boot like a little kid caught telling a fib. "I guess I should cut him some slack. But damn it, I can take care of myself!"

"Yes, you can. But he's worried you might do something foolish. Although I can't imagine how he got that impression. Looks like you both have to give a little. Compromise, I believe it's called?"

"Yeah, I think I've heard of it. Well, I'm not calling him right away. He can just sit around and growl a little longer."

Lissa threw her hands up in the air in mock despair. "You young people will drive me to drink! Listen, Miss Lonely Hearts, I have news. I finally finished the biography about Catherine Thorpe. She was definitely off center. The book also suggests she might have committed a 'foul deed', as they used to say in them days. Reene, I'm convinced she killed Josey."

"We've got to be sure about this, Lissa. Otherwise, Josey will never find peace."

"Agreed. That's why I'm going straight to the source. The author."

"Who is the author? Does he live nearby?"

"His name is Scott Collins. He wrote the book under a pen name," Lissa replied. "He's a lawyer with a practice here in town. I've got an appointment with him next week."

266

"A lawyer?" She rolled her eyes. "Wonderful. He may not give you a straight answer if he's protecting someone."

"What else is new? Maybe I should take a page from Andrea's book and go on the principle there's nothing I can't get if I want it badly enough."

A week later, Lissa drove into Westbrook's business zone. She wasn't too familiar with this section and took one too many wrong turns locating the address. Ironically, Attorney Collins' building stood only a block from the police station.

"Atty. Collins will see you momentarily, Mrs. Martin," smiled the receptionist. "Won't you have a seat?"

She barely had time to thumb through the latest copy of *Newsweek* before the gracious receptionist ushered her into the attorney's office.

"Atty. Collins, I really appreciate your seeing me, especially as this visit has nothing to do with retaining your services. If I may, I'd like to ask a few questions concerning your book on Catherine Thorpe's life."

"I'm flattered you've even read the book," the attorney responded.

"Circumstances forced me to read your book." Then she blushed as she realized how that sounded. "I'm terribly sorry, Atty. Collins," Lissa apologized. "That didn't come out the way I intended."

"Don't apologize," Collins smiled. "Some of my friends who have read the book feel the same way. What sort of questions do you have?"

"Is there a possibility some information got left on the cutting room floor, so to speak?" Lissa asked. "I'm particularly interested in circumstances surrounding Catherine's decent into madness. You mention in Chapter Twelve that Catherine had been overheard crying 'Go away! I killed you' or words to that effect. Can you verify she was rambling or were you basing your statement on reality?"

"May I ask why this is so important to you? My great-great grandmother has been dead for nearly a century. I can't imagine anything she did or said so long ago is of current importance. Moreover, I do not wish to have her reputation further tarnished due to speculation."

"Your great-great grandmother!" Lissa echoed. "I had no idea. The book jacket doesn't mention your relationship to her."

"No, it doesn't. But you didn't answer my question."

"No, I didn't, did I?" Lissa answered. "Actually, the reason I'm so interested is we, that is, my friend Reene Anderson and I, believe Catherine Thorpe may have caused the death of Josephine Taylor

Williams. Perhaps you've heard we found letters hidden in our inn confirming that Josephine Williams spied for the North during the Civil War?"

"Yes, of course. The news has been well publicized. Congratulations on your accomplishment. I also understand your inn is now listed on the National Register of Historic Buildings. Quite a feather in your cap."

"We think so. But some of the letters we found strongly state that Catherine hated Josephine and became insanely jealous of her. We've delved further into the connection between these two women, and we are certain Josephine's death was not an accident. I'm sure you can understand we'd like to bring closure to this story in every way possible. Can you confirm Catherine had a darker side? Darker than you portray in your book?"

"Mrs. Anderson, as my family's lawyer I can neither confirm nor deny anything. What you suggest is purely speculation. However, strictly off the record, there were some references to past incidents, which ended up on the 'cutting room floor', as you so delicately put it. Some statements Catherine made while confined were so unrelated to her story, the editor felt it unnecessary to include them. As I recall, some nonsense about 'shooting a horse' and 'marrying a darkie'. Great fortunes often mask great crimes. You may draw your own conclusions."

Lissa locked eyes with Collins. He was clearly throwing out a thread and it was up to her to catch it.

"I see. Unfortunately, those are not the conclusions I'd hoped for."

A look of mutual understanding passed between them. "I'm afraid I've wasted your valuable time. Thank you so much for seeing me."

"Not at all, Mrs. Martin. I trust I have been of some service?"

"Most definitely. We'd love to have you as a guest at our inn. You would enjoy a lovely break from your hectic schedule, right here in town. You might even be interested in learning more about the young woman who stirred our curiosity. An amazing person who risked everything for her country and the man she loved."

"You have intrigued me. I believe I will find the time to visit your inn. Good day."

Driving home, Lissa mulled over the interview. While she had hoped for an outright admission of guilt on Catherine's part in the 'accident', Scott Collins had given her a confirmation of sorts. Was he being noble by protecting his great-great grandma or was there another reason?

After lunch, sitting at the kitchen table with steaming mugs of tea, Lissa gave Reene the short version of what she had learned at Attorney Collins' office.

"Basically, without saying the words he said Mad Catherine committed murder, right?" Reene asked. "We're almost one hundred percent sure she killed Josey. That she staged the riding accident. No one would've questioned what happened. Catherine was a clever girl."

"Too clever for her own good. Even though she got away with murder, Catherine eventually paid the price. She went insane and died alone with no family to comfort her. Finally, Collins lobbed a tidbit about Catherine. I returned it. Game, set and match. As you've told me once or twice, what goes around comes around."

"Exactly. I'm tired of all these hidden secrets and long-lost relatives. Now that we've solved the mystery, we can only hope Josey is satisfied and decides it's time to leave."

Chapter 38

"You should welcome this exposure, Andrea," Grady Ferguson argued. "A major part of a politician's life is public speaking. And it won't hurt to polish your skills in front of a large group."

Mayor Stuart had challenged her in print to meet him to debate the issues. Furious at his one-upmanship, she accepted his challenge. Tonight's debate between the mayoral candidates would kick off the official race for votes.

"Keep pushing the off-ramp plan. Make it sound like it will happen tomorrow. The mayor may wake up enough to point out that the ramp could stall years in the planning stage or that the budget would require an approval by the town counselors. And don't even mention that homeowners and businesses could lose their land to eminent domain."

"I *know* that, Grady," Andrea snapped. "I'm quite prepared to tap dance around the issue, thank you very much."

"And flash that new engagement ring around," Grady said. "Nothing warms the women voters' hearts like an old fashioned love story."

Andrea stared at her ring, a two carat emerald surrounded by baguette diamonds that Lloyd had mockingly slid on her finger. *"A token of my love and fidelity."* The memory froze her into immobility. Oblivious of her silence, Grady continued to pepper her with his campaign strategy.

"Speaking of women, what's your stand on Affirmative Action? I wouldn't think it'd be a high priority out here in the sticks. The gooks and spics already know they'd have a hard time collecting welfare in this corner of the state."

"Is there anyone you *do* like?" she asked sarcastically.

"Yeah, a few. So where do you stand?"

"I believe in equal opportunity under the law," Andrea responded.

"A brilliant, ambiguous answer. I'm impressed," Grady said. "Do you plan on appointing some of your women friends to cushy jobs?"

"Don't be ridiculous," she snapped. "I don't intend to hand out 'cushy jobs', as you nastily put it, simply because of gender. No one gave me a break. I had to earn my way just like any man."

"Just the same, you should be ready in case His Honor drags out 'righting past wrongful discrimination'. That's hysterical considering he has his own network of friends and there's not a Black or a Jew among them. Let's go over your notes one more time."

When their bull session finally ended, Andrea, none too graciously, ushered him out of her conference room. But not out of her mind. His biting remarks struck home.

"That son of a bitch! Who is he to judge?" In frustration Andrea swept the notes off the table. "And if I bitched to Lloyd, he'd only laugh in my face and call me a hypocrite. Once this election is over, I intend to eliminate both Lloyd and Grady from my life. Permanently."

Chapter 39

"Damn those amateur sleuths!" Sgt. Edmondson griped. "If they weren't hiding evidence, they were trying to solve problems that put them in danger. Then it's up to us when it's almost too late to clean up the mess."

Earlier that day he'd conducted a thorough search of the woods adjacent to where the women had claimed Anderson's dog went into a barking fit. After an exhausting hunt, he returned to his cruiser with what appeared to be proof of a planned attack sealed in a plastic bag. He'd found the BB gun among broken branches and trampled ground.

"I'll drop this off at the station with the horseshoes," he decided as he sped down Breckenridge Road. "Paul and his boys can handle this job."

Back at his office he had just finished writing up this latest development when his phone jangled. It was Randal Simms.

"How is the investigation going?" Simms barked. "Any progress in finding the killer?"

"Sir, we're handling the situation. I can't reveal any of our leads."

"I understand. But I want to do all I can to help solve Stephen's murder," Simms declared. "We were friends in college, you know."

"We're doing all we can," the sergeant said. "Now if you will excuse me, I really must get back to work."

Simms persisted in his efforts to help. "I took numerous photos that day and I'll bring in all the pictures of the parade if you think they'll do any good. Other people may have videos. Have you investigated that angle?"

Keeping a lid of his temper, Edmondson thanked the banker for his cooperation and urged him to send over his photographs. Then he hustled out to his cruiser.

Next stop, office of Mr. Lloyd Collins, Esquire.

"Wilson's alibi, bird watching or whatever the hell, with her future husband was hardly new or clever," Edmondson mused. "Without a doubt they were covering for each other. Rank amateurs."

"May I help you?" Lloyd asked as he opened the door.

"Sergeant Edmondson of the State Police," he stated as he flipped open his wallet and flashed his identification card. "Sir, I'd like to ask you a few questions if I may."

"Of course, sergeant. Please come into my office. I don't have any clients at the moment. We won't be interrupted."

"I presume you know why I'm here," Edmondson said pointedly.

"In fact, I do. You wish to know my whereabouts at the time Stephen Marshall was killed."

"That's correct, sir."

"As I'm certain Ms. Wilson confirmed, we were picnicking in the Berkshires. Actually, I brought her there to propose. Everything went exceedingly well. We arrived around noon and left a little before six. It gets dark so early now and we didn't want to find ourselves lost in Pompanoosuc Park."

"Anyone else see you there?"

"Only a few hikers and other nature lovers. I don't believe there's a ranger station in that particular park."

"How well did you know Stephen Marshall?"

"Only on a casual basis," Lloyd answered. "I met him once or twice when he and Andrea were married. We didn't travel in the same social circles."

Edmondson noted the slightly bitter edge in his last comment. Had this guy been jealous enough to kill?

"Then you wouldn't know any of his close friends?"

"No, Officer, I'm afraid not. Possibly Andrea could help in that department."

"You became engaged to Ms. Wilson soon after Mr. Marshall's death, didn't you?"

"I realize it may seem in poor taste, Officer, and I admit the timing could have been better, but we had talked about marriage months ago. We only made it official the day of the unfortunate incident. Stephen's passing had nothing to do with our decision."

"Timing is everything, isn't it?" the officer responded. "Is there anything else you'd like to tell me?"

"Only that I can truthfully say I had absolutely nothing to do with Stephen's murder," Lloyd replied.

"Thank you, Mr. Collins. That's all for now. I may want to talk to you again. If I were you, I wouldn't make any plans to leave town just now."

"My word of honor, I have no intentions of going anywhere."

Lloyd closed his office for the day and called Andrea. The interview with the state trooper sent warning signals flying. To his annoyance she insisted on meeting at her office. His aggravation grew the longer she kept him waiting, the door to her office shut.

Lloyd paced back and forth like a caged tiger. Furious at being left hanging, he flung open her door.

Andrea stood by the window, violently wringing and massaging her hands. Incoherent mutterings punctuated the eerie silence.

"Having a spot o' bother, Lady Macbeth?"

Andrea whirled, her eyes wide with madness. "I didn't invite you in! Get out!"

"Temper, temper," Lloyd snapped. "May I remind you that the blood on your hands is permanent?"

"It's not Stephen's blood I'm trying to wash away. It's my own blood. And I'll never wash it away."

"Wash away your guilt, you mean. I'm afraid the late unlamented Lady M went mad trying to rid herself of her guilt. If you start sleepwalking anytime soon, I may have second thoughts about our upcoming nuptials."

"Sleepwalking? You just gave me the perfect excuse to sleepwalk through our 'upcoming nuptials'." Andrea seated herself at her desk and now regarded him with a serene smile.

"Touché. Andrea, is it too much to ask that we could meet at a restaurant? Or my brownstone? We have to talk."

"And is it too much to ask that you could remember I'm in the middle of an election campaign?"

"How can I forget? It's an all-consuming subject with you."

"Damn right. I won't have time for frivolous lunches or *tête-à-têtes* until I'm elected."

"You're so determined to protect your 'dark secret', you've lost sight of everything else," Lloyd retorted.

"You idiot!" she rasped. "If I don't protect my 'dark secret', I'll be treated exactly like my ancestors."

"You're acting like it's the fifties!" Lloyd snapped in exasperation. "You can drink from the White water fountain now."

"Don't patronize me! And spare me the usual platitudes about freedom and equality. The bottom line is the North cloaks its true feelings in civility and breeding. Now everyone is so politically correct:

'I *adore* Black people. Why, my dear friend Alida is Black and our children play together.'"

Her expression hardened. "If I had been born in the South, at least I'd know where I stand. They're in your face telling you they hate you," she snapped, eyes flashing with hatred.

"I must admit you've revealed an unpleasant truth about New England," Lloyd said. "Trust me, I do understand. But look in the mirror, Andrea. Ask yourself if you see a woman empowered by her own accomplishments or a woman shamed by her own self-loathing. There's the rub, my dear future mayor. I'll leave you with some of your favorite words. 'Watch your ass!'"

Chapter 40

"I'm so saddle sore I can't stand myself," moaned Lissa. She hobbled down the aisle with her saddle, heaved it onto the rack and trundled back for the saddle pad and bridle.

"Me too," admitted Reene. "I'm beginning to have second thoughts about our brilliant idea."

"What do you mean, 'our'? I must've been delirious when I agreed to this stunt," Lissa grunted as she led Bravo out to his paddock. Their training had paid off. His coat was shining and his flanks were muscling up nicely. Unfortunately, *her* flanks were muscling up a bit too much.

"Seriously," Reene said when she joined Lissa outside, "I'm worried if we can pull this off. Our hoedown almost turned into a tragedy. I can't shake the image of those bloody horseshoes. What if he tries again? During the ride or when we dedicate the plaque?"

"Reene, he's a coward who got chased off by your dog! He won't dare bother us."

"Brave little Andes! If I'd lost him—," Reene choked.

"But you didn't. He was our hero that day," Lissa said lightly. She smiled at her friend. "Think of all the long trail rides we've done, just the two of us, deep in the wilds of Maine and New Hampshire. We didn't fall off, we didn't get lost, and our horses never put a hoof wrong. Believe me, we won't put a foot wrong this time either."

"We have had some adventures, haven't we Lissa?"

"Yes, and this will be an amazing adventure. We just have to make sure we're careful. The mayor will be there. So will Tom, Gina, and all our new friends when we come galloping triumphantly up the road. Think of Josey. If she could do it in the middle of a war, we can do it now."

"Exactly. You've given my courage a boost. Good point about the war. She and Shiloh were under fire in terrible danger. I won't disappoint her—or you."

Trying to relax in her bedroom, Reene jumped when the phone jangled intsistently. "Hello," she signed.

"Hi, Reenie," At that moment, Tom's sexy voice was the last thing Reene expected to hear. His quick changes of emotion were driving her crazy.

"Tom, I am glad you called. Our last visit ended on a sour note."

"I know, Reenie. I get bull-headed some times."

"You most certainly do. You have to realize I'm a big girl and can take care of myself. Even though Lissa and I have had a hellacious time lately. Ever since we found those Civil War letters, a lot of weirdos have come out of the woodwork. We almost got run off the road when Sissy was deliberately spooked. She took off for home at an almost dead run."

"What the hell! Why didn't you tell me?"

"You were away helping your friend who lost his barn. I didn't want to be a burden."

"You are *not* a burden and I don't ever want to hear you say that again."

"Yes, dear," she said in a small voice.

"That's my girl," he said tenderly. "Your horse wasn't hurt, was she?"

"Yes, she was. She suffered some painful cuts to her legs. Sissy's okay now. But Tom, it was a close call. Lissa thinks we were the victims of a hate crime. We've gotten weird phone calls, and crude messages in the mail."

"Good God! Lissa is right. You are victims of a hate crime."

"If you'd heard the rotten things the guy yelled at us..."

"Son of a bitch! I'd like to punch the lights out of this jerk."

"Tom, maybe you can help us in another way. I think the guy's truck had farm plates, but it happened so fast I'm not sure. It was a dark green older GMC pick-up. half ton, I'd say. A NASCAR decal pasted on the back window. Have you ever seen a truck like that?"

For a long moment, there was silence on the other end of the line. When Tom answered, Reene was startled by the change in his voice. It was cold and flat.

"Don't you go hunting for that truck, Reenie. It belongs to a real bad ass. That guy is a loud-mouthed jerk who can't hold a job for more than five minutes. He's for sale to the highest bidder whenever there's a dirty job that needs doing. Keep away from him. I'll take care of this."

"Tom, please don't think I'm ungrateful, but I just told you I can take care of myself. Besides I don't want you to get into any trouble. I'd be

277

devastated if anything happened to you because you were trying to help me."

"Would you, Reenie?" he asked softly. "You're definitely worth it."

She blushed like a bride on her wedding night. Thank God he couldn't see her face. "You are sweet to say that. Do you know who owns the pickup?"

"Yeah, I do. But I'm not telling you. I'll handle it my own way."

"Tom, don't be stubborn! Let the police do their job. We're already in enough trouble."

"Don't worry, Reenie. If push comes to shove, I'm just going to have a little pleasant conversation, is all."

"Stubborn!" she yelled again. "If you get killed, don't come crying to me!"

Tom's low chuckle made her even madder. "As I believe I mentioned, you're worth it."

The call disconnected and she stood frozen in exasperation.

"Well, at least I used my brain and didn't mention the hoedown. He'd go after that guy in a heartbeat. And do something stupid. It would be my fault! If anything happened to Tom, I'd never forgive myself."

So much for not getting emotionally involved with him. She loved him. She'd fallen in so deep she might never climb out. She didn't *want* to climb out. Ever.

Chapter 41

"Remember when you got the heebie jeebies about this ride?" Lissa asked as they groomed their horses. "Now our day of reckoning is staring me in the face and I'm a basket case. First that nutcase nearly killed us. And as for our hoedown, I won't even go there."

Since their encounter with the truck, the phone calls had stopped and no more weird letters or horrifying packages had arrived. Chief Frechette had called with the depressing news that neither the bloody horseshoes or the BB gun revealed any readable prints.

To their relief, everything had fallen into place for the grand finale. Their ride would follow designated roads and return them to the inn for the dedication by Mayor Stuart.

Reene popped out of Shenan's stall. "I know. We're turning into nervous wrecks. But we've got to go through with this, especially after we made such a point of reenacting Josey's ride. We'll be extra careful and watch for trouble makers."

"That's not too comforting when I think of all the hiding places along our route. Oh, man, I'm not doing myself any favors. I'd better calm down or Bravo will feel every nerve twanging in my body." Lissa put the brushes back in her tack box and threw the saddle pad over his back.

"We're right on schedule. It should take us just a little over an hour to go the distance from the center of town and return here. The mayor and his entourage will be camped out at the inn. Gina plans to have her photographer set up on the farmer's porch."

"In that case, how do I look?" Lissa asked, tilting her cap to a more rakish angle. An old pair of Hank's pants covered her Western riding boots. A worn flannel shirt and suspenders completed her outfit.

"Marvelous! We're like twins!" Reene answered.

"More like twins separated at birth," Lissa grumbled. "You look like a fashion model while I look like Boxcar Willie. But I'm ready if you are."

She led Bravo over to the mounting block and climbed on. She checked the horn bag for her cell phone. If they ran into trouble, she wanted a phone handy to dial 911.

Reene quickly clipped Shenan's breastplate in place and hopped on. "Let's go! We're off on another great adventure!"

"Josey, I hope you appreciate what we're doing for you, girl," Lissa muttered while she adjusted her stirrups. "This is going to feel like the longest five miles of my life."

"Who are you talking to back there?" Reene asked.

"I'm talking to Miss Josey. She's probably riding along with us. If I'm not mistaken, we're going to need every bit of help she can give us."

Reene laughed and twisted around in her saddle. "Trust me, she's here. She wouldn't miss this for anything. Come on, partner, we can't let her down!"

Reene lightly squeezed Shenan who settled into a comfortable rocking-chair canter. Lissa cued Bravo and they loped along side by side until they reached their first designated turn off.

To their delight, despite it being the middle of the week, more than a few spectators lined the road. Some had staked out good vantage points and had brought lawn chairs and coolers.

"Good morning!" Reene called. "Thank you so much for coming!"

Lissa nodded and smiled her thanks. Everyone's warm response helped calm her fears. She was silly to worry. He wouldn't dare.

As they continued on, young children jogged alongside asking questions. Some waved small American flags and surprisingly, a few waved Confederate flags.

"Reene, look at those flags! I didn't think you could find any north of the Mason Dixon line."

"That's awesome! Everyone's really getting into this! Let's pick up a trot."

Their horses settled into a slow steady trot. The October air was so clear they could almost taste it. Overhead a great red-tailed hawk soared effortlessly, hunting its prey.

Both riders kept a constant watch along the road. While Lissa was determined to enjoy every moment, she was also on the alert for trouble. Their narrow escapes only a few weeks ago still remained fresh in her mind.

"How far do you think we've come?" Lissa asked when they slowed down to a walk. "We've had such an enthusiastic reception the time has flown by."

"We're about halfway there. I'd say we're right on schedule," Reene replied.

"I've noticed a lot of folks taking pictures. I hope they shoot my good side—whichever side that might be."

When their route took them back toward the inn, Shen and Bravo's internal compass kicked in and the last few miles were eaten up by their eagerness to return to their paddocks. Curious onlookers had dwindled to an occasional spectator.

"We should rest them a bit," Reene said, taking a healthy gulp from the water bottle hanging from her saddle horn. "So they'll be full of beans when we gallop up to the inn as if the Confederate army were after us!"

"I'll be satisfied with a rather sedate grand entrance, but I gotta admit a full gallop is much more exciting. Let's give them another five minutes to get their wind."

"All set now?" Reene asked when the allotted time was up. She pulled her cap lower on her forehead and settled deeper into her saddle, ready to run.

"As set as I'll ever be," Lissa replied, her heart pounding in anticipation.

In response, Reene let out a rebel yell that nearly scared Lissa out of her boots. Shen and Bravo's heads flew up. They pricked their ears and began dancing in place.

Suddenly, fist-sized rocks rained down on them from the hillside above. Dirt flew off the road as the rocks landed near their horses' feet. A jagged chunk narrowly missed Shenan's head. Reene flinched when a missile hit her shoulder.

"Oh, my God! He's here! He's trying to kill us again!"

"You rotten son of a bitch!" Lissa yelled. Another large rock sailed by her head.

"Let's get the hell out of here! Go! Go!" Reene hollered.

Before Lissa could collect herself, Bravo screamed and bolted forward with a spurt that nearly put her on his neck. Desperately she tried to regain her seat. She could hear pounding hooves behind her. Shen ran right on Bravo's heels. Terrified their horses' legs would tangle, Lissa swerved her horse to the left to give Shen room.

"Let them have their heads!" Reene cried. "We've got to put space between us and that crazy rock thrower!"

Side by side they raced along the road. Even in their frantic attempt to escape their attacker, the frightened women noticed more spectators clustered along the road. The unknowing crowd cheered and waved as the two riders, using all their skill to keep the horses separated, pounded down the road.

"I think we're safe now!" Lissa gasped. "Where can we pull them in?"

"Head for that open spot up ahead! Last mailbox on the left!"

The two horses made up ground so fast they nearly overrode the opening.

"Come back, Bravo! Come back!" Lissa cried. His frenzied gallop shortened only marginally at her command. With all her strength, she pulled his head almost around to his shoulder and aimed for open space. Bravo had no choice; jerking his head in protest, he broke into an uneven canter, throwing his body left and right. The abrupt change in rhythm nearly yanked Lissa from her saddle.

"Watch out! I need room!" yelled Reene. Onlookers scattered in fear when Reene swung her horse in a wide circle. Mothers grabbed their children and dragged them to safety. A young boy tripped over his lawn chair, sending it flying.

Reene was struggling to control Shenan, who tossed her head dangerously and danced sideways. No one on the sidelines dared to help by risking a kick from Shen's powerful hind legs.

After a few more headlong strides, both horses slowed to a ragged trot. At last the two frightened animals began to relax. When they lurched to a halt, both were blowing hard and covered with sweat.

"That cowardly bastard!" Lissa raged. Quickly she dismounted to check Bravo for injuries. She had never heard him scream like that, and the sound had chilled her to her core.

"Is everything all right?" a tentative voice offered. "Your horse looks distressed."

Lissa's attention swung toward the stranger, an older gentleman with the weathered look of a farmer. A tall woman with short salt and pepper hair stood at his side, her arm linked with his.

Making an effort, Lissa smiled at him gratefully. "We've had a bit of a dust-up down the road," she explained. "Our horses got spooked and so did we. But we're handling it okay now. Thank you so much for your concern."

"You're welcome," the man smiled. "We'd been enjoying your exciting horsemanship." He glanced at his companion who nodded her head in agreement.

"We were afraid it looked a bit too real for comfort," she said, care radiating from steel-blue eyes behind wide rimmed glasses.

"Our sentiments exactly," Reene chimed in as she dismounted. "We just need a breather and we'll be good to go. If you all can stick around, join us at the Barn Swallow Inn for the big finish. And refreshments!"

"We'll take you up on that!" another man hollered. "Good luck to you!"

"Thanks again," Lissa waved.

"Good cover-up, Lissa. We don't need a mob scene right now. Are you okay?" Reene asked. "Is Bravo hurt?"

"The asshole missed me. But Bravo took a hit. Dear Lord, if that bastard hurt my horse, I'll break every bone in his body."

Lissa patted Bravo's neck and whispered sweet nothings in his ear. Although he couldn't comprehend her words, she knew he could understand her touch and the tone of her voice.

"Damn it! He's got a nasty welt on his rump and a big scratch on his flank. His legs seem sound. What about Shen?"

"She's fine. No thanks to that prick," Reene answered, hurrying over to look at Bravo. "The rock must have hit a big muscle in his butt. Thankfully that cut doesn't look too deep. He's such a good boy," she added, stroking his sweaty neck.

Lissa noticed the motion made her wince in pain. "Reene! Were you hit too?"

"My shoulder. Purple bruises are probably blossoming as we speak. Nothing I can't stand."

"I am so done with this! It's probably the same creep who tried to run us off the road! And I thought he'd been scared off when Andes attacked him! The minute we're finished with this ride and the mayor, I'm calling the police. If we'd gotten hurt, I'd be on that cell phone right now and the hell with the plaque dedication!"

"What kind of a madman hides in bushes to throw rocks at women and animals? Are you kidding me?" Reene railed. "He's lucky I didn't catch him. Shen and I would've trampled his ass!"

Lissa's first concern was for her horse. "Reene, what do you think? Should I ride Brav?"

"He certainly ran down the road like there was nothing wrong with him."

"His adrenaline had kicked in. I'm worried how he'll feel once the rush subsides."

"We'll take it easy and see how he goes. Then if he seems sound, we can try a nice slow canter up the drive."

"That'll work. But if he shows any signs of lameness, I'm hopping right off." Lissa paused to peer at her friend's sweaty, dirty face. "Do I look as I bad as I feel?"

Reene nodded in agreement. "I'm afraid so." She grinned wickedly. "You look like you just crawled out of a coal mine."

"I *feel* like I just crawled out of a coal mine. No one can say we didn't recreate this ride right down to the last detail. When we get back to the inn, let's not mention what happened. At least not right away. I don't want anything more to spoil this ceremony."

"I totally agree. We've put our heart and soul into this project."

"We've also added blood, sweat, and a few tears," Lissa said as she checked her horse again. His coat was matted with sweat, but his chest felt barely warm. She walked him over to the shoulder of the road and climbed into the saddle. Reene mounted as well and they slowly moved out.

"Goodbye and thanks again!" Lissa called over her shoulder. The friendly onlookers waved and smiled. Their response calmed other spectators who had fled to safer ground. Cautiously they emerged from hiding to holler words of encouragement.

"Lissa, I'll trail behind you for a bit to see how he goes." Reene leaned over Shen's shoulder to watch Bravo's progress. "He's not off at the walk. Ask him to try a little trot."

Gingerly Lissa lightly kicked Bravo's side and he responded with a slow, steady gait. "He doesn't feel off either and his head isn't bobbing," she called. She patted his neck again. "Thank heavens for your hearty Quarter Horse breeding. But if a rock had hit your legs... I can't even go there. Reene, I'll *never* understand why our beautiful horses were designed to carry all their weight on such delicate legs."

Reene trotted to her side, reached over and pressed Lissa's hand in sympathetic agreement.

By the time they were halfway along the carriage road, shade and the long walk had cooled the horses enough so they could make a dramatic and thrilling finish.

"Are you ready?" Reene asked. "Your boy looks like he's gotten his second wind."

"We're both more than ready," Lissa answered. "Now my adrenaline is pumping. Let's give 'em something to write home about!"

In response, Reene let out another rebel yell. Bravo and Shen leaped forward. Galloping out of the woods, they surged up the long driveway.

"Here they come!"

"Ride 'em, cowgirls!" Tom whooped.

The crowd of dignitaries and friends on the farmer's porch applauded loudly. Whistles and cheers accompanied them as they skidded to a halt a few feet from the inn. Lights flashed and video cameras rolled.

"Congratulations, you two!" beamed Gina, hurrying down from the porch. "It must have been so exciting. You looked as if the Devil himself were after you!"

"Thanks, Gina, but you don't know how right you are," Reene replied as she dismounted. She lowered her voice, but Gina heard the anger in it.

Under the pretext of stroking Shenan's neck, Gina whispered, "Did something go wrong? You sound angry."

"Yes. The Devil himself *was* after us. We'll give you the full story later. We've got to take care of our horses before we can join the mayor for the ceremony."

"I'll keep things moving here," Gina said. "With a little persuasion, I can convince Mayor Stuart to make a speech about the upcoming election. Needless to say, as long as there's film in the camera, he'll keep smiling and posing."

"You're the best," Lissa said as she walked up leading Bravo. "We need a distraction so no one will miss us."

"I understand. Take your time. Leave His Honor to me."

Leading their horses to the barn, they swiftly removed saddles and bridles. Lissa cleaned the cut on Bravo's flank and covered it with an antibiotic cream. Then she applied cold cloths to the lump on his rear while she thoroughly checked the rest of his body for damage.

"Lissa? Reenie? Is everything all right?" It was Tom.

He had sensed something happened when the two women abruptly left without a word. He decided to find out what they were hiding.

"Tom! You startled me! Nothing's wrong. Honestly," Reene said hurriedly.

"If nothing's wrong, then why does Lissa's horse have a nasty cut on his flank and a lump the size of my fist on his butt?"

Lissa walked over to him and laid her hand on his arm. "Tom, we had another incident out on the road, but we don't want to spoil the dedication ceremony by having a squad of police cars flying up here with sirens wailing and blue lights flashing. We decided not to call the police until after the plaque dedication."

"We just had a bad scare," Reene said. "Seriously, Tom, we're all right."

Tom regarded the two women. "You are as stubborn as two mules in harness!" he exploded. "Neither of you realize how much danger you're in. All you can think of is dedicating that damn plaque!"

"You're wrong, Tom!" Reene cried. "You don't realize how important this is to us!"

Tom glowered at both of them in silence, his face unreadable.

"Well, are you going to keep yelling at us 'till we say we're sorry?" Reene said heatedly. "That's the usual male reaction."

"No, but someone I know could use a good paddling on her behind!"

Reene stared at him in stunned disbelief. Lissa burst into welcome laughter. If she hadn't laughed, she would have dissolved in tears.

"I'll give you two hell-raisers a bit longer to take care of your animals. You probably won't listen to a word I say anyway, and I wouldn't want you to disappoint the mayor in his fifteen minutes of fame."

Tom stomped out of the barn without a backward glance.

"Do you think he's mad?" Lissa asked, now dangerously close to getting the giggles.

"I don't give a damn if he is mad! That'll be the day he paddles my behind!" Reene stormed.

"I can't stand it! You'll have me in hysterics in another minute and we've got to hurry. Mayor Stuart is waiting!"

"Sorry. But he made me so angry! I'll have a little talk with Mr. O'Brien later. Here, I'll help you with your tack. We'll get the horses settled and then throw some water on our faces so we'll look human again."

Faces scrubbed clean, they hustled back to the inn. The mayor had covered his agitation at the delay by hustling a few votes. Scattered applause broke out as they joined him on the porch and shook hands.

"Thank you so much for waiting so patiently, Mayor Stuart," Reene said, summoning her brightest smile. "We had to scrub off a lot of dirt before we dared stand next to you."

"Not a problem, Mrs. Anderson. You both look charming," he smiled. "It was worth the wait, I can assure you. Shall we proceed?"

With Reene and Lissa standing on either side, Mayor Stuart proclaimed that henceforth the Barn Swallow Inn would be listed on the register of historical buildings. His aide quietly handed him the bronze marker and motioned the two women to crowd in a bit closer for the cameras. Sharing the marker between them, Mayor Stuart read the text Lissa had written.

To her amazement, he brought an emotional depth of expression to her words she had not dreamed possible. Tears formed under her lashes, and she blinked rapidly to keep from bawling.

"Congratulations to you both for your sincere and honest efforts to bring this chapter of Westbrook's history to light. By recognizing the heroism of one of our former residents, Mrs. Josephine Taylor Williams, it is sincerely hoped that an injustice has been rectified. As mayor of Westbrook, let me state unequivocally we are forever in your debt."

Applause and cheers erupted once more. The mayor took advantage of this opportunity to hug both women and plant kisses on their cheeks. Reene blushed furiously to the roots of her hair while Lissa found herself enveloped in a bear hug by the mayor's enthusiastic aide-de-camp.

Before the situation developed into a free-for-all, Gina emerged from the shadows where she had been watching the ceremony and directing the photography.

"Ladies and gentlemen, and I include Mayor Stuart in the latter category," Gina paused to savor the good-natured laughter that ensued, "Mrs. Martin and Mrs. Anderson are pleased to invite all of you to enjoy refreshments in the Gathering Room. Mayor Stuart, would you lead the way?"

Gallantly he offered an arm to each woman and they squeezed their way through the coffin door. His booming voice drifted above the crowd. At home in his element, he was having the time of his life.

Meanwhile, the enjoyment of the day had gone sour for Tom. He was angry Reene was in danger, but angrier still she hadn't turned to him for help. Little wildcat. But she'd get his help whether she asked for it or not. He slipped into his truck and quietly drove away from the inn.

"Time to pay a man-to-man call on Griffin McGuire," Tom growled.

Chapter 42

Election Day that November dawned grey and overcast, with air cold and raw with a hint of snow. The hardy souls Lissa spotted who stood outside voting headquarters and at traffic lights were warmly dressed. But after standing for hours waving and smiling at passing drivers, even their spirits had begun to sag.

Reene parked her truck behind the high school, their precinct's designated voting place. After registering earlier in the year, they were anxious to cast their votes.

"This election will be close," predicted Reene. "We gave the mayor a boost by our plaque ceremony, but Andrea certainly has her supporters."

"Well, she's lost my vote," Lissa decided. "Ever since we locked horns when she caused your accident, she freaked me out. I don't think anyone should trust her."

To their surprise, they had to stand in line to cast their ballots. Voter turnout was heavy. When they reached the voting booth, they discovered Westbrook still hadn't advanced past the pencil and paper method.

Civic duty done, they hurried down the steps. Reene suddenly clamped her hand on Lissa's arm.

"Lissa, that truck over by the dumpster! Unless I've gone senile, it's the same truck that tried to run us off the road!"

"I'll be damned. Let's march over there and check it out."

Cautiously they approached the truck. The make and color were right. Prominently displayed on the back window was the multi-colored NASCAR logo.

"This is it, I'm sure of it!" Lissa exclaimed. She dug in her pocketbook for a pen and paper. "I'll copy down the license plate. You were right! Farm plates! Should we hang around to see if the owner shows up? We can't accuse the wrong guy of attempted murder."

"Part of me itches to confront the son of a bitch, but the sensible part of me says no way! No telling what he might do if he sees us. Let's lurk around for a bit longer and if he does show up, we can call the police."

"Agreed. He's tried to kill us twice, and I intend to make sure he's punished."

"If it is him, I wonder why this fine, upstanding citizen is here. Casting his vote for duty and humanity?"

"He doesn't seem like the kind of guy who would be bothered about the election, does he?"

"Not in the slightest. Come on, Lissa. Let's sit in the truck. I'm freezing."

Two cups of coffee later, Lissa's bladder was about to burst. Enough was enough. "Either this guy isn't here or he's not coming out this century. Let's get out of here."

"Yeah. We can't kill time forever," Reene admitted and started the engine. Just as she pulled the gearshift lever down, a tall, heavyset man, hunched in his winter jacket against the cold, approached the green truck. The temperature had dropped so fast icicles dripped off his mustache.

"Lissa! Is that him? It can't be. He looks way too old."

"Maybe it's his dad or an uncle. Or no relation at all," Lissa added dryly.

"I'm going back in. Someone will tell us who he is."

"Not without me. You can ask questions while I hit the Ladies."

When Lissa emerged from the restroom, she spotted her friend making her way across the packed room.

"C'mon, let's go! I've found out who the guy is. I'll tell you in the truck."

"That was quick work," Lissa said as Reene whipped her truck out of the parking lot.

"That guy is Billy McGuire and he's our tormentor's father. From what I heard from the locals, sonny boy is a bad dude. Tom told me the same thing when he not so politely warned me not to go chasing after said dude."

"Which advice you ignored, of course. We should go right to the police with this information. They can haul his ass in for questioning."

"Can't happen soon enough for me."

From his office Chief Frechette heard their familiar voices. *Now what?* He wondered, as he came out of his office to meet them.

"Chief, we think we found the truck that ran us off the road," Lissa reported.

"Are you positive it's the same vehicle?" he asked.

"Positive," Reene confirmed. "Right down to the NASCAR decal on the window."

"Officer," the Chief said to his desk sergeant, "take down their information." Chief Frechette nodded to Reene and Lissa. "Good work in spotting the truck. I'll keep in touch."

By the time they returned to the inn, Shen, Bravo and Sissy were hollering to come in. A biting wind had picked up. They hustled out to the paddocks, brought them in and set up hay and night feed. Before she left, Lissa checked Bravo's nasty cut one more time.

"It's healing nicely. If that miserable bastard were here right now, he'd be wearing his nose on the other side of his face," Lissa growled.

She liberally slathered hydrocortisone cream on the cut. Untreated, the cut could prevent his hair from growing back. Happily, the lump had disappeared into his already oversized butt.

She snugged the barn door and hot-footed it back to the house. She had promised to cook tonight and already her tummy rumbled and growled.

While Lissa prepared her only culinary specialty, American chop suey, Reene checked the answering machine. As Lissa sauted onions and added stewed tomatoes to the scrambled hamburger, Reene slowly walked into the kitchen reading the evening paper. Even in the soft light, Lissa could tell she was clutching the paper with a white-knuckled hand.

"You look like death warmed over. What's wrong? Has anything happened to Tom?"

"No, no. Nothing like that. Lissa, Gina left us a message. She tried to reach us before the evening edition came out. There's a new development about Stephen's murder."

"For heaven's sake, hand me that paper! You're acting awfully weird about this. I would think you'd want to know..." Lissa grabbed the newspaper from Reene's hesitant hand and looked for the story.

"It's on page 3," Reene said quietly.

Lissa eagerly began reading. Eagerness turned to rage as her eyes flew over the page.

Murder Victim Had Local Ties
State Police Probe Continues

Two months ago Westbrook was shocked out of its complacency by the unexpected murder of Stephen Marshall, a prominent New York businessman. Marshall, 58, had been staying at a local inn when he was poisoned during the Yankee Homecoming Day Parade.

At the request of Police Chief Paul Frechette, Sergeant David Edmondson of the Massachusetts State Police has been called in to conduct an investigation.

However, Marshall had ties to a local town official. He was the former husband of Andrea Wilson, Town Treasurer. Ms. Wilson is currently running for office of mayor in Westbrook.

Due to this new development, several Town Hall employees were interviewed. More interviews are expected by the end of the week.

Sgt. Edmondson acknowledged that 'a few workers and supervisors' would be questioned.

"The investigative process has taken longer than expected due to logistics and a lack of witnesses," Sgt. Edmondson continued. "At present, no one has come forward with additional information and we have not singled out a person of interest."

Mayor Robert Stuart declared that his people were cooperating fully with the State Police investigation. "I am confident the identity of the killer or killers will soon be discovered," the mayor concluded.

State and local police are seeking the public's assistance in connection with the murder.

"Andrea and Stephen were married?" Lissa cried in disbelief. "No wonder he didn't want to tell us her name. He was 'afraid to risk his luck'? Poor Stephen! If he'd only known the woman we know, he might still be alive."

"Maybe Steve did know, but was too blind to see her for what she really was."

Lissa stared into Reene's eyes. "You've jumped to the same conclusion I have?"

"Andrea killed Stephen," Reene replied. "And right in front of the whole town. She's one ballsy woman. She's the mysterious clown the police are looking for."

"Damn straight. She *poisoned* him! I feel like driving over to her place and beating a confession out of that murdering bitch." A burnt-pan smell assailed her nose. "Oh hell! My sauce will be ruined!"

While Lissa tried to rescue her dinner from disaster, Reene reread the story. Straight forward reporting, no suggestion Andrea may be guilty of anything more than being an ex-wife.

"It's pissing me off to say this, but no one has any proof Andrea killed Steve. What's bugging me is why? Why would she want to kill such a nice person? What could he possibly have done?"

Lissa filled a pot with water to cook pasta, cranked the burner up to high, and stared into the burbling mixture as if it would reveal the answer.

"Reene, in every divorce there are three versions of what happened: his, hers and the truth. Unfortunately, we may never know any of these versions. Maybe they simply grew apart. Maybe the Stephen we knew was a womanizer. Or a wife beater. Although I'll never believe that in a million years. Whatever the reason, real or imagined, it pushed Andrea to do the unthinkable."

Sergeant Edmondson reviewed the article in the *Hampshire Times*. His only person of interest was definitely Andrea Wilson, but he couldn't prove she'd murdered her ex-husband. Yet. After an enlightening visit to the 1761 Old Mill restaurant, he'd discovered Wilson was the 'mystery' woman Marshall taken there shortly before his death. She had an alibi, that on paper looked solid, but he had a feeling if he and Frechette played good cop vs bad cop with Wilson or her alleged fiancé, Collins, they'd be singing like two canaries in a not-so-gilded cage.

His gut instinct told him Collins was the weak link. Now all he had to do was break that link.

Chapter 43

Mayoral Race Comes Down to the Wire

First-Time Candidate Unseats Incumbent.

Mayor Stuart to Demand Recount

Banner headlines proclaimed the upset in letters almost two inches high. Andrea's hard earned victory was front-page news.

"I won! My God, I won!" she gloated.

Shaking with excitement she savored the article, reading it again and again. *Stephen would have been so proud of me. Damn shame I had to kill him.*

She reread Mayor Stuart's concession speech which regurgitated the usual platitudes regarding his opponent. He pledged to make the transition as easy as possible if the recount went against him.

"Damn straight he would."

The article concluded by saying it was the closest race in Westbrook's history.

All night long Andrea had sweated out the results at campaign headquarters. Returns from various districts trickled in at a snail's pace. Grady and Lloyd had sweated with her. The room, littered with discarded coffee containers and empty pizza boxes, felt like a prison. In the heat of the moment, she forgot her aversion to Grady and her antagonism toward Lloyd. She was grateful for their support.

But as the night wore on, she had grown increasingly aggravated. Reporters shoved microphones in her face. Grady constantly counseled her not to lose her poise at the eleventh hour. Not when she was so close to winning.

When the results were finally announced, she and Lloyd had shared a chaste congratulatory kiss at the podium, his arm possessively locked around her waist, during her acceptance speech.

"Kudos are due to my *wonderful* campaign manager, Grady Ferguson," Andrea said, tongue planted firmly in cheek. "He will never know how much his political expertise and personal insight contributed to my victory." She beamed a professional-model smile in Grady's direction.

Grady had hovered in the background wondering when she'd mention his name. Her words of praise stroked his already over-inflated ego. Then he stopped listening, and she suspected he was calculating how much he could increase his fee.

She continued her 'I'm glad I won, so sorry he didn't' speech. Lloyd smiled and nodded at each cliché.

Conniving son of a bitch! He has maneuvered to share in the center of my spotlight. The spotlight I've craved for nearly half my lifetime. Maybe this is what's he's been after all along.

Mayor Stuart had approached the podium to offer his congratulations. His wife stood stolidly by his side, a wan smile pasted on her face.

"Well done, Andrea. I wish you the best. However, I warn you; I haven't given up. I'm filing for a recount in the morning."

"I wouldn't expect otherwise, Bob. But thank you for your good wishes. Bernice, you should be proud of your husband's accomplishments. And you're looking *lovely* this evening."

"Thank you, Andrea. I *am* proud of my husband," she stated.

"If you will excuse me," Andrea replied, eyes bright with victory.

Stupid cow! If she'd been raised in the South, she'd know she's just been insulted. 'Lovely' is Southern for 'you look ridiculous'. Condescending blue bloods! Always looking down their well-shaped noses at women they didn't consider good enough to run in their circles. Now I'm running in her circle.

When the emotionally exhausting evening had finally come to a close, Andrea exulted in her triumph. She forgot her irritation toward Lloyd's commandeering her Great Moment. When their eyes met, the glow in his eyes matched hers. Power!

She came into his arms and they savagely kissed as they had in the early days of their affair. Caught up in the drug of success, they had reverted to their 'what-the-hell-let's-go-for-it' abandon and reveled in each other with an all-consuming passion.

Hours later, dawn peeked under drawn shades in Andrea's master bedroom. She rolled across her now empty bed. The scent of frenzied love making lingered on her sheets.

"Christ, what was I thinking?" she groaned. "That prick better not think a piece of ass comes with the territory. I'll kick his butt from hell to breakfast."

Lissa unfolded the *Hampshire Times'* morning edition. "Oh my lord!" By a narrow margin, Andrea Wilson had been elected mayor of Westbrook. Incumbent Mayor Stuart was demanding a recount, but Lissa had little hope a recount would overturn the election results. She sighed in resignation.

"Reene, take a gander at this," Lissa urged, holding the front page high in the air.

Reene craned her neck around the pantry corner. Her eyes widened when she read the blaring headline. "Damn! I hate to say it, but I'm not really surprised. Andrea's one of those love her or hate her types. People are drawn to her. And maybe a lot of people wanted a change from the same old, same old."

"You're probably right. I'm not being a poor loser. I don't appreciate a killer, excuse me, *alleged killer*, becoming our mayor."

"Don't lose hope. The cops may find some evidence against her. Just remember we did our best for the cause."

"Interesting choice of words, my friend. 'The Cause' was how the South referred to the war. And the South lost too," Lissa said. "When is the inauguration or swearing in, or whatever it's called?"

"Are you hoping for a pardon from the recount?" Reene asked.

"You got that right. Andrea doesn't deserve any kind of pardon."

"I liked her at first," Reene admitted, "but after she pulled that stupid stunt when I got kicked, I lost all respect for her. With any kind of luck you might get your wish. The inauguration won't take place until January."

"There is a Supreme Being after all! I'll keep my fingers crossed our sergeant will arrest the murdering bitch. Anything can happen between now and then."

"Come!" Andrea barked.

Lloyd opened the door but poked his head only part way in. "Dare I enter the sacred office of the mayor-elect?"

"What the hell to you want? Can't a day go by without you having to check in with me? I assumed you had a business to run."

"I beg your pardon, Andrea. I didn't think you would take umbrage at my playing the devoted fiancé," Lloyd said as he dropped languidly into her visitor's chair. He saw her lips tighten and knew she was in no mood for idle banter.

"Janice gave her notice today. She couldn't even put off leaving until I take office," Andrea fumed. "She'll be gone by the end of the month. Unless she pisses me off. In fact, I'll tell her I won't stand in her way and she's free to go. I'll personally escort her out the door."

Lloyd regarded Andrea impassively, but his heart thudded painfully. At least Janice would be leaving with some semblance of dignity. After spending so much time in Andrea's company, Lloyd realized he had trapped himself in a web of his own spinning. Once the euphoria of victory had worn off, their relationship had turned prickly. Before he had engineered their engagement of convenience, they had seemed to enjoy badgering and baiting each other. But always underneath lay a mutual regard and respect. Now animosity and distrust remained the only bond between them.

"Pray tell, what terrible crime did she commit to rouse your ire?" Lloyd stressed the word 'crime' hoping she would back off. She didn't.

"Damned ungrateful bitch. She didn't give me a chance to fire her ass. I hate disloyalty."

"My dearest fiancé, you are the biggest pretender on the face of the earth. Hardly worthy of our future mayor."

She glared at him, obviously ready for a battle royal. Fortunately for Lloyd, her private line rang. She snatched up the phone.

"No, let things settle down. Do you want me to spell it out? You've stirred them up and the cops are on alert. Besides, from the outlandish stories you've told me, you scared the shit out of them. Well done. Your payment will be sent out in today's mail. You're getting the full amount I promised despite the fact you let a dog run you off! I'll call you again if and when I need you."

"Should I ask about that mystifying conversation?" His stomach lurched when Andrea smiled enigmatically over her shoulder. To his horror he felt like a very small mouse being watched hungrily by a large predatory cat.

"Nothing for you to concern yourself about," she replied, swinging around to confront him. "I decided a little intimidation might be in order. It didn't exactly work out the way I expected, but you get what you pay for, and I'm not paying very much."

"And just who, or is it whom, was the object of your intimidation for hire?"

"Since you'll sit here all morning until I tell you, I hired Griffin McGuire to bring a little mayhem into the lives of those two shining stars at the inn. Is your curiosity satisfied?"

296

"Most assuredly. Was either of them hurt?" he asked. As he casually adjusted the handkerchief in his breast pocket, he hoped his shaking hand didn't betray him.

"Unfortunately, no. One of their horses did suffer an injury. Maybe now those bitches'll keep their noses out of things that don't concern them."

"Up until this moment, I had no idea their noses were any concern of yours."

"Use your vivid imagination. If they hadn't discovered all that old Civil War shit at the same time Stephen showed up, my secret would have been safe. And I wouldn't be engaged to you."

"You forget, my dear Andrea. I already knew your secret. Harming them makes no sense."

"You're so wrong, *darling*. Everyone will assume it's a racial hate crime. I chose Mr. McGuire as my fall guy because of his reputation in town. Even if he is arrested, I doubt anyone would believe I hired him. My word against his. It's as simple as that."

"Your cleverness never ceases to amaze me. Let's move on to a more germane subject. At the risk of incurring your displeasure, must we attend any cocktail parties or one hundred-dollar-a-plate dinners this week? I had hoped to spend a couple of quiet evenings at home for a change."

"Poor baby. Drinking champagne and eating caviar is such a trial. But you've been granted a pardon. Nothing is scheduled until after the holiday. Smiling cherubs sitting 'round grandma's table with their eyes on the drumsticks. Relatives you can't stand the other three hundred sixty four days of the year posing for pictures while passing the mashed potatoes. Stupid hypocrites!"

"Our future holidays should be filled with such joy and love. Although I feel we should forego producing any cherubs."

Andrea's eyes never left his as he rose to leave. Her face was unreadable. In the old days, she would have made a biting comeback to his raillery. Not any more.

"Stay in touch. I never know when I might be asked to produce my devoted fiancé for a social outing. That's the term you used, didn't you?"

"Be careful, Andrea. Don't push me too far. I don't take orders. Try to remember that."

He left her office as quietly as he had come in. Her assumption that he would stay at her beck and call rankled, but he held his temper in check. He did not intend to give her any reason to suspect his intentions. Not if he wanted to stay alive.

"Scott, I'm in trouble. No bullshit. It's bad. Can you see me tonight?"

"Get your ass over here right now."

"Thank you for not asking too many questions," Lloyd said when his brother answered his knock. Their eyes met over Lloyd's hesitantly extended hand. For the first time in many years no animosity or jealousy kindled between them.

"Damn Lloyd," Scott said. "You look like a hunted animal. What the hell is going on?"

"Mad Catherine has come back to haunt me. It's a long, convoluted story. Can you take it?" Lloyd asked.

"If you can, I can."

Scott listened without interruption as Lloyd poured out the entire sordid story. Much to his relief, Scott refused to pass judgment.

"I assume you want me represent you," Scott stated. "You can be sure I'll get you the best deal possible."

"I know you will, Scott. I've always admired your skill." Lloyd held up a self-deprecating hand. "Even though I had a hell of a way of showing it."

"There may be hope for you after all. I'll call the D.A. and make an appointment. Wally Higgins is a little flinty, but fair. Remember, for once in your life, keep your tongue out of your cheek and act humble!"

"Behold a changed man," Lloyd replied in a humble tone.

"That's a start. Now, let's go over this charming story one more time."

Griffin McGuire couldn't sleep. Lying on his disheveled bed, he had been awake for hours thinking and plotting. Now he was totally pissed off. A week ago that son of a bitch Tom O'Brien had used his face as a punching bag. Bastard had hauled him out of his truck when he drove into the yard. Before Griffin could holler for help, Tom had dragged him into the woods behind the garage. O'Brien had grabbed him by the throat and rammed him against a tree. Scared shitless, Griffin gagged when Tom's hand locked around his neck.

"McGuire, I always figured you for a creep and a low life," O'Brien growled and backhanded him across the face. "But even you've hit a new low."

298

"What the hell are you talking about? I didn't have nothin' to do with those broads!"

"You dumb shit! You just gave yourself away. Listen up, McGuire. If anything happens to those two women again, I don't care if you are fifty miles away with fifty witnesses, I'm coming after you."

Griffin's eyes bulged as Tom's huge fist connected in a sharp jab that broke his nose. Griffin gurgled in pain and shock.

"Tom, stop! For Christ's sake!" Griffin cried.

"I'll stop when you stop," O'Brien snapped and landed a solid punch to McGuire's ribs that left him sitting on his ass, gasping and spitting blood. "Last chance."

Then O'Brien disappeared into the shadows.

"Oh, God," Griffin moaned. He struggled to his feet and stumbled into the house holding his bleeding nose. His father hardly noticed him. When Griffin finally emerged from the bathroom, his father raised an eyebrow.

"You'll want to put some ice on that busted nose," said the elder McGuire as he reached into the fridge and tossed Griffin a beer.

Together they sat in silence, watching television and drinking beer. Griffin held an ice pack to his bruised face. Not a word was spoken.

Griffin's nose had slowly healed, but two black eyes made him look like a raccoon. He knew people were snickering at him behind his back. No one believed he'd had an accident.

Now he'd made his decision. "It's time to put the hurt on those women. Then I'll split before O'Brien works me over again. If I don't split, I'll get locked up. Dad told me the cops have been nosing around. I've saved the money that miserable broad paid me for those other jobs. She'd gotten her money's worth. Besides, she'd won the damn election. This piece of work will be strictly personal."

Griffin threw on dark pants and a black hooded sweatshirt and quietly left by the back door. As he passed his father's room, he could hear his old man's window-rattling snores. He'd be back before his father dragged his fat ass out of bed.

He drove out behind the old farmhouse on Breckenridge Road. He parked his truck and worked his way through the dense woods.

"Once I find the house and barn, I'll decide where to start. I've got some creative plans in mind for those two broads and for that friggin' beagle. The little shit won't take a bite out of me this time."

Griffin's ankle turned over and he nearly fell. "Shit!" he yelled, glad there was no danger of anyone hearing him. "It's darker than a witch's ass. Damn fields are all rutted and weeds are freakin' ten feet high!"

He struggled doggedly through the undergrowth. Head down and sweat pouring down his face, he swore when he bumped into a chain link fence.

"What the hell? Must be a pen to keep their damn animals in." The fence was only about six feet high. "Easy enough to climb over. I've climbed higher fences with a cop chasing me."

Nimbly, he scaled the fence. With a final heave, Griffin lurched over the top. He dropped heavily to the ground and set off toward the house.

He never made it.

He had taken only a few steps when he plummeted into a black hole. A black hole filled with bitingly cold water. A black hole with no bottom.

"Son of a bitch!" he screamed. Griffin tread water as he tried frantically to find a handhold. His fingers clawed at the crumbling dirt walls. But there was nothing he could cling to, nothing he could grip.

Griffin shivered violently. His clothes were soaked through, and the water felt brutally cold. As he tried to dig into the walls, his hands began to go numb. He thrashed as much as he could in the confined space to keep the circulation going in his legs.

"Oh, God, I can't breathe!" Griffin's voice was getting weaker as his breathing slowed. His breath came in shallow spurts. "Help! Help!" he gasped. But he knew he was too far away for anyone to hear his cries.

Griffin's head lolled on his shoulders in exhaustion. *I'm screwed! I can't get out!*

A burst of wind above the hole snapped his head back up. Leaves whirled and dirt trickled down into the well.

"Who's there?" Griffin twisted around and tried to peer into the darkness. "Can you hear me? I need help!"

The wind increased its intensity and danced around the opening. Pebbles clattered against the walls and dropped into the water.

"Is someone up there?" he yelled again. "Answer me!"

A long drawn-out wail answered his plea. The keening cry, like a banshee foretelling impending death, echoed all around him.

"Christ Almighty!" His scalp prickled in terror. He pushed away from the awful sound as far as the walls would allow and cowered, trembling, until the appalling voice suddenly vanished.

Unexpectedly Griffin felt a warm sensation spread through his body giving him new hope. *I can make it now!*

He braced his back against the wall and planted his feet against the opposite wall. With all of his strength, he heaved upward. But it was too late. His muscles wouldn't respond to the physical demand. He slid back down the wall into the frigid water.

"Shit! This can't be happening! Help me! Someone help me!"

Silence enveloped him as he struggled to stay above the waterline. The longer he stayed in the water, the less chance he had for survival.

"Thish is her fault! Goddamn hard-nosed bitch! I'll fix her assh when I get out of here!" Griffin smiled at his sudden brain wave. As much as he loved taking her money, he hated that woman. "Yeah, I'll get even with her if it's the lash thing I ever do. She won't put me in jail!"

And while he was at it, he'd pay back Tom O'Brien. Who the hell put him in charge? Yeah, he'd fix his ass too.

"Tommy, boyo, I'm comin' to get you!" He giggled and played with the brackish water. All he had to do was walk up the walls and crawl out. Or fly out. Easy as pie.

"Hell! The shun is in my eyes! I wanted to slipp late." Feebly, he covered his eyes with a leaden arm. "I gotta get some slipp. Jush ten more minutes! I'm not gettin' out of thish bed."

Turning aside, he burrowed his head under the water. It felt warm and inviting. Griffin pushed further into the soft, feather pillows. Slowly, he sank into nothingness as his body relaxed and embraced a peaceful oblivion.

Chapter 44

"Did I invoke the Supreme Being a few days ago?" Lissa muttered. Evidently, the Supreme Being enjoyed a good joke as much as anyone. According to the *Hampshire Times*, the recount tally had come in. Mayor Stuart picked up a few more votes, but not enough to change the outcome.

"Damnation! We're stuck with Andrea Wilson for three years!"

Despite this unwelcome news, Lissa was breaking even. The well contractor called to say he'd finally obtained their license to start re-digging; he'd be coming with his crew at the end of the week.

"Good news and bad news, girlfriend," Lissa announced when Reene joined her for breakfast. "Good news: we can have the well business finished before the holiday, praise the Lord and pass the turkey. Bad news: our less than brilliant voters of Westbrook have officially elected an ex-husband-killer."

"We can't blame the voters. She promised them the moon and they jumped at the chance. And she hasn't been implicated in Steve's death. Let it go, Lissa. What goes around, comes around. Ye gods, Thanksgiving is right around the corner! Are we going to stay open? Or, should I ask, do we have any guests?"

"Yes and yes. I've taken reservations from folks who, stuffed full of turkey and pumpkin pie, are using our inn as a stopover point between here and grandmother's house."

"Maybe it'll snow," Reene sighed. "Our inn'll look good in snow. Especially now that we finally got the insulation blown in. A single white candle in each window. We'll go caroling! Wouldn't that be perfect?"

"Norman Rockwell would be proud. Do you want to invite Tom to fight over the wishbone?"

Reene's face darkened. "We don't need a wishbone. We're still fighting over the fact that I won't obey his every command."

"Men in love can be a pain. I'd tell you to cook him a fancy dinner and wear your most seductive outfit, but that'd set women's lib back fifty years."

"Women's lib wouldn't approve of my using sex to get my way, but that's not a bad idea. The way to a man's heart et cetera, et cetera. Maybe I can get my point across between courses," Reene said, a determined look in her eye.

"Good. Just make sure you're all lovey dovey by Turkey Day."

Friday morning Lissa stood on the back deck watching trucks, backhoes and vans rumbling their way to the fenced off area. Yellow hard hats bobbed up and down as heavy machinery jockeyed into position. The foreman unlocked the chain link gate and signaled the backhoe closer.

As he peered into the dank opening, he threw up his hand and hollered something Lissa couldn't hear. He dropped to his knees and leaned further into the opening, then motioned for two other men to join him.

"What in bloody hell is happening over there?" Lissa fretted. "I hope their equipment didn't break already."

Suddenly she noticed a flurry of activity as men ran back and forth. The backhoe cautiously backed out. Men climbed in their vehicles, truck doors slammed shut and the little convoy headed back up the field toward the house.

"Oh Lord. I have a terrible feeling this isn't good news."

The foreman roared up in his truck. She recognized the young man she had met a few months ago.

"Mrs. Martin, you'd better call the cops right now," Craig Zylak said as he jumped out to meet her.

"Why? What's wrong?"

"There's a body in your well. We're pretty sure he's dead, but you'd better call 911."

"A body? But there can't be! It's a person, not an animal?"

"Yeah, it's a man, all right. Three of us looked to make sure."

Lissa started to feel lightheaded and her knees gave way. She sat down, hard, on the deck.

"Are you going to pass out?"

"No. Yes. Give me a moment," Lissa gasped as the deck tilted and spun. She clutched the foreman's arm. "Don't go yet."

"No problem. Take your time."

Lissa stared numbly at the ground wondering if that man crumpled in their well thought he had plenty of time. She was tired of dealing with

303

death, the ultimate stealer of time. Death had stolen the two loves of her life and laughed in her face.

"I'll go make that call." She hauled herself to her feet. "Will you tell the others not to leave? I'm sure the police will want to question everyone."

"No problem," he said again. He watched her walk down the path before he went back to his truck.

"Man, she looked almost as bad as the guy in the well."

Ten minutes later, the yard swarmed with police, fire and ambulance vehicles. Lights flashed and sporadic messages crackled from the cruiser's radio.

"What on earth has gone wrong now?" Reene groaned when she returned from a dentist appointment. She found Lissa outside, deep in conversation with a police officer. As she hurried to Lissa's side, the fire engine and ambulance moved off toward the field.

"Why are the fire engine and ambulance here? Is someone hurt?"

"Reene, it's a horror! The construction guys found a dead body in our well! We don't know if he fell in or got dumped there."

"Oh my God! Officer, do you have any idea who it is?"

"No, ma'am," responded the officer. "The fire department is removing the body right now. The body's in pretty bad shape, bloated and covered with muck. We're checking to see if he carried any identification. The Chief will want to speak to you both."

"Reene, the crew found him before they started to lower their equipment," Lissa explained. "Their foreman drove up here with his hair on fire to tell me. Who can it be? What was he doing on our land?"

"Come on, Lissa, let's go back to the house. We're not needed now, are we, Officer?"

"No, but don't go far." With a nod, he released them. Before he could change his mind, they took cover in Lissa's office. Reene wanted to get her friend as far away from the chaos as possible.

"Reene, I'm so afraid this latest episode is going to ruin us! No one will want to come here ever again! We've become the murder capital of Massachusetts."

"We can't blame ourselves, Lissa. We got caught in the middle of something over which we had no control." As Lissa fought back tears, Reene put her arm around Lissa's shoulder. "It'll come out all right. I know it will."

"It didn't come out all right for Stephen," Lissa choked. "You know what else is bothering me? We may be indirectly responsible for the

304

deaths of two people! All because we wanted to help a spirit cross over that only we believe exists. We should have just left things alone!"

"I wish I could convince you we did the right thing."

The front door slammed. Seconds later, a glowering Tom burst in nearly colliding with Reene who ran to investigate.

"Reenie, what the hell is going on now? I heard on the scanner that a body was found on your property."

"Well, hello to you too! I don't know what's going on! I just got here and Lissa is close to having a breakdown. There's a dead guy in our well, the cops are all over the place again, and you come charging in here like the Cavalry and—"

Tom pulled her into his arms and crushed her mouth beneath his.

Reene pulled away and ducked her head into his chest. "Tom, it's terrible. I don't know what we're going to do."

"Shut up, Reenie." He lightly showered her face with kisses. "Shut up and let me love you."

"I guess this means you two have made up," Lissa said from the doorway. She'd ignored the agitated voices for as long as she could.

Reene and Tom broke their embrace and stood with their arms around each other.

"Yeah, I guess we have," Tom agreed with a grin. Reene smiled up at him with a promise in her eyes.

"Well, that's good because we all need to be on the same page if we're going to survive this latest disaster. If the inn is shut down, we're finished," Lissa said. She struggled to hold back a fresh set of tears.

"Oh no, Lissa! Did the police say they'd close us down?"

"No, not yet. They tell you just enough without telling all. Keeping everyone guessing is their favorite sport."

"Bide your time, Lissa. Don't jump to conclusions," Tom counseled. "I can't see the authorities doing anything for a while anyway. They still have to identify the body and—"

Reene nudged him in the ribs to stop any further comments. Lissa's composure was hanging by a thread. "Sorry, ladies. Take one day at a time. And you're not to feel guilty for any of this."

"Thanks, Tom," Lissa said gratefully.

A blue flash outside the window caught Lissa's eye. "Oh joy, oh rapture. Here comes our dear friend Chief Frechette. Doubtless he's ready to clap us in irons on general principles." She yanked the door open before he could knock.

"Good day, Mrs. Anderson, Mrs. Martin…"

"Please, Chief, call us by our first names. After all that's happened around here, I'd feel better if you were less formal," Lissa requested.

"That's fine with me, Lissa," he responded. "The body we hauled out of your well is Griffin McGuire. We recovered his wallet, what was left of it. If I'm not mistaken, he's the same guy who almost drove you off the road and tried to attack you with a BB gun. No doubt he threw rocks at you and Reene the day of the dedication. His face is nearly unrecognizable. Lots of old bruising around the eyes. Doesn't look like it was caused by the fall into your well."

Tom stiffened and Reene glanced up fearfully.

What had Tom done? Lissa worried. Then she forced herself to calm down. Reene's boyfriend was not a murderer.

"You're certain he caused all the trouble, Chief?" Reene asked quickly.

"Not yet. But I can put two and two together. I'm forwarding a report to Sgt. Edmondson. We need to find out if McGuire was working alone, or if someone else put him to the job. Now, let's go over the details. I want to know how and why this guy ended up in your well."

"I'll go out and see if there's anything I can do," Tom said. He stroked Reene's cheek lightly with his hand.

"Tom, I want to have a word with you before you leave," Chief Frechette said, his tone casual. But his eyes locked on Tom's. Tom hesitated, then nodded and slipped out the door.

"All right, ladies," the chief said as he pulled out his notebook. "Let's get this done as painlessly as possible. You know the drill."

Chapter 45

"Thank goodness, we're still open for business," Reene said as she set out water buckets to clean and fill. In Sissy's paddock, Lissa scooped up manure and heaved it into the wheelbarrow.

"Yeah, but we might as well have a skull and crossbones over our door. No one will come within a country mile of this place."

"Let's keep our options open until we hear the autopsy results," Reene advised. "Maybe it was an accident."

"Accidentally fell in, you mean? If McGuire was prowling around here in the middle of the night on the wrong side of a chain link fence, he wasn't out for a moonlight stroll. He was intent on hurting us or our horses. If he'd succeeded, we'd definitely be on the list of main suspects!"

Reene stopped to rest on the handle of her pitchfork. "Silly woman! No one would *ever* believe we could do such a thing! Naturally we wanted to kill him, but we'd be more subtle than dumping him down our own well."

Lissa laughed ruefully. "All the dead bodies finding their way to our door are making me paranoid."

"All? I only count two. Of course, two is two too many."

"Beg your pardon? Since we're keeping score, the count is three, but Josey's murder took place over one hundred years ago." Lissa maneuvered the wheelbarrow closer to the water trough. "Hey, I caught the look you threw Tom when the Chief identified our latest dead body as Griffin McGuire. What was that all about?"

"Did you also notice how Tom reacted when the cop told us about the bruises on the creep's face? I have a nasty hunch Tom did or said something to that guy before he 'accidentally' fell into our laps."

"That's ridiculous. I'm sure it wasn't more than a well-deserved punch or two. Let's face it, in Tom's male mind, he was protecting the woman he loved."

"It's sweet of you to stick up for him. He's just got to stop running interference for me."

"Let's put Tom's testosterone fit on the back burner," Lissa said. "Unless more guests are clamoring for our services, it is going to be extremely quiet around here."

"I know," Reene agreed dejectedly. "The setbacks have really piled up. We need a change in our luck."

"Speaking of luck, did you ever have any researching those names in the Bible?" Back in the house, Lissa peeked into the pumpkin-shaped cookie jar. "Hermits! You go, girl!"

"Sorry to disappoint you, but those came straight from the bakery aisle in the market. And no, I never did get around to checking out those names. I'll do that tonight."

"Great. These are yummy!" Lissa mumbled between mouthfuls of the sweet molasses and raisin cookie. "Come on, Reene. We haven't gone for a long ride since the late not-so-sadly-missed Mr. McGuire made our lives miserable."

"Absolutely! But hold on a minute. I'll fix some hot chocolate to take with us. No doubt Shen and Brav will be frisky now that weather's turned cold. Should I ride bareback? Shen will keep me warm."

"Excuse me, woman, but I don't want to scrape you off a rock. Use your saddle and if you think you'll be cold, put on some thermal underwear and your leg warmers. Not that frou-frou stuff either."

"No sleazy sleepwear?" Reene laughed. "I'll meet you in the barn in a few."

Lissa was halfway out the door when the phone rang. She glanced quickly at the caller ID. Happy days, it wasn't any of her new best friends from the police department.

"Good morning, Barn Swallow Inn."

"Good morning!" An incredibly vivacious woman's voice halted Lissa's eagerness to escape. "Might you have a room available for this weekend?"

"This weekend? I'll look. How many people for how many nights?"

"My significant other and I are looking for three nights."

"It must be Fate. We just had a cancellation," Lissa said glibly. Fibbing was becoming too easy. "Would you prefer a queen bed or two twins?"

"Fabulous! The queen works for us! Just one more thing. Are there any hiking trails nearby?"

Lissa spent a long time chatting and taking down information. Finally she begged off, telling the friendly guest-to-be that she heard her horse calling her.

"By all means, go and tend to your beastie!" the woman responded with a deep, throaty chuckle. "Ta ta for now!"

Reene was saddled and ready to go when Lissa finally arrived. "What took you so long?" she asked as Lissa hurriedly groomed Bravo and settled his saddle pad evenly on his back.

"Excellent news! Not everyone thinks we're Typhoid Mary. I just took a reservation for three days. An outdoorsy couple, Cindy and Jeff, are arriving on Friday," she answered.

She threw her synthetic saddle on top of the pad and tightened the girth. "The caller told me she'd ridden in the show jumping circuit for years. It'll be nice having a guest who's a horse person. She mentioned they'll be geocaching. What the heck *is* geocaching?"

"Oh, that's a blast! It's like a scavenger hunt, but you hunt for prizes buried or hidden somewhere. Some people make up simple clues to find hiding places. You're supposed to write your name and date in a notebook that's hidden with the treasure."

"I gotta get out more," Lissa grumped and slipped the bit into Bravo's mouth.

"Too bad they didn't show up earlier. Maybe they could have helped us salvage our reputation."

"I suspect they haven't heard about our infamous crime spree. At this point, I'll take any guests willing to overlook a few dead bodies."

Not long after Reene and Lissa returned from their ride, Tom called. Reene's trip to the library was put on hold.

"Reenie, I want to explain about my involvement with Griffin McGuire. Can you come over?"

"Scat," Lissa smiled as her excited friend burst into explanations. "If you aren't back in time—which I highly doubt—I'll take care of the night feeding."

Confronting Tom in his barn, Reene stuffed her shaking hands into her jeans. "Tom, tell me everything! What happened between you and that bastard?"

"Bastard is the word, Reenie. Before I begin, let me say that I talked to Chief Frechette about this and he believes I had nothing to do with McGuire's death."

"So what happened," Reene demanded again.

"I beat Griffin McGuire to a bloody pulp. You wouldn't let me help, so I gave McGuire something to think about."

"Oh, so it's my fault?" she flared.

"Let's not get into a dog and cat fight, honey. If I had it to do over again, I still would have clobbered the guy, but I didn't help him take a header into your well."

Reene glared at him for a minute. But only for a minute. With a yelp of joy, she jumped into his lap. Wrapping her arms around his neck, she kissed him so hard he nearly dropped her. But he recovered quickly and scooped her up in his arms.

"Reenie, could I interest you in a roll in the hay?"

I'll never look at a pile of hay the same way again, Reene blushed. Wheeling her truck into the library parking lot, her mind reverted to more pleasurable activities. Tom had found an old blanket in the hayloft, but it had worn thin and hay poked through at inopportune moments. Despite a few punctures, she'd found out that he was *extremely* good at everything.

Back to researching those family names. Brushing away imaginary pieces of hay and twitching uncomfortably, she hopped out and made her way to the Reference Desk.

Reene went directly to the 'Births and Deaths' volume and dug out her notebook. She began hunting for names and dates she'd taken from the Bible. Sighing heavily, she matched all the entries until her fingers cramped. Finally, one last name remained.

"George Wilson married Elaine Barry in 1952. That must've been the washed-out name in the Bible. Any children? Only one child, Andrea Elizabeth born in 1960, Andrea Wilson. *Andrea Wilson?*" Reene cried out in horror.

Heads turned toward her stricken face. "Would you mind keeping your comments to yourself?" an elderly matron asked frostily. "This is a library, young lady."

Reene barely heard the woman's reprimand. Shocked into silence by the revelation, she stared at the page. The revelation that confirmed what only she and Lissa had suspected.

The missing puzzle piece that had eluded them for so long had finally fallen into place.

Chapter 46

"Lissa, I know why Andrea killed Steve."

Lissa's head jerked up from *Heiress to Madness*. Rereading Catherine's tragic story, she never heard Reene's footsteps echo on the hardwood floor.

"What did you just say?"

Reene walked over to Lissa's easy chair and sat down heavily. She tossed her notebook on the desk.

"It's all in there. This afternoon I went to the library. I looked up all the names written in the Bible you drove yourself crazy trying to find. I wish now you hadn't found it. Know that saying 'be careful what you wish for'?"

Reene looked away for an instant and Lissa braced herself.

"I was writing and writing, copying down names and facts. When I reached the last set of names, the truth hit me so hard I nearly screamed. I guess I must have made too much noise 'cause an old lady yelled at me." Reene's attempt at humor fell very flat. "Lissa, it hurts me so to have to tell you this. Andrea is Josey's great-great granddaughter."

Lissa gasped as if she'd been sucker punched in the stomach. Whatever she had expected to hear, this was not it. Slowly and deliberately she placed the book on the wicker table beside her. She swung her legs onto the floor and looked straight into her friend's troubled eyes.

"Reene, have I lost my mind? You're telling me *Andrea* is Josey's great-great-granddaughter?" Lissa gripped Reene's hand in hers as she struggled to keep her composure. "There's no mistake?"

"No mistake. I traced all those names down to the present. Andrea Elizabeth Wilson, born in 1960 to George and Elaine Wilson. Their names were the last entries in the Bible."

"The Bible I drove myself crazy to find," Lissa repeated. "With all my heart and soul, I don't want this to be true! Andrea is ashamed of her own family?"

"Yes! Remember her hysterical reaction at our tea when she almost choked over that Sally Laplander reference? She was so paranoid that anyone would guess her secret! My God!"

"That time she stayed here, just before she caused you grief, I caught her staring at Josey's portrait with genuine emotion. But I never guessed she was filled with such hate. A cold blooded murderer descended from an unselfish patriot. A heart-breaking descent from Josey's point of view. Because Andrea couldn't accept her heritage, an innocent man died. Better people than her suffered because their skin was the 'wrong' color. They never resorted to murder. "

"She must have revealed the truth to Steve the night he took her to dinner," Reene said. "That's why he was too upset about their relationship to face us."

"Even though he tried to hide it, his sadness is forever burned into my brain." Lissa paused to rub her pounding head. "I'll never forgive Andrea for what she did to Stephen."

"Then she focused her hatred on us when we found those letters. I'm certain she's the one who tried to steal them," Reene said. "When that didn't work, she hired that jerk McGuire to make our lives miserable."

"Miserable? He almost killed us!"

"She's pure evil, isn't she Lissa?"

"She's the unstable thread between Josey and Stephen, two caring and loyal people who were murdered years apart for virtually the same reason: an unbalanced mind that never learned a person's worth isn't judged by skin color."

"Paul, it's Dave. I just had an interesting phone call. Are you in your office the rest of the day?"

"Yeah, I am. No more DOAs cluttering up the landscape. You sound excited. For you."

"I'll ignore that," Edmondson grunted. "But you'd better not make any more smart remarks or I won't let you in on the arrest."

"Arrest? Have you made someone for the Marshall murder?"

"Not exactly. But I have the next best thing: the guy who's blackmailing the murderer. Or to be politically correct, the murderess."

"Get your ass over here right away."

"Lloyd Collins made a deal with the DA?" Paul said incredulously. "Did you have him fingered as a suspect?"

"Number two behind Ms. Wilson. I figured he was involved somehow. His sudden engagement to Wilson. No witnesses to confirm his story, excuse me, 'alleged story', about the picnic in the mountains with Wilson. No doubt they assumed they'd cover for each other. You know what they say about assuming. Right now he's looking at obstruction of justice and extortion."

"It could have been a lot worse if he'd helped Wilson put her husband away. If he cuts a good deal with the DA, he could be back overcharging his clients in a couple of years. Always kind of an odd guy, but kept out of trouble. Patronizing as hell though."

"Well, he's in trouble now," said the trooper. "He even rolled on Griffin McGuire. Said Wilson hired McGuire to harass and intimidate those two women."

"Yeah? Why am I not surprised? Autopsy report came back on McGuire. Cause of death was hypothermia. No bullet holes or broken bones on the body. Tox screen came back negative. I was sure he'd been drinking or using."

"So you're saying there's a pretty good chance his death was accidental."

"Yeah, that's just what I'm saying. Collins' confession confirms it. Guy probably went out there, sneaking around, intending to cause more trouble. Except trouble found him, and he ended up on a cold slab in the morgue."

"I'll leave this case in your capable hands, Chief. Tomorrow Mr. Collins — and his attorney — will be presenting himself to the DA's office while I'll be escorting Ms. Andrea Wilson to jail. Guess the town will have to hold another election."

"Damn," Paul snorted. "We'll have to go through that bullshit all over again." He walked over to his ever-present coffee pot and poured a mug of what appeared to be black sludge. "Coffee?"

Dave grimaced. "No, thanks. I plan on living a little longer. How can you drink that stuff?"

Paul took a tentative sip of the steaming liquid. "Nectar of the gods. I wonder what brought about Collins' sudden change of heart."

"Collins said Wilson threatened his ass and made him fear for his life. He gave her up in a New York minute. From the story he told me about Wilson, I'd say he had good reason to worry. He claims she's a cold-hearted bitch who'd stab you in the back and smile while twisting the knife."

"Too bad he didn't realize that before he jumped in bed with her. I'd say congratulations, but you didn't have to break a sweat," Paul said. He raised his mug in mock salute.

"Put that god-awful stuff down and let's get a real drink. I'm off duty and, despite not breaking a sweat, I'm thirsty."

Lloyd walked silently down the central hall of his apartment. He went from room to room running a hand over the polished wood of his antique desk and adjusting the watercolor landscape over the breakfront to its best advantage.

"I could have lost all this. I still might," Lloyd murmured. "Tomorrow morning at the unreasonable hour of nine, I'll turn myself in before that big sergeant hauls me off in chains."

Scott had assured Lloyd that in exchange for testimony against Andrea, he would have a good shot at getting immunity. Even with the small risk of imprisonment, Lloyd was relieved to end the charade between himself and Andrea. Her suspicious mind, not to mention her violent mood swings, made her increasingly hard to handle. Her failed attempt to humiliate Janice hurt him more than he was willing to admit.

When Andrea had confessed she'd hired Griffin McGuire to ratchet up the body count, it was the final straw.

"Undoubtedly I'd be next on her hit list. I made a pact with the Devil, but she can go straight to Hell without me."

He continued his tour through the rooms. He should never have let it come to this. But he had wanted all the power and position as much, if not more, as she had.

"Where did I put that manila folder with the copies of my latest tax returns? I should put them into the safe. Don't want to leave any loose ends," Lloyd muttered. "Hell! I left it in my car. I'll bet the cell phone is there too. Might as well make sure everything's tidied up before I try to unwind."

Without bothering to throw on a jacket, he hurried out to the street. Lloyd unlocked his car door and the overhead light revealed the folder lying on the seat. His cell phone perched in the cup holder. Just as he reached for the forgotten articles, a familiar voice penetrated the darkness.

"Hello, Lloyd. I've come to kiss you goodbye."

"Andrea!" The back of his scalp tingled with fear as he whirled to face her. "Listen to me! You must understand why I—"

314

"Darling, you sold me out," she said, her white face expressionless. Andrea's right arm twitched by her side as she walked closer. Something metal clanked against the pavement, but Lloyd was too terrified to take his eyes off her.

Instinctively he moved away, but found himself backed up against his car. He was trapped by a will stronger than his.

"You rotten prick!" she shrieked. She raised both arms overhead, lips curled back like a rabid dog. With all her strength, she flailed at Lloyd with a heavy iron rod.

He dodged to one side and threw out an arm to ward off the blows.

"Andrea, stop, for God's sake!" Lloyd screamed as blow after blow landed on his arms and back. In desperation he hurled the cell phone at her face. It missed its target but glanced off her shoulder.

Andrea's maniacal cry pierced the air. She raked the sharp point of the rod across his face.

"Help! Help me! Someone call 911!" Lloyd cried. Pain shot through him and blood spurted from his cheek. He crumpled to the ground. As he forced his battered body not to shut down, he heard the faint wail of a siren.

Like a huntress, Andrea poised for the death blow. Suddenly, lights flashed on in adjoining houses. Howling like a vengeful animal, she struck him one last blow. As the blinking blue lights raced toward them, she turned and vanished into the night.

"Thank God!" Lloyd mumbled before darkness closed in.

Chapter 47

A full moon hung in the night sky as Andrea crept silently toward the barn on Breckenridge Road and slipped in the side door. It was just past midnight. She glanced over her shoulder at the house. No lights were burning. With any luck, everyone was asleep.

With the moonlight streaming through the windows, Andrea could see that the three horses were definitely awake. They eyed her curiously and nickered as if questioning her presence.

"You'll be yelling your heads off in a few minutes. But it'll be too late. I'll make damn sure of that."

Less than twenty four hours had passed since Chief Frechette and his deputy had read her rights and politely informed her they would arrive in the morning to take her into custody. Andrea, a total professional, had assured them she would be waiting.

"What trusting assholes!" she laughed aloud now. "Like I'm going to make it easy for them? And after the cops find what's left of Lloyd, they might not wait till morning. But I'll leave those two broads a farewell present. Only this present will haunt them the rest of their lives."

She set down a container filled with kerosene and dug in her pocket for her flashlight. She flicked the light on, cupping her hand over the lens to keep its light from being seen from outside. Once her eyes adjusted to the dim light, Andrea searched the barn while she slowly moved down the aisle.

"Where are the damn hay bales?" she cursed. "I'll light them first. They'll go up like wildfire." A quick search with the flashlight located a stack of bales near the tack room.

Andrea splashed kerosene on the bales and the walls. Feeling her way toward the front door, she paused to catch her breath. Suddenly, a small furry creature bounded over her head, its bushy tail brushing her face. She shrieked in fright and stumbled backwards against the wall. She knocked two manure forks loose and they clattered to the floor.

"Shit! Shit! Shit!" Andrea shone her flashlight into the rafters where two emerald eyes stared back. "Son of a bitching cat!" she snarled in fury. If only she had something to throw at the wretched thing!

"Damn! I've made enough noise to wake the dead!" she hissed. "Hell, maybe I woke up dear old great-great-granny. I'd better work fast in case those bitches heard the noise and come out to check on their nags. When I'm finished, there'll be nothing left of them to bury."

She lifted the container. The pungent smell of kerosene made her nose wrinkle. Almost all the liquid had spilled onto the floor. Disgustedly she splashed the remainder of the kerosene over the grain bins. She tossed some matches into the hay bales.

"Good bye, you four-legged hay burners. Only this time the hay'll burn you."

Reene and Lissa endured another emotional day from hell. Sgt. Edmondson had dropped by with news that Andrea Wilson would be taken into custody the next day; her fiancé had turned state's evidence. To their relief, Edmondson reported McGuire's death was accidental. But their jubilation was short-lived. Too many lives had been shattered.

When Lissa dragged her weary body upstairs, the grandfather clock chimed midnight. She flopped down in her comfy bed. Stress started to leave her body, but her mind still raced like a hamster in a wheel. She hovered in the twilight zone desperate to fall into a deep sleep. Out of nowhere a tremendous clanging jolted her wide-awake.

"What the hell is making that noise?" Lissa cried. "Damn it all! I was almost asleep!" She flung herself out of bed and stomped out the door where she nearly collided with Reene.

"Did you hear it too?"

"I sure as hell did! Lord save us! I'll bet Josey is conducting a midnight haunting. I'm too tired for this nonsense."

Another horrific noise made them both jump.

"Quick!" Reene hissed. "Those god-awful noises are coming from the kitchen! Let's get down there before She wakes up the whole place."

They hurried down the back stairs to the kitchen where Lissa flipped on the light switch. All the cooking pans and skillets had been ripped from their overhead rack and were strewn in every corner.

"Look at this! What the hell! Something has really ticked her off," Reene growled. She collected the cookware and hung the pans back on their hooks. "Well, at least nothing's broken."

Lissa walked across the room to fetch an iron skillet hiding under a chair. When she passed by the window, she automatically glanced out toward the barn. She stopped abruptly and stared out into the darkness.

"What's wrong?" Reene asked.

"I thought I saw a light in the barn. Not the overhead but...there it is again! Quick, come look!"

Reene hurried to her side and pressed her face against the glass.

"Look!" Lissa pointed. "A beam of light is definitely moving inside the barn."

A quick sharp scream made their hair stand on end. A woman's scream. Then something metal banged against wood.

"We have a prowler," Reene said.

Lissa listened intently, eyes fixed on the barn as she strained to see in the dark. Then Reene gasped and grabbed her arm.

"Oh, no! No! I see flames! Call 911, Lissa! Someone's set it on fire!"

"Our horses! Oh, dear God, no!"

Lissa's heart pounded as she ran for the phone and punched in the numbers. But as the 911 operator answered, she was horrified to see Reene snatch up her biggest carving knife. Before Lissa could stop her, Reene dashed outside.

The bales had caught fire, and the glow from the flames illuminated the frantic horses. Andrea watched as they circled their stalls in terror and futilely kicked at the walls. When they snorted and stomped and called to each other, she reveled in their fear. Anger and thirst for revenge encompassed her entire being. Her eyes glowed with excitement.

As smoke poured into the barn, she struggled to breathe. She pulled a bandanna out of her pocket and covered her mouth and nose. She wanted to enjoy this moment as long as possible. But she wasn't stupid. She knew there were only a few minutes at best to make her escape.

"Shen! Sissy! It's all right! I'm coming!" Reene cried. She rolled the heavy door aside and rushed forward into the smoke and flames.

A figure in front of her whirled, clutching the flashlight like a club.

"Hello, Reene."

"Andrea! My God! You did this? Why?"

"Stupid bitch! I wanted to be mayor! You ruined my life. Now I'm ruining yours."

"You ruined yourself! You killed Steve!"

318

"'Steve'? Does every man love you?" Andrea lunged forward but stopped short when she spotted the knife in Reene's hand.

"You're crazy! Get the hell away from me!" Reene shouted. She brandished the knife in Andrea's face. "I'll kill you before I let these horses die!"

"Whore!"

"I'm getting the horses out of here! Back off!"

Fear for her animals made Reene cool as an iceberg. The two women faced off as the fire grew and the horses screamed.

Lissa flung open the side door in search of her friend. "Reene?" Lissa hollered.

Without warning a small panic-stricken creature, its body slung low to the ground, streaked by her. "Jesse!" she cried, but he had already disappeared through the open door.

At the sound of Lissa's voice, Bravo whinnied anxiously. Blinded by smoke, she ran toward his stall and crashed headlong into Reene. Reene staggered and fell to her knees. The knife flew from her hand.

Out of the smoke and flames, Andrea, snarling like a tigress, charged Lissa and the two women slammed to the ground.

"Reene! Save our horses!" Lissa shouted. Entangled with Andrea, she was in the fight of her life.

"Burn in hell, bitch!" Andrea snarled.

"You first!" Lissa yelled and kicked out at the woman's midsection.

Andrea grunted but grabbed Lissa's arms in a grip of steel. Lissa, twisting to break Andrea's hold, brought her knee up and again connected with her stomach. Shrieking in pain and rage, Andrea loosened her hold and Lissa drove her thumbs toward Andrea's streaming eyes.

Ignoring the life and death struggle, Reene managed to get to her feet, grabbed a lunge whip and ran to open the stall doors. She flung the doors wide, but the animals stood trembling in fear. Heartsick, she knew they'd never leave their familiar home, the haven where they always felt safe. Not unless she made them leave.

"Go! Go! Run!" Reene yelled frantically and cracked her whip against the wall. The smoke thickened and fire raged. Time was running out.

"Bravo! Git! Git!" she screamed and cracked the whip again. Bravo spun and raised his hind legs in a threatening kick. Without a second

319

thought, she slashed her whip hard across his butt. He whipped around, mouth open and she leaped aside. She lashed his rump again. Ears laid back, Bravo surged out of his stall.

Reene rushed to Shen and grasped her halter. "Shen! Move! Move!" she choked. Deadly smoke swirled around their heads. If the horses didn't get out now, she'd die with them. Wrenching a water bucket from the wall, she hurled it at the horse's shoulder. When the mare jumped forward in fright, Reene brought the whip down hard.

"Go! Go! Go!" Shen jigged and hesitated. Reene raised her whip again. With a terrified squeal, Shen leaped out of her stall.

Shen rushed down the aisle while Reene ran to Sissy. At the sight of the upraised whip, eyes rolling in terror, Sissy lurched out of the stall and followed the fleeing horses.

"Heee-yaaa!" Reene hollered, smacking Sissy's flank to keep her moving.

"Lissa! Watch out! The horses are coming!"

"Oh my God!" Lissa cried.

Andrea, clawing and punching wildly, still clung to her. In desperation she head-butted the crazed woman. Andrea's head snapped back and she lost her death grip. Lissa used her remaining strength to push Andrea from her. Lissa barely rolled out of the way when three horses came charging toward the barn door.

Lying in the aisle, smoke and flames all around her, Andrea screamed. Three terrified horses were racing toward her.

"Shit! No! *No!*"

To Lissa's mounting horror, the horses trampled over the fallen woman. The creatures Andrea sought to destroy pitilessly destroyed her.

As the horses thundered out of the barn, Reene ran to Lissa. "Hurry! Hurry! Let's get out of here!" she cried, pulling Lissa up. "We've got to keep them from running back in! Help me close the door!"

"Wait! Andrea!" Lissa gasped. "We can't leave her behind!"

"The hell we can't!"

Staggering outside, they tugged together at the barn door, but they only managed to close it a few feet before the intense heat drove them back. In the distance, they heard sirens screaming.

"We've got to put the horses in the outside paddocks before the fire engines show up! Where the hell are you going?" Lissa screamed as Reene ran toward the flaming barn.

"Lead ropes! We'll never catch the horses without them!" Shielding her face with her arm, she ripped ropes off the wrought iron hooks on the front of the barn and fled.

"I could only grab two leads!"

"You brave idiot!" Lissa stormed, grabbing a rope. "Let's try to herd them toward us!"

With their arms spread out like a makeshift barricade, the desperate women ran toward the frantic animals to keep them from running back into the inferno. The horses were so frightened they clung together in a tight pack. Ears laid back and eyes wide, they spun and wheeled as if joined at the hip.

"Whoa! Whoa now!" Lissa yelled.

Shen was rearing and plunging so hard Reene couldn't get near her.

"Shen! Whoa!" Reene cried, desperately dodging her frenzied horse's front legs. When Shen finally came to rest, Reene hurled herself forward, locked her left arm around Shen's head and snapped the lead onto her halter. Running beside her jigging horse, she led Shen into the paddock.

"Easy, Bravo!" Lissa commanded. "Easy!" Abruptly Bravo stopped. Even as his ears flicked toward her in response, he tensed, ready to speed away.

"It's all right! You're okay!" she cried.

Eyes wide with fear and fixed on her, Bravo trotted forward. He came on so fast, she feared she'd be knocked down. But she stood her ground, and he halted inches from her feet. She grabbed his halter and clipped the lead line to the ring.

"Good boy! Come on!" Lissa urged.

Behind them a burning timber snapped and crashed to the ground. Bravo reared straight up, forelegs pawing the air. She clung desperately to the lead rope. When his legs slammed down, she cried out when his hoof sliced her leg.

"Oh God! Whoa, Bravo! Whoa!" she shouted as he struggled to break free. He dragged her back a few steps, but she jerked the lead rope. Bravo halted but swung his body away from her, anxiously rolling his eye.

"Git, Bravo! Git, damn you or I'll break all your legs!" she begged. Muscles straining, she hauled him into the middle paddock. She latched the gate just as a fire engine, its siren wailing, rounded the corner of the inn.

"Lissa, help me with Sissy!" Reene hollered. "She's freaking out!" The big mare tossed her head and fought her efforts to drag her forward.

"Sissy, come!" Reene pleaded. "It's all right, little girl. Easy, easy." Sissy was shaking with fear.

"Sissy, listen to me!" But the mare was too scared to respond.

"Lissa, help me! Run the chain over her nose!"

With fumbling fingers, Lissa unclipped the lead rope from Sissy's halter and threaded the brass clip through the left halter ring. As she ran the chain across Sissy's nose, the mare nearly jerked loose before she rehooked it to the ring on the other side. She gave the rope a sharp jerk to get Sissy's attention.

"Now hang onto her as hard as you can!" Reene ripped off her fleece bed jacket. "Sweetie, I won't let anything hurt you! Don't be afraid!"

Before Sissy could toss her head again, Reene blindfolded her with the jacket and knotted the long sleeves under Sissy's throat. Unable to see and relying on blind faith, Sissy yielded. While Lissa applied pressure on the mare's left flank, Reene dragged her into the paddock with Shen.

"Stand, Sissy! Stand!" Reene begged. "Lissa, help me get this jacket off!"

Lissa wrenched the jacket loose and rammed it behind the water trough. Shen and Bravo, even more terrified by the piercing noise and blinking red lights on the fire engine, ran back and forth in the paddocks. Flames reflected the fear in their eyes.

"Oh my God! I was never so scared!" Lissa quavered as she slammed the gate closed. "Are we still in one piece?"

"Yes! Just a little battered and bruised!"

"Get your breath. I'll take care of that ear-splitting noise!" Lissa ran to the truck and jumped on the running board. "Turn off that damn siren and the lights! You're scaring our horses to death!"

"Okay, Cap?" asked the firefighter inside the engine's cab.

"Shut everything off," the captain ordered.

The flashing red light and screaming siren were replaced by men's voices, clanking equipment and the crackling fire. Two firemen leaped from the truck. One threw switches on the pumper while the other released the hoses. The captain jumped down from the engine.

"Glenn!" he directed, "attack mode! Keep the fire away from the main house!"

"Right, Cap!" Glenn hollered as he picked up the hose.

322

"Marco, pull out another line!" The captain returned to his truck and picked up a radio microphone.

"Watch it, ma'am!" yelled Glenn as he dragged the heavy hose along the ground. Lissa hopped over the hose and leaned against the truck. She watched the firefighters' valiant but losing effort to save their barn. Her head whipped around as another engine pulled in behind the first truck. She dashed around the front of the first engine and careened into the captain.

"Is anyone else in the barn?" he demanded.

"Yes! The woman who set the fire is still in there!" Lissa cried.

Reene ran up and tried to explain. "She wanted to kill our horses! We tried to stop her, but she nearly killed us! When the horses broke out, they trampled her. We think she's dead."

The commander ran to the second engine and spoke to the lieutenant. Two firefighters equipped with breathing apparatus jogged toward the crumbling structure.

"What's happening?" Lissa asked when he returned.

"Search and rescue. We have to recover the victim. What about your animals? Did you get them all out?"

"Yes!" Reene answered. "They fought us every inch of the way, but we put them into the paddocks just as you got here."

"I'm glad, for your sake. You won't like hearing this, but our first responsibility is to save people. Then property," he said as he nodded toward the barn and house. "Then animals. If you had run back to save your horses, I would've stopped you," the captain declared somberly.

Reene gasped and Lissa clamped her teeth into her lip.

"We have another problem. Is there a lake or pond nearby?" he asked. "The pumper only holds seven hundred and fifty gallons of water, and the fire is taking it all."

"Yes, yes, we have a pond out back," Lissa recovered. "It's about a quarter mile away behind the fences. Can you reach it from here?"

"Yes. We can draft water from one engine to another." He hustled to the second engine and again conferred with the lieutenant.

As the other engine backed down the drive and navigated the field, a car followed by an ambulance drove in.

"Good Lord, the whole fire department's here!" Lissa exclaimed.

A familiar figure climbed out of the car. When he walked over to speak to the commander, Lissa recognized him. Stressed out as she was, she still remembered him from their High Tea.

"Chief Bourassa!" she called.

He nodded in acknowledgment but continued his conversation with the captain. While they talked, two firefighters emerged from the smoldering barn carrying Andrea's body.

The chief signaled and the paramedics moved forward. Reene and Lissa watched in silence as they placed Andrea's body on a gurney and rolled it to the ambulance.

Chief Bourassa joined them. "Are you all right, young ladies?"

"Yes, Chief, thank you!" Lissa cried.

"What happened to your horses? Were they rescued?"

"Yes, but they're still flipping out!" Reene answered. "I'm scared they'll hurt themselves!"

"Right now, they're a little too close to the fire," the Chief answered. "But there's nothing we can do."

"Oh God!" Reene sobbed.

"Reenie!" Tom, his face smudged and sweaty, ran toward her. She threw herself into his arms. Tom released her and hugged Lissa in turn.

"Tom! Your face! I didn't see you..." Reene faltered.

"That's because I was busy trying to save your barn. Just doin' my job, ma'am."

Lissa watched as they exchanged a deep look. Tom's expression was more serene than she'd ever seen it.

"Our horses are having a hard time dealing with the fire, Tom," Reene said. "And the captain told us we might have to move them again."

"Cap's right," Tom agreed. "There's not much space between them and the barn."

"Excuse me, ladies," Chief Bourassa interrupted, "Sgt. Edmondson is here. He would like to speak with you."

Edmondson detached himself from the firefighters. As he approached, smoke and dying flames framed his tall figure. "I realize this is a bad time for both of you, but you'll need to come to the police station to make a formal statement."

"Bad time? We almost lost our horses, our lives and our barn is a pile of smoking rubble!" Lissa snapped. "Sergeant, I can't imagine a worse time!"

"Please don't misunderstand," he replied. "I am sympathetic to your situation. I'll expect you when things settle down here. And I do appreciate your cooperation."

He nodded and walked over to the ambulance. He pulled back the sheet from the trampled figure and shuddered.

"One hell of a way to die. It must have been horrible."

In the dimming firelight, Reene and Lissa exchanged a knowing look.

"No more horrible than what she had planned for our innocent animals," Lissa retorted. "But Andrea forgot the cardinal rule, sergeant. The horse *always* comes first."

With Tom at their heels, the two bedraggled women raced back to the inn where more chaos greeted them. Lights burned everywhere and their only guests were huddled on the farmer's porch.

"Are we in danger?" Cindy cried.

"Good God, what's happened?" Jeff demanded.

"No, no! Please! Listen to me!" Lissa pleaded. "The fire is under control."

"I'm one of the firefighters," Tom said. "You are in no danger, but I'd advise you to go back inside."

However, fascinated by the flickering flames and bustling firemen, the geocaching couple were reluctant to leave the porch.

"I'm familiar with horses," Cindy said. "Please let me help!"

"I'm not a horse person," Jeff added, "but I can haul water and hay."

Reene graciously thanked them for their offer and shepherded them back in. "Maybe tomorrow when things calm down," she promised, "we may just ask you to pitch in."

When she returned to the porch, Tom asked, "Reenie, is there anything I can do?"

"Yes! Now we're moving the horses further away from the barn until the fire is out. Can you handle that?" she demanded.

"Anything you need!" Tom promised.

"Come with us!" Lissa cried. "We have extra lead ropes in the mudroom!"

"There was a message on my cell phone!" Tom hollered as they sprinted through the kitchen. "Jill Stanton called. She heard about the fire and is driving over with bags of grain."

"Horse people!" Reene exclaimed. "They're the best!"

First light had appeared in the night sky when, a lifetime later, Tom finally shooed an exhausted Reene and Lissa into the Gathering Room and closed the door. Lissa noticed that her friends looked like zombies, and figured she looked the same.

When Tom brought in a tray of hot coffee and cookies, the steaming liquid banished chills the drained women were trying unsuccessfully to hide, returning color to their cheeks.

"I'm glad our horses are in their paddocks safe and sound," Lissa said, "but they're still acting a little squirrely. Not that I blame them. I think they'll need a lot of TLC for a while,"

"Lissa, your leg!" Reene exclaimed.

Lissa looked down at her calf which had taken on Popeye proportions. A goose egg was raised on her shin, and a long gash oozed a trail of blood.

"That doesn't look good," she murmured, gingerly touching her swollen extremity. "Looks like Bravo accidentally nicked me."

"The understatement of the century," Tom laughed. "Where's your first aid kit?"

While Tom cleaned and bandaged Lissa's leg, they poured out the whole unbelievable story.

"I rescued the horses while Lissa rolled around on the ground with our late, and I do mean late, mayor-elect," Reene explained. "She's the one who set the barn on fire."

"Reene, you were amazing," Lissa praised. "You performed a miracle. I never could have handled those terrified animals. Thank you, dear friend."

"You would have done the same thing! We'd risk our lives a thousand times to save our kids and you know it!"

Tom's jaw dropped as he stared at them. "Wait. Back up. Are you telling me *Andrea Wilson* set your barn on fire? Lissa was in a fight? Man, you two have a lot of explaining to do."

He sat quietly, listening as they continued their story, looking more and more furious at what Andrea had done.

"She nearly succeeded," Reene said angrily. "Andrea knew just how to hurt us. Her revenge would have been complete."

"If Josey hadn't awakened us, I can't imagine what would have happened. I can't even go there. It's too terrible," raged Lissa. "I don't care if I get struck by lightning for saying this, but that bitch got what she deserved."

"Josey?" Tom asked with a puzzled look. "Who's Josey? Now I'm really lost."

"I guess we'd better tell him, huh, Reene?"

"Tell me what?" Tom almost hollered in exasperation.

"Can I tell you the whole story later? First we've got to check on the horses and then report to the police and—"

"Yes, sweetie," Tom broke in. "You can tell me later. Both of you have been through enough tonight." Lissa looked at him gratefully as he busied himself collecting dirty dishes and departed for the kitchen.

"Reene, if you let him get away, I'll make you eat my cooking for a year!"

Epilogue

Barn Swallow Inn
2 Months Later

"Our new barn is shaping up nicely, isn't it Lissa?" Reene asked as they stood on the deck and watched workmen hammering and sawing. At the pace they were setting, it wouldn't be much longer before the inn could again accommodate equine guests.

"It certainly is. I'm pleased the insurance company was so prompt with our check. And I'm happy our favorite contractor is reconstructing our new-new barn just like the old one," Lissa answered. "His crew put up the temporary run in shed in record time. We might even have enough left over for you to buy a new wagon, Reene."

"To be honest, Lissa, I need a little more time to recover from our terrifying adventures before I go wagon shopping."

"Good point. I still get the shakes anytime I see someone strike a match. Reene, have you noticed no strange happenings lately or things going bump in the night?"

"It has been awfully quiet," Reene agreed. "Funny thing, I almost miss the tricks Josey used to play on us. We'll always be grateful to her. She saved us all that awful night. But now I truly feel her spirit has crossed over, and she is finally at peace. I picture her riding her splendid Shiloh on long trail rides. I know Peter and Josey are together again, reunited in love and harmony."

Lissa handed Reene a tissue as her friend's eyes filled with tears.

"Here," sniffled Lissa, "we'd better stop this before we turn into blubbering idiots."

"No kidding," said Reene, dabbing at her eyes. "I'm so glad we brought justice and closure to Josey after so many years. She certainly deserved it." She shoved the tissue into her pocket. "Now, let's get cracking. Five new guests are coming later this week, which means the rooms need cleaning, I've got to order grain, and our trailer is due for inspection..."

"Slow down, woman! Come on, I'll race you. Zip up your jacket and grab your gloves! First one to finish makes dinner reservations!"

As the two friends set off to complete their multitude of chores, their laughter wafted back to Bravo, Shen and Sissy, enjoying morning hay in their paddocks. Noses down, they foraged in the snow for every morsel of hay.

All at once their heads snapped to attention. The horses stood like statues, their eyes fixed on something only they could see moving across the pasture. Ears flicking back and forth like radar, they honed in on signals only they could hear. Wisps of dry snow whirled around as if a presence was trampling a path through the field, but the air was unnaturally still. No footprints showed in the unbroken white of winter.

Bravo neighed loudly, and Shen and Sissy added their calls. Somewhere in the distance, an answering whinny drifted back. They whinnied in unison and again a faint reply floated back. They returned the greeting once more, but this time there was no response.

Sensing their message sent and received, with one accord they broke ranks and lowered their heads to their hay.

Marilyn C. Long - Biography

Living in Methuen, MA for over sixty years, Marilyn moved to the beautiful New Hampshire countryside where she plans to enjoy life with her husband, adult children, three beautiful granddaughters and her still feisty thirty-two year old Quarter Horse Rio Bravo. When the real 'Reene Anderson' told her about a fantastic dream she'd had, Marilyn incorporated her great love of horses and Slay Ride is the result of that dream.

Made in the USA
Middletown, DE
16 February 2020